THE GEOGRAPHICAL CURE

Also by Michael Parker

HELLO DOWN THERE

The
Geographical
Cure

NOVELLAS AND STORIES

Michael Parker

CHARLES SCRIBNER'S SONS
NEW YORK

Maxwell Macmillan Canada
Toronto

Maxwell Macmillan International
New York   Oxford   Singapore   Sydney

Copyright © 1994 by Michael Parker

Some of the stories in this book were originally published in the following periodicals: *The Georgia Review, Carolina Quarterly, The New Virginia Review.*

Charles Scribner's Sons   Maxwell Macmillan Canada, Inc.
Macmillan Publishing Company   200 Eglinton Avenue East
866 Third Avenue   Suite 200
New York, NY 10022   Don Mills, Ontario M3C 3N1

Macmillan Publishing Company is part of the Maxwell Communication Group of Companies.

Library of Congress Cataloging-in-Publication Data
Parker, Michael, 1959–
    The geographical cure: novellas and stories / Michael Parker.
      p.   cm.
    ISBN 0-684-19682-4
    I. Title
PR6066.A66G46   1994
823'.914—dc20   93-40188
CIP

Macmillan books are available at special discounts for bulk purchases for sales promotions, premiums, fund-raising, or educational use. For details, contact:

Special Sales Director
Macmillan Publishing Company
866 Third Avenue
New York, NY 10022

10 9 8 7 6 5 4 3 2 1

Printed in the United States of America

For Hallie and Jim

Contents

THE GEOGRAPHICAL CURE

The Little Marine Went Over to France

I

They left that town in the middle of a night so hot that sleep was a shallow tossing, sheets wet gauze dressing prickly skin. Mosquito bites ringed both Mac's ankles even though they were covered with the sheet he'd tried to thrash off earlier, which was wound around his feet now, tethering him to the thin pad. Headlights from the highway streaked across the pine paneling, needling him awake during those sweaty hours before his mother stuck her head in from the bathroom and told them to get up, get packed, they were leaving.

Beyond her, Glenn's lathered face loomed in the bathroom mirror. Only one of the globes above the sink was working, and the shadowy image of Glenn—head cocked toward the light, his razorless hand straddling his Adam's apple to stretch his neck skin—lingered after Mac's mother closed the door.

"What's he bothering to shave for?" said Mac's sister Cindy. It was dark again and in the bathroom low voices mixed with running water. Cindy lay above him on the couch in the alcove sitting room of this cabinette somewhere west of Raleigh, North Carolina. Or was this South Carolina? Coming from Wisconsin, Mac confused the two.

"I knew all along we'd leave tonight," whispered Mac.

"You are *such* a liar," Cindy said. Mac knew that more than anything his sister hated his claims of clairvoyance, and she took each claim with an uncharacteristic seriousness, as if Mac was accusing her of being stupid. At fourteen and a half, Cindy was older by fourteen months. If either of them could predict the next caprice, it should be her.

"He's shaving because he needs a shave," said Mac. "Your beard grows while you're sleeping. It doesn't go to sleep, too. Besides, Glenn's probably been up all this time."

"You better hope he hasn't if he's going to drive us out of here." As she spoke, Cindy swung her legs down to Mac's bed, or his pallet, as she called it: a piece of thin foam rubber, two yellowish sheets, a pillow. "Pallet" reminded Mac of the Sunday school his father had made him attend back in Milwaukee, where a Bible story was favored in which the word pallet figured prominently. Mac couldn't remember much about the story except that it contained some type of miracle, some act of transformation. A healed man borne through awestruck throngs on a pallet . . . or, wait . . . wasn't there a midget with a funny name watching from the top of a tree? This was all he remembered of his religious training, a stray detail from a parable, the point of which escaped him. Of course there was no one he could ask to verify it, because his mother slept in on Sundays and Cindy had recently managed to evade their father's decree that they attend church. Mac did everything he said— always, everything—without argument, whether he wanted to or not.

"I don't know how you could actually believe that Glenn never sleeps," said Cindy, "but it doesn't surprise me that you do. I was just asking why he needs to get all clean to drive us to another hick town. In the middle of the damn night, with nobody up to see him anyway."

"Just pack, Cin," said Mac. He went into the kitchen to dress, then rolled his pallet up and tightened it with a belt.

After stuffing his knapsack with comic books and high-top sneakers, he tiptoed outside to the Cortina, dumped his gear on the ground beside the driver's side and climbed in. For a few minutes Mac dozed, his cheek leaning against the cool glass, until tapping roused him and he jolted up to see a cigarette glowing in the near dark.

"The Macman had us fooled," Glenn whispered when Mac rolled down the window. "We thought he had the car all packed."

"I'm not asleep," said Mac.

Glenn held his laugh low. "I didn't say you were. Help me pack. Plus we have to pop the clutch."

They loaded the gear Glenn had carried out, lashing most to the luggage rack. When Cindy came shuffling through the thick sand of the driveway, Glenn ordered her into the driver's seat and told her to crank the car when they hit pavement; he pointed out a spot in the darkness where a stand of trees loomed alongside a field, said she should wait for them there. Cindy took his orders sullenly, but she didn't talk back to him the way she sometimes did, the way she always had to their father.

"What's with Mom?" she called out the window.

"Keep it down," said Glenn.

"Sorry," Cindy said, her whisper wildly exaggerated. "It's just not my natural state to be always trying to get away with something. It's hard for me to wake up sneaky since I'm basically an honest person."

This made Glenn chuckle—too loudly, Mac thought. While Mac checked the office of the motor court to make sure all the windows were dark, Glenn stuck his head in the window and said, "You're getting pretty good at it, Cin. I know you have it in you." Cindy responded with another whisper which Mac could not make out. She was always vowing not to talk to Glenn but everything he said made her frantic for a quick comeback. Mac liked listening to their ban-

ter—it could be entertaining—but this time he tuned them
out when he saw his mother pause on the stoop of the cabinette. She bent over; moths circled her head. Above the
whispery bickering of Cindy and Glenn, Mac heard the
hum of the porch light. Moving closer, he watched his
mother pluck cotton balls from the screen door. The daytime
desk clerk had told Mac's mother that the cotton balls were
there to ward off flies. Mac watched as she opened her
pocketbook and stuffed the cotton balls inside. Moving
around to the side of the car, he pretended to listen to the tail
end of the teasing, which his mother interrupted by tossing
her pocketbook in the front seat and saying, "Okay."

The sand was deep and thick and even with Glenn's
strength the tiny English Ford barely moved. "Heave ho,"
half-sang Glenn, and Mac dug his heels into the sand for
traction, the three of them groaning and wheezing, noses
touching blue metal. Tire tread patterned the ruts beneath
them, ten seconds and they were running, Mac between his
mother and Glenn, trying to match their strides, synchro-
nize his steps with theirs, though it didn't matter that they
were in step so long as the Cortina picked up speed. As
they hit the blacktop the tires whirred at a higher, louder
pitch. They pulled back their fingertips and, bending toward the blacktop, placed them on their kneecaps and
wheezed; they hunkered in the middle of the road while
Cindy popped the clutch; the motor sputtered, caught, settled into an idle. By the trees the Cortina slowed, brake
lights blinked. The three of them took off in a trot, Mac's
grin widening with the building wind. Every few steps he
swiveled to check for lights. Inside the car, Cindy and Mac
slumped in opposite corners of the tiny backseat, as far
away from each other as possible. Their mother was the first
to speak: three dark miles down the road she looked back in
the rearview one last time and sang out, "Two weeks in another town," which was a phrase they'd seen on a movie

marquee a week or so before, a title lit in yellow bulbs which seemed to speak to her.

ALL DAY LONG they drove east, past tobacco farms and hogs rooting through cornfields, past cows standing in muddy ponds which came only to their knees, through funneled passages where dusty-leafed trees dripped shadows over the highway. The further east they drove the more the land seemed to dip and puddle, the more lush, sunken and secretive the roadside woods grew.

"There's nothing tame *about* this place," Cindy said once. "I see no difference between this South and South America. Ugly jungles and sleepy people who speak a different language."

"Don't you just love the music down here though?" said Glenn. He twisted the dials of the Cortina's radio, which didn't work. Nothing much worked but the engine, yet the car was sporty and imported. Gas attendants gawked at it and even the laziest among them checked under the hood out of curiosity; the idea of a Ford made in England and shipped to the United States elicited a flurry of technical and patriotic skepticism. Mac liked the car, despite its shabbiness. It was four on the floor, and Glenn was going to teach him to drive it. Only reason he'd taught Cindy first was because she was lighter and Mac was needed to push during their midnight getaways.

"Oh, well," said Glenn, drawing static on the radio, "Guess I'll have to sing." He sang lots while he drove, usually the same song. Cindy detested it, and Glenn proceeded to belt it out in his scratchy tenor.

> *The little Marine went over to France,*
>   parlez-vous
> *The little Marine went over to France,*
>   parlez-vous

> *The little Marine went over to France,*
> *kicked the kaiser in the pants*
> *Inky dinky* parlez-vous, parlez-vous.

"Ignoring for right now the fact that you sound like hell, those lyrics make absolutely no sense," said Cindy. "The little Marine went over to France do you speak?"

"She's translating," Glenn said, winking at Mac in the rearview. "Parlayvoo France-A. And only a minute ago we were in South America."

"Not to mention the fact this little marine goes to France to kick the kaiser instead of to Germany, where kaisers originate from."

"Maybe he was sick of sauerkraut and crossed the border for some snails," said Glenn.

"Completely ridiculous," said Cindy. "Stupider than most nursery rhymes."

"You sure know your European history," said Glenn.

"My father is a veteran," said Cindy.

"He is most definitely that," said Glenn, and Mac's mother, who had been staring at the greenness flashing past outside, laughed and tried to elbow Glenn's ribs, but when he feigned injury before she even touched him, she dropped her hand.

"I guess you were too busy taking pictures of brats to serve your country," said Cindy. Mac watched his mom draw her hand from Glenn's lap, as if she'd been burned.

Glenn and Mac's mother met in the department store where both worked, she as a salesclerk in the children's department, he as a photographer on a six-week stint to hawk his portraits. He worked in the far corner of Boys' Shoes, scrunched up behind shoved-aside displays, their former positions demarcated by ghostly squares in the carpet. Glenn needed lots of room for his setup: several feet between the camera and the black boxes he posed his subjects

on, and room also for the scrims and backdrops he project-
ed behind—library settings with rows of tightly shelved
books bound in fake leather, a forest, an amusement park
with a red Ferris wheel spinning in front of a roller coaster
trestle. When she considered the way he'd been crammed
between the back wall and Boys' Shoes, Mac's mother suspected that management was less than impressed with
Glenn's operation. She made herself walk over and talk to
him one afternoon, and at first she talked to him in the
same superficial, distant way she talked to all those she felt
ashamed of feeling sorry for.

One morning a few weeks later, Cindy and Mac rode
the bus downtown to eat lunch with their mother in the
top floor cafeteria. They found her leaning in the doorway
of the stockroom talking to Glenn, a green and dingy curtain draped across her shoulder. Other employees bumped
past them carrying handfuls of wire hangers, and Mac and
Cindy noticed the looks those employees leveled at their
mother before disappearing through the low door. But
what kept them frozen there, what kept her children from
approaching or even speaking was the way the curtain fell
over her shoulder like a tress of twisted fungus. It seemed to
Mac that something foreign and new had washed up from
an out-of-the-blue ocean and she was too oblivious to feel
it draping her. Cindy had been so disgusted she'd gone
down to the cafeteria alone, paying for her food with money she'd saved for records.

"Actually, I'm a little younger than your father," said
Glenn.

"This is just more than we need to know right now,"
Mac's mother said. She folded the magazine she'd been
reading, snapped open her pocketbook; Mac could hear the
clink of coin and nail clipper which always drifted in the
bottom, and remembering the cotton balls plucked from
the screen door, he wondered if she was about to pull one

out and dab her face with it. He was relieved to see her pull out her sunglasses instead. Putting them on, she twisted around in the bucket seat to face her children. "Why don't we sing something else?" she said.

"Something that makes sense?" said Cindy.

"Why do you want everything to make sense?" said Glenn. "That makes no sense. Does that make sense to you, Mac?"

"He wouldn't know the difference," said Cindy. She was staring at her mother. "Did you sit on those glasses?" she asked, but before her mother could check the rearview and reply, Cindy said that they didn't have to sing anything, that she needed her sleep.

Near dusk Mac watched a town rise from an hour's stretch of swamp and wide sky, announcing itself in fits of billboard and gas station. They crossed a body of water which Glenn identified as the sound and came finally into the town. Glenn stopped at a store in its center and bought a newspaper from a curbside stand. The three of them watched as Glenn stood just outside the car, his foot propped on an island of gas pumps, leafing slowly through the paper.

Suddenly Cindy, who had been asleep since the last verse of "Little Marine," woke, squinted at Glenn and said, "Are we getting gas here or reading the damn newspaper?"

Their mother spoke without turning around. "This newspaper, they're supposed to be looking for a photographer. If he gets the job, we'll stay here for a few weeks, then head south again."

"So wake me up when we leave." Cindy shut her eyes again. Both Mac and his mother looked at her as if she were a vaporous figure in a dream. Was she serious? Then Mac's mother turned to him with her brow pinched, held this quizzical gaze until he shrugged. "Well, what do you think?"

Mac looked around. Idle old men in work clothes sat in

front of the store. Across the street sagged a row of shingled houses, gardens and clothes lines dividing the scant yards separating them. The door of one flew open and a throw rug flapped a wave of dust across the porch, then receded into the dark foyer like the flicked tongue of a snake. Kite string dripped from a power line. From all sides rose a close, medicinal smell like the overheated rooms of someone ancient and bedridden, a smell Mac would rather die than become accustomed to.

"Two weeks in another town," he said.

"Looks good," said Glenn, climbing into the car. "Job's still open. Pictures stink. I'm Karsh compared."

"Whoever Karsh is," Mac's mother said into the windshield.

Glenn stuck a cigarette in his mouth but didn't light it. "They don't know who he is either. Just as damn well." Spreading paper across the steering wheel he punched a spot above a grid of grocery prices.

"Look here, Mac." Leaning forward, Mac studied the dotted black rectangle Glenn pointed to, a rounded silhouette in a Stetson standing by an even darker, blocky form. "What d'you see?" asked Glenn.

"Two dead in Oak Stump collision," read Mac aloud. "Is it a wreck?"

"Can't make out much," said Mac's mom.

"I could pick up blood spotting the damn steering column," said Glenn.

"If that was something that they wanted," Mac's mother said. "There's the victim's family to consider."

"This is how they sell newspapers," said Glenn. "They might not need Karsh, but they do need better pictures of what passes for trauma around here."

"Y'all lost?" They looked up to find an attendant from the station crouched by Glenn's window. He pointed to the paper, which he must have mistaken for a map.

"She's lost," Glenn said, jerking his head back toward Cindy.

"I wish," said Cindy, springing awake to smile at the confused attendant, and to whisper, once he backed away from the Cortina, "Grease monkey's not used to gringos, no?"

II

Mac's mother had some money: a chunk of inheritance when her parents died and monthly dribbles from the profits of a grapefruit grove south of Tampa. Now they were on their way to Florida to see this grove, a quarter of which was lost now, trees sold off or killed by frost during the winter of 1957. Mac's father lived to make fun of the grapefruit grove. What he called his work ethic did not allow him to feel comfortable with income earned from something he neither laid hands nor eyes on.

He ran an office supply store. On Saturdays and during the summer he dragged Mac and Cindy downtown to *the office,* as he called it. The showroom was dank and airless, cluttered with khaki-colored swivel chairs, adding machines with dust-caked keys, yellowing day planners. Winter and summer, floor fans oscillated from black corners, rising above bulwarks of pushed-together desks to ruffle cobwebs above Mac's head. He and Cindy were supposedly there to work, but more often than not, Cindy sank into a plush swivel chair with a magazine or her transistor, leaving Mac to the task at hand.

Their father was rarely around; he held court at a Polish restaurant across the street, where at a back table he led assassination attempts against the character of Adlai Stevenson. Mac and Cindy were left to the supervision of the salesgirl Irma, who was famous between them for never thumping her cigarettes. Despite constant and reckless gesticulations, her cigarettes remained all ash, as if petrified. They dubbed these ash formations "Irmas" and made a game of cataloging the most outrageous specimens, of being the first to notice them, of clocking the seconds between first sighting and final crumble. "Check out that spirma," Cindy would whisper, and Mac would point to the pyramid of butts heaped in the ashtray on Irma's desk and say, "The Spanish Irmata."

Though the office supply store steadily lost money, Mac's father refused to give it up while his wife's inheritance was still sitting in the bank, drawing interest. When the account was finally drained and he announced his plan to start in on the grapefruit grove, she staved him off by taking the department store job.

Mac found it odd that the measure she'd taken to save her grapefruit grove (and it was a drastic measure, this job following haughty moms around, kneeling to wrench tape measures around the waists of fidgety kids) had led her to Glenn, and eventually would lead her to see—to actually lay eyes and hands on—the grapefruit grove.

In the car that afternoon, on the way out of Milwaukee, his mother had launched into a manic tirade about how they were on their way to rescue the grove from the greedy clutches of their father, though he was never mentioned by name. It was like a war in which the real enemy was acknowledged to be not the state but the Church, yet no one wanted to commit heresy by saying so.

Substitute enemies became the weather, the orchard keeper, the produce brokers, the trucking industry. As his mom railed, last light glinted off Lake Michigan, and Mac leaned back in the seat, feeling as if he'd been born for this moment of escape, even though he'd been reluctant to leave at first. He'd been halfway home from school, midway through the maze of alley, vacant lot and railroad track he called his shortcut, when he'd spotted the Cortina. The car bucked and lurched, braked and coasted as if trolling for something lost, and at intervals a head hung out of the passenger's side window. And even from a distance it looked funny: instead of the standard four-door, sleek-curved, high-finned Detroitmobile this car was bulbous and squat, with no real trunk and bugged-out headlights.

When the Cortina idled alongside and his mother hopped out, Mac kept walking. She swept up on the sidewalk wearing her work clothes and a wide moony smile. Mac glanced quickly at Glenn, who smiled, touched his forehead as if it was a hat bill, blew smoke into the street.

"We've been looking all over for you," his mother said. "Kind of a circuitous route you take home, isn't it?"

"No killer dogs."

"Cindy already home?"

When he shrugged, his mother told him that she did not read shoulders and would appreciate it if he would stop walking and turn around and talk to her.

Mac knew this was done for the benefit of Glenn. She did read shoulders—in fact, when alone, they communicated mostly by body language—and it irritated him, her putting on a show for Glenn, who was out of earshot anyway.

"Why aren't you at work?" he said in a tone borrowed from his father. He slowed down, let her catch up, stopped walking, jerked his head dramatically in the direction of Glenn. "Who's he?"

"You know who he is."

"Didn't recognize him outside of Boys' Shoes."

Close by, a man laughed, and both turned to see that Glenn had eased the Cortina up behind them. "Told you it's time to go," he said. "Stayed so long Mr. Mac here's got me confused with a shoe rack."

"Go where?" Mac asked his mother.

"Florida." She drew him close and leaned over, as if she was about to measure his waist. "To the grapefruit grove."

Lately he'd been worried about her. Staying home all the time, hovering in the same airspace between fights with his dad about bank accounts, grapefruit, small change. One morning at breakfast she had spoken in a low and unbroken voice. Every night she was awakened by the clink of her dwindling fortune, she said. Even with her head hidden between pillows she could hear it, the pillaging of her future, her insurance against a life of boredom and dangling tape measures and mouthfuls of safety pins, broken into pocket change too piddly to collect. Your father acts as if silver is beneath him, she said. He left nickels and dimes for her to sweep into a Mason jar marked House Account, its jingly refrain the song of the sleepless night before.

Mac's mother had told them other things when their father wasn't around: all about this man she met, this talented photographer.

"Stay put for a minute," his mother was saying to Glenn. She swiveled Mac around, placed her hands on his shoulders and marched him down the sidewalk as if it were a schoolhouse corridor and she was a stern teacher guiding an upstart to the principal's office.

"You're going to Florida with him?" Mac asked as they huddled in a patch of shade beneath an awning.

"We are going to Florida with him."

"You told Dad *you're* going to Florida with him?"

She pretended to ignore his substituted pronoun. "He's up at Sturgeon, looking at a cabin to buy with my money. I left him a note."

She told Mac about the note, which said that she was pulling the kids out of school a few weeks early and heading to Florida with a friend. On the sidewalk in mid-afternoon, with Glenn a distant silhouette in the front seat of his boxy foreign coupe, she quoted her Dear

John letter in its entirety. "Not to worry, talk soon," was how she signed off. The ink started to run dry in her pen, she said, and she bore down so hard signing her name that it went through the paper and etched itself into the dining room table. Noticing her name—Carol in blocky letters—when she moved the paper, she thought of adding "was here."

"Cindy's probably *there* right now, reading the note and overreacting," she said. "Probably flinging furniture around the room. She needs a tan is what she needs. Come on, let's go get her."

"Why are you going to Florida?" he asked.

She glanced quickly back at Glenn, as if the sight of him could renew her patience. "I told you. To see our grapefruit grove."

"And then we turn right around and come back?"

She smiled slightly at his switch from singular to plural, but knew better than to acknowledge it.

"Not immediately, no. Glenn knows the country real well. He'll show us around." She put her hands on his shoulders again. "I want you to pay attention to everything."

"I always do."

"I know," she said.

"What's he going to show me I can't already see?" he said, annoyed again: at her, at the idling English Ford in the background, at the world.

"Who knows?" she said. "Maybe nothing. . . . You're one of the main reasons I'm going," she said. "I thought for sure you'd want to see the grapefruit grove."

So she's doing it for me, Mac thought. So I can pay attention to things which may or may not be there, which Glenn may or may not be able to point out to me. She had cast herself in the role of Mom Who Sacrifices So That Her Children Might See More of the World, and it did not fit her, this selflessness. Yet he liked the change in her, the spunky tone she'd picked up since Glenn had set up shop in the crowded corner of Boys' Shoes. Sometimes she sounded like Cindy, but without the sarcasm, bound to make light of things but careful never to ridicule. Before, Mac felt as if he could say anything to his mother—when she was miserable, there was no part of her life off limits to him. But now, since Glenn, Mac did not feel as if he could ask what *she* was getting out of this trip.

A new and sacred layer of the unsaid appeared, and though it was never mentioned, it seemed to Mac to grow deeper and more powerful with each mile they put between themselves and Milwaukee.

III

Tendrils were only a fingernail's width above ground in Wisconsin, but the farther south they burrowed, the more the country warmed and greened as if the Cortina plowed the zipper track of winter, exposing the towns in its wake to spring. The motels Glenn chose were always the cheapest—slanted, sooty-paneled rooms smelling of ten-year-old smoke—but they were exotic. The type of people Mac rarely got to see went in and out of them at all hours.

Glenn would stop whenever you asked him to, unlike their dad. Mac's dad was a severe man who had been sick when very young and had the purplish-lipped fastidiousness of someone who had been spoiled and bored very early in life. He was angry—driving, he'd often talk to himself at intersections, lingering when the light was green and saying things like, "He's trying to butter me up, the son of a bitch," while backed-up traffic beeped at him to get a move on. Mac didn't miss him. Despite his profligate streak he was strict and humorless and too often too tired. Mac didn't talk much as a result of life with his father. Cindy didn't

normally talk much at home, either, but on this trip her
tongue gradually loosened. With each state southward she
mouthed off more. Glenn was the only one who bothered
to talk to her much after Mammoth Cave, where she stumbled into a guide three times accidentally on purpose and
shouted Stalactite, Stalagmite in an unbelievably bad mock-
ery of German tourist speech that echoed like firecracker
reports through the tamed and spotlit innards of the cavern.

But at night—during those times when she and Mac had
rooms to themselves—she whispered things against Glenn,
serious things which bothered Mac though he didn't believe them. Glenn was after Mom's grove too, only he
wasn't content to sell them off one by one. According to
Cindy, Glenn was giving them a ride to Florida in exchange for the grapefruit grove—that was why he paid for
things, that was why he was being so nice. That was why he
brought them along in the first place, she argued, because
he was buttering their mother up. He would leave them
destitute among gator-infested mangrove swamps. They
would be forced into migrant labor, forced to pick their
way back to Wisconsin through fields sticky with tobacco
juice, forced to wear long-sleeved shirts and jeans in Georgia August to protect themselves from prickly squash vines.
Last-leg buses prone to accidents and crooked crew leaders
who overcharged you for toilet paper sold piece by perfo-
rated piece—the list of horrors circulated like fan blades
throughout the night.

Mac fell asleep to this list of Cindy's. She was his sister,
he told himself, she was *this way.* It was natural for her to
find the campaigns of others lacking in ambition or otherwise suspicious. As for Glenn, Mac liked him, and he
thought he always would.

There *were* times when Cindy's list got to him, but then
along came one of their midnight escapes—they'd sneaked
away without paying three times so far—and these flights,

though he knew they were wrong, restored Mac's faith in the trip. He liked the way they all worked together to flee, liked the quiet, smooth way their luck ran, saving themselves money under the light of the moon's rays with strength roused from sleepy bodies. It wasn't a question of right or wrong but of extracting weight, conserving energy: loading the car in the dark without the requisite flashlight his dad always carried, keeping quiet, threading the Cortina though pines and the other cars in the parking lot. Pushing the car out to the road, synchronizing his steps with his mother's and Glenn's, kneeling with them at the moment when they discovered that their energy was no longer needed and the car bucked away on its own power. Even Cindy enjoyed it; Mac could tell by the surreptitious hunch of her body over the steering wheel, and by the way Glenn would practically have to lift her from the driver's seat so he could drive them away. And there were those resplendent moments afterward, one or more of them swiveling back to see if they were being followed, suppressed smiles on their faces during that slow-motion lag following anything for which you could be caught and punished.

It had been like a vacation, but not a vacation he'd ever been on. They took two weeks a year in a cabin near Sturgeon Bay, the very cabin that Mac's father had gone to buy when Glenn came for them. Sturgeon Bay was always a regimented, fitful time for Mac, his father ordering him around and checking up on him if he even went for a walk down to the pier. This was restful in comparison, despite the hot nights once they came down from the Alleghenies into the valley of Virginia, despite the mosquitoes and the predawn orders to get packed, this was it, they were leaving.

Mac felt particularly rested the next day when his mother came into the motel room that he was sharing with his sleeping sister. They had splurged on a separate room instead of a kitchenette this time, because Glenn was going to pick up a few days of work. His mother drew open the blinds, pulled the earphone cord out of Mac's transistor, which lay beside him on his pillow, turned up WLS out of Chicago, sat down on Mac's bed and pulled things out of a paper bag: a carton each of grapefruit juice and milk, three cheeseburgers, three oranges.

"Sleepyheads," said Mac's mom.

"What time?" said Cindy. Since the opening of the blinds and the sound of Sam Cooke through the tinny transistor, she had covered her head with a pillow; her voice sounded faint and foreign, as if it were echoing back to them from Mammoth Cave.

"Noon. I brought breakfast *and* lunch. So get up."

"We're leaving?" asked Cindy.

"Not exactly."

Cindy threw the pillow in the crack between the beds. The shapeless way her nightgown clung to her shoulders made her seem even sleepier, younger too.

"I thought we were going to Florida," she said.

"I told you last night while you were pretending to be asleep. We need money. We thought we'd stay here for a while, save some. That way we can stay longer in Florida."

"You phoned Dad?" said Cindy. She had retrieved her pillow from the floor and was cradling it to her chest.

"Sure," said Mac's mom. "Line was busy." She wasn't smiling.

"Probably talking to the FBI," said Cindy.

"CIA," said their mom.

"VFW," said Mac, and his mother, grateful for this intervention, handed him a carton of milk which he opened and upturned, drawing a "Hey, wait, yuck" from his sister.

"We found a house." Their mother sounded oddly solemn, as if she didn't believe this herself.

Cindy, who had unscrewed the lid from the juice and taken a gulp, clapped the lid on and froze. "You bought a house in this hick town?"

"Rented, Cindy. You don't go around buying houses when you're only planning on staying for a month. We rented it because it was cheaper than paying motel rates." She looked around the motel room. "Besides, you haven't even seen this place. You were asleep when we came in, remember? You can't really base it on this one room." She continued looking around the room, staring at things. Mac tried hard to look where she looked; he wanted to see this whole trip through her eyes. She was staring at a photo of Crater Lake on the wall above the scuffed bedside table. The water of Crater Lake was very blue, the rocks that rose around it the color of real rust. It looked touched-up, so glossy it could have been laminated. What was it doing hanging here in a motel room in eastern North Carolina, Mac imagined his mother was wondering. He wanted to think what she was thinking, just for now.

"Sometimes when I act like I'm asleep I'm really not," said Cindy, breaking the silence. She reached for a burger.

"Which is another way of saying something else entirely," said their mother.

Cindy giggled and said, "So what's old Olan Mills up to? Taking pictures of little snotsters down at the Feed and Seed?"

"He's working at the newspaper," said Mac, turning to his mother. "Right?"

She peeled an orange with a thumbnail, a fine spray visible in the blind-slatted light as she carved. "Special assignments," she said.

"White House correspondent or what?" said Cindy.

"He's on-call sort of, like a doctor. A stringer they call it. When they need a photographer someplace quick they call Glenn."

"What kinds of things would they need pictures of quick down here in Crackersville?" asked Cindy.

"From what little Glenn has told me," said their mom,

reaching for Mac's milk carton and ignoring the face Cindy made when she drank from it, "I gather that he will be handling mostly disasters and sudden tragedies."

"Like grisly wrecks?" said Cindy.

"Mostly grisly wrecks I believe."

"Can we go along?" said Cindy.

"I don't see why in the world you'd would want to."

"I don't see why in the world we wouldn't want to."

"You'll have to ask him."

"Oh Olan please Olan oh Olan Olan please please please," sang Cindy, and the way she squeezed her cheeseburger in one hand, her pillow in the other, made Mac forget trying to think what his mother was thinking, made them all laugh.

IV

Mac liked the furniture in their rented farmhouse, most of which seemed to have been dragged, kicking, from a landfill, legs, drawers and cushions lost in the struggle. They had two bedrooms, a parlor, a saggy kitchen connected to the rest of the house by a breezeway of buckled porch boards which Glenn called a dogtrot. The house was back off the road in a grove of pecan trees, and it was quiet. The first day they sat in the yard where it was cooler, waiting for the telephone man to come so that Glenn could get his first assignment.

"Since I'll soon have access to a darkroom, I can take pictures of everybody." Somewhere in the world of curling snapshots exists a sheaf of pictures from this day: Cindy hugging a pecan tree, sleeveless blouse knotted at her midriff, jeans rolled up past her ankles, and her hair tossed over one shoulder; Mac unlashing his pallet from the luggage rack, the tip of his tongue protruding from his grimace suggesting a difficulty with his own intricate knots; Mac's mom behind the wheel of the Cortina, her hand dangling over the steering wheel holding a cigarette. In this picture her wrist is prominent, sleek and sculpted as the neck of a goose. Her eyes look to the farmhouse where they will spend the next couple of weeks.

"If we could maybe move more toward candids where I am concerned?" said Cindy.

"Impossible," said Glenn. "*You* forget to pose? It'll never happen."

After lunch the phone man finally showed, and they watched his slow stringing of wires impatiently, as if the moment he finished, bells would ring with news of fresh disaster. In fact, more than a day passed. Late the next night when Glenn got his call, Mac went rigid with the first ring. Underneath the thin sheet of his pallet he sweated, dressed already in cutoffs and a T-shirt. All he needed to do was pull on his hightops, poised bedside like fireman's boots. When he heard Glenn say "wreck" in response to his mother's mumble, he slipped out the screen door and waited in the Cortina.

"Where's big sis?" Glenn said when he climbed into the car.

"She sleeps heavier than she wants you to believe."

"Or than she wants to admit." Glenn handed his camera gear over for Mac to hold. "I'm going to need a navigator until I learn these roads," he said. "Pilot to co-pilot: get the map out and fasten your seatbelt."

They didn't talk much on the way, Glenn concentrating on the road, Mac on the county map. The roads were marked both by number and folksy names like Thick Neck Crook, Bear Gut, Bro John. It was confusing, but they made good time, thanks to Glenn's speeding. They beat the ambulance to the wreck site, which was on a straightaway above alfalfa fields, an odd place, Mac thought, for a wreck.

He mentioned this to Glenn as they pulled onto the shoulder behind the police cruiser.

"Curvy roads require you pay attention," said Glenn. "It's easier to nod off on a straight stretch." He grabbed his equipment and told Mac to stay in the car until he came back for him. "Let me see how bad. I'll come back and get you."

But he never did. Mac sat in the Cortina for a half-hour, watching the blue lights of the cruiser churn through the tops of nearby pines. Other cars happened by and stopped, people hurried past him, among them a child who could not have been more than seven or eight. He wasn't exactly mad at Glenn—he knew that he was protecting him from something he had no business seeing—but he was disappointed. He felt there was something out there he could learn from, something on that lonely straightaway that he needed. Curves require you pay more attention, he thought as the ambulance finally arrived, bleating its siren and inching through the tight corridor formed by the abandoned cars of the curious.

"Was it real bad?" Mac asked when Glenn returned.

Glenn shook his head. "Crash course. You'd think I could wade into this. Maybe a broken nose or collarbone to begin."

"You've done this before?"

"Take pictures?" said Glenn.

"Of wrecks and stuff, I mean." In Milwaukee they did not print pictures of wrecks on the front page of the newspaper. Mac found it an amazing idea, backward and uncivilized, fascinating and exciting.

"Not exactly," said Glenn. "I suppose you get used to it, but it's not like what I was doing when I met your mom. Though the thing is, I guess I distanced myself from that, too. Got away from the day-to-day by looking at the big picture. That job called for a different kind of distance, though. Lots would think that would be a cheerful job, but the families that come to get their pictures taken in a place like that . . ."

The tow truck passed, dragging the crushed automobile; a sapling, caught in a bend of the bumper, swished the pavement. When the patrolman turned his blue lights off and pulled away from them into the night, Glenn seemed to be pulled away from the big picture, shocked back into the moment. "Hell, it's a product," he said. "Something to sell papers to damn fools."

Mac expected Cindy to be jealous, at least curious, but the next morning at breakfast she acted as if nothing had happened. "You didn't hear the phone ring last night?" he said after ten minutes of coffee slurp and spoon chinking the sides of cereal bowls. "We went out on assignment."

As soon as she looked up from her cereal, Mac realized that he had said something stupid.

"Of course I heard it," she said. "What, pray tell, was your assignment? Mouth-to-mouth to some drunk corn-pone mama?"

"Why didn't you come?" Mac kept on even though he was blushing, even though he knew she would make every-thing he said seem impudent.

"I'm not interested in gore, Mac. Besides, if I go along to see the real thing, I would probably be very disappointed with the pictures he took." She turned to Glenn. "Don't you have to crop out the real gory stuff?" It was evident from her enunciation that she was proud of using "crop," which she'd picked up from her days on the yearbook staff.

"Yeah," said Glenn. "Sure do, Cin." He finished his cof-fee and toast and headed outside. Mac's mother followed him, her hands fishing through the pockets of her house-coat for something she seemed to have lost.

"Somebody got decapitated, right?" Cindy said when they were alone.

"Why would you say that?" said Mac.

She pointed at the plate abandoned across the table from him. "Olan didn't hardly touch his over-easies."

V

A few days after the wreck, Glenn came home from the newspaper and announced that he had a surprise for them that afternoon. Riding through town an hour later, Mac watched the short block of businesses give way to a street of high old houses and finally an outskirt of duplexes and bungalows. For several days his mother had complained of the heat, and that afternoon the heat began to get to him, too. While stopped at a light, Mac heard the popping of aluminum awnings which shielded the windows of tract houses. Dogs slept under bushes in cool dirt dugouts; everything was dust-coated, timed to the tick of postlunch stillness.

They coasted up to a lot on a deadend street where a house sat on a low trailer. As they arrived, a battered truck cab was backing up to the trailer. "Hole up" a half-dozen men called out of the sides of their mouths as the truck inched up to the hitch. There was a brake hiss, a grinding; the house wobbled then resettled, its chimney grazing a sycamore limb. Who would want to move a house like that, Mac wondered. Its bottom shingles were chipped and mudstained, several of its windows were missing panes, a street number was scrawled by the screen door in a primitive hand. Wrenched from its foundation, the house looked victimized, useless.

"What?" Cindy said, rising from her backseat slump to stare.

"They're moving it across town," said Glenn. "I'm supposed to take pictures of it for the paper and I thought you'd like to see how they do it."

After a string of "oh brothers" and "whoop-de-doos," Cindy said, "I thought maybe you were going to take us someplace fun. Like maybe Florida?"

"Just wait, Cin," said Mac.

Glenn twisted the rearview, focusing its slant on Cindy. "I take it you've seen a house moved down Main Street at the height of rush hour before?" he asked in a cartoonish voice. Mac smiled and shielded his eyes, as if the rearview were a naked thousand-watt bulb, as if *he* were the one being interrogated. Cindy thrust herself between the bucket seats, refusing to play along.

"Well you know, Olan, geez, where I come from"—she stopped to slant a sidelong look at her mom—"where *we* come from, people when they move they generally leave their house where it is. We move to another house, you get it? We don't carry it along with us, we aren't turtles."

Clasping his hand around Cindy's neck, Glenn said, "That's what you think."

Cindy shrugged his hand off. "Olan's being weird, Mom."

"Just wait, Cin," said their mom, managing to sound simultaneously hopeful and weary.

And they waited for an hour almost while the moving men stood in circles smoking and pawing the driveway with their workboots. When Glenn got out to join them and Cindy, assuming the air of a fireman called out to rescue a cat from a tree, slumped down in the sticky vinyl with a magazine, Mac felt constricted inside the stifling Cortina. They seemed to be sucking up each other's dwindling energy; the reptilian pulse of the wait caused the afternoon to feel draped and molten. The hour became an airtight box dumped into a river; occasionally someone spoke in an attempt to break free and swim to the surface, but things said were insignificant, and if they drew any response it was only after a pause that belied interest or courtesy. Mac thought of going outside to stretch his legs for a few minutes, yet he knew that if he joined the clump of men he would be both self-conscious and invisible, a combination he was trying to avoid. It seemed to Mac as if their lives had dead-ended here, as if leaving Milwaukee had led them smack into this static moment.

Finally the men ground their cigarettes out and climbed into their trucks. Glenn handed the keys to Mac's mom and told her to drive slowly backward so he could take pictures. In reverse the Cortina whirred like a windup toy. The house spilled over the sides of the trailer and towered over the truck cab. People gathered on their lawns to watch the bruised house bear down on this tiny foreign car with out-of-state tags. Something extraordinary was happening and they were a part of it, Mac realized. His mom twisted her head around to see behind, and Glenn pushed himself out of the window and sat on the door, tucking his feet beneath the car seat so that only his legs remained in the Cortina.

Framed by the windshield, the house seemed to be gaining on them. Cindy and I are the only ones who can see it, thought Mac; Mom's too busy driving and Glenn's too busy taking pictures. He longed to yank Glenn inside and tell him to forget about making money at a moment like this, to hell with selling papers to damn fools. He wanted his mother to see it as well, wanted them all together during these few moments in which they seemed to have achieved an independence from the daily and the domestic, a freedom enviable to the crowds lining the sidewalk, witnessing this uprooted house chase them toward the grapefruit grove, toward Florida.

VI

"We're being kidnapped, you know," said Cindy. She was standing in the doorway of the kitchen, where Mac sat at the table paging through the newspaper. He had started a clip file of all the pictures he'd helped Glenn take—the house-moving ones which made the front page, a handful of traffic accidents. Most of the wrecks had been minor, cars running off the road into fields so sodden with summer rains that they functioned like pillows, victims more mud-crusted than bloodstained. But there was one, just a few nights before, in which a girl was thrown from a car and killed. No one at the scene had even known there was a girl. They assumed the boy driving had been alone, but when he came to, he asked about his passenger.

"Everybody fan out now," the patrolman said to the small crowd. Glenn put his equipment away and jumped the ditch; Mac stood by the car until the patrolman spotted him and said, "You too, son. You got eyes." At first he shadowed the patrolman through the roadside scrub, but the patrolman seemed to feel him back there and he motioned Mac to the left with the wide beam of his flashlight. Mac spotted Glenn highstepping through the field and trotted toward him. He kept his eyes framed on Glenn, not on the ground. He tried not to touch earth. He tried not to let himself think about what he was doing. He was positive he would be the one to find her and when someone else called out "Over here," and they dragged the body out and laid it on the highway behind the mangled car, Mac was able to ignore the injured boy's wailing, so thankful was he to be spared the discovery.

"We're not being kidnapped either," he told Cindy. "This is just our summer vacation."

"You think life in this shitty town is a vacation?"

Mac looked out the window to where Glenn, his mother, and a reporter from the newspaper sat under the pecan trees drinking beer. Radios played in both the Cortina and the reporter's car, an American Ford which seemed boxy and plain alongside the Cortina. The three sat in lawn chairs in the last light, smoking and listening to the radio, their posture showing that slightly relaxed rigidity of people who don't know each other well but who've had a few drinks. Jimmy Rogers on the tuned-together radios, one crackling slightly with static.

"Yes," he said. He thought of his father, the way he dropped Mac off at Sunday school, the interminable rides to and from church, his father quiet all the way except to say, if anything, the same thing: "My parents made me go to Sunday school and it gave me a lot to think about." He remembered the stubby yellow pencils found in church pews, thought of the other places he'd seen the same type of pencil: putt-putt golf courses, bowling alleys, any place with a scorecard.

"You're too young to understand the situation at hand," said Cindy.

"You're fourteen going on twenty trying to make something of it that ain't there."

"That ain't there, that ain't there. Already talking hickster."

"They say ain't in Wisconsin."

"Certain kinds of people do, true."

"Go away, I'm busy." The picture of a wreck he'd covered had cropped up on the sports page, and Mac went after it with his scissors.

"As long as you fill your morbid quota you're happy. But I'm telling you, Glenn's a jailbird. Skipping out on those motels? They're looking for us right now, dumbass. That's why we're here—laying low. And don't think they'll let us go because we're minors."

Cindy knew the two things he was most afraid of: war and prison. When Mac was younger, he'd had recurring nightmares about being sent to either place; in a moment of slack judgment he had confided in his sister. Of course what he wanted was for someone to tell him that he'd never have to worry about going to war or prison, that he wasn't a coward for being scared. His mother would have told him this without hesitation, but also without consideration—a doled-out act of motherhood reflexive as the shaking down of a thermometer. Wasn't there, to be honest, a chance that he would go to war? Bay of Pigs was in the news then, Communist rebels had come down out of the mountains just two years before in that country only ninety miles from the crust of the state where they were headed now. Cindy had assuaged his fears in a bluntly tender way: *I can't see you in prison,* she'd said. *Not at all, Mac, not you.* He'd been afraid that there was something in him that would lead him to commit actions punishable by incarceration, something that everyone but himself could see. Cindy's answer would have seemed evasive, even mocking to some, but to Mac it was perfect.

And if you go to college you don't have to go to war, she said.

No contest, thought Mac. Dorm room vs. barracks? World Civ. versus ten-mile marches wearing combat boots? She had even provided some semblance of balance by confessing that some baby splitting her wide open terrified her no end, kept her up nights too. Her confession made him feel better, but not exactly masculine or at peace.

"They won't put us in jail. We didn't do anything."

"It's called accessory. Who pushed the car onto the road?"

"Who steered?" This kind of return-fire argument, as instinctive within him as his father told him prayer should be, always made Mac feel sticky and ashamed. But then she started it, and what does pushing the car have to do with it anyway? Stiffing the motel is the illegal part, who cares *how* you leave.

"All I'm trying to say is that Glenn's not who you think he is. Neither is Mom these days."

"What's that mean?"

"Whatever he says, she does. She's lost her marbles."

Mac looked out the window at the three of them in the

near dark, at his mother waving her cigarette in tight circles to shoo away mosquitoes.

"She'll do whatever he wants. We're never going to see Dad again."

Mac bent to his paper and started cutting. "Think Dad's looking for us?" he said softly. He imagined his father on the phone all day, talking to people he referred to as officers of the law, drinking scotch and milk in the skinny kitchen, looking out over the backyard and racking his brain for the name of a neighborhood boy he could hire to mow it.

"If he's not, he will be soon," said Cindy. "The only thing she told him in that note of hers was that we were going to the grapefruit grove."

The grapefruit grove: it was the first time Mac had thought about it since the house had chased them down the street. It did seem silly now, a ridiculous destination. What would they do when they got there? Stroll around like they did at rest areas? Summer wasn't even grapefruit season, and Mac only liked the pink ones, which his mom said didn't grow in her grove, and he only liked those with plenty of sugar on top. The way Cindy had said "her grapefruit grove" made it clear that she doubted its existence. Or thought there was nothing much left of it to see, a few gnarled trees bearing swollen yellow globes, people poorer than they'd ever be climbing ladders to pick them.

"How do you know what she wrote in that note?"

"She told me. She'll tell me anything, see? Any question I ask, she just answers. That's why I say she's loony tunes. She's too far gone to tell her own daughter a lie."

"Why should she lie?"

"You think this is really all about grapefruits? You're even dumber than I thought, Mackie."

"Don't call me that."

"I guess you think Glenn's some kind of grapefruit expert or something," said Cindy. "That's why they share a bedroom. They stay up all night talking about vitamin C."

"Just stop it, Cin."

"Just look at her, Mac."

Glenn and the reporter leaned forward with their beers pointed in the air as if to launch bottle rockets, talking to each other across the still airspace of Mac's mother's lap. Her bottle sat in the corner of the lawn chair, wedged between her hip and the loose green and white webbing, half-full, forgotten. She seemed glad that she did not have to talk, could just bask, nod, smile and watch the sunset stripe the space above the treeline red and yellow.

"She's forgotten us. Never meant to bring us anyway."

"Why did she then?"

"She wouldn't have come without us because she would have felt too guilty. With us along she can ignore us in a way she couldn't of if we were back home with Dad."

"What'd you come for then?"

Cindy's face went as dreamy distant as their mother's at the same moment.

"Florida," she said, and without taking a breath, a little too quickly, she added, "But not the Florida of grapefruit groves."

VII

In this town where they hesitated there was going to be a total eclipse of the sun. Of course the eclipse would occur all across the path of totality but because it was so odd for Mac to be in this town in the first place, living his new life—days lying under trees in thick sand, thin pallet-sleep at night, disentangling back roads from veiny maps by moonlight, searching fields for bodies—he felt as if the eclipse would affect *only* this town. It seemed a likely location for him to be when something so monumental occurred as the moon blotting out the sun, bringing darkness down to noon.

Back home there would have been a buildup: in school, eclipse reports to write, scientists from Madison visiting his class, a hokey assembly during which some fat teacher's pet dressed up as the moon passed in front of a skinnier teacher's pet dressed as the sun just as the custodian cut the lights, teachers exhaled firework oohs and aahs, students cuffed each other and snickered.

At the least there would have been something in the newspaper. In this town there was no news, no hoopla. When Glenn came home the day before and told them about the eclipse, Mac wondered aloud why they had not known about this for days. He was treating it like a presidential election or a Cape Canaveral blast-off, and although his mother suspected his promotion of the eclipse was a carryover from overcelebratory attention paid such events in grade school, she was infected by his exuberance.

"Yeah," she said, standing at the kitchen sink washing vegetables a neighbor had given her which she knew nothing about: okra, field peas, wilted greens. "Yes, yes, you're right, Mackenzie. Nobody let us know. They should have let us know a long time ago so we could prepare."

"But why would anyone down here give a yeehaw hot damn if the lights go out for a minute or two," said Cindy. "It'll be a little siesta for them. Catnap in their pickup trucks."

"Cin still thinks we're in South America," Glenn said.

"Our driveway's really the equator," said Mac.

"Might as well be," said Cindy.

"It's a lot hotter in Florida, Cin," said her mother.

Cindy flipped the crisp page of a magazine and said, "What do I care if we're never going to get there?"

At breakfast the next morning, Glenn announced his special assignment: he was to locate a barnyard and take some pictures of befuddled hens taking roost in the artificial darkness of noon.

"But wherever will you find a barnyard around here?" said Cindy. She sat at the table with a magazine, refusing to be interested.

Mac helped Glenn load film into his camera and stowed the flashes he had brought home from the newspaper in the car. They stamped their special barnyard boots on the sloped linoleum and announced that it was time to go.

"We're not going," said Cindy.

Mac's mother had pushed her cup and saucer aside and was halfway out of her chair. She slanted her head down at Cindy, making a face almost identical to one her daughter often made at her.

"I'm going. You can stay if you want. Do the dishes."

"No, Mom. You're staying too."

Cindy slumped further down in the chair, her feet reaching the bottom rung of the ladderback across the small table from her. This slackening seemed a trump, as if she were gaining control by turning invertebrate, the way Mac had seen civil rights protesters do on television when picked up by police.

"Why, Cin? Exactly why am I staying too?"

"Because I need to talk to you in private now."

"About what?" said Mac.

"That's for me to know and you never to find out."

Mac's mother sat back down at the table. There seemed a draft in the kitchen created by her acquiescence, and Mac watched her closely for signs of disappointment or an instinctive summoning of maternal duty, but what he saw was only his mother in a farmhouse kitchen on the morning of an eclipse.

In the car he tried several lines—"Female trouble" . . . "Girl talk" . . . "My ears are buzzing"—none of which drew anything but maddening silence from the driver's side. He tried to cover one remark up with another, which was a mistake, he realized, that people often make; that he often made. Glenn's silence seemed stronger, weightier, respectful of whatever was taking place back in the kitchen. Mac gave in to it, forgetting in this unimpaired silence all about what they were on their way to witness.

As it happened, there was not much witnessing from either of them during the magical moment itself. Setting up their equipment in the barnyard took a long time; cows in an adjacent pasture and the farmer's three young children stopped to watch, a sameness in their slow eyes. They blinked occasionally to dislodge gnats but otherwise they were still, fixing him with the unwavering lenses of their stares. Mac was unsure of how to help with the preparations, and having an audience made him nervous. He slipped his hands in the back pockets of his jeans and started whistling "The Little Marine," but stopped when the youngest of the farmer's children began singing along, supplying the words of a children's song called "If You're Happy and You Know It," which shared the same tune. Mac felt as if he would never be able to talk to someone his own age again, and he hurried back to work, tightening the butterfly toggles on the tripod, standing on his tiptoes to sight the henhouse door through the tiny lens of the Pentax.

Slowly the sky began to change, growing not the gradual and variegated greys he'd expected, but a strange, warm pink: Mac thought of how, when his eighty-year-old grandfather used to sit on the porch, light would seep through the lobes of his overgrown ears. He remembered the hair on his grandfather's ears, silhouetted singly and brilliant, like trees on a ridge behind which the sun was sinking. Mostly he stayed too busy helping Glenn set up to concentrate on the eeriness of the moments leading up to the moment, but once he ignored Glenn's order not to look up and saw that the sun was already half-covered by the ragged cutout of the moon. The eclipse looked crude to Mac, slapped up in the sky like kindergarten art pushpinned to a bulletin board. It reminded him of this place, of the cardboard covering the windowpanes back at the farm-house, the sawed-off, spray-painted lattice used to display merchandise in the show-windows downtown.

Back in Milwaukee he would be watching with hun-dreds in a park or a school playground, peering through some specially devised instrument made safe for schoolkids. There would be information about the hole in the sun's outer atmosphere known as the corona, warnings against using improvised viewing devices such as darkened film or smoked glass. Down here he watched when he could, be-tween orders from Glenn, alongside cows and cow-eyed kids oblivious to any aspect of nature save gnats that must be blinked away. He took his chances looking up; he risked his eyesight for a minute of high noon here in this place where they had hesitated.

Mac tried to think of how his father would react to the eclipse, and decided that he would treat it as something Mac should attend. He would compare it to something stel-lar from his own youth which had given him a lot to think about.

During the moment of darkness roosters began to crow. A lone cow broke from the herd and trampled up the pas-ture. Glenn cussed the hens who took a few tentative steps toward their house, pecked each other, jerked about in tight clumsy circles.

"Herd 'em in there, Mac, hurry," said Glenn, and Mac moved toward them, flailed his arms, hammering the ground with his boot heels. Three clucked at each other calmly and the other two rose in a flurry of wings and dust, terrifying Mac who had forgotten or perhaps never known that hens could fly.

It wasn't their fault if the hens didn't cooperate. It was after all a shock, this darkness at noon, and not long enough to convince anyone, even senseless hens, that night had fallen. "Oh hell," said Glenn, and he pulled himself up out of his stoop, rubbed the photographer's squint from his eyes, became Glenn again. "Oh well," he said, and he walked over toward the farmhouse where the farmer and his hands sat under trees in slack-webbed lawn chairs. Mac started to load the equipment into the car, but midway though his first trip, Glenn stopped him.

"No need for that now. We're coming back."

"When?" said Mac. There wasn't, to his knowledge, such a thing as a doubleheader eclipse.

"Dusk."

"What for?"

"To get a shot of hens taking roost."

Mac didn't say anything. He helped Glenn stow the equipment in the barn. The rest of the afternoon they crisscrossed the county on back roads, killing time before dark. Mac wondered why they didn't go back home, but he remembered the scene they'd left and figured Glenn felt his mother and Cindy needed more time alone. They spent the day in a fatigued and respectful silence. Mac's moods were as many as the kinds of crops they passed in the flat countryside. Farmers had to rotate them, Glenn explained, in order to preserve the nutrients in the soil. It took them a long time to figure this out, said Glenn, pointing out fields which looked thirsty and depleted. Mac found it hard to think of something as elemental as the earth wearing out; it bothered him to think of the acres and acres of played-out land in this world. He didn't think he could take another of nature's secrets, and wished the afternoon would end.

Finally—it must have been well past seven—the sun started its descent toward the pine forest. They stopped at a grill for cheeseburgers. Sitting at a picnic table, wiping splatted mosquitoes off his arms, Mac decided that this return-to-the-scene-of-the-crime-under-cover-of-darkness scheme wasn't proof that Glenn was, as Cindy liked to claim, not the man Mac thought he was. It bothered him, this deception, but it didn't make Glenn a kidnapper or a jailbird. Was it Glenn's fault that the hens weren't fooled? Some things don't last long enough to make much of a change in how you act, and Glenn, after all, had orders. He had to do what the editor told him or he wouldn't get paid and they wouldn't get to Florida. They'd be imprisoned here in this place that Mac was beginning to doubt.

It was just something to sell papers to damn fools. Like Glenn had said earlier, you distance yourself from the day-to-day by thinking of the big picture. And there was a larger deception surrounding them to consider. Mac didn't really want to consider it; he acknowledged it by pushing it away.

As Mac wiped his plate clean of ketchup with a french fry, Glenn tilted his head back to see the sky and said, "Now it's going dark for good." Mac, tilting his head back like Glenn, felt glad the hens had not taken roost, for they would have just had to get up again in a minute, when the moon moved away and the sun streamed again through the wide cracks of their house.

Back home, walking into the flood of overhead light which brought out the shabbiness of the farmhouse and caused both of them to squint, they found Cindy and his mother at the kitchen table, just where they'd left them. Their plates were filled with barely touched pork chops, large portions of okra and field peas. Both chairs were scooted back from the table, both bodies sunken in an after-dinner slump.

"Supposed to put ketchup on those field peas. That's what the reporter said."

Cindy pushed her plate away. She pushed her hair out of her eyes, drew herself up in the ladderback. "Tell him, Mom."

"Cindy wants to go back home."

Mac watched Glenn walk across the kitchen to the stove, stir the pot of beans. Watching Glenn's calm reaction, he wondered if Glenn had expected this to happen. As much as Mac loved to predict the not-yet, as often as he felt things before they happened, he was shocked himself. He began to doubt his talent for clairvoyance, wondered if it was a useful talent to have.

He'd thought Cindy had been whining as usual, thought she'd whine until they escaped this town and continued to Florida. Not the Florida of grapefruit groves but her Florida, the one where tiers of trick water-skiers threaded cypress trees, the Florida of high-rise hotels and driving right on the beach. Why couldn't she just hold on? He knew Glenn as well as anyone, as well as his mother did; he knew that if Cindy could just hold on, Glenn would take them where they wanted to go.

"To Milwaukee?" said Mac. "She misses Milwaukee?"

"Plus," said Cindy, ignoring him, prodding her mother as if she had forgotten her lines and Cindy was standing in the wings with a copy of the script.

"She wants to leave tomorrow."

Glenn opened a cabinet, found a plate, dished himself some field peas. He dolloped ketchup on the top, stirred the peas around with a spoon. "Well, okay, Cin. Sure, baby. Okay. The thing of it is I hate to quit this job right when I'm starting to salt some away. So what if we put you on a bus?"

Cindy leaned across the table to her mother. "Mom. Olan doesn't seem to be really getting it, Mom."

"Olan's name is Glenn, Lucinda."

"And Lucinda's name is Cindy, Beatrice."

"Get out of this room, please," said Mac's mother. Glenn had turned away, was putting his plate down.

"It's called a kitchen," said Cindy. Mac flinched when his mother bolted up; the slap of her chair against the linoleum was anticlimactic. Her name's not Beatrice, Mac was thinking, her name is Carol. It *actually* was a kitchen that they were standing in, but there was more than simple teenage recalcitrance in Cindy's statement; it was an honest appraisal of where they stood that moment in their lives. Cindy refused to be fooled. Calling the room a kitchen made more sense, and cut much deeper, than if she'd called her mother a slut, Glenn a kidnapper, Mac a gullible little mama's boy. This room was a kitchen. Mac looked around at the rust-spotted sink, at the oven door pulled down, its grease-splattered hollow exposed. Glenn ate with his back to them, but he ate. Mac was amazed not that such a thing was taking place but that he had been able to read it so well after all that had gone on that day, after all he had seen. Another time he might have thought his sister's reaction irrational, only immature retaliation, might have missed out entirely on the significance of what she'd said.

"You too, Mackenzie," his mom said now. "Get out." In the hallway he swerved close to the door of Cindy's room but heard nothing; he went outside and climbed onto the hood of the Cortina, leaning his head back on the windshield and staring up at the stars, which, he thought, must be as tired as he was. They'd worked overtime today too, and had to be weary still from their noon matinee.

AT DAWN his mother woke him. She sat on the edge of his pallet and shook him, her fingers clamping his collarbone as he stirred. She had on clothes he'd last seen her wear to her job at the department store: beige blouse, pleated skirt, knee socks. She hugged her legs, rested her cheek on her kneecaps and peered sideways at him while he blinked and stretched himself awake. First light through the curtainless windows sparked her heavily glossed lips and he remembered waking earlier in the night to noises in the parlor, where his mother slept with Glenn. Since he'd started assisting Glenn he had trained himself to sleep lightly, and when he heard the thumps and rustlings he felt ashamed for sleeping through the phone ring. He'd tried hard to struggle up from the sleep that seemed to pin him to the pallet; the will to rise (*get up, get dressed, we're leaving*) filled his head to overflowing but refused to make the trip to his limbs. His arms and legs lay heavily across the sandy sheets, splayed there as if some unidentifiable force hovered above, holding him down. All the while the noises continued, and it seemed as if Glenn was having as hard a time getting into gear as he was. Low voices not quite distinguishable as language; more music, a gurgly background wash like the faint song of schoolhouse radiator. Mac had his shorts on and was lacing his boots when he heard his mother cry out, heard Glenn's finish line heaving, and realized what was going on.

"You don't have to sleep on the pallet from now on," his mother said. Mac rolled over, stared at the cobwebbed corners of the room, wondering how he'd managed to go back to sleep so easily. He did not even remember getting undressed, yet there he was in his boxers; it bothered him more than if he'd slept through a call from the newspaper.

"You woke me up to tell me that?"

She laughed at this, which angered him until he remembered the scene the night before, how it had ended: his mother banishing both her children from her sight, from the room which Cindy called a kitchen. He remembered Cindy calling his mother Beatrice, and against his will he smiled. Although it wasn't funny, really—it made no sense—the harder he tried to keep a straight face, the more his lips spread and his cheek muscles ached under the strain of keeping silent. A half-giggle escaped, which he masked as a cough. His mother was fooled; she patted his back like she was burping a baby, and he thought that his mother's stint as Beatrice was awfully short. She had come back to him, her sweet helpless self, Carol, Mom.

"I only meant you can sleep in Cindy's bed if you want. Cin and I are leaving this morning. There's a bus to Chicago at nine. Glenn says you can stay here with him until I get back. A week or so, okay, Mac? But you don't have to sleep on the floor the whole time."

He liked the pallet, was used to it. He'd started out this trip sleeping on it and felt that sleeping on it prolonged the temporary.

"I thought you'd rather stay here than ride a bus to Milwaukee," she said. When he didn't turn to her or answer she said, "Stay with Glenn, I mean. Until I get back?"

"Then what?"

"Then we go on down to Florida. Pick some grapefruit. Out of somebody else's grove of course."

Mac pictured the three of them stealing into a roadside grove, inching the car past the caretaker's cabin. He would take Cindy's place behind the wheel, popping the clutch and steering by moonlight to the appointed spot. To his sleepy mind it seemed a seductive rearrangement.

"Then what?"

"Quit talking to your pillow and I'll tell you. Look at me."

"Then what?" he asked the wall.

"Then I'll have you back for the first day of school."

"Cin misses her friends and stuff," he said. It seemed silly, an immature thing to say apropos of nothing, but it kept him from saying other things. It kept him from asking his mother what she would do after his first day of school. There was nothing she had to be back for, no deadlines, no first days. This was no summer vacation, for her at least.

"Cindy's at that age," his mother said. "Still, I can't just put her on the bus to Chicago. She's not that old."

"Thinks she is." He heard his mother snicker, heard her move, a second later felt her weight against him on the pallet. Her arm sneaked around his bare rib cage and he thought of and rejected things to say to get her away from him: *"You'll mess up your bus clothes."* Too much a thing Cindy would say. *"You've already done one floor tonight."* Even Cindy would not say a thing like this, and he felt sick for thinking it.

"I've got to tell your father *something,*" she said into his ear. "I left him a note and I've sent a postcard, but that's really it."

"What do you have to tell him?"

She was quiet for a few seconds, and her hands grew sweaty on his ribs and he remembered the midnight noises and twisted away.

"Well, he's your father."

"He knows that."

"I know he does, Mac."

"If he doesn't, it's too late."

"Why is it too late?"

"Just, I mean, I don't know, just go away."

"What's too late?"

"Mom!" He let go an exaggerated Cindy sigh, dramatic gasp designed to transmit without another word—they were beyond words—his impatience.

"Okay, baby. Don't wake up Glenn. It's not often he gets to sleep the night through without being called out. You'll be all right here with him."

Mac was quiet. "Of course you will," she said. "Look, you know how your father is. I can't do a thing about it, it's just how he is. You know what I mean."

"Yes," he said, although he had no idea.

"He's worried about you, I'm sure."

"What will you tell him?" asked Mac, but he was too ashamed of having started the conversation up again to pay attention to her answer, though he could tell by her face that she was making it all up anyway. When she left the room he lay in bed for a long time wondering if there had been an eclipse in Wisconsin, if the path of totality had extended that far north. If it was something he would have gotten to see if he'd never left, or if it was something that followed them down here like weather, fate or luck.

VIII

Mac's mother and Cindy left on a Sunday morning. In that place, Sundays seemed longer than two weekdays spliced together; the farmers stayed home to doze on their porches, there was no traffic on the highway, the tractor hum from surrounding fields gave way to swells of cicada chorus. The stillness made Mac want only to eat, mumble and sleep. Glenn's reporter pal came over to the farmhouse in the early afternoon with a box of beer and a burlap bag filled with peanuts. The peanuts looked as if they'd been dug up that morning; dirt clung to their tiny roots and they tasted so raw that Mac decided they'd come from a field in which all nutrients were depleted. He ate only one. Glenn went into the shed and returned with two rusty ashcans. He and the reporter sagged back in their lawn chairs and jammed the ashcans between their legs, filling them with shells as the flat afternoon burned slowly onward. Mac leaned against the Cortina or sat in front of them in the drive drawing stick figures in the dirt with a twig.

"These are hog peanuts technically," said the reporter. He told a story about stealing the wrong kind of corn, hog corn, getting caught stealing hog corn, the embarrassment of buckshot in your ass due to stealing corn meant for hogs. Glenn, who had not said much all day, eating peanuts and drinking quietly as the reporter talked on (Mac was sure Glenn missed his mom, and maybe even Cindy), started to laugh during the middle of the reporter's story.

"I wouldn't think your ass would give a damn what kind of corn it was."

"Neither do you speaketh from the pain of personal experience," said the reporter.

Glenn laughed harder. Once he started laughing he abandoned himself to laughing at everything said. The reporter talked his trash. He was thin, and had the Adam's apple of an iguana. Mac watched it bob to the time of his syllables; he wished he'd shut up, wished Cindy was there to hear him so at least they could sneak away and make fun of him. The reporter went to great lengths to belabor the scant payoffs of his stories. Cindy would have something to say about his great lengths; she would blame him and his interminable delivery on the place, the heat, the equator, the fact that they weren't yet in Florida. Mac would not necessarily agree with her—he thought her judgments about this place too colored by the fact that she missed her friends, that she was *at that age*—but still he missed hearing them.

"Give the boy a beer," said the reporter. "Give Mr. Mac some icy-coldy."

All day Mac had wished for a phone call, an urgent summons to the site of a wreck, a fire, even a drowning in an irrigation pond. But this Sunday was like a cease-fire, and his mother and Cindy's absence made it drag all the more.

"You can have a half one, Mac," Glenn said. "Go get yourself a cup."

Mac sipped the beer. It bubbled up inside of him like a clogged sink, the foam rose to his nose and he hated it.

Between stories the reporter turned to him. "You miss your mama?"

Before Mac could answer the reporter said, "Hell, I miss my mama and she don't live but just up the road." The reporter started pointing, giving directions. Mac listened, catching the names of some of the back roads they'd taken, but Glenn's beery grin grew bigger and finally burst into hilly laughter which the reporter talked right through. "You know where Crumpler's is at?" the reporter said to Mac. Mac shook his head no and Glenn laughed so hard that beer shot in lava-like beads from his bottle. "You know where Hoop the bootlegger's place is back up here off Number 242?" The reporter leaned in so close that Mac could see peanut skins stuck to his teeth. "Surely you know where Suzanne Bledsoe stays?"

Mac's grin was meant to correspond to Glenn's wild laughter, but he knew it did not connect. Glenn's behavior seemed a part of a code he could not crack, and he wondered if all this time—since he'd left Milwaukee—some kind of joke were being played on him. There had been times before in his life when he'd realized well after the fact how he'd misjudged a situation and had thought that some unidentifiable force was conspiring to make a fool of him. He hated feeling this way—it seemed something he'd picked up from his father—but it also helped him overcome embarrassment or shame. Yet this time it failed to make him feel better. It didn't matter who was responsible for the joke; the fact was that the joke was on him. Casting about for someone or something to blame, Mac decided that men grew meaner during cease-fires.

Finally the reporter got in his car and bumped up the drive at five miles an hour. Glenn smiled vaguely at the trunk of the reporter's car until it was out of sight, then fell asleep in the lawn chair. Mac sat down in the reporter's chair, straddled the ashcan brimming with peanut shells, settled in between Glenn's snores and a fermata of tree frog song rising from the bottomland. When Glenn awoke near dusk, he fished a bottle from the tub of melting ice, splashed some of the tub water on his face and neck, twisted the cap off his beer and said, "Well, now, Mr. Mac. Fell asleep I guess."

"What if they had called about a wreck or something?"

Glenn smiled. "I got my navigator with me."

"Still," said Mac.

"Forget it," said Glenn. "Everybody's driving careful today."

"Yeah. Like the reporter?"

Glenn smiled, but it wasn't the same smile he'd flashed when laughing with the reporter. "You're starting to sound like big sis," he said.

"You don't like Cindy much."

"Hold on," said Glenn. Mac could tell that Glenn found his petulance irritating, but Glenn didn't seem to know exactly how to act, with Mac's mother on a bus back to Milwaukee. Instead of denying Mac's charge, Glenn said, "You've got to admit she's a person who'd rather rock the boat than not."

"She's my sister," said Mac. He felt a weary allegiance he remembered feeling when much younger. He'd hoped that calling Cindy his sister would be as powerful and as ir-refutable as Cindy calling a kitchen a kitchen, but Glenn saw things differently from Mac's mother, and calling a thing by its name seemed to have no effect on him.

"I don't know why Mom brought us along," said Mac.

Glenn leaned over, twisted his beer bottle into the sand and said, "Because she loves you two." It seemed too easy an answer to Mac, and it irritated him.

"Not much of a vacation for you," said Mac.

Glenn, laughing again, said, "Well now you know, Mac, I don't really take vacations. I mean I'm not that kind of guy."

Mac considered this. Taking off for Florida at the first hint of spring, staying in motels, eating cheeseburgers. It looked and smelled and tasted like a vacation to him, yet there was something else—something at once desperate and carefree—about Glenn's life that made him think Glenn was telling the truth. You think life in this shitty town is a vacation?

Cindy had asked him. Rather than stick it out, she'd gone home, and he wondered if he'd made a mistake in staying.

"You're thinking about your father." Mac looked up to see Glenn studying him. "You miss him?"

"No," said Mac. He looked at Glenn defiantly, but Glenn didn't seem shocked, only sleepy. He thought of saying, "He's like Cindy," or "Cindy is like she is because of Dad," but that wouldn't be fair to Cindy or to Glenn. What did Glenn care about Mac's father? Glenn had risen already, as if he'd asked the question because he felt he needed to but didn't want to stick around for the answer.

"Let's go into town and get something to eat," he said. He reached for his beer and poured it out slowly, both of them watching it fizz up, turning the blond sand muddy.

"Okay," said Mac, thinking as he watched the parched sand absorb the foam that it was not going to be possible for him to rush things, that he wanted to speed things up.

IX

It was a slow week: two AWOL soldiers from Fort Bragg took out a tree on Seven Bridges Road, but neither was seriously injured because they were drunk.

"Bones give when they got all that liquor in them," the patrolman told Glenn. "If they'd been holy roller abstainers, they'd been dead."

A barn caught fire on Railroad Street in town. Mac and Glenn arrived just in time to get a picture of its skeleton quiver and implode.

"If I'd have been alone, I wouldn't have been able to make it in time, much less get set up," said Glenn. Mac had read the map, Mac had loaded the camera on the way. Driving home, Glenn sang; he was in a good mood, he had his picture. Mac lost a battle in which he tried not to laugh at

Glenn's singing—the "Little Marine" again, this time in a patchy falsetto which Glenn claimed beat hell out of Dion.

A couple of nights later Mac's mom called.

"Your father says hello." Glenn stayed in the room while Mac talked. Several times Mac cast frowns his way, but Glenn kept his head in the folds of the newspaper and stayed put.

"He said it was okay for me to stay?"

"Sure," said Mac's mother.

"Is he there?"

There was a delay during which the phone crackled with static, reminding Mac of the distance between them. "I'm staying over at Mim's. You remember her from the department store?"

"Cindy's there?"

"Not right now. I'll be back soon. Get Glenn to tell you because I have to get off Mim's phone now." Lowering her voice, she unleashed a juicy, muted laugh that Mac had never heard from her before. "Mim has a hot date tonight with an exterminator. She's in there fumigating herself so he won't I guess."

Hanging up, Mac tried not to think about what was going on up there. In a few weeks the summer would be over and these weeks in Mac's mind were chock-full of things: his mother's return, the Cortina speeding finally south through states he'd never been to. Florida: the three of them giggling in the hot predawn dark, trying to dislodge the Cortina from the sprawling roots of a massive magnolia. They would rock the car, laughter would rock them, dogs would chase them, the electric eyes of animals would flash from the roadside while they made their getaway.

Later that night, just before they went to bed, the phone rang again. Mac thought for sure it was his mother—maybe Cindy was home now and wanted to talk to him. He could tell her about the Irma he spotted on the reporter's Lucky

Strike, but he had a premonition that Cindy would act as if
Irmas were a thing of the past, a thing consigned to the
slow showroom afternoons, a thing she'd outgrown. Still,
he wanted to talk to her and he hurried into the kitchen,
but Glenn pinched the receiver to his neck and made a
scribbling motion in the air and, when Mac brought over a
pencil and pad, covered the paper with directions.

"A whiskey still," Glenn said when he hung up. "They
discovered it in the woods and the paper wants pictures tak-
en before they blow it up. Must be the granddaddy of them
all from the way they described it. Get your shoes on."

In the car, Glenn seemed so charged up about this liquor
still that Mac could not bring himself to ask what his mother had said. He wanted to be excited about this shoot,
too—Glenn had promised him that they could stay to see
the still blown—but he'd rather it had been his mother on
the phone. He'd rather have stayed in tonight, and if she
and Cindy had been there, he might have.

County maps spread across his lap, interior light blazing
above, Mac read directions and called out turns. Dark
houses, pine forests and fields slid past and Mac marveled at
how accustomed he'd become to moving at night. It didn't
really matter what his mom had said as long as she was
coming back. She, too, had grown used to traveling by
dark. Those nights they'd sneaked away from the sleepy
motor courts had changed her, changed both of them in
similar ways. This world that Glenn had shown them was
one that Mac and his mother had not known and had
feared. Glenn defused the danger by taking pictures; he
even let the pictures be used to sell papers to damn fools.
Mac wished Cindy was along now so that he could tell her
how wrong she'd been about Glenn, how much he'd shown
them.

At the end of a long logging trail they met an officer
who was waiting to lead them through the woods to the

site. Glenn and the man walked quickly, talking about the still in tones as low and tangled as the brush underfoot. A branch stretched back by the men snapped into Mac's face, stinging his cheek. They've forgotten me, he thought, and he hurried to catch up, to huddle in their draft where he'd be protected from the sidelong assault of the periphery.

But he couldn't keep up. The feeble halo diced from the dark wood by the officer's flashlight was not meant for him to share. Beyond its ray things moved through the wood. There were rustlings, twig snaps, the sound of far-off feet splashing through water. Mac looked over his shoulder, swiveled his head from side to side. Hunching over, he bounced on the balls of his feet, a stance he remembered from war movies. More footfalls behind; Mac spun around to investigate, but the trail was swallowed by blackness. He felt he was being watched, and wondered if this trip was not part of the joke, and if all the creatures of night as well as everyone he knew—Cindy, his mom, even his dad—were gathered under cover of darkness to watch him be tricked.

Once again he wished he were back at the farmhouse asleep on his pallet, Cindy and his mom just beyond the walls. He conjured up an image of his mother loping along between him and Glenn, and he managed to hold this image by borrowing from his memory of those midnight flights from motels, when Mac, Glenn and his mom were possessed by an illicit and rarefied energy, strong enough to push cars through thick sand with Ouija board fingertips.

But this fantasy didn't last. His mother might have agreed to come along, but only for the ride. She would have stayed in the Cortina; she would not care to see a still blown up. After all, she'd stayed inside with Cindy during the eclipse, she'd looked behind her when the house had chased them. Perhaps it was enough for her that these things happened, that Glenn had come along to take them to a place where they existed. Or perhaps she had a hand in creating these things along with Glenn, thought Mac. Maybe she'd just grown too bored to see them through.

Rising sun lighting this middle of nowhere place would have found her smiling through the windshield at the played-out fields, waiting for Glenn to come back and take her away, farther away.

Mac followed the voices into a clearing where a half-dozen men, Glenn among them, stood around a fire. Mac hovered at the edge of the clearing, cameras and flashes strapped across his shoulders. He felt stupid, half-hidden there in the shadows like a pack mule led into camp and then ignored until provisions were needed. The men huddled around the fire, their talk constant and indecipherable. He stood still in the farthest reach of campfire light, watching the shadows flicker up the tree trunks. Some moments passed until a deputy spotted him, did a double-take and said something low to the others, who fixed him with the efficient glares of men interrupted.

"That your boy?"

"Brought my helper with me," Glenn said sheepishly.

Mac felt like calling out to them that Glenn was a friend of his mother's. *She left him,* Mac felt like screaming, *she's gone back to my daddy,* but he realized that saying it aloud might make it true, and if it was true then she'd left them both, abandoned them in this place where they had hesitated.

Glenn turned back to the fire. Backlit by the blaze, his silhouette seemed to glow.

"Bring him on over here, let him see how they make this shit," one of the men said.

Mac unlashed the equipment, laid it carefully in a bed of pine straw. He felt lighter as he approached the fire. The still was smaller and simpler than he'd imagined, yet nothing fit: pipes and barrels were held together by baling wire, at one end was an open vat, the type of rust-flaked brown can favored by country stores for makeshift incinerators. Mac noticed a car radiator hidden in the middle of the still, pipes running from top and bottom. Tattered sweatshirts hung from low limbs around the clearing, as if pinned to dry on backyard clotheslines.

"Radiator's used to condense it?" asked Glenn.

"Blind you in a goddamn heartbeat," someone said.

"Naw, hell, Gil," said another man. "Never blinded you."

"Yet," someone added.

"What Gil does, he picks him up some strange? Pours some this mash down her and watches those legs spread."

"Lickety split."

"And stay damn spread, too."

While the men kept this line stoked with their clipped, guttural contributions, Glenn turned to Mac. He watched him for a while, looked past him to where the camera equipment nestled among pine straw, turned back to the fire.

"Giving the boy ideas," a deputy said, and all of them turned and watched him closely for a reaction. Their bellies rose with heavy breath which verged on snores. Their leather holsters creaked.

Glenn said, "Show him what you showed me."

One of the men pulled a glove on up to his elbow, an industrial-looking glove made of black rubber, and grabbed up a fishnet, the type that Mac's father bought every summer at Sturgeon Bay. The deputies grew sober and quiet while the man waved the net through the vat. He struck something, leaned into his scoop, brought a dead, dripping possum up to the surface. While the man lifted the possum higher and pushed the net toward Mac, the rest watched him closely. Mac decided that instead of teaching him a lesson—warning him away from tainted homemade hooch—these men were making fun of him in their thick, secretive way, like the reporter had been doing with those endless directions to his mother's house. And Glenn, once again, was in on it.

Suddenly, Mac knew that when the sun rose in a few hours, things would be different. Glenn would pay less attention to him, would go about his business and leave Mac to fend for himself. By insisting the possum be fished again from the vat, Glenn was either insulting Mac's intelligence with a too-obvious lesson, having fun at his expense, or sincerely trying to instruct him. Perhaps a little of each: Mac thought of his father, whose attempts at illustration consisted of dropping him off at schools—Sunday, Vacation Bible, elementary—and coming back for him a few hours later. As different as the two men were, Mac felt them pulling away from him together at that moment, leaving him alone in these woods, and though he missed his mother the most, he was thankful she was miles—an entire solar system—away. Tuning out the possum-died-happy jokes, Mac catalogued those things he'd looked to mistakenly for meaning: Irma's miracles of ash, plucked cotton balls, midnight motel escapes, a kitchen called a kitchen.

"Take your pictures so we can blow this thing to kingdom come and make the world safe again for drunks and possums," a deputy said. As Glenn snapped pictures, Mac watched the men tuck dynamite beneath the barrels, then followed as they walked backward through the thick wood, uncoiling the fuse wire. Halfway to the road they stopped in a clearing. Mac moved behind Glenn, who did not notice him. A column of men between him and the dynamite did not make him feel safe, but he didn't feel afraid either. What Mac felt in that moment before the charges were detonated was that Glenn was going to stay in this place or someplace like it, and that he, soon—tomorrow perhaps— was going to leave. In that long moment of silence before the blast, Mac saw that he was glad to have come to this place and that like his mother he would surely need to return.

The woods went quiet. As someone counted softly down from ten, Mac wondered if he'd ever come to trust his judgment in such places where hens weren't fooled by nature and alongside straight stretches of road, bodies littered fields; where houses chased cars down streets and where, in seconds, smoke would rise from a sleepy wood and bad, bad liquor—stuff that could kill you, that could make you go blind—would rain down from a sky lit white as noon.

Love Wild

Bouncing up the rut-and-gully trail, late for work again that morning, I half-turned in my seat to check on Tony. His war paint had already started to run down his cheeks and chest. A fly lit on his chin and he slapped at it, finger painting. The fringe on his chaps was stained black and red from where he'd wiped his hands on it.

The driver had been watching me study Tony. He leaned in close like the jeep was hugging a curve and whispered, "What's wrong with him?"

I pretended I couldn't hear him for the wind. I cupped my hands under the bucket seat and hunkered, shivering in my uniform of loincloth, beaded headband and moccasins.

The train whistle blew, one short blast up on the ridge. The rearview had shaken loose from its mount, and when it swung my way I saw Tony's hands clutching the sissy bar. Another swing and I saw his face; his mouth was wide open like he was singing, but the jeep muffler was Swiss cheese, I couldn't hear note one. "What?" said the driver.

"I'll tell you later," I said, speaking low and sideways, as if later, I would motion him around a corner and take him into confidence. But later, I would avoid him. It's none of his business what's wrong with Tony, and besides, I couldn't explain it if I wanted to. Nobody really knows except Abby and me, not even Tony himself.

TONY'S SISTER ABBY left me for a string of men leading to the latest, an optician who peddles eyeglasses from the back of a drugstore in the mall. He's balding blond and pink-skinned, with a forehead as broad and shiny as a windshield, and he's got Abby clerking for him, wearing a long white lab coat like she's suddenly some kind of specialist. They drive around town in a two-tone van, all its windows tinted black.

Abby and I started going out in high school, but even before then I used to give Tony rides home from school, taxi him into town—they lived ten miles out—just so I could see his sister. And she has always appreciated it, my taking care of Tony. When we started going out I'd let him come along with us sometimes if we weren't doing any-thing special, just riding around on a Sunday afternoon. Abby'd make him sit in the backseat but he'd always lean forward, his arms hugging the headrest, his head thrust be-tween us like a partition, as if he was our chaperon.

Tony was sixteen when Abby and I graduated and moved over to Asheville. We'd been gone for a few months when we started hearing things: Tony lost his after-school job at the hardware store, was expelled from school, ran away to Orlando. One night Abby's mother called with news that Tony hadn't spoken a word to anyone for a month and a half. They had no choice but to commit him to the hospital down in Morganton. He was there for six weeks, and the night before they were supposed to let him out, Abby's mother called again and asked us to pick Tony up at the hospital. Said she couldn't handle him, so Tony came to stay with us.

Abby felt guilty about having left him alone in our

town, which is like most towns of its size I know now, except higher up in the mountains, more isolated. The air is thinner, the winters are longer and there's no work unless you get on at one of the ski resorts or theme parks that have sprung up since we've been away.

When Abby and I split the last time—the time she refers to as *for good*—she asked me to take care of her little brother. Actually, what she asked me to do was to keep an eye on him. It was the last thing we talked about before I left that day. We were standing in the driveway of the little bungalow we shared, the back of the car sunken with all these things we'd bought together that she claimed she didn't need anymore. This favor she was asking seemed to me like a gift, something that made up for all those boxes in the backseat she didn't want any part of, something that we could *share*. And it was something I knew I could do. Tony has always listened to me, more to me than to her sometimes.

WHEN WE WALKED into camp that morning, I was a little worried that Chief Vincent would try to fire us for being late again, but I figured by lunchtime he would have cooled and things would be back to boring.

Of course it never got too boring up there on the mountain, what with Vincent and Tony at each other's throats all day long. One of the things I liked about the job at first was how we only had to work thirty minutes out of each hour. I'd imagined the rest of the time I'd read or sleep or just sit around the fire and talk trash; turned out I spent most of my time trying to keep Vincent or Tony happy. Seemed like Tony had gotten worse since we'd been working up there: moodier, slower, lazier. It was all I could do to rouse him out of bed in the morning and sometimes I couldn't even do that.

Even though he went along with it when I decided we ought to apply for the job, he made it plain in the interview that playing Indian at Frontierland was not his idea of gainful employ. After we'd filled out all the forms, the manager asked about our experience in the theater. Before I could answer, Tony was telling about that time in Tacoma when the woman sitting beside us rose suddenly during the second Russian roulette scene of *The Deer Hunter* and screamed, "What the bloody hell were we doing over there in the first place?" The usher figured she was with Tony, and both of them were escorted out of the theater, Tony cussing his way up the dark aisle.

I was sure that Tony's little story might cost us the job, but the interviewer only sighed, chewed the cap of his ballpoint and said, "Well, y'all sure look the part. Last guy in here would have had to spend a week in a tanning booth just to pass for half-breed."

We'd just spent a year on an oil rig off Pass Christian and were both near black from two-week stretches in the Gulf sun. We needed work, and this time we planned on staying. Even if there was no decent work around, there were other things to consider: the chance to lay eyes on her, even in passing. Wherever we happened to be over the years, Abby had always called regularly to check on Tony and she'd always ask him to put me on the line. Back home for visits, I would manage a few hours alone with Abby, and more often than not we spent those few hours in bed.

Of course these hours were my happiest and of course they always ended with her crying and saying, "You know we shouldn't be doing this." And I would agree with her even though I didn't agree with her, because I wanted her to think I had grown and because I knew if I tried to convince her otherwise it would only make her feel worse. But she knew I was still taking care of Tony and I knew she loved me for it.

Early one Sunday morning when we had been back in town for about a month, I went out to get a newspaper. I was stopped at a light, staring dead ahead without seeing, like you do sometimes when you can just *feel* the lights changing by the motion around you. All of a sudden I felt something change, and I looked up and saw the optometrist's van passing in front of me. The tinted windows were rolled all the way down and Abby drove slowly, an arm thrown out the window, fingers trilling in the breeze.

In the mall parking lot I spotted her walking toward the back door of their shop. As I pulled alongside, she was sifting through a clump of keys. Abby smiled, shook the key ring and said: "Twenty keys and only three of them fit anything current."

"What *are* all those?" I was coasting and braking to keep up with her.

"One night he went through them for me, told their stories," she said. "Took two bottles of wine to get through the whole ring. One's to a motel room in Lauderdale. One's to a liquor cabinet in the beach house of an old girlfriend. Nags Head or Kitty Hawk, I believe." She flipped through the ring, tracing the cuts at the end of each key with a forefinger. "These two are old dorm rooms. This one's to a motorcycle he sold before I even met him. This tiny one goes to a locker at an athletic club down in Charlotte."

We'd reached the service entrance. I parked and followed her through a maze of dumpsters and stacked pallets. "I don't know why he keeps them," she said.

"Not that I like defending him, but a certain amount of nostalgia won't kill you."

"Is that why y'all are working up there on the warpath?"

We'd been through this before; like most natives, she resented the historical theme parks less for the liberties they took with the truth than the fact that they were the only place left for the people of our town to find work. They paid only minimum wage and you had to wear coonskin caps and bonnets, flour sacks and buckskin to earn it.

"Only job we could find."

"I just don't see how you can drive to work in feathers and a loincloth without losing your dignity."

Dignity has always been her thing. I decided years ago that you can't love wild like you're supposed to and worry about acting dignified at the same time. Sometimes when Abby talked about dignity, seemed to me what she really meant was a thin paste of vanity and pride. And it was easier for her to act dignified behind those tinted windows.

"When you're riding around in that van of his, don't the clouds always look like the bottom's about to drop out?" I said.

She ignored this. "It's the pits for Tony, that job. He's got scars left over from this place, and going up there and play-acting like a native. . . . I mean, you might as well be pouring salt in his wounds."

"People around here take all that stuff too seriously if you ask me. It's only acting. Besides, I'm right there with him," I reminded her.

She tried a couple of keys in the lock. The third clicked deep inside the thick steel.

"You shouldn't have come back this time," she said. She turned the knob and shoved, and the door swung open to darkness. When I stumbled and toppled a stack of boxes, she reached for my hand and led me over to a couch.

As we sat, waiting for our eyes to adjust, I could feel her breathing beside me, and I thought of all the times we'd talked in the dark. I remembered the little cottage halfway up Beaucatcher Mountain we'd rented years ago in Asheville, how we'd pushed the bed beneath the window and stayed up listening to bugs bounce off the screen. I remembered nights we'd spent in a sleeping bag by Hound's Ears Falls, waking the next mornings to mist between us and the sound of the creek wearing away its thousand stones.

I wanted to talk to Abby in the dark, but instead I asked: "Is this where he tests for astigmatisms?"

"He's one reason why you shouldn't have come back. I think I'm going to stay with him."

"Free bifocals when the time comes, I guess."

"He's stable," she said. "None of this up and down."

I told Abby that since I'd been looking after Tony for so long, our problems and personalities must have blurred in her mind.

"That's ridiculous. I hope I can still tell you apart. Look, if you're tired of Tony you know I can take him any time. Just leave him here with us any time he gets to be a burden."

But she knew my answer, and it was quiet except for our breathing and the sound of zippers chewing track and, in some far-off part of the mall, a burglar alarm that rang the entire time we spent in the dark stockroom, as if it had been tripped accidentally too many times and was being ignored now.

AFTER THE MICA TRADE dried up, the tracks laid to haul it from the mines down to Piedmont sat rusting for twenty years until some developers bought it. At the base of the mountain they slapped up Frontierland, a two-block run of clapboard storefronts that opens when the snow melts, sucks busloads of tourists up from the flatlands until first frost. At twelve bucks a head you could stumble along plank sidewalks or have your picture taken behind bars in a jail that doubled as a mop closet for the saloon next door. Down by the depot, three mules the color and texture of worn leather gloves packed bored kids around a hoof-pocked ring.

But the train was the thing. The developers found this old steam engine and painted it up like a rack of thrift-shop prom dresses. It was the most undignified train you'd ever seen.

Our Indian camp was a clearing on the edge of the gorge. There was a circle of charred stones lining a fire pit, a dry-rotted army tent set up to the side for shelter during the afternoon rains, five hammocks strung between trees and a dammed-up creek with a spout rigged for drinking. No one spoke that morning when Tony and I came around the bend. Larry and Vincent were sprawled in lawn chairs by the fire, smoking and gulping thermos coffee. When I apologized for being late, Vincent said something under his breath which I paid no attention to because I expected it from him. Vincent and Larry were cut midseason from the cast of *Trail of Tears,* a local outdoor pageant about the removal of the Cherokee from western North Carolina. Vincent disliked us because we weren't actors, because we landed the job without one hour of theater experience between us. The manager decided that somebody had to be in charge up there, so Vincent was given the waist-length headdress to wear and made chief.

What Vincent wanted was to turn the train ride into one of his outdoor pageants. He was always coming up with ways we could fine-tune our performance so that it would seem more lifelike, but Tony never paid him any attention. Tony did what he felt like, something different every time; I thought he was the most convincing of us all, and the crowds seemed to agree. Whenever he bounded into a car the kids either hushed or screamed louder, and the grown-ups swallowed a lot and stretched their mouths into thin, tight smiles, like they were trying hard to convince the kids that Tony was just pretend.

"How'd it go first run?" I asked Larry.

"Pitiful. Bet there weren't forty people on all five cars. A few kids even fell asleep during the ambush."

"They'll wake up now that the local yokels are here," said Vincent. He had his compact out and was making faces into the mirror, dabbing paint across his forehead.

"Damn right," I said, though I've never really cared if the kids slept or screamed. I've always figured that if I didn't take the job seriously, it couldn't bother me. Tony took it too seriously, though when he was on the train he didn't seem to be acting at all. Even Vincent would have had to agree that during the runs, Tony was a natural.

Vincent lifted his gaze from the compact and smirked. "It has to do with numbers, not ability," he said. "It's weak with only two Indians to ambush a six-car train. I had to send Larry up to the cowpoke camp to tell them to leave somebody at the ranch."

The train whistle blew, three long blasts. The number of blasts told where the train was, how long we had until it arrived. Another thing I liked about the job: moved right along. There was always a train to catch, so you knew that all the little in-between arguments couldn't last but so long, and were usually forgotten once the fifth whistle blew.

Vincent stuffed his compact into the backpack and squatted to do his breathing exercises. "You guys take engine this time," he wheezed.

"We ran engine yesterday," I said. "It's our turn to caboose."

Vincent exhaled dramatically before he replied. "But you missed the first run and I had to cover for you."

It was always better to run caboose because all you had to do was trot down the mountain, breeze up the back steps when the train stopped, like you were home for lunch. Running engine meant you had to sprint alongside until you could take the hop. Vincent made sure the engineer kept it at a "realistic" clip, at least ten miles an hour. We traded tasks, alternating days.

"Breathe deep, Vincent," said Tony. "And hold!" he sang, like an aerobics instructor.

"You know what I decided when you guys didn't show up this morning? I decided we should call you two the Affirmative Action Actors, since it seems your presence here is a concession to this hillbilly backwater on the part of the developers, who must feel guilty for lopping off a hillside or two. Must be a quota: a couple hometown boys to every two competent outsiders."

Four blasts, our get-set. The train was just below us, starting to climb the ridge. We had about ten minutes before the run, but it was a five-minute climb and Vincent liked to get up there plenty early so he could do his deep-knee bends. Larry went first, then Vincent, Tony and me. Halfway up the trail, Tony began to lag. He watched Vincent out of sight, then sat down on a boulder.

"What?" I asked.

Tony didn't look at me. "I don't much like Vincent," he said.

"He doesn't like you much either. Or me, for that matter. So don't take it personal. Come on, we're behind."

He rose and began to climb, but slower than before. After a few yards he found another rock and sat again. I almost asked, "What's wrong with you?" but stopped myself when I felt his mood shift, felt the hate rising off him like waves of heat from an August blacktop.

"Get up, Tony. We've got to move."

"I can't be the only one to see how stupid this job is. It's just a bunch of lies put on for people who don't give a damn whether they're being lied to. As long as the kids are quiet and the wife's happy, Daddy figures the lies are worth the bucks he shelled out for them."

Tony twisted a tendril from a huckleberry bush. "It's wrong," he said. "Wrong for me, wrong for those poor brats on the train, wrong for the world." He shredded leaves and sprinkled them in the air.

People coming up the trail might think we were taking a break from hiking if it weren't for the way we were dressed and the hatred rising from Tony, which even a stranger— even a child, an animal—could sense.

"Wrong, wrong, wrong," said Tony.

"Train's almost here. If you get us fired, that's it. There's nothing else for us this time."

"So we move," he said. His tone suggested that moving was as simple as shredding huckleberry leaves.

Surely he knew why we were back, I thought. "I don't want to move."

Vincent called from the path above, but I didn't answer. His words echoed through the hollow and ricocheted off the walls of the gorge.

"Oh, so you're home for good now?" said Tony. "You think you're finally home? You ready to make a down payment on one of these mountainside chalets? After you figure out how to get rid of the glasses grinder, I mean. I'd like to know where you're going to put me. Convert the garage? Mother-in-law apartment in the basement? Be just like Beaucatcher, back when y'all were happy in love. And you can divvy up your new life into little chores and give me some to do so I won't mildew down there in the cellar. Chores of my very own."

"Tony."

He aimed his voice down the mountain, speaking softer and faster. "I'll mow the lawn until I'm sixty-five, then I'll sit in a lawn chair by the side of the road and wave at passing motorists. Rain or shine. But if anyone should lay a hand on my mower I'll go *hey no way get your hand off that's my chore mine alone.*"

"Let's go," I said. I had never seen him act so pitiful; it was as if suddenly he'd turned into the helpless ward we'd always made him out to be.

He straightened up and said, "You still love my sister?"

"Of course," I said, and I smiled at him, but I was hoping for the train to finally save us.

Tony smiled back. "Good," he said, and he took off. "Least that hasn't changed," he called down to me as he scrambled up the slick hill.

And I thought things were fine then, back to normal. Tony and I might be on the road for a year or two, Abby and I might have to wait a long while between those stolen hours in borrowed places—astigmatism sofas or the blue-black innards of a tinted-windshield van—but sooner or later we'd meet. As long as I kept an eye on Tony, as long as he continued to listen to me, those hours would arrive, just like the train that I could hear down the ridge then, its chug rising as beautiful as cicada song.

We reached the others, who were bunched up below the track. Suddenly the top of the engine was over the crest and Larry took off. Vincent ran toward the engine, which confused me since he made such a big deal about it being our turn, but I followed anyway.

Tony was hardly moving. I passed him easily and when I was a good ways ahead, alongside Vincent, I turned to see Tony stumble and fall.

And then I heard the shrieks, and saw hundreds of kids sticking their heads out of the windows, pointing and laughing at Tony. Vincent and I both made the hop easily. Inside the cab Vincent leaned out the window to watch Tony struggling along. "What's wrong with him? he said.

"He's coming."

But he didn't come; he shuffled alongside and for a time it seemed certain that the train would leave him behind, until I talked the engineer into ignoring Vincent's orders not to slow, until the brake hiss drowned out the laughter of the hundred heads.

"They'll hear about this down the mountain," said Vincent, but I didn't answer because I was busy wrenching

Tony's tomahawk from its sheath and wrapping his fingers around the grip.

BACK AT CAMP, Vincent and I sat by the fire while the others searched the weeds by the trestle where the conductor dropped our lunch each day. A wind brought in quick fits of rain, but the rhododendron was so thick above that only a few drops reached us.

"How come you came with us?" I asked Vincent. "You make such a big deal about taking caboose and you're first one on."

"Mixed up in the thrill of the chase, I suppose. Although it wasn't a total waste."

"You're not really going to report him, are you? He just got a little winded. You're not in top form for every run."

"I always hop the train. And I always make it look good."

"Indians got tired, for chrissakes. It's a train we're trying to outrun, not a tricycle. Besides, the kids loved it."

Vincent tossed his cigarette into the ashes and turned to me. "Why are you always protecting him? I don't get it. Are you his legal guardian or something?"

I took up a stick and stirred the ashes. Why should I answer him? Abby wouldn't appreciate me discussing Tony's problem with strangers. My loyalty was to her, and to Tony of course.

"Whatever your connection is, beats me what you see in him," said Vincent. "The guy's a loser. Talk about arrested development. I bet you have to pull his chaps on for him every morning."

"His sister is an old friend of mine." And as soon as I said it I wished I hadn't. Because he didn't need to know, did not deserve to know. I poked the coals, listening for the whistle.

"So you *are* sort of like his guardian."

"He's a friend of mine. Just so happens his sister is too."

"Right. What's wrong with him?"

"His dad used to mine mica on this very mountain. Used to load boxcars on the track that our choo-choo uses now. One time he brought us up here—me and Tony, Tony's mom and his sister—and showed us where all the mines were."

"But what's wrong with him?"

"I'm trying to tell you a little about this place," I said.

"Don't mean to offend, but I'm not the least bit interested in the local lore." Vincent took out his paints and started dabbing at his face. He pursed his lips into a careful "o," as if he were warming up for a song.

The sun reappeared, and after the storm everything seemed too new, too fresh, too wild to face. Water dripped from leaves, wet branches twitched. Vince's garish face glistened in the light, blending with nothing in the black and green woods around us; it seemed he really was painted up for war. Voices filtered through the thick pin oak and laurel. When the others filed into camp, Vincent said, "I want to hear more later on. About what's *really* wrong with him."

Lunch was fried chicken, biscuits, a paper tub of lukewarm slaw. We sat around the fire and ate with our eyes on our plates, as if we'd made camp after a long day's journey, were worn out and starving. After several minutes of this silence, Vincent said, "I'm reporting you for this morning."

First whistle blew. No one said anything, but everyone knew who Vincent was talking to.

Chewing chicken, Tony held a finger up to signal he couldn't talk, then pushed one word up from a half-swallow.

"Verisimilitude."

Vincent looked up at him. We all did.

"Verisimilitude. You didn't think I'd remember but I do."

That's the word you're always tossing at us to justify all the artsy-fartsy bullshit you ask us to do."

"What's that mean again?" asked Larry.

"Lifelike. So my busting ass is verisimilitude with a capital V."

"You can save your excuses for down the mountain," said Vincent. "But as long as you brought it up: these people don't want realism. They're on their week's vacation."

Two fat blasts interrupted him.

". . . a week away from their meter-reading jobs down in South cracker Caroline—these people don't want history. They want to be entertained. They want pageantry, amusement, drama."

"I'm not at all interested in what they want," said Tony.

Larry chuckled and went back to lunch, but I set my plate aside. Tony seemed different, like on the train when he tore down the aisle and the kids either went quiet or screamed louder. Most of the time I could see Abby in Tony—they have the same nose and during a certain caught-off-guard smile, the same mouth. But at that moment I could not find the slightest resemblance.

There was barely time for a cigarette before four blasts. I walked over to the creek and smoked, with my feet in the water. After a minute of watching the current, I felt Tony squatting behind me.

"Verisimilitude with a capital V?"

Tony tossed his cigarette into the creek and watched its filter bob and spin in an eddy. "Nothing lifelike about this job," he said.

The first of four blasts shocked me. I jumped, even though I'd been waiting for the noise as if it were a quitting-time whistle. "Bad time for another one of your powwows, boys," Vincent called down to us.

"So get another job, Tony," I said.

"I will," he said.

"By yourself, right?"

"Sure."

"Okay," I said as I pulled on my shoes. "Call me when you're all set up and we'll be by to see you. Right now you better get your ass in gear because there's a train to catch."

FIVE BLASTS: no trees to filter the rain up there and the wet clay was like ice. I led the way, then Tony, Vincent, Larry. I slipped once, then moved over to the grass and worked myself up by roots. When I was up I turned to help Tony and saw that he'd slipped too. He couldn't get any traction with the slick-soled moccasins, and he fell to his hands and knees.

When he slipped again, Vincent hopped right over him instead of helping him up.

"Go," said Vincent. He gave me a push as the train topped the grade, then started running toward the caboose. Six heads stuck out of each window, and above them I saw the smirking faces of grown-ups, pointing at us or moving their children's heads with both hands, framing them on us like movie cameras. I looked back at Tony, who was standing at the top of the hill dazed and mud-covered, watching Vincent sprint away. Larry popped up behind him and yanked him toward the engine.

During most runs the screams blended into background—I didn't hardly hear it after the first week—but that time it seemed I heard each separate voice and saw each face as we rushed down the corridor after the conductor, tomahawks unsheathed and cocked in the air, rope coiled and ready. Toy rifles clicked away like castanets as we terrorized each car; when we reached the middle car the porter was there but no Tony, no Larry. We had no choice but to go ahead and lash the porter to the conductor while the kids and their parents crowded around. We had them circled loosely twice when Larry stumbled into the car. The kids jeered at him—they grabbed the fringe of his chaps and tried to pluck the feathers from his headband—but when Tony appeared behind him, even the older kids stopped laughing, and the toddlers screamed louder. His war paint was mixed with streaks of mud; his eyes were red and wide and fixed on Vincent. He shoved the bundled-up porter and conductor out of his way, pushed past the rest of us to get to Vincent. The car fell quiet as Vincent struggled to free himself from Tony's headlock.

I watched Tony drag Vincent through the car for a few seconds before I recovered enough to push through the kids and grab Tony's arms. He threw one arm behind him, backhanding my face so hard that I fell backward onto the platform.

Lying there, I saw Tony throw Vincent off the train.

"What's wrong with him?" a child asked and without thinking I answered, "Vincent went too far this time." But as soon as I spoke I realized Vincent had little to do with it. I understood that Abby and I were to blame for what was wrong with Tony, and I saw that he wouldn't even have been on that train if we hadn't held him hostage all these years for a love we liked to call wild.

A cheer echoed through the crowded car, and I realized what was going on—that everyone thought it was an act, that Tony had them all convinced—one second before a small boy rushed up to Tony with a wide vacation smile on his face and a plastic squirt gun in hand, aimed at Tony's stomach. Tony turned to me and smiled that smile he shared with his sister; then he grabbed the gun, bit off the end of the barrel, and spit pieces of green plastic into the air. Sunlight glinted the pieces and water from the pistol, mixed with spit, dropped in beads. I watched the boy's thin legs scissor-kick under Tony's arms as he lifted him.

The train slowed, but all else was still. Tony was the only

one of us then who was not acting, and no one could touch him because he held all the power, all the dwindling energy of our lies. No one moved as the boy went limp in Tony's arms and Tony hugged him close. None of us moved until we heard the sound of horses' hooves in the gravel of the track, until the cowboys finally arrived.

Cursive

That night they carved their initials under the eaves of the overpass. Blocky letters in the rusty girder, flakes the color of dried blood floating in the dark down to where cars flashed past. From that angle they could not see drivers' faces—only triangles of elbow-and-arm thrust from windows, and streaky lingering lights.

"Put the date down too," said Bev.

But the pocketknife was incapable of curve. Nine and one were recognizable but the three looked like a backass-ward hillbilly E.

"Okay, caveman," Walker said. Criticizing his efforts out loud made him feel workmanlike. He'd heard plumbers do this, act as if there were two of them working on the same project: one who screwed up bad, another who fixed the leak. Grabbing the handle, he attacked the bottom ell of the three.

"That reminds me," Bev said over his shoulder. "I'm famous for my stick people. In ninth grade the art teacher would study my pictures like she liked them. She'd get all serious and pinch her jaw like people do in a museum. But then, whenever the bell would ring? She'd keep me behind and ask me about LIFE AT HOME."

"You must have put a lot into each stick," said Walker,

struggling with the eight now, which was looking more like an hourglass.

"I had some good titles. 'The Inside Skinny by Bev' was one that I personally thought good. She didn't go for it. 'What does it refer to thematically?' she asked. I mean, Jesus." Bev laughed her gargling baking soda laugh, delivered it defiantly, as if someone—her mom, this art teacher—were watching over her in a cramped half-bath and Bev was trying to imply without speaking how the soda burned her tonsils instead of soothing them. Sounded to Walker like a laugh she'd been asked to tone down or leave at home.

"I did a whole series called 'Life at Home.' See, my stick people lived in treehouses and in these bamboo cabanas stuck up on stilts. All they would eat was celery sticks, carrot sticks, fish sticks. Whiled away their days doing jumping jacks."

"That why you quit school then? Because of this art teacher?"

"She had a hyphenated marriage," said Bev.

Walker studied her in the seepage of violet streetlight which made her cheekbones look like twin bruises, blue-blackened the smears of three-day-old eyeliner. She scrunched her face up, as if remembering back to the ninth grade—last year—was a chore.

"She got married in the middle of the semester and even though she didn't tell nobody, everybody knew. I hate how she didn't ever mention her life to her students but even the brain donors in her study hall knew when she'd hooked up with old socks-and-sandals, that boyfriend of hers. Meanwhile my life at home is like the weather to her. The Monday she came back? I drew a picture of her wedding night: two sticks on a bed of lettuce with a hyphen in between."

"She had it in for you after that." Of course the art teacher had it in for Bev—otherwise why talk about her—

but Walker felt he had to say *something*, and to show he understood her, never doubted her, he kept the intoned arc of questioning out of his last syllables, pitched his statements level and low.

"She held me back. Literally 'cause she was going to flunk my ass but also because she didn't get it, what I was doing. She didn't *want* to get it. Plus I think she had something to do with them keeping me from taking driver's ed. I wouldn't be surprised if she got together with the coach and brainwashed him into believing something was screwy with my depth perception. I believe they figured I lived in a one-dimensional world and that to me an intersection would be like the background of one of those billboards painted with mountains that look like you can drive right up on them."

Walker stopped carving. "Wait, now: how come they wouldn't let you take driver's ed?"

"'You got to be able to judge distances in order to properly operate a motor vehicle,' the coach said whenever I went to sign up. He had this big Ban-Lon stomach, picks and runs all across it I called gut zippers."

"You didn't miss a thing," said Walker. While the bridge thundered with truck traffic and pigeons rustled on the lips of the girders, Walker told Bev that coaches couldn't teach driving, that they just leaned back on the headrests and went to sleep with their mouths and eyes open, giving directions in the language of cops being interviewed on the local news: 'Turn left at the next home of a private individual.' 'Follow that maroon vehicle attempting to make a sharp right-handed turn.' Safe beneath their bridge, Walker told Bev that driving lessons are like loving lessons, that everybody almost is born with the instinct within, we don't all end up racing at the Indy or starring in live sex shows but everybody knows enough at the outset to get in a wreck or pregnant. Bev, said Walker in the words of the gut-zippered coach, I will show you how to drive as soon as we can gain access to the vehicle of a private individual. Bev, said Walker, proud to have found a sphere of experience to hold over her, "I'll show you, Bev, it's easy."

His real name was Walter. The k had been substituted by his classmates, who renamed him because he walked: straight lines, swaths unswerving, miles every day, before school, after, on weekends; through neighborhoods and woods, down the littered medians of boulevards and thruways. He did not walk for exercise, nor because it was conducive to meditation. He walked because he heard a cadence, steady and undeniable, too slow for freestyle, cross-country or crew.

While walking, he did not search ditches for the glint of aluminum or glass; he never foraged, salvaged or collected. He did not dress like the walkers he sometimes encountered on the roadsides, inappropriately attired for the weather or climate even, complete wardrobe carried on their backs. Walker dressed seasonally always, jeans or cuffed khaki shorts, polo shirts and Tretorn tennis shoes shiny white save for grass smudges along the rubber-rimmed soles.

Dressed so generically, Walker appeared to friends and passing motorists simply on his way somewhere. It took repeated sightings of him all over town, in odd places at odd times, for them to say anything, and even then they contained their ridicule in a nickname, which Walker suffered with smiles. Hard consonant exchanged for another: such an insignificant substitution that Walker barely noticed the difference after a week. He'd heard crueler nicknames—the square-headed boy in his Biology class called "Box," a girl known around school only as "Burnt Cheese."

Only after he had missed many meals, disappeared all day for six straight weekends, gone AWOL for most of a Thanksgiving family reunion, did questions arise at home.

He answered these questions by filing past them, kept on walking right past supper, home, parents, time. Past school in the mornings, which eventually led to a pause: a six-week stay in a solar-heated hospital where other patients sat in something called a "day room," glibly describing the voices *they* heard. Listening, Walker felt relieved that his dictation was rhythmic, wordless, a backbeat, a laid-down track against which he could improvise, against which his real life ran like salmon fighting upstream to spawn. He was grateful for this freedom, yet his doctor suggested that the cadence was in truth a suppression of syllables, that Walker was ignoring the words which could free him, keep him off the streets.

In the days before Bev, it seemed that every time he opened his mouth a cloud of steam emerged. He tried to convince himself that it was only the age, that no one his age used words particularly well, that their sentences mimicked the mercurial pitch of their voices, the elastic surge of their limbs. People fifteen should either nod or scream, Walker decided, or just sit around glumly like spider plants and shoot out tendrils.

A week before Walker met Bev, a group of boys from Bev's side of town stole a sign from a school crossing— SLOW CHILDREN AT PLAY, it read; they stuck it up late one night in front of Bev's house. The next day her father yanked it from the ditch bank but not before Bev, startled by the sight of her dad wrestling a sign from the mud in the early morning mist, saw and read.

She inquired around. "One good thing about being our age," she would tell Walker later, "is that everybody's a snitch. I gained access to the vital statistics of the individual positively identified as the perpetrator," she would say after coachese became the official language of the eaves.

What happened next Walker was present for, though he heard little, saw even less. A few days after the sign appeared, on this very night that Walker and Bev would spend beneath the eaves, a circle of cars pulled up in a strawberry field at the edge of town, closing ranks like a wagon train. In moments a slow and ragged drunk was underway, music so loud it flushed rabbits and possums from the scrub. Walker was there on the periphery, circling the circle, head tilted heavenward as if charting stars.

Midway through an orbit he heard wet screams. Bev had lured the perpetrator into the back of a van. Kneeling on an air mattress, hair grazing the rippled plastic, she licked red dirt-road dust from his forehead and proclaimed herself a tattoo artist of the tongue. How would he like a mermaid emblazoned upon his lower stomach? Go for it, said the perpetrator. Bev shut his eyelids gently with her fingertips, kissing them closed as if he were her own tucked-in offspring and demanded they stay shut so that she might concentrate.

Skin gives better than steel girder. The smallest blade of the pocketknife performed like a finger in sand and Bev had the fluid crook of a capital B going before her victim was able to rouse himself from his shock and scream. This departure from pure stick figure existed long afterward, a raised and purplish wound the width and length of a caterpillar, a breakthrough for Bev.

Bisecting a circle so cleanly sketched it could have been drawn by a compass, Bev brushed Walker at field's edge. In the stunned second following she tried to scream, but what emerged was a trapped version of her salty laugh, which struck Walker as last-ditch, desperate. Somebody's after you, he said. Close enough, said Bev, unable to admit that the sight of him in button-down oxford cloth, creased Levis and Wallabees terrified her even more than the scene she'd fled. Heels spraying dust as he trampled the overgrown furrows, moonlight striping his forehead, Walker appeared to Bev like the ghost of a boy from a good family. Yet she'd taken his hand when he'd offered it, followed the path he beat through the woods.

ONCE BENEATH the overpass they'd cleaned the knife with trash, set about carving their skinny initials.

"We'll come back in five years, see if they've sandblasted us," said Walker. He folded the knife and turned to see Bev staring down at the scant traffic. A wall-eyed headlight traced her midriff, then slid across the alphabet of spray-painted initials on the slope. Bev and Walker shared a build—all rail and slat—yet as he watched the light streak her, Walker noticed that parts of Bev seemed older than others: her breasts looked twenty instead of fifteen. Maybe it was the trapped air of the underpass, warm Piedmont night working her skin; but the same baggy air surrounded him too, and he felt the same age everywhere.

Suddenly he felt miserable sitting beside her; he was all angle, growing evenly, stupidly. It seemed forever that men must abide by the breathtakingly sudden surges of women. Bev could tap into a burst tomorrow and streak away. Passing herself off for far older, she would veer out into a world real with apartments, jobs, cars. He'd only been with Bev for a few hours and was already worried about losing her.

All day long they tucked themselves under the eaves to talk and toss gravel at the pigeons. Emerging at dusk, they split up like veteran predators, she to a sleepy grocery to shoplift cigarettes and a quart of beer, he to a phone booth to order pizzas with unpopular ingredients, giving the address of a shut-tight storefront near the underpass for the delivery.

Four hours' sleep in a machine shed, burlap feed sacks spread across oil-slick concrete slab. Walker woke before her, sat up to watch her sleep: she did not seem in hiding, her limbs splayed as if she'd dropped through the ceiling.

Walker studied her arms, pasty and blue-veined as notebook paper, and reminded himself that she had carved half an initial into a boy's belly. As she rose and fell slightly in sleep, Walker's cadence returned, rising gradually until metronomic, throbbing. It'd be better if I slipped away now, he thought; how long can we hide under that bridge? Someone would spot them soon: carloads of men who'd steal up the slope, pin him to the pocked concrete, lower themselves on her like helicopters, her hair blown back by the wind of them. Afterward they'd turn them in—there must be a reward by now—and more men would come, cars clogging the cool darkness beneath the bridge, high antennae swaying like saplings, static coachese crackling over radios.

When he thought the shift had ended for the pizza deliverymen he woke her. She pulled on her fuzzy black sweater, stuffed tapered jeans into knee-high boots, lit a long cigarette, huffed smoke signals to wake herself. Followed him down back alleys, watched the corners for cops as he dove the Dumpster. They picked off the pineapple and extra anchovy, took their dinner back to the bridge. After they ate they talked of teachers, a recurring topic though neither would admit to much missing schooldays. Walker told her about his English teacher, who claimed that in those prissy ancient poems he made them read, sex equaled death.

"Let's curl up and die, then," said Bev, and they did. Greater than, less than, equal to it was the inside skinny by Bev.

"Roll over and we're roadkill," she whispered once. Glancing at the two-inch margin of concrete, Walker remembered how she'd lured the perpetrator into the back of the van.

"Sex equals death," Walker whispered back, but his words seemed meaningless, grace notes for his mounting cadence.

"Mmmmmmmmm," said Bev, her hum washing over his beat, water rising to his ankles, calves, knees. He remained angle and line while beneath him Bev bloomed into curve and bulge. He could feel them inching toward the slope which would funnel her away with traffic, catch him against the guardrail. Sex equals not death but a few minutes of life, he thought as the water crested and began its quick, cold, draining away.

Because he knew that he had little more to offer her than these angled eaves, Walker did a one-armed pushup, yanked his Levi's to his waist and said, "Let's go."

"Go where?"

"Walking," said Walker. He emerged from his T-shirt to see Bev's hair spring frizzy through the sweater hole, watched her limp sleeves ripple with arm like garden hoses surging with water. Wincing, she crammed her feet into her boots and crawled along the ledge.

"I wasn't going to say it," she said when he caught up a half-block away, "but they pointed you out to me in the parking lot at school one day. You were power-walking to class, man, holding stacks of books to your side like an apeman? My ex-boyfriend Kent goes, 'Check him out, they call that dude the Walker.' Everybody giggled but we weren't high. 'Cause I don't know, you looked so normal and all." She made wide eyes at his blue oxford cloth. "Kent and them said how you walked everywhere all the time, how they'd see you way out by the airport or almost to Morningside? At the time I thought it was a weird way to get off, but now I understand. Now here I am walking with the Walker. Check it out. So where all'd you used to walk to?"

He couldn't tell her. Destination and scenery were irrelevant, and he had neither the inclination nor the words needed to make something up. She accepted his mumbled "all over," didn't bug him, fell behind as his cadence cranked up.

Walking with the Walker, check it out. They kept to side street and back road, Walker concentrating on route, a new regard for him and distracting—like being tethered by earphone to a transistor radio. He began to notice, to focus on things passing. Around a curve a long station wagon appeared, plastic-wrapped newspapers shooting from a back window. Walker jumped at the sodden thwack of tube against dew-soaked lawn, hid from the paper man in the shadows, but Bev didn't bother. She marched up the street oblivious, Salem Long waving like a fire baton, boot heels clacking out a tap dance. She held her cigarettes aloft in one hand, a pack of matches tucked into the cellophane, her pants pocket stretched too tight to take anything thicker than a ticket stub. Suddenly Walker felt none of the dread of losing Bev that had needled him under the eaves. It didn't even matter that they were looking for her; any time with Bev would seem to him like life-on-the-lam, its desperate pleasures derived from knowledge that it would not last.

He slowed to let her catch up, took her hand and led her into and through the boxy subdivisions, all right angles and corners as if drawn on an Etch-A-Sketch by a tight child. In his front yard he parked her behind a shrub and crouched by the left tire well of his father's Skylark. Pulling the key box from its hiding place he dropped it, magnet clanging against the blacktop. He turned to Bev and whispered, "Smooth move," and again that night there were two of him: one who screws up bad, another who fixes the leak.

Seconds later she was rising from the front seat floorboard and laughing as he ran the stop sign at the end of his street and headed for the freeway. As they passed over their underpass, Walker tapped a tribute out on the horn. Bev blew loud kisses, then leaned outside to yell, "We'll be back in five years to check out our skinnyass initials." Walker rolled down his own window, let the wind-roar drum over his dwindling cadence.

He angled onto an exit ramp, followed a country road threading hills still milky with early morning mist. Down a dirt road past barns, shacks, a patchy grove of pines, deep into someone's abandoned back forty. He inched the Skylark onto a field and when he did not tire-spin or mire he threw the car into park, turned to Bev and said, "Driver's Education, Session Number One."

"No way," said Bev. She scooted across the seat, tugged his zipper tongue. "Need some of these on your gut, Coach."

"Did I not inform you that I would soon gain access to the vehicle of a private individual?"

"I will not inquire as to how you happened to ascertain the whereabouts of this private individual's extra set of keys." She bent across him to open the door, pushed him into the field, slid behind the wheel. "Check it out," she said when he climbed in beside her. "Walk with the Walker and learn to drive, all in one day."

"You're supposed to view about a hundred hours of boring filmstrips before I technically let you even sit behind the wheel," said Walker. "This will have to be a crash course."

"Literally?" Bev gunned it, and for the next half-hour they plowed back and forth across the field, Walker letting the wind suppress those syllables which it was said could free him.

"Pull over by those pines, we'll practice our parallel parking," said Walker.

But Bev ignored him. She drove slowly to a far part of the field where the dirt was virgin except for faint, long-fallow crop rows.

"What'll it be, Walker?" said Bev, patting the seat next to her.

"What'll what be?"

"We're going to leave a message for Sky Five. The one

and only weather chopper, Piedmont's premier eye from the sky. What should I say?"

"I don't think that's a good idea," he said, even though he suspected that any effort would be illegible to the powers-that-be-up-above, a swirl of dirt tracks, carelessly layered graffiti.

"He's back, the ghost of a boy from a good family," Bev said. In the distance he heard it, dim percussion propelling an approaching parade. It grew closer. It had words: *get-out-now and walk, left, get-out-now and walk, right.* His father would forgive him for borrowing the car, but what about Bev? He tried to convince himself that Bev was real, that she was dangerous, that staying with her would be standing still.

"How about 'sex equals death'?" she was saying. "That ought to boost the ratings for old 'News at Six.' How about 'The inside skinny by Walker and Bev?' How about . . ." She stuck her cigarette in her mouth and curled her knuckles around the steering wheel at textbook ten and two o'clock. ". . . 'slow children at play'?"

They were moving. There was no sound but Bev's laughter and the wind, and as Walker grew giddy and began to inch toward her across the seat, he told himself something that people like to believe, that people need to believe even when it's a lie. This is just a stage. *This is just a stage.* For a moment it stirred his cadence—for a moment it seemed something he could walk to—but when Bev whipped the car around he lost it, lost both word and beat as he hugged and trusted the bend.

As Told To

I

On the eighth page I discovered a decent line: "The road in winter was red with mud." I circled it, drew an arrow out to the margin, where I slanted two exclamation points. I'm not sure why. Perhaps the rhythm of the sentence whetted my subconscious; I'm certain it was something aside from the subject at hand. Yes, the road in winter led to a country schoolhouse during the Depression. Yes, the traveler on that road, my oldest brother, Wilson, was underdressed for the inclement conditions, hatless and bare-necked and poorly shod. Yes, the passage reeked of sanctimony and the threat of hardship and homily to come. Yes, the reader mired down in the banality of the scene as if it were red wintry mud.

I read over the sentence several times. What will Wilson make of my attraction to it? Better yet, what do I make of it?

I thought of another time when I had written something in the heat of first impression, and of what came from it: just last night, in fact. We had all been sitting around Wilson's Florida room drinking brandy. It had been growing dark out, the hedges bordering the yard receding into the river beyond like a silent surge. Daylight waned in its protracted, mid-summer way, keeping the

yard barely aglow, land reclaimed from night. We'd finished a long and satisfactory meal, the smokers among us
were shooting their milky tendrils toward windows and
corners. The disagreement over some minor point of the
Civil War had passed (the Shelby Foote, shucked from its
tight shelf and brandished, had been returned to the case
behind Wilson's wingback). The evening had loped
along, the six of us marooned somewhere between the
Shelby Foote and coffee.

I'd gone to the kitchen for more brandy, and this is
where Wilson had cornered me and pressed his memoirs
into my arms. And where, after my reticence was misin-
terpreted as . . . as what? . . . willingness? enthusiasm?
Let's just say that after my reticence had been misinter-
preted and Wilson had returned to his company, I'd
scrawled on the pocked roughness of a paper towel in a
hand which seemed shaky and geriatric the words:
Chapter LXVIII: IN WHICH I TRY TO STOP MY
BROTHER FROM WRITING HIS AUTOBIOGRA-
PHY. Back with the party I'd passed the note to my
younger sister Elaine. She had excused herself, and when
she'd returned to her place beside me on the love seat,
had passed me a wad of tissue which I'd saved to read until we were leaving. I had pulled the car around and was
waiting for my wife Alex, who had been lingering with
good nights on the front stoop. Leaning across the seat,
I'd flicked on the map light: the tissue was the green of
reception punch, lipstick-kissed in places. Holding it in
my hand, I'd thought of the deep and sensuous clutter of
a woman's purse, and it may have been this association as
much as the tenor of the message which had caused the
words in my sister's looping hand—OR: THE STORY
OF YOUR LIFE—to seem more than slightly maternal.

⋆   ⋆   ⋆

THOUGH I AM by no means a scholar, I like to read, and I would say that it has been my reading which has supplied me with the necessary and vital distractions, living as I have for the past forty years in the town where I grew up. Ours is a family of readers, and though it sounds presumptuous to say so, I suppose that our reading is what has set us apart from most of the people around here. Apart—I did not say above. I am talking about something subtle and restrained; we are not aloof, we don't distance ourselves from neighbors based on something as abstracted from the daily thread as the reading of books. Yet a gap exists between us and the others which has to do with language and abstraction.

A love of reading binds us as a family, even those of us who are far-flung and rarely in touch—Peter out in Portland, Virginia Anne up in her Boston suburb. Wilson was for some years a consistent and intelligent reader, though dating from his first job abroad in the early sixties, he has concentrated on books set in or dealing with the problems of the many places he has lived. According to his wife Jen, he has since his retirement become a quarrelsome and dyspeptic reader, always ready to pounce upon a slight error of fact, the type who would slam the cover of a novel in which its author had succeeded in creating a parallel universe replete with mystery and nuance but described inaccurately the gear box of a cherry picker or botched slightly the fauna native to southeast Wales.

Yet if it weren't for Wilson, I doubt any of us would read much more than the occasional piece of genre fluff while on vacation or a doctor's office *Reader's Digest*. To Wilson we owe this significant change in the quality of our lives. Elaine and I have talked about this debt many times over the years, more frequently since Wilson moved back to Trent two years ago. And our talks have validated its importance in a way that makes it seem both crucial and slightly like a curse.

II

Wilson spent his childhood not in the Victorian house on Church Street where the rest of us were raised and where Elaine now lives with her husband, but in a small cottage in the country near Speed's Crossroads. Speed's Crossroads falls in the Lower Sawyer School District, and the county schools were then inferior to those in town, which were not much of an improvement. Wilson was precocious. He had an intimidatingly nimble mind, a phenomenal ability to anticipate steps in math and science and he wrote well for Lower Sawyer standards (though he was and still is a lousy speller). He carried like a force field the testy bravado of the firstborn, and as early as sixth grade he sometimes scared the lectures out of some of his teachers, local girls who had gone off to teachers' colleges to fit themselves with something-to-fall-back-on-until-they-got-married degrees. Competent and considerate teachers by and large, yet Wilson was too much for them. My father met with the principal of Lower South Sawyer High and argued weakly that he was a taxpayer, that public schools should be equipped to handle whatever was thrown their way. His argument was weak because he didn't believe it himself, because he was begging none too subtly for compliments, because he was proud of what he would describe for years to come as "his oldest boy Wilson having thunk himself right out of the Sawyer school system."

His use of the word thunk, and the throaty way he delivered it, making the act of thinking sound masculine and risky, barely concealed the high school dropout's pride in a son who had surpassed him. Yet my father's odd choice of words was more than the result of his patchy schooling, and seems as significant to me now as it was then.

And it was hugely significant then, to all of us. As I've explained, our family was attuned to language, and we made a game out of scrutinizing the sentences of those around us for solecisms, wildly mixed metaphors, malaprops. It was, I see now, an elitist exercise, and I'm more than a little ashamed to admit it, yet I *must* admit to it simply because it happened. We played this game daily, and we eavesdropped not only upon ignorants or innocents but also—I should say primarily—on our father.

He chose words which were approximate, inappropriate or downright incorrect. We listened out for them, shared them with each other when they arrived. Occasionally we called him on them.

One of his choices has been particularly prevalent in my thoughts lately. My father had once made a little pocket change off three acres of peanuts planted behind the cottage, and because of this windfall his favorite American hero became George Washington Carver. He was always talking about the man who *discovered* the peanut. *Discovered* brought to our minds antiseptic laboratories. It seemed all wrong. Did George *discover* it in a brick building on a university campus or while walking home from church through the woods? Did he spot its squat and wrinkled shape camouflaged amid an autumnal carpet of leaves? Shelling it, did he discover the pods curled against each other like newborn rodents nesting? Or perhaps he discovered the peanut in the way that I discovered that sentence on page eight of Wilson's memoirs—weary with the task at hand he was ready to attach significance to anything, in this case an unattractive and subterranean legume.

George Washington Carver discovered the peanut. I remember well my father's spirited defense when we tried to tell him that his verb seemed wrong.

"What would you say instead? He didn't find it. He for damn sure didn't invent it. It wasn't is-o-lated like a virus. Wasn't concocted. Discovered's what the man did to it.

Everything is out there, it's just for us to discover how to manipulate it."

So the phrase became a kind of catch phrase for us. Its meaning was for years irrelevant, subverted by the skill with which we wove it into the subject at hand. Our quirky appreciation of it was what counted, at least until recently, when the question of discovery versus invention became relevant to me.

On the school issue my father conferred with the Methodist minister here in town, a Mr. Foreman from Connecticut, who supplied my father with a list of the five best preparatory schools in the nation, all of which were well north of Philadelphia. My father asked Mr. Foreman to write some letters of recommendation, and within a few months Wilson was offered a scholarship to a school in New England.

For the next four years we saw him only on holidays, and I began to associate Wilson with trips to the train station in Raleigh and with something else: with books. Wilson brought home books; he left books around for us to read.

I believe my father felt threatened by the sudden intellectual flurry. Though he'd had only a tenth-grade education, which in his day was more than adequate, he read little. In the front hallway of both our houses, books were kept in a glass-front case along with my mother's miniature thimble collection, a juxtaposition which did little to enhance our respect for their contents, at least before Wilson was sent away. Among them were sets of Cooper, Irving, Scott, an eight-volume set of primer-sized works called *Wit and Humor in America,* and a two-volume complete Shakespeare, neither of which I ever saw disturbed from the top shelves. For ten years they sat there, slouched against each other like children shaken asleep on a bus seat.

My father distrusted the authors whose books Wilson

brought home to us. He had doubts about what he called their moral integrity and often he voiced these doubts. Years later, reading *Long Day's Journey into Night,* I came upon the scene where Tyrone Senior admonishes Edwin for his taste in literature:

> Voltaire, Rousseau, Schopenhauer, Nietzsche, Ibsen— Atheists, fools and madmen! And your poets! This Dowson, and this Baudelaire, and Swinburne and Oscar Wilde, and Whitman and Poe! Whoremongers and degenerates! When I've three good sets of Shakespeare there . . .

We read the whoremongers and degenerates, the atheists, the fools, the madmen, their works imported from the far cultured North. One of the degenerate authors Wilson brought home after his second year away was Evelyn Waugh, and I remember well the summer we surreptitiously passed around *A Handful of Dust* and, after we had all read it, spent hours on the porch debating whether poor Tony Last would ever escape from the reprehensible Mr. Todd, who held him prisoner in deepest South America, forcing him to read aloud without pause Dickens's complete works—a fate we thought worse than the bleakest poorhouse scenes those works contained. From *A Handful of Dust* we got the idea of renting the empty rooms above Rivenbark's and transforming them into a *salon.* Virginia Anne came up with the idea—she was enamored of Brenda Last's taking an apartment in London where she would meet her lover. Those were the days before the downtowns were turned inside out like emptied pockets and outskirts siphoned off businesses, and the rooms above Rivenbark's were the only downtown rooms not let. Now each second-story window in our business district reveals ghostly shadows thrown by stored furniture or, worse, the high wintry whiteness of barren rooms.

We even chose patron saints for our salon. Beiderbecke

I believe was one, and Dostoevsky. There was a third, a woman, chosen by Virginia Anne and Elaine, though I can't for the life of me remember who it was. Helen Keller? Josephine Baker? I'd have to ask Elaine. The plan was to spread posters of our saints across the walls. Where we were to find posters of Dostoevsky in eastern North Carolina in the early forties was a problem that was not considered; the main concern was renting the rooms. That summer between Wilson's sophomore and junior years we held many planning meetings, and one afternoon we even sent a committee to Rivenbark's to inspect the rooms. Not all of us could go, so we drew straws: I took the shortest one, Elaine the next-to. Whatever we encountered in the rooms above the hardware store (I remember nothing of this day) must have been encouraging, because we kept up our plans for our salon until mid-September, when Wilson went back to school.

It was during that autumn that the rest of us began to grow restless with our own schooling. We waited impatiently for our father to take us aside one day with news that we had been accepted at some bastion of preparatory education, and were to leave in the middle of the school year. Some of us were more impatient than others. Since Wilson had gone first, it was assumed that we were to be shipped off in chronological order. Yet when Virginia Anne turned fourteen and announced nightly her boredom with what passed for scholastics at Trent High—and then fifteen, offering the same refrain several times a day—some of us assumed that "going away" was limited to the men in the family, a position which Peter and I withheld any opinion of, since we had a vested interest.

Peter took up Virginia Anne's complaint at the supper table, which went ignored by my parents until one night well after Peter's fourteenth birthday when my father condescended to respond. Wilson, he said, was a special case. It was not that he was any smarter than the rest of us, nor that he was favored in the slightest. It was just that he would have become, had he stayed in the Sawyer schools, county or city (and once again my father's choice of words shocked and confounded me), handicapped.

Peter's blond hair appeared to redden at the roots, as if an artery in the back of his brain had burst and blood was being drawn through his scalp. He bolted up, his ladder-back tipping over and slamming hard against the chair rail. Thumping his chest with both hands, Peter screamed, "What about me? Just how much more handicapped can you get?"

"Very well put," Virginia Anne said softly. She clasped her hands behind her head, leaned back from the table and looked out the window into the dusky streets. She had decided months before that this whole prep school thing was nothing more than male chauvinism, though we did not call it that back then, and despite new evidence to the contrary she was already too far away to cumber herself with argument. Even then she was well into the stoic buckling under which would earn her a scholarship to Wellesley and life thereafter in Brookline, Massachusetts.

But I was not so strong, and I was incapable of distancing myself. I was horrified at the thought of four years in Trent when I had accustomed myself to escape. The others at least were halfway through it. I felt as if rising water had lapped the last air bubble from a sinking automobile in which I was trapped; craning higher for available air I hit the roof, my lungs tight with oxygen debt.

"So you're saying what you're saying here is that no more no prep school for none I mean any of us you mean?" I said.

"Very well put." Elaine said it this time, and both girls giggled sadly.

"Correct," said my father.

Peter rose and left the dining room just in time to miss the most infuriating statement of the night.

"Seems to me your big brother has been working hard to educate you all," my father said. "Bringing down his books and poisoning all your young minds with filth and heresy. I see no need to subject you all directly to something you've picked up secondhand."

"Sort of like five for the price of one," Virginia Anne said without lifting her gaze from the window that seemed to frame her future, her fate in the frosty and sophisticated North.

"Money is a factor, I'll admit," Father said. "We're by no means wealthy and even though your brother was lucky enough to attain financial assistance—and I'm sure you would all qualify as well, since as I told you before it is not a question of one of you being any smarter than the others—even with the scholarship, well, there's train fare, and unforeseen expenses. Though truthfully, the point is, and your mother will back me up on this: if you work hard enough and apply yourself and accept the limitations of this school system I will guarantee you all, and you can relate this to Peter when he comes down from his high horse, I will guarantee you will get into the college of your choice and I will do my best to send you wherever you'd like to go, within limits of course. But for now I suggest you all settle down and enjoy yourselves in this place, which after all is good enough for your mother and me and should be good enough for you too. You're young, you'll leave here in good time and it will be good for you to get out for a bit but for now you're young so settle down, work hard but enjoy yourselves."

And after that night, some of us did some of those things sometimes.

III

It has long been my custom to spend Saturday mornings strolling through the streets of our downtown. Late on the Saturday morning which I spent looking over Wilson's memoirs, I stacked the pages of his typescript on a corner of my desk, anchored them with a stapler, and called to Alex that I was going out and would be gone for lunch. Leaving the usual tasks neglected—swollen doors in need of planing, the edging of the lawn—I walked south down Main. The river glinted where Main dead ends, and a boat in full sail passed by, billowing white above the lawn of Waterfront Park. I walked, grinning, into Saturday downtown, oblivious to how I might appear to passing motorists. Traffic on Main was steady—Buicks in from the country sunken with laundry and cousins, new cars dripping from the car wash down Church or freshly waxed and flashing in the hot noon whiteness. Teenage drivers steered one-armed, silhouetted behind tinted glass, the bass of their radios vibrating so loud that it seemed the chassis shimmied in time. I associated this bass-dominant music with my Saturday strolls, and with these cars and the gauzy features of their young drivers who, according to an article I read recently in the human interest section of the *Daily Trentonian,* often work two and three jobs in order to meet strapping payments and quite often remain in their father's house well into their twenties as a result. A vainglorious sacrifice to say the least, but they take such pride in their machines, and they keep them so spotless. Why should I care? Soon enough the cars will go unvacuumed and the pail full of special-ordered tire brushes and chamois buffing pads will sprout cobwebs in garage corners and the human impulse to acquire and flaunt will be lost to the day-late, dollar-short struggle of middle age.

But I didn't want to think of what things are traded with age. I was feeling charitable as I passed into downtown Saturday, for in a small town such as mine, Saturday morning is a slow and lovely parade, and observing it never fails to soften me. I was still smiling—though I took care to disguise it behind an exaggerated squint—as I passed First Baptist and the Sir Trent Hotel and entered the eight square blocks of my kingdom.

I turned south on Malette. A cab slid by, the handlebar of a lawn mower protruding from its trunk. Malette is two lanes but one-way; due to some terribly approximate surgery by our boys from Water and Sewer, a substantial hump runs down its center. I watched the cab shift lanes, rolling over the rise as if it were a skiff crossing the wake of a tanker. The trunk lid bobbed, loosely secured by a wide blue necktie. The cabdriver knew everyone on the street, and he slowed in time to the tap of the trunk against the metal grip of the mower, trolling the streets for greetings and waves, tap and beep and "Look out here," honk, tap, "All right now!" His fare sat up front, rather familiarly, dividing the long seat of the Chrysler into thirds and abandoning the far share for the sunken warmth of the middle. Like a hot date, my son would have said. I wished he could be there with me then—I wished someone else were there to experience this with me—but then there would exist the possibility of having to point out or far worse explain. I watched the car creep toward the stoplight and pondered the relationship between cabbie and fare. Lover? Wife? Third cousin? Did he or she belong to the lawn mower and was the necktie yanked from the slot of his own frayed collar when he picked up lady and mower or did it accompany him wherever for just such a situation, coiled like a snake and hidden in the rusty tire well?

Such mysteries lay everywhere in my Saturday downtown morning. Waiting in line at the Everything Under

Three Dollars Store, a tube of caulk in my hand, I could not ignore the particulars of the life of the slow clerk. I sneaked glances at her slender arms, the skin of which appeared varnished, freckled and cancerous blemishes laminated beneath a glaze of fresh sun. Did she live by the Sound in a trailer with, out back beneath a canopy of yaupon, her very own fish-cleaning station? I saw her in a spread of green after-supper light, shucking oyster or snapping bean while a sprinkling of less industrious relatives ignored her in favor of lawn furniture and beer. I saw her working herself toward a pinched and final thinness. In a furniture store five years hence she squints into a Canaletto painting of a Venetian square, her eyes adjusting to the minute renderings while grandchildren to whom she is oblivious bounce upon couches of brushed velour. After I made my purchase I loitered about in the aisles, scrunching my face up as if I'd forgotten what I'd really come to buy and staring at her for another quarter hour.

At the intersection of Malette and Water streets I turned left toward the river and met my brother Wilson on the sidewalk.

"I was just headed over to your place," he said.

"Come take a hot dog with me down at Captain's," I said, and he smiled. "Guess take is the wrong verb," I added before he could answer. "Take sounds kind of British. You take tea, not hot dogs, right? And I'm sure Captain's not giving them away today."

I have this tendency to overanalyze my own sentences; this self-consciousness amuses some people and annoys others. Wilson (though he was of course guilty of once doing the same to the sentences of others, a much more egregious act if you ask me) fell into the latter group.

He clung to his smile. "I know what you're talking about, Matt," he said.

"Well, then?"

Wilson looked at his watch. "Let's do some hot dogs," he said, and his stiff smile loosened into an infectious one, the one he summoned to express his delight in being irreverent or jocular, the smile he'd worn as he led his younger siblings away from the plains of illiteracy into the forest of language and idea. The Wilson smile: it transposed plodding time, promised adventure, hinted at states feverish, combustion spontaneous. Hinted at the right—the Carleton birthright—to find mystery where most would find repetition or peeling paint. I hadn't seen this smile in months, and I was glad I ran into him.

"So what are you doing down here this mawning?" Since he'd moved back to Trent he sometimes affected a Southern accent. His affectations always stood out to me and Elaine, as if rendered in an aural italics. We could think only that he was being facetious rather than trying to assimilate, since the first thing Wilson shed when he left for the North was his accent. Abandoned first was the long "i"— that was the trashiest, the swampiest. Another giveaway was ole for oil. Wilson came back after six weeks asking if the oy-ol had been changed in the clunker Chevy my father let him drive. I remember how we made fun of him, circling him and singing "O-yee-ole! O-yee-ee-ole!" to the tune of the "Volga Boat Song." He took it well because he felt superior: betrayed by our vowels, we could never be taken for serious intellectuals outside of the coastal plain. In no time, he'd perfected what I think of as a California accent. Bland as pavement, generic, a go-anywhere-and-blend-in manner of speech. Perhaps that was his motive—anonymity, preparation for his life overseas—yet denizens of Djakarta are not likely to distinguish between the sluggish tones of a Mississippian and the pungent nasalese of someone from Syracuse. And back then, if I remember correctly, Wilson had plans to become a lawyer, not a State Department grind.

"I come downtown every Saturday morning." For obvious reasons it irritated me to have to say this. Everyone who knew me even slightly knew of my weekly ritual. Wilson had been back for two years, and during all his years away he came home frequently for visits, often staying at our place. His offhand question seemed deliberate to me. He knew what I was doing downtown.

"Of course you do," he called over his shoulder to me. The sidewalk on Water Street was narrowed by a string of light poles placed in the middle of the pavement. We could no longer walk abreast. I followed as close to him as I could.

Perhaps he'd forgotten what day it was, I thought; perhaps he was preoccupied with his own affairs, with some scene in his memoirs. I longed again to be free of him. I could flee down the alley between Universal Printing and Shugart's, could stand still and let him move away and round a corner. He never glanced back as he talked.

But we were going to lunch. We were going to do some hot dogs. Might as well; I was in the market for a diversion. The thought of his typescript shoved to the side of my rolltop, a breeze from the shuttered windows of my study riffling its pages, had transformed my morning into a mundane rut. People in the streets walked with purpose; loitering was no longer epidemic; cars were on their way somewhere.

You might as well eat. Alex always says this to me when I enter into a period of black and selfish brooding. She calls me to the table with the pitch and clarity of a church camp dinner bell, yet she cares little how many helpings of baked beans I take, whether my plate remains feather weight or dips under a load of deviled eggs. Might as well eat, I thought as I walked along behind my brother, my eyes on the sidewalk cracks. I could be ten. I can be twelve. Arrested for development, farcically tried, falsely imprisoned. Always a life sentence: you are twelve forever.

I was on the verge of slinking off down the alley when I happened to glance across the street into the tall windows of the rooms above Rivenbark's. At the sight of them I reached out and cuffed my brother lightly on the shoulder.

"What?" he said. I suddenly realized he'd been talking again, describing some trouble he was having getting the roofers to reset the flashing around his chimneys. Since his retirement, Wilson had been busy orchestrating work crews of various specialties, all of them shiftless, overpriced, late, drunken, inept.

"Rivenbark's," I said, nodding. "Remember our Rivenbark's plan?"

"I haven't been in Rivenbark's in twenty-five years."

"I'm talking about when we were kids. When we wanted to rent the rooms up there for a salon." I pointed to the second story. In the years since—fifty almost—I had kept loose track of these rooms. They had been occupied rarely: once for a couple of years by a dance studio whose tap classes reportedly drove Rivenbark the elder so crazy he'd thrown them out in mid-lease; once in the fifties by a vacuum cleaner outfit; finally in the tail end seventies by a Pakistani dentist, whose work was cheap and good—I went to him several times, and not just for the nitrous oxide like a number of younger people in town—but who was driven out of business due to racism fueled by the Iranian hostage crisis.

Since then it had sat empty, nearly ten years now.

"Salon," said Wilson.

"Not as in hair. As in Gertrude Stein. Natalie Barney." I tried to think of some famous non-Parisian salons, but came up blank.

"This was when?" Wilson had the traces of a smile on his face, as if what I was telling him was something he wanted to doubt. *I am at war with my own memory,* I thought, *I don't need battles with yours or anyone else's.* For the second time on my walk that day I wondered if what inspired me the most, what gave these walks their magic, was nostalgia—and I pledged to give them up if this was the case.

I crossed the street.

"Matthew," Wilson said, and I called over my shoulder to him, glad to be taking the lead, to feel him behind me for a change.

"We're taking a detour." I stopped near the back of Rivenbark's, in front of Fred Rivenbark's grandson Gray.

"Mr. Carleton," he said without looking up at me. He plunged his hands into a bin of screws as if it were a sink full of dinner dishes and brought out heaps of silver, dropped them into the scoop of a scales, began to flick them back into the bin, counting.

"Mr. Carleton," he said again as Wilson coasted up behind me.

"Mr. Rivenbark, Mr. Rivenbark," I said.

"What for you gentlemen this Saturday?"

"We'd like to take a look at the rooms upstairs."

Rivenbark's grandson kept on counting, his scrunched brow reflecting the difficulty of counting and conversing at once. His lips moved slightly, as if he'd had a stroke.

"You two thinking of going in business together?"

"House of ill repute," I said, and Rivenbark chuckled, his eyes still registering digits, silver screws.

"Don't know if I can recommend a family business situation," he said.

"We're too old to argue," I said.

"And too old to agree," said Wilson. He stepped forward, smiling, and I felt a thrill for having forced him to participate.

"Seriously, gentlemen," said Rivenbark.

"We're considering renting some rooms. Office space for a joint business venture."

"Those rooms ain't been cleaned since Dr. Gujihari or

however you called him left us. Back about ten years. All kind of junk up there."

"We're just looking, Gray."

Without taking his eyes from the scoop, Rivenbark called to a man on his knees in the paint section and said, "Tell Ricky I said show y'all up there. Be careful don't break a leg and sue me for all the money I'm making off these two-cent screws."

Ricky left us at the head of the stairs with the key. There were three large rooms, a walk-in closet, a small bathroom. The front two rooms showed roots of the plumbing and wiring done for the dentist's office. Fifty-pound bags of fertilizer were stacked on slats in the middle of each room, and the sweet pink-ish chemical odor of the pellets made me think of life before we moved into town, of loam and sand and muddy discs—until a moment later I remembered that when we lived in the country the only fertilizer in use was manure.

"This isn't exactly how I remembered it would be," I said, looking around the rooms at the peeling molding, the bubbled light slanting through the thick window glass.

"That's because you've never been up here before."

I'd been talking to myself, and had forgotten for a moment that Wilson was with me.

He sat down on a stack of fertilizer. "At least you didn't come up here for this salon business you're talking about. I remember now how that went. Peter came, with Virginia. We drew straws."

"I'm afraid you're wrong," I said. "I remember asking Fred Rivenbark's daddy if we could go upstairs. All the other rooms in town were rented out. This was our only option."

"And he let you see them?" He was smiling his "I doubt it" smile again. What could I expect to find out about our lives from the autobiography of someone exhibiting such a poor memory?

"Yes, he let us see them."

"So what did you say to get him to let you up here? I mean, why would anyone show two kids the last available piece of downtown real estate?"

"We made something up," I said to Wilson. "Like I did just now to get us up here. I don't remember."

"It was fifty years ago," said Wilson. He was both agreeing with and accusing me. And, as if by his having said it, it became true: it was fifty years ago, and I was a teenager again. Wilson was through his first year at prep school, and had already transformed himself into the person who stood before me now, making me feel as if I were lying, making everything I said seem obvious or incorrect. I saw then how wrong it was to have climbed the stairs to these rooms. The barren windows had hovered above me all these years like levitating ghosts, invoking the summer of the salon, when our family had merged into something more than siblings sharing a house and a last name. That summer we had gained a common vision, both skeptical and infinitely curious, attuned to nuance and irony everlasting. How could that have all dwindled down to polite battles of memory and fact? To names, dates, places?

I wished I had stayed single file behind him on the sidewalk instead of trying to change fifty years of petrified history. He would always treat me as if I were twelve. I stood across from him, unsure of the simplest things: what to say next, how to get us down the stairs and outside.

"Anyway it doesn't matter," he said. "I'm starving, aren't you?"

Downstairs Rivenbark looked up from his counting as we passed. "So what'd you decide?" he asked.

"We decided to go get a hot dog," I said as I pushed past him.

And Wilson, ever the diplomat, tagged Rivenbark paternally on the shoulder and said, "Thanks, son. We'll be in touch if we can afford you." Putting things right with a pat and a sentence as I moved outside into an afternoon so flat and dispirited it could have been a Thursday.

WALKING IN SILENCE to the restaurant, I meditated upon the nature of autobiography, which I decided was almost always an exercise in inadvertent irony. Even the most controlled and veteran writers reveal more than intended when writing their private lives; for the less accomplished or nakedly inept it is a vainglorious undertaking which leaves its author looking foolish to all but relatives, sycophants or the thickest of readers.

I have had to read my share of these disasters. I am at that age. People—friends, acquaintances—who fancy themselves storytellers succumb to pleas to "put a few things down on paper" so that their great-grandchildren will be able to know them. Posterity: that's the motivation they use to justify these projects. Often they claim to have been blackmailed or coerced. *"My daughter Margaret Anne said she'd write it down if I didn't; might as well do it myself and get it right."* The work begins and for a fortnight they burn at the dining room table with the hard gemlike flame of diligent reminiscence.

Lest I appear too cynical, I'll admit to an understanding of the impulse. I am old enough to have occasional thoughts of what I'll leave behind. If I have twenty years left I'm lucky; it's time to consider what will remain of me afterward besides a closet full of unfashionable suits to be boxed and carted down to the thrift shop. A little record of where you've been and who you've met and what you've thought about—it's too easy a thing to deny yourself when the time comes. From what I've observed, it is a project which normally occupies a few weeks at most, days and nights during which meals—both baneful and pivotal during the last quarter of your life—are taken like breaths and the stiffness of your bones fades; sitting at the dining room table for six-hour stretches on the old Underwood it's as if you're disembodied, hovering above your history like a plane following a river as it twists out to sea.

So why should I be wary? Because ninety-eight out of one hundred autobiographies I've read take great liberty with a thing I've always tried to hold in some regard: the truth.

SETTLING INTO a back booth of patched green vinyl, Wilson and I leaned into the menus we held in our hands. I didn't need a menu at Captain's, having eaten here twice a month or more for forty years, but I had not brought a newspaper along and had nothing to do with my hands while Wilson pondered, vacillating between a Chicago dog and sliced barbecue.

"I was headed over to your house this morning," he said from behind the plastic. "Morning" he said like a Californian this time, not like a native. I wondered if our encounter at Rivenbark's had made him feel the need to distance himself from Trent, and from me. In my resentment I imagined he felt that my poor memory was the result of a life lived narrowly, for the most part in one small place.

"That's what you said. Anything in particular you wanted?"

The waitress came. When we had ordered and she was gone, Wilson said, "I was wondering if you'd had a chance to get to the book yet."

"You mean your *manuscript*?" I didn't look at him as I spoke—I watched Captain scrape his griddle with a spatula, edging a crust of grease toward the trough. The way I bore down on the word manuscript was a cheap shot, but it was out in the world now, and I couldn't take it back.

"Book, manuscript, whatever you want to call it," Wilson said, smiling. "I know it's not a book until I publish it, but I can't just call it a project. That makes it sound like goddamned macramé. You know how it is when you're retired—any inkling of the shuffleboard set and you're sunk."

Sometimes, talking to Wilson, I think of so many things to say that I grow frantic, anxious that I'll lose a response and go around for days plagued by that horrible "I should have said X" feeling. I wanted to respond to the retirement question—I work mostly half-days now down at the print shop because I'm trying to train a boy to take my place and don't want to intimidate him by looking over his shoulder all the time—but I am by no means retired. Like Wilson is retired, with his pensions and his sailboat and his extended vacations. I tagged this thought for later and pushed ahead with my most pressing point.

"So you want to publish this?"

"Well, of course. Why spend time on it otherwise?"

"Some people write their memoirs so that their grand-children will know what their life was like. For posterity."

He shrugged, which shocked me a little; it was an un-characteristic gesture for him. Maybe I just imagined it—maybe what he said next seemed the type thing that a shrug would accompany.

"My grandkids can buy the book."

I chuckled at this—Wilson trying to be callous.

Wilson relaxed with my laughter, the vinyl of his booth crackling as he spread into it. "I'll give them a discount."

"Of course."

Our food came. Between bites of barbecue and slaw Wilson said, "So you don't like it?"

I put my hot dog down, smiling. "I've only read ten pages."

"But so far you don't see it as something that's publish-able."

Even though I knew this was coming, I was unprepared for it. I am not a writer and I know nothing about the business of book publishing. My tastes in art are like everyone else's—subjective. Yet it was quite a different question to be asked if I "liked" his memoir and if I thought it publishable. Did he mean like in the sense of aesthetic appreciation? Did I "like" the prose? Did I find the work well put together, illuminating, subtle, filled with levels and layers I require in order to be entertained? Or did I "like" how Wilson had presented his—ours, my very own—life?

Two very different things to consider. What I should have done at that moment was to point this out to Wilson, but instead I gave way to the question I really wanted to ask him, had been wanting to ask all day.

"Let me ask *you* a question," I said. "Why did you give this to me to read?" I did not expect Wilson to tell me that I had, in those years since he'd left behind a few beat-up Penguin classics, become better read than he could ever hope to be, surpassing him in knowledge and an appreciation of life's mystifying twists. I thought then of teachers whose knowledge *I had surpassed*—Mrs. Bacon under whose twelfth-grade tutelage I first read Shakespeare. Her knowledge of the plays seemed in retrospect too tidy, anal-retentive almost—stock readings of Hamlet's personality, an irksome emphasis on recitation. And there was my mother, whose passion was psychology; she kept up as best she could, given the resources available in our area, with developments in the field. Once in high school I decided to write a paper on Freud, and my mother was very helpful, spending hours at the kitchen table explaining the terms; yet years later when I actually got around to reading Freud I was embarrassed by how little she understood of his work, how she seized the convenient interpretations and ignored the deeper, more unsettling discoveries altogether, like everything that dealt even remotely with sex.

Shakespeare without language, Freud without sex. Still I find it hard to feel victorious over either of them, because back then I knew nothing. If they knew little, I understood less. And it is in this light that I judge them still.

"Because you're my brother," said Wilson, nibbling a hush puppy. When I didn't respond to this—what was there to say?—he looked up suddenly, startled, as if by remaining silent I was disputing our relation.

"And you're a big reader," he added. His choice of the word "big" to describe my reading reminded me of my father. I felt like saying: I've seen bigger. Wilson ate slaw and barbecue and hush puppies as I searched his face for any sign of the man to whom I owed what little intellectual prowess I could claim.

"You read more than anyone I know," he said. "You read good things, too."

"I don't read a lot of autobiography," I said. Thinking that I'd sounded too harsh I added, "Elaine reads a lot, too."

He shoved his plate to the side. "I can ask Elaine. Elaine will do fine. Either way. I just thought you might be interested. But if you're too busy you should have said so."

Crossing my arms over my chest, I relaxed into the booth. "I'm not too busy, Wilson. I *want* to read it. I was just curious as to why you asked me and not Jen or Elaine."

"Jen's my wife. She's paid to love everything I do," he said. "Seriously? I just happened to nab you first when you were over last night. You know, when you came into the kitchen I'd just gone up to my study to get the manuscript and hadn't decided who to share it with first. If Elaine had come into the kitchen instead, I'd have asked her."

That he would try to make it sound so random was shocking, pathetic. I was embarrassed for the man.

"Maybe we can both read it," I said.

"Of course. You can give it to her after you're through. I welcome feedback from anywhere I can get it."

I changed the subject. We made plans for swimming. Three times a week I drive to Wilmington with Wilson and Jen to swim laps at the YMCA's indoor pool. Alex is not a lap swimmer and rarely goes with us. We talked about who would drive when, what errands there were to run while in town.

Standing at the counter, waiting for Captain to take our money, Wilson said, "So have you read any of it at all?"

"I told you, Wilson. The first ten pages. Early this morning."

"Of course there's work to be done." I could tell that he was waiting for me to open up. Every time a few seconds would pass without my saying something he would nudge me with another comment. "I find it easier to write it all out at once." Twenty seconds later. "I had almost all of it outlined, but I abandoned the outline after the first twenty pages." Thirty seconds later: "I'm sure I'll have to go back through it several times." Forty-five seconds later: "What do you think of the way it opens?"

"It's interesting," I said.

"You can say whatever you want."

"I found a beautiful sentence on page eight." I regretted saying it immediately. Of course I couldn't say whatever I wanted.

He hesitated, as if he'd been holding his breath all this time and could exhale now that something positive was in the air.

"What sentence was that?"

"About a road leading to a school. Something like, 'The road in winter was red with mud.' Very nice. I like the economy and the rhythm there." The last sentence I rushed through, hoping he wouldn't follow up, wondering why I had ever mentioned it. It was the type of thought I had long since learned to squelch.

Wilson, looking baffled, said, "Thanks." Then, after a pause: "That road, you could hardly walk down it. You'd be too young to remember. You'd stay drier taking the damn ditch. What else?"

We were outside now, strolling down Main toward my house. The streets had thinned, the sky had clouded. Squat buildings, none higher than two stories, cast canyon-like shadows. Awnings billowed in a sand-laced breeze, and the mood of downtown stretched toward the windswept sanctity of Sunday morning.

What else?

"I liked the part about how we played so much horse-shoes that summer," I said. In fact this was the first thing I could think of—a set of horseshoes in the display window of Wyrick's Sporting Goods had saved me. I felt the need to temper this with something critical, so I said, "I think you could beef that part up a bit, though."

"Beef it up?" Repeating it made the expression seem juvenile and approximate.

"Make it sharper. Get in more details. Remember how we were so little and the horseshoes were so big and heavy that we'd always graze our legs swinging them? And at the end of the day our kneecaps would be bruised and swollen? We'd all limp down to that irrigation pond in the woods and stand frozen in the warm water like cattle."

"Oh yeah. I do remember that happening a few times. To some of us."

His response made it clear whose memories were important. It seemed to occur to him for the first time that I was witness to some of what he chose to describe, and that this might cause problems.

"Well of course it didn't happen with every toss. We'd all be in wheelchairs, as many games as we threw. But it seems like a nice metaphor to me."

What I remembered then but did not mention was how

desperate and competitive those long days of play were—
how frenzied they had ended, with my skin itching from
various chafes: the elements, the insults. It was hard to sleep
or even rest after days of such fury. And I felt that other
families were not like ours even then—that they left each
other alone, which was better, and worse.

"Maybe you're right," said Wilson. "But this is just an
autobiography. I'm not so concerned with metaphors as I
am with the facts. What happened, how it happened,
how it shaped me. This isn't supposed to be Somerset
Maugham."

"Thank God," I said. Wilson tagged me on the shoulder
like he would a drinking buddy and called me, with what I
recognized as sincere brotherly affection, an "A-number-
one smartass."

IV

The road in winter was red with mud. In the margin beside this
underlined sentence I erased the exclamation points (the
sight of them after my lunch with Wilson embarrassed me)
and replaced them with another sentence: *George Washington Carver discovered the peanut.*

Alex must have heard me chuckling. She came into my
study and leaned on the arm of my desk chair, draping an
arm around my shoulder.

"What?" she said, reading over my shoulder. "George
Washington Carver discovered the peanut?"

"Didn't he?"

"I get Booker T. Washington and George Washington
Carver mixed up."

"It's been a long time since sixth grade when we learned
that stuff."

"Is this passage about peanuts? Is that a criticism?"

"The scope and breadth of Wilson's autobiography is deep and wide," I said.

Alex was quiet; I could tell she was reading over the other pages splayed across my desk. "I hope you're not being mean to him," she said.

"I'm being honest with him."

"Why did you write that in the margin, Matthew? About the peanut. What does that mean?"

I sighed. I wished she'd leave. She was so unbearably fair. She understood the battles between Wilson and me with a clarity and wisdom which led me to deny every observation she made.

"I'll erase it," I said, rubbing the words so hard a rent appeared in the margin, blowing the flecks of rubber onto the blotter, sweeping them onto the rug with the flap of a business envelope.

"Well? What does it mean?"

"It was something my father used to say. He was a big fan of both the peanut and its discoverer."

"But why did you write it there?"

I considered her question: because the red road in winter reminded me of my father's muddy peanut field? Because I knew I should have said no to Wilson when he stopped me in the kitchen the night before, manuscript in hand, and the peanut comment was a way of admitting that I could not read his manuscript without petty reactions, sarcasm, guile? Because the use of the word "discover" to describe what I might find in Wilson's manuscript was as approximate as it was when applied by my father to Mr. Carver's work?

"I erased it," I said. "It doesn't exist anymore except in sixth-grade history texts and the minds of people with good memories." I felt suddenly anxious, as I'd felt years ago after those long summer days of horseshoes: bottled-up, cross, bruised.

"Self-awareness is a horrible thing." I meant to think it but spoke it instead.

"What do you mean?" said Alex.

"The lack of it causes all the problems in the world. People doing things without considering the implications. It's always: I am, therefore I am invincible."

"So it's better to cower?"

"It's better to be sensitive," I said.

"A chameleon of a word," said Alex. "The people who you're trying to describe use it to mean touchy and defensive. But you mean something else entirely, don't you? Don't you mean considerate?"

Maybe she is not unbearably fair. I like to think she is because she is my wife and I'm in love with her, but she often takes the opposite side of mine, even in a family battle. Especially in a family battle.

"There's no better word for it, though," I said. And I felt at fault for not being able to find one, as if the right word would make her agree with me.

"Maybe you better put this away for now," said Alex, reaching down to straighten the pages on my desk.

I stared at her fingers on the pages until she quit.

"Okay?" she said.

"Soon."

"Elaine called and asked us to dinner."

"Tonight?"

"Seven-thirty."

"We just saw everyone last night."

"It's the weekend again. You don't want to go?"

"Not really."

"Too late," she said. Grasping my chin between forefinger and thumb, she pulled it away from the window.

"You said you saw Wilson. Did you two have a fight?"

"No," I said. "We had a hot dog from Captain's."

She must have sensed my humiliation, because she took

my cue and spared me. "That explains everything," she said
before she closed the door.

V

Aside from being dishonest, most memoirs suffer from a
staleness of structure. Conventional autobiography begins at
birth, with a slap and a child's first wail, proceeding inter-
minably through the horseshoe games and irrigation ponds
of childhood. Nothing is more tedious to me than the
obvious chronology—childhood, puberty, college, first job.

There is also the question of authority. The majority of
memoirs contain a tonal ambiguity which, despite the author's presumption of complete control, establishes an "as-
told-to" relationship. Here the "to" is not ghostwriter or
personal secretary, as is the case with those showbiz bios
that line the racks of grocery stores; here the "to" is an in-
termediary—the reader—whom the author, often unwit-
tingly, trusts with his life. The author tells you everything,
and you tell yourself only what you need to know. Should
you rise to the occasion and see your task as less collabora-
tion than tug-of-war over veracity and fact, should you allow yourself to feel less the hack hired to transcribe
monologues and more an artist who finds in the notes not
sung a tune filled with too much truthful sound and fury
to ignore, that second-party *you* to whom the tale is told
becomes omnipotent. Between the straight and uninspired
lines of memoirist's milestones you trace those secret
curves which make up the life not presented, the life de-
nied. Real Life.

The more I read of Wilson's "life," the more I took
refuge in questioning the true nature of autobiography.
Perhaps this was only another way to put off reading the
damn thing, but all this theorizing led finally to a charitable

conclusion. Wasn't there more than an outside chance, I asked myself, that the act of autobiography is an *act of faith*, a search for life's lowest common denominator?

It occurred to me that I might treat it in the way one chooses to treat small talk—not as a meddlesome waste of time but as a metaphorical expression of our common existence.

Yet when someone behind me in the grocery store line yammers on about wind chill, it is rare that I smile and think charitably: he's not really talking about the weather. What he's really saying is: isn't it wonderful and terrifying that we're all in this together.

Instead I think, yeah, yeah, yeah, yeah.

Sitting at my desk in a lull of quiet, I think instead: autobiography is an act of naked vanity.

I must call Wilson now and tell him I've changed my mind, I thought; bundle this sheaf of paper up and take it over to Elaine's. She's so much nicer than I am, and a better reader, too: not as "big," but not as picky either.

I'd begun to pile the papers together when I noticed the ghost of my sentence in the margin, a faint cursive trail that seemed to fade slowly, like skywriting. The curlicues intrigued me: what else lurked beneath the surface? There was always the chance that he would reveal something of significance, something that might alter the way I see his life, or my own.

As I considered this, I remembered another Saturday afternoon that I had spent at my desk. Years ago, a day in early February, but warm out, unseasonably so after weeks of chilly rain. I had both windows raised and was enjoying the tepid wind when I heard rustling beneath me. I thought it was Jake, the neighbor's dog, confused by the heat wave and come to burrow beneath my shrubbery.

I smelled sulfur and then, a half-second before smoke streamed in through the screen, cigarettes.

My pen remained frozen above a tax form as I heard the voice of my middle son Peter, then fourteen. "You know that fat-ass policewoman downtown?"

"That humongous bitch that always wears men's pants?" said another voice in the squeezed pitch of postpuberty.

"She tried to arrest my ass for jaywalking yesterday."

"No shit?" The other voice I recognized as the Davis kid from down the street.

Their words rose with the smoke, the window screen sifting but not censoring. I could not believe this was Peter, who had never given me more than the minimum amount of trouble, whose familial persona was so rigidly good scout that I'd begun to worry.

Not that this scene made me relax. Their language, while completely and typically boyish and by no means coarser than anything I'd heard in the Army, shocked me nevertheless, perhaps because of the way it rose from a bush, accompanied by cigarette smoke. And it grew worse.

"She said she could send me to fucking walking school if she wanted," replied Peter. "Said I needed to learn how to cross the goddamn street."

"Fuck her," said the Davis boy.

"You first," said Peter. Wincing, I bolted up and, pushing my face as close to the screen as I could get it, so close that I could see through the shrubs a spike of brown hair, I opened my mouth to upbraid him, but before I spoke I realized how long I'd been listening to them without making my presence known. In the end I settled for dropping a stapler hard on my desk, sufficient enough disturbance to flush both boys into the afternoon.

There was the chance that by slugging through Wilson's manuscript I was going to overhear something shocking, something that would show me a side of him I'd not seen and, like Peter's offensive bush talk, would rather not see. But of course the comparison is flawed, I told myself as soon as I thought of it: Wilson was not outside the window hiding in the bushes. I was not overhearing, I was *hearing*; he had given this to me to read. Yet there remained something voyeuristic about my reading it, something significant about this as-told-to situation that I had not yet discovered, which prevented me from bundling it up and dumping it on Elaine, which cajoled me to read on.

In order to avoid the sluggish structure I decided to skip around and ended up on page twenty-nine, in a dorm room during Wilson's college years. After prep school, Wilson applied to a slew of colleges: Harvard, Haverford, Dartmouth, Brown, Davidson, Chapel Hill. Davidson was a concession to my mother's family, who were staunch Presbyterians—and of course it is a fine college, crown as they say of the kudzu league—but I don't think Wilson ever seriously considered attending. Unless you were mechanically inclined or interested in animal husbandry, Chapel Hill was then a magnet for every good mind in the state, if not the entire Upper South. Haverford reflected Wilson's interest in the pacifist philosophies of Quakerism. Harvard, Dartmouth, Brown—need I explain why Wilson, strolling through the quads which in winter were white with snow, would dream of attending such schools?

He was accepted everywhere he applied except Harvard, and awarded scholarships to Chapel Hill and Brown. He chose Brown. And was happy; according to page twenty-nine, he made many lifelong friends during his two years there. Describing these years, Wilson's prose has less of a style than a kind of anachronistic raccoon coat, goldfish-swallowing swagger.

Old Bill Findstrom was a scrapper. I knew that the first time I laid eyes on him in Box Bondurant's dorm room down the hall from mine. Findstrom was brilliant and fun-loving, scion of a West Coast shipping family, majoring of all things in Psychology for which Bill spent many the hour of research in the Portuguese bars of Providence.

He went on to use his well-researched psychological insight to scare himself up a seat on the Stock Ex. Bill and I shared a love of the seedier parts of Providence. On Friday afternoons we embarked on EAT AND DRINK AS THE NATIVES EAT AND DRINK excursions which took us as far away as Pawtucket and filled our bellies with all sorts of combinations of quahog and rotgut. After college we kept up and often has been the time when Jen and I have blown into New York from some far, godforsaken corner of this earth without a prospective roof over our head only to be offered unlimited nights in the guest room of Bill's Fifth Avenue triplex. Bill and his Helen are special folk—down-to-earth and you wouldn't know their riches unless someone waved their bank book in front of your face. Even then you'd ask to be taken to the vault for proof. Bill and his Helen came to see us twice while we were in Beirut . . .

Bill and his Helen, I repeated. Bill and his Helen. I imagined what Wilson would say if I called him on this.

"*His* Helen? You mean Helen to his Paris, Wilson?"

"Lord, no, Matt." Wilson would chuckle as if he thought classical allusions the silliest thing in the world. After all, this wasn't supposed to be Somerset Maugham. "That's her name."

"But why *his* Helen?"

Wilson's face would cloud. "Because they've been married for forty years."

"But why can't she be her own Helen?"

"Good heavens, Matthew," Wilson would say. "I wouldn't have figured you for a militant feminist reading of such a harmless figure of speech."

It's neither militant, feminist nor harmless, I would say

before Wilson would smile his I-doubt-that smile and I would redden and go back to pointing out misspellings.

I read on. Brown ended and Chapel Hill began. This was a pivotal time for Wilson. Though his tuition was taken care of and he had a small stipend to cover most living expenses, sending Wilson to Brown was still a strain for my father. Train fare to Providence was expensive. We had no relatives in the Northeast and Wilson ended up coming home often. During Christmas holiday of Wilson's sophomore year my father took Wilson aside and told him he'd have to transfer to Chapel Hill.

A sulky Wilson poked around in the corners of that holiday season, sneaking across town to a bootlegger's for beers at night and spouting off during meals about how his career was done for. He had decided then to be a lawyer and had his sights set on Harvard Law; he was certain that he'd never be admitted if he left the Ivy League, and he maintained that the only thing Chapel Hill's law school was good for was the training of lawyers who could negotiate contracts dealing with timber rights or livestock sales. My father was, like many other scantly educated North Carolinians, inordinately proud of our university, and he extolled its virtues nonstop during those three frigid weeks. Unlike other rabid supporters, he cared little for college athletics. His praise was reserved for the scholars, living and dead, whose reputations had penetrated even the thick of the state, and although he was proud of Wilson's scholarship to Brown, he made it clear in his eulogistic monologues that he considered these scholars at least the equal of Wilson's Ivy League professors.

As soon as my father was out of the room, Wilson would begin to mock him: " 'Our Horace Williams is as damn fine a Classics scholar as you're apt to find above or below the Mason-Dixon. There's Prof. Koch got good work out of Thomas Wolfe years before he went up to Harvard,' " Wilson would bellow in a fair mimicry of my father's bark. "'Old Al Coates is doing fine work over to the Institute of Government, and don't forget Howard Odum and Dr. Frank Porter Graham, both of 'em the darlings of even your Yankee liberals.'"

Wilson became more and more maudlin during that holiday, and more insufferable. By New Year's traditional extended family lunch he had been exiled to the card table with the eight- to ten-year-olds. I watched him sit there as if he were by himself in a crowded restaurant, trying to ignore the other tables, acting as if he ate alone—or with four fifth- or sixth-graders—every day of his life. He didn't seem to notice when milk bubbled from the mouths of his giggly tablemates, when catapulted dollops of candied yam and marshmallow landed on his cuff.

We would not see him again until a weekend in late May. That summer our father allowed Wilson to work as a bellhop in a Newport hotel, which smoothed the transition. By the time he arrived in Chapel Hill, tanned and full of stories to tell, he had decided to make the best of it.

Staring at the shrubs beneath the window, I was anxious to read Wilson's version of his college years. I lowered my eyes to the page and dragged them across the type, hoping to skim meaning instantaneously.

After two years at Brown I transferred to Chapel Hill. Though I missed Providence and the many friends I had made there, the move to Chapel Hill was a wise one for all involved, for I found many like minds in my home state as well, and my two years there were satisfactory in a number of ways.

I was mildly shocked to find bland synopsis where I expected vituperation. Satisfactory in a number of ways? Perhaps.

Wilson immediately scouted out the prep school crowd, joined a good fraternity, and by Christmas of his junior year began dating Jennifer, who had known Virginia Anne slightly at Wellesley and was in Chapel Hill working on her master's in Romance Languages. Perhaps it was satisfactory in a number of ways: Wilson had friends; he found my father's ravings about academic excellence to be maddeningly true; he fell in love.

But there is another side of the story which I was certain would not appear in Wilson's autobiography.

At the same time that Wilson transferred, my brother Peter was entering the freshman class and since both were new to the university, they spent the first few weeks eating together each day in the cafeteria and studying together at night. Peter was nervous about college—like the rest of us, he'd rarely been away from home. Having Wilson around was reassuring during those few weeks, Peter later confided. He was solicitous in a way he'd never been during the years he came home from up North. Together at college it seemed that their view of the world—a shared skepticism, a cultivated sense of the bizarre and the absurd, the slightly pretentious literary leanings which had led us to search out a room for our own salon—emerged in sharp relief against the sensibilities of the pimply tide clogging Franklin Street.

Three weeks into the semester Wilson ran into an old friend from prep school. Within a week he was ensconced in a preppie clique, within two weeks he'd pledged his fraternity. "It would have been fine if he'd dropped me then and there," Peter told me later. "I'd've found my way—it's just those first few weeks when you're anxious, anyway— but Wilson hung in there, taking me to all his fraternity functions, introducing me to all his friends. They were nice enough to me. I was Wilson's little brother after all, but I was still public school, worse yet a rural public school where French came only in the form of a twist in Mrs.

Darlington's hair. Remember her, the big red Geometry teacher? I couldn't keep up. They talked big constantly—you know how you are when you're twenty—and even though there were times when I could hold my own, every time I opened my mouth I felt like what came out was mud. Swampy mud."

Peter became Wilson's Little Brother. He wanted to break away but he was still flattered by the attention Wilson was paying him, shackled by the loyalty he felt he owed the family.

He was terrorized by nightmares in which a volume of *Yackety Yak,* the UNC yearbook, was riffled by a black wind to the page bearing Peter's picture above the bold caption: "WILSON CARLETON'S LITTLE BROTHER." He suffered through the semester with Wilson's friends talking of foreign things: coxswains and commons, tea dances and trips to the bar at the Biltmore Hotel. Jennifer's arrival late in the semester helped—she was attentive to Peter in a sincere way, not only because he was Wilson's brother—but Jen and Wilson were falling in love then, and her priorities understandably were with her fiancé.

February is a month I happen to love. I have always cherished the way it arrives down South, in a damp curtain of greyness that makes me fantasize about foreign things—England, its fens and moors, its dour periods of history and literature. During that month it is if I've finally, after all these years, left Trent. The colorlessness settles in my marrow like the mist of inspiration; it is a fertile time for me, a time during which I log millions of imaginative miles.

Yet most find the shortest month intolerable. Peter spent the February of his freshman year either drinking too much in a dark corner of Wilson's fraternity house or sleeping away the abbreviated days. He skipped classes, missed midterms. He hid from Wilson and fell out of favor with his dorm mates when he told them to lie to his brother should he call (there was only one phone, in the downstairs lobby) and threatened to expose their violations of dorm rules if they did not comply.

A drunk, a blackmailer, an indifferent student, a basket case: this is how Peter described himself during that infinite and torturous February, when each short day lingered like a separate and insidious disease. By mid-March he was sharing a bedroom not with the long-suffering Religion major from High Point, but with me again, at home in Trent. He read and rested, rested, read. Walked through the Trent streets without appearing to look where he was going. Wilson came home several times that spring—short missions of mercy during which he would clear everyone out of the house and lock himself in my bedroom with Peter. Once Elaine and I sneaked around to the back of the house to spy through the window. From what little I know of psychoanalysis, these sessions seemed to reverse the role of doctor and patient, for based on what Elaine and I heard through the buffer of hibiscus, Wilson talked nonstop for fifty minutes, Peter nodded thoughtfully throughout.

By late April Wilson was too busy with school and the frenzied spring social schedule to visit. Despite the discontinued therapy sessions Peter emerged, in sync with the greening of summer. One night in mid-May, a week before he left, he related to me most of what I've just told you. Later that night he announced to my parents that he was taking the rest of the money he had saved for tuition and traveling out West for a while. My mother protested; my father thought it might do him some good. Both expected him to return, which so far—it's been forty-six years—he has done a half-dozen times, for one-week stints to a rented cottage near Cape Hatteras.

Of course, some people would blame Peter for his buckling under, would suggest that there were links already weakened in my lost brother's psyche, and that Wilson acted with compassion and loyalty. Sometimes it appears that way to me, too. Why couldn't Peter have extricated himself sooner? Why was Wilson's shadow so constricting? I am Wilson's little brother also—I have been so almost as long as Peter, and while it has never been exactly easy, I never flunked out of school or drank to excess because of it, and it has never caused me to consider living in a walk-up apartment crammed with books and cats in Portland, Oregon, working for nominal wages in a bookstore and living a life which sounds to us as ascetic as a Trappist's.

To distract myself from such thoughts I shuffled the stack of onionskin in front of me, cut to page sixty-two. It took only a few sentences to deduce that Wilson had moved past his college years, past his two years in the Seabees building tarmacs in the Philippines, past his year at Duke Law and was into his life overseas.

During his years abroad—and he and Jen must have been out of the country for twenty years altogether—Wilson relocated a great deal, as low-level State Department bureaucrats are often required to do. He was tightlipped about the specifics of his work—to anyone who asked, I was programmed to reply that he worked as an "economic attaché"—and he was nonemotive about his job. In my more generous moments I attribute this stoicism to those of us so conditioned by growing up during the Depression that we accepted any hardship in the workplace with the rationale that we were lucky to be working at all.

Yet by keeping quiet about his job, Wilson gave many the romantic impression that his foreign details involved a bit of espionage. I have it on good authority that the closest Wilson has ever come to the CIA is traveling the Capital Beltway where it passes closest to Langley, but if Wilson wants to cloak his work with that romantic notion, I see no point in denying him such deception. What he did during all those years was fairly mundane desk work involving the tabulation of economic data. His work is conspicuously by-passed in the overseas chapters of his memoir, where a feel for landscape that I never knew Wilson had takes prece-dence over all other details.

Nowadays Beirut is ravaged and war-torn, yet in the years when I knew it, it was truly the jewel of the Mediter-ranean, unequaled in natural splendor by any other city ex-cept perhaps Rome on a clear day, a blend of hill and blue water so majestic as to make San Francisco seem like Akron.

Terraced fields rose upon the hillsides of the Dominican Republic. Our son Jonathan, then five, noticed many cows dotting the mountainous terrain that were in possession of, in his young words, one set of legs shorter than another.

Strolling those Thai beaches I thought many times of Robinson Crusoe, for if ever there was a place to be ship-wrecked it was here on this sandy cusp by the lush, steamy jungle.

This last passage contained Wilson's only literary reference, which is fortunate, since this description caused me to pic-ture Crusoe as a man on a quest for the greatest-beach-to-be-shipwrecked-on, sort of a location scout for Club Med.

I would like to claim that I enjoyed these passages about Wilson's overseas experiences, but to be honest I found them intolerable. I always have, and not just when Wilson is concerned: when anyone starts telling me about their travels I tune out. It sounds rude or provincial I'm sure, but I can't control it. It's damn near a phobia with me, and like most who have developed phobias, I have sifted my past for an incident which could have triggered such fear. My only conjecture involves a family trip to the 1939 World's Fair in

New York. This was of course the largest crowd I'd ever seen. When you are five years old and have come from a world that is sparse and wan in winter, lush with tendril and corn thicket in summer, scant always of people, you are less fascinated by pavilions showcasing cars and appliances of the future than you are by the throngs. The future to me was not what was inside these peculiar glass-and-steel structures, nor what appeared above them—the dirigible-laden sky, the spiky columns which scraped it—but what teemed and milled outside of them.

After a lunch of things foreign to me—Coney Island–style hot dogs, sliced pizza—we were walking toward the Japanese pavilion. Elaine and I brought up the rear, Mother and Father leading, and Peter, Virginia and Wilson in an aloof flank between. Pushed along by the crowd, I grew sleepy, lulled by the afternoon heat, the involuntary shuffle, exotic lunch settling in my belly. The only thing that kept me awake and barely moving was the clash of languages around me, cacophonous rumble of foreign tongues—other countries and distant parts of my own. Someplace in the Orient, Russia, the seductive cadence of a Windward Island; Brooklyn, a Midwestern state, just-across-the-water Jersey. I was fascinated, but the clash had a different effect on Elaine. Each different accent seemed to stroke her in another place where she was ticklish, and her laughter caused others to look down and away, as if she were afflicted.

Which is how I reacted as well. Pretending I'd never seen her before in my life, I stopped walking and watched Elaine disappear.

Some time passed—five or six minutes—before I began to feel anxious. By this time I had been passed back through several groups like a collection plate, had landed in a clump of sweaty and garlic-breathed Baltimoreans. The bluntness of their language—their words hit the air like brickbats hurled through plate glass—both shocked me and made me homesick. I struggled away from them, pushing into the next group, the next. I was fighting through thick scrub in the swamp at home; fingernails scraped me and once a bony elbow lodged like a tree limb between my third and fourth rib.

Suddenly I saw, through the blur of the crowd ahead, a flash of chalky white: Wilson's cast. He'd broken an arm in a baseball game a month before. I lost sight of it, spotted it again, lost it. I swam toward it, saw it blink among the olive and sunburnt skin like the fleshless limb of a skeleton. I did not see the rest of him, only the cast as it rose and fell like a life preserver in turbulent seas. Finally I swam close enough to lunge: plaster flaked into my palm as I grabbed it; I ran my hand down its roughness until I found the tips of Wilson's fingers, which were clammy, forced by the cast into a fetal curl. I drew so close to him that I could smell the putrid skin beneath the cast.

"Stay with me from now on or we'll leave you here in the future," said Wilson.

Could this be the root of my let-me-tell-you-about-my-walking-tour-of-Wales phobia? For five minutes at the age of five I was tossed about the continent, a fly alighting on a spinning globe. Wilson saved me from a future of rootlessness and condemned me to a life lived within a single square mile. I had latched onto his handicap and pulled myself to safety, yet I had him to thank for another rescue, another debt which over the years had become slightly like a curse.

There was a knock on the door, and Alex stuck her head inside. I swiveled my desk chair around to stare at her.

"How's it going?" she asked.

I looked through her, rolling a pencil between front teeth. "Thinking."

"You're missing the Texaco."

Another Saturday custom: late afternoon hours on a couch in the den we added to the rear of the house, on my back in the deepest sheltered reach of all the land I own in the world, listening to the weekly opera broadcast. I nap some, rise from shallow sleep into the passion of *Cavalleria Rusticana* or a little Wagner made warbly by the interference of Hoot McCallister's weed whacker. A bookend to my morning walk and often as soothing. Yet that day, my morning ritual tainted, I was wary of trying to make up for it with the opera.

"Thanks. I'm busy now, but I'll probably be out in a little while," I said, though I knew she could tell from my gaze—which, though steady, seemed to want to rove like the beam of a lighthouse—that I would not be.

She closed the door. I tried to remember what she'd interrupted. It came back in shards, a dissolved dream linking piecemeal: my father . . . Wilson . . . Wilson's travelogues . . . As I sought to recover these threads I stumbled upon a memory which promised to weave them together into something more than speculation.

I thought first of a wall of steamed glass. An indoor pool before breakfast, the timed slap of swimmers, wheeze of regulated breath.

When Wilson announced he was planning on retiring to Trent, he'd cabled Elaine and me to tell us he was flying in to look for a house. A month later he'd arrived alone, and I'd taken a few days off work to help him search. On the second day he'd found the place where he now lives, the Malette place out on Oak Stump. It had been on the market for two years, they were eager to unload and the agent thought he could work a quick closing. Wilson had accumulated leave and cabled Jen that he would stay. Several times over the next few days we had driven down to Wilmington to swim laps before breakfast. It was on the last of these trips that this connection had been made between my father's fear of travel and my own.

We'd been sidestroking so that we could talk as we swam. All this chatter had made us flag and we'd drawn stares from the taut, pace-clock, flip-turn types as we'd sculled slowly and noisily down the lane.

But we couldn't *not* talk, even in the pool; we hadn't stopped talking since I'd picked Wilson up at the airport. It had been a wonderful visit, and we'd gotten along splendidly. His stories were airy and brief, he'd asked us questions about our lives and listened to the answers, he'd been funny in the mornings and had helped with the dishes, he'd carried an energy that made the middle of the week seem like the golden crust of an extended holiday. The possibility of returning to Trent had seemed somehow to fill him with a spirited ease.

"I'm surprised you want to come back here," I'd said. We'd been talking about real estate, and it had seemed an appropriate segue.

Wilson had smiled, an "I was waiting for that" cast to his face. He'd swum ahead and when I had caught up he'd said, "Sounds trite, Matt, but I've seen the world."

I had tried to nod but remembered that I was on my side in the deep end of a swimming pool.

"Not that I'm saying I know it," he'd said. "Sometimes seems the more I see of it the more disoriented I become."

I had been perplexed by this admission—what did he mean "disoriented"?—but amazed. I'd always thought of Wilson as the type who equated travel with knowledge, the type to believe that a man who had not traveled to at least four continents and could not pass himself off as a polyglot could never enter the kingdom of the worldly, the sophisticated. Of course I'd always sneered at such an attitude, in keeping with my belief that the well-traveled became so only to add to their baskets of bath soap from four-star hotels worldwide; that the majority of them would benefit more from watching slide shows in their rec rooms.

My goggles were beginning to fog. Wilson churned powerfully alongside in the mist like a tug towing a barge.

"So you're tired of traveling?"

Wilson must not have heard, because he had not answered. Suddenly I'd felt silly carrying on this conversation in the YMCA pool. This can wait, I'd thought, but it had been hard to suppress the questions I'd had for him, and I'd been concerned that suppression would stifle the spirit of this visit. Our sidestroked conversation had seemed proof that we *could* get along and that Wilson's return to Trent would add immeasurably to my life.

At the end of the lane, I'd clung to the lip beneath the high dive. Water had lapped into the gutter, the drain gurgling as we'd rested. Wilson had started to push off again but I'd reached out to tag him on the shoulder.

"So you're tired of traveling?"

"Jen and I deserve a rest." Wilson had draped his arms in the gutter and hung limply, letting the delayed wake rock him. "And it will be nice to be back in a place where people know me."

How many times since had I heard him describe Trent in the hackneyed language used by all small-town detractors—everybody knows everybody, everybody knows your business. Trent had not been what he had thought it would be that day in the pool; his return had not been the coup he'd fantasized. I suppose this disappointment should make me feel sorry for him, but really, it seems so simple to me; people should take more care with the end of their lives.

There at the edge of the pool, on that day two years ago, Wilson had turned to me and said, "What did people say when you told them your brother was living in Zaire or Beirut?"

"What?" I'd shook my head, as if to empty my ears of water.

"What did they say around here when they asked what I was up to and you told them I was with the State Department in Djakarta?"

I couldn't very well have told him the truth: that people in a place like this forget about you if they don't see you on the street for a month, that the warm clannishness of church bulletins listing the sick and the home-for-the-weekend-from-the-city is deceptive, a compensatory gesture by a town trying to mask its own indifference. I like to think it hasn't always been this way but except for four years of college and four following I've been here forever, and I like to think a lot of things about Trent that aren't at all true. Only a megalomaniac could convince himself that everyone here "knows your business." Here, as everywhere else these days, they could care less. This town has seen as many come and go as a Baltimore block, most of them struggling families making the small-town rounds—fathers on the insurance or loan officer circuit, mothers who taught you in grade school for only a half-year, not even long enough to appear in the yearbook. And their children, whose names you can't remember, who brushed against your life brief as something blown by in a storm. The trail of transients stays warm in a place like this, and when they are gone there's no commiserating in the vegetable aisle or across fence or church pew. You move, you're lost.

True also of native daughters and sons. Perhaps people did ask me about Wilson and Peter and Virginia Anne for a time after they left—staunch and pillared friends of the family whose questions were obligatory or even rhetorical. How is Wilson these days was not to be answered with, "Well, he was recently transferred to Dakar where he reports that the diet consists largely of . . ." At high school reunions, back when I still felt obliged to attend them, inquiries about siblings surfaced when people ran out of things to say, and then the band came back from a break.

"They'd ask if Djakarta was up near Norfolk," I'd said.

Wilson's laughter had echoed in the high hollow of the pool. I'd looked around, a bit embarrassed. Other swimmers, finished with their workouts, had disappeared into the locker rooms. Besides the lifeguard, slumped above us in his high chair like a gull on a piling, we were alone.

"No, now really, Matt," Wilson had said. "What was their reaction?"

"They say, 'Oh,'" I'd answered him. "They nod. They say, 'Un-hunh.'"

I thought my reply was gentler than the truth. *They never ask. They don't care.* But I could see the hurt in his face, which he'd turned away from me toward the steamed wall of glass and the patio beyond, where morning sunlight had spread yellow across chaise longue and concrete.

"I guess they're too provincial to consider anyplace farther away than Raleigh or Wilmington."

I should have agreed with that remark. After all, what he'd been saying was true to an extent, and I'd understood from this statement how much Wilson wanted to be a local celebrity, finally home from the wars.

"Not *that* so much as it's been forty years since you left."

"I think . . ." Wilson had said, and it had been clear without even looking at him that he hadn't been listening. ". . . I think the only reason I chose to come back here, to answer your question, is not because I need a rest but because I feel I can afford to take a rest."

Looking past him, I'd noticed the lifeguard staring at us. I'd put myself on his perch and had pictured the two of us, old men hanging off the side of the deep end, talking in tones that rose and fell with the formal and familiar, and it not yet seven on a Tuesday morning.

"The problem with these people is—Lord knows I'd never criticize someone who has not the means nor the education to broaden themselves—but half these people have more money than you and me put together and they end up giving it away to churches and athletic departments."

"And you think they should spend it to get to Chartres and the Louvre?"

"They'd be better off."

"You've been away longer than I thought. You're going to have to revise some opinions if you're really moving back here."

"Of course I'm really moving back here. I didn't take time away from my job and my family to come down here and swim some laps."

It had seemed more and more unreal for us to be having this conversation in a room full of water, a sleepy teenager frozen in the air above us. Most of the time we spent there he seemed less a lifeguard than a kouros put there to remind me of that vulnerable stage at which my own development had been arrested.

"Look," I'd said. "It's just that your moving back surprised us. It's still an *idea* to us."

"You might see this place differently if you'd been away."

"I see it differently anyway." I'd stared into the gutter at soggy Band-Aids suctioned to the drain.

"Of course you see it differently from the rest of the town. You're a Carleton, and *we've* always seen it differently."

In a minute the battle had grown intricate, the ranks dividing: I was one of them; I wasn't one of them; I was one of them, and had been since birth.

"It's not as if I've never been away," I'd said.

"No—you've traveled a hell of a lot more than most."

Than most xenophobic provincial bourgeois? Next he'd mention my trip to the Virgin Islands and I *would* swim away. My St. Croix to his Mombasa. My beach-side cabana and rum punch to his base camp on Mount Kenya, fried plantains. I should have told him that I had learned more of the world on one of my Saturday walks than he had in thirty years abroad. That these walks were my travels, microcosmic and enriched, filled with insights which had escaped him in five continents. But such a claim would have been wasted on him. What he'd said next proved just that.

"You know, you're right. I probably will have to revise some opinions like you say. Our daddy never saw the Louvre and he was not a stupid man by any means. Hell, you probably know more about Chartres than I do, and I've set foot in the place six times if I've been there once."

Remembering that conversation, I understood finally what Wilson was trying to say: that I had allowed myself to become our father, and that through his travels, Wilson had escaped fossilization and could return home triumphant. And though I again felt the horror which accompanied understanding something years after the fact, I also felt physically stronger, as if all the shocks I'd experienced in the last few hours were conditioning me. I felt my legs growing solid beneath my desk, as if I were just now getting my land legs back from that day in the pool.

OUTSIDE MY STUDY, shadows had begun to puddle and bunch. Over the back fence I saw Hoot and Sally McCallister seated in lawn chairs under their trellis, having drinks with the Dardens. Hoot and his Sally, I said aloud; Hoot and his Sally. It was late, I had missed the Texaco, frittered the afternoon away staring into space, indulging myself in half-baked memories. Wilson's manuscript sat barely disturbed on the desk before me; I should have discovered something innocuous to say to him by now.

There was a knock at the door again. Before I could wheel my chair around, Alex had her head in the door.

"Mr. Diligence," she said.

"Diligently daydreaming."

She opened the door a skinny width and slid inside

quickly, as if keeping out children or pets, though we no longer have to worry about either.

"How far along are you?" she asked, looking over my shoulder at page numbers.

"I'm skipping around."

"You know he's going to ask you about it tonight."

"He only gave it to me last night. I can't speed-read the damn thing."

"Better get back to work." She leaned over to read a few lines; I reached up and covered her eyes, pulled her close, whispered in her ear, "I think we should take a nap instead."

"I've got work to do," she whispered back. "And it's late."

Alex slipped out as quietly as she'd entered. I checked the depth of shadows in my backyard: five-thirty at the latest. Time left for a thirty-minute nap, a length at which I am undisputed master.

Climbing the stairs I selected a sentence, one of my *sentences*—talisman-like lines I've hoarded over the years and summon in times of need. The sentence I chose—*Snow was general all over Ireland*—is preventive in nature, repeated when I want to curb an onset of indulgence. To explain further I must tell you how I came to collect such a line.

Some years ago, our local library held a program to commemorate National Library Week during which select citizens were asked to read passages from their favorite books. On the program I noticed, across from the name of a high school girl who lived down the street from us, Joyce's *Finnegans Wake*. How bizarre and brave, I thought—for though I try not to be snobbish about the literary tastes of my neighbors, the second most literary selection on the program was a few paragraphs from *All Quiet on the Western Front*. The master of ceremonies was the Methodist minister whose humor and hawker's bray seemed better suited to

Jaycee Park than the library's carpeted quiet. He would be sure to get off a philistine quip at her expense, I decided. Sure enough his introduction did not disappoint—or did, as I'd predicted. "This next little lady's gonna read us some James Joyce. He's a author I had to read in college. Well, I was supposed to read some of him. I searched from here to kingdom come for a translation of one of his books till somebody told me that Pig Latin of his was supposed to be English." Unanimous laughter from adults and children both. I actually didn't mind it because I'd rather it come before than after. And the joke, of course, was on him.

The girl—she was a young woman then, this being the spring before her first autumn away in college—took it well. She was cheerful and poised as she reached the podium and said, "I've decided against reading any Pig Latin tonight." No trace of sarcasm in her words—I would not have been able to resist spitting the words Pig Latin back at the preacher, but she was more mature than that. "I would still like to read to you from James Joyce. From his long story 'The Dead.'"

Programs rustled, children along to hear their older siblings read from *Green Eggs and Ham* whispered and fidgeted, their nervousness forming an undercurrent while she read. I remembered something Mozart was supposed to have said upon returning to Salzburg for a performance: "When I play here it's as if wooden chairs and not the people in them are listening." I felt for her, and leaned so far forward I was in danger of toppling into the next row to prove that I, as well as my chair, was interested. She started very near the end, when Greta has fallen asleep after telling her story to Gabriel, who sits beside her on the bed deeply moved, unable to sleep, staring out the window at the falling snow. I looked at Alex beside me, smiled at her as if to say, listen to this extraordinary thing taking place. For this young woman found the words and the sentences not from the page but from somewhere deeply hewn and luminous. Around me kids fidgeted. I detected kicks and shrugs on the periphery like serpents in grass underfoot but it didn't bother me and in a minute I could no longer hear them—words took over, Joyce's words, filtered through this girl who had triked and biked, walked and driven past my house all her life, whom I'd never noticed. *One by one they were all becoming shades,* she read. *Better pass boldly into that other world, in the full glory of some passion, than fade and wither dismally with age.* Alex smiled back. I hear, her smile said, and it's lovely. A lovely little moment. But it was more than just lovely and little; it was the moment isolated, the moment suspended and enriched, the very moment Joyce had created, Gabriel in his hotel, Dublin and all of Ireland paralyzed outside—this moment was ticking away now, for me among greenish carpet, snickers, Pig Latin jokes. *Other forms were near. His soul had approached that region where dwell the vast hosts of the dead.*

All around, my life crackled and hummed and stretched. I pitched forward as if throwing my head out a window to watch something down on the street; my breath touched the backs and necks of those in the next row. I could feel Alex look at me every so often and her looks were warm but bemused, even quizzical. *The time had come for him to set out on his journey westward. Yes the newspapers were right: snow was general all over Ireland.* At this line I fell back into the cool iron of the folding chair. Dramatically, and sighed. People down the row swiveled to see; a kid snickered; Alex touched my elbow. The young woman continued to read, the snow fell on the living and the dead and then it was over and we were in the car driving home.

"What was all that?" Alex asked from the darkness of her side.

"A lovely moment," I said, conceding to the ineffability of what had passed.

The moment passed, but the sentence lingered. I repeated it as I flopped fully clothed across the bed. Our bedroom faces the street, and a late Saturday nap coincides with the last spurt of activity before supper, the penultimate spasm of the day in fact, until teenagers emerge to cruise up and down Main. A nap at this hour must be necessarily light, a comforting if not restful bout with the subconscious and the sensual: puddle dribbled on a clutched pillow, quarter dreams scored by patches of drumbeat from passing cars, playing cards slapping bike tire spokes, dog bark, lawn mower, siren. Settling in my bed I heard the timed clack of stroller tires across sidewalk cracks; a kid dragged a stick in the gutter and called out to someone named "Onion."

Snow was general, snow was general . . . I repeated it until another sentence overtook its cadence, insinuated itself into my vulnerable consciousness. *The road in winter was red with mud.* I sat up suddenly in bed, opened my eyes to a fresh sweep of yellow: the entire room, even dusty cobwebbed corner, was sallowed like an ancient photograph, toe molding warped like the border of snapshot curled by years. *The road in winter was red with mud.* I tried to drown it out with another. *Snow was general all over Ireland.* After a moment's tug-of-war in the disquieting brilliance of new light, the red wintry road won out.

Swinging my feet to the floor, I sat at the edge of the bed, my hands gripping the edge of the mattress. Could it be that this sentence returned because it represented my desire to be loyal to the boy who brought us all books, and consequently, a new life? For a moment my breath grew short and quick and shallow, and I thought I was ill until it occurred that both sentences were trapped somewhere within, straining to escape, their syllables fluttering like the flapped wings of a bird caught in stovepipe.

I forced myself to picture Wilson in the Trent Public Library on that fateful night a decade ago. He would have been a chair; he would have heard only words, a lovely little moment. And it seemed he'd given us all he had, and that I had taken what he brought and blamed him since for bringing. The white plaster of his arm cast flashed again, floating back to me through the crowded future.

I watched the light settle in the corners of the room, leaving the waxed floor dark as mahogany, and I decided that Wilson's being sent away was the best break any of us could have had. We sent him out into the world like a sentry and because he was oblivious to certain nuances, he survived, and sent back the provisions necessary for us to survive. Anywhere. Here even. And though I never left, I've never lived here, not since Wilson was sent away. Our lives, had Wilson stayed or had we gone in his place, would have been different. And at my age, at that hour of the day, I allowed myself to think only that different could mean worse.

VI

"I like when people laugh so hard they shake," said Elaine's granddaughter Claire. Claire was four and lived down the street from Elaine and Bill, though she spent most of her time at their house. "Can't y'all do that?" she asked Wilson and me.

"We're not people," Wilson said. Claire put her chin on his knee and gave him a patient look which made it clear that she did not accept his answer. "Shake," she commanded.

We were having drinks on Elaine's front porch. Elaine, studying Claire, said, "I'm so glad she's not boring. The only worse thing than a boring adult is a boring child."

"You were a boring child, Elaine," Wilson said.

"I was not!" Elaine pretended to be wounded. "I was enthralling."

"To the sheets on your crib maybe," Wilson said.

"You were boring," I agreed.

"All you did was lie around like a picture in a baby blanket catalog," said Wilson. "We all thought you were stuffed."

"I was just well behaved," said Elaine.

"Exactly," said Wilson.

When we all laughed, Claire got excited, twirled, shrieked, begged us to keep laughing. She wanted us to laugh so hard we shook, shake so hard the porch shook, shake the porch so hard the earth shook, town shook, state shook, shake the world. Comfortable in my porch rocker, with Claire bumping against my knees and the laughter of my family surrounding me I was convinced we could shake it, shake the world.

When I came back into the moment, Elaine was midway through an elaborate description of the crewcuts we Carleton sons wore until age fourteen, in which she compared the backs of our heads to concrete blocks, then packing crates, finally American Legion huts.

When she was through and the laughter had died down, Bill said to Alex, "What amazing memories these Carletons have. I can't remember anything before I entered the Army."

"Sometimes I believe they remember things that didn't happen," Alex said, and though she traded winks with Bill and I knew she was joking, her remark threatened my mood.

The next few minutes of conversation were as familiar and as comforting as one of my Saturday morning walks: an anecdote about the time Peter tossed blocks into Elaine's crib and how she hid them until nightfall before returning fire; a somber aside about the time Virginia Anne got tangled in the cord of the venetian blind above her crib and almost hanged herself—this one whispered as Claire still threaded our legs and chairs, but she perked up at the rasp of lowered voices and draped herself across Bill's knees, asking, "Granddaddy, who got hung who got hung who who?" as Bill listened to the end of the story and then looked down at Claire as if she'd just appeared there. "Hush now, nobody," Bill said. And then looked again at her and blinking said, "Time for you to go home, sweet. Granddaddy'll walkya home now." While Claire protested, clinging to Bill's knees like a draped afghan, Jen and Alex decided to go along to visit Claire's parents, who were refurbishing an older house down the street and had recently added on a room that everyone was eager to see.

"Somebody's got to stay here and help with dinner," said Elaine.

"Matt and I will stay," said Wilson. And in the very next moment I was alone with my brother and sister on the porch of my father's house.

Wilson immediately excused himself to use the phone, muttering something about needing to call some house-painters before they tied one on.

Elaine settled into the wicker glider beside mine.

"I wasn't really that boring was I?" she asked.

"Of course not," I said. "You responded to stimuli, however sluggishly."

"And still do today." She took a sip of her drink and leaned way back, resting her head on the wicker. I looked across the street at rows of houses and hedges, a view I'd known well since I was sixteen, and the way not much had changed since—a tree taken out in a side yard, aluminum siding over the Caldwells' clapboard—surprised me. When Wilson returned, it would be as if we'd all just gotten home from school and were waiting on the porch for dinner.

"So: what chapter are we on?" asked Elaine.

"Chapter?"

"In which you try to stop your brother from writing his autobiography."

"Not trying to stop him anymore."

"Talk about responding sluggishly to stimuli. Are you going to tell me how the thing is or not?"

"The thing?"

"Alex told me you spent all day on it."

"With it, not on it. And it wasn't all day. I took my morning walk."

"Well, of course. It's Saturday."

"And met Wilson for lunch."

"What you call a working lunch?"

"We talked a little about his manuscript. To be honest, I didn't get much done today. Sat at my desk and daydreamed mostly."

"Is it that bad?"

"It's not bad at all, really. Actually it's sort of, umm . . . innocuous."

Elaine lifted her head from the back of the chair.

"I went here," I said. "This happened. Then I went there and that happened."

"Well, considering whose hands the 'went here and did this' is in . . ."

She let the sentence trail off, but her tone surprised me. Concerning Wilson, Elaine has always been much more charitable than I have. When he announced that he was going to retire here, Elaine expressed doubt—it was hard for her not to suspect he'd grow bored and age with an accelerated bitterness—but she never once complained about his decision. There are things about Wilson that I know upset her—she has intimated once or twice over the years her suspicion that Wilson does not consider Bill her equal, and never has. Yet these intimations were done with such characteristic Elaine-ish opaqueness that five seconds afterward I wondered if I had not made it up. "How's his memory?" she asked. It occurred to me that she was simply curious about her place in Wilson's memoirs—whether he mentioned her, in what context. Suddenly I found an opening which would allow me to be truthful without seeming petty or bitter. These conversations called for artful construction; one must compose them with the quality and care of the finest craftsman or be exposed.

"One major gap," I said.

"Let me guess. Chapter umpteen, in which our protagonist grows bored with bucolic life and is whisked off to tony prep school."

I continued to be shocked by Elaine's bluntness. And grateful: she was so caught up in her own resentment it seemed mine might be camouflaged. I felt validated by her reaction. All these years I'd borne such lonesome guilt, as if I was the only Carleton who kept score.

"No, this was in life actually, not in his book. The gap wasn't in the book at all. A conspicuous omission if you ask me.

"I met Wilson downtown. Tail end of my walk. We were walking by Rivenbark's, and I guess because I'd been reading his memoirs and had lots of old stuff on the brain, I remembered when we tried to rent the rooms above the hardware."

"Our salon," Elaine said. She smiled, but her smile was as faded and wan as the rooms above Rivenbark's had appeared earlier.

"Rivenbark's grandson let us go up and take a look. And when we got up there, it looked different. Of course it's been fifty years since that afternoon you and I went up there but still, it looked like a different building. So I said so, and Wilson said that the reason it was unfamiliar was because I'd never been there before."

"Above Rivenbark's?" Elaine stared into the street; the question and her tone suggested that she was half-listening.

"Rivenbark's Hardware, on Malette. He claimed it was Virginia Anne and Peter who went that day."

"He's right. It was."

Monosyllables made it sound unequivocal, her simple words small bullets producing clean wounds.

"I've never been up there. No, I take it back—when the Indian dentist was up there, once to have my teeth cleaned. Never before or since."

I didn't say anything. What was there to say? Elaine, you're wrong. Wilson, you're mistaken?

The screen door creaked and Wilson plopped down beside me. I looked across the street instead of at him and this time the view struck me as sublime. Light and shadow striping rooftops, highest limbs of chestnut and pecan trees, top panes of attic windows and I thought, I am here on the porch of the house I grew up in, sitting in between my brother and sister, because there is nowhere else for me. Which is to say that I chose to be there. Aware that the next glance across the street might make me feel like a prisoner again, I joined the conversation.

"Matthew's been telling me about your book, Will," said Elaine.

Wilson set his fresh drink on the Parsons table, lining it with the ring left by his last. "I'm sure he said manuscript."

"Actually, I said book." Elaine gave me a stern look, similar to the one Alex uses to warn me of some modulation I seem oblivious to called tone.

"Oh. Well, then I must have done something right since I've seen you last."

"Sure," I said, aware of the vagueness of this response.

"Matt's a tough critic," Wilson said to Elaine. "He did like one of my sentences, though. Which one was it now, Matt?"

"The road in winter was red with mud," I said in the flat tone of a grade school recitation.

"That's right. Road in winter was red with mud." Wilson ravaged the cadence beyond recognition.

A ruminating hum from Elaine, who seemed on the verge of being either polite or perplexed. I didn't pay any attention to her reaction because in that moment this sentence which had been haunting me all day lost its magic. And though I continued to feel stunted in my brother's presence, I knew then that I would have found books on my own, that ideas would have come to me even if Wilson had stayed right here in this house all these years.

"Tell me again why you like it so much?" Wilson said.

"It's an awfully *pretty* description," Elaine said when I neither spoke nor acted as if I'd ever speak again.

Pretty but bland. And literal: this time it was accompanied by image instead of mood; I pictured a low dirt road running through the frozen stubble of February coastal plain countryside. Puddles. Red mud. The Depression. Ten miles to school in brogans the thickness of an envelope.

"Yes, it's very visual," I said. Desperate for an escape, I reached for my empty glass, but before I could stand, Elaine was up. "Sit," she commanded, and she took my glass. "I've got to go check on dinner. I'll get you another."

"I've been thinking about what you said at lunch," Wilson said. "I suppose my first aim in writing this thing was so I wouldn't forget it all. So the grandkids could hear it as it was. Still now, be honest: you don't think the general public would be interested?"

"In your manuscript?"

Wilson grinned. "I guess I'm back to thinking of it as a book now. What I had imagined while I was working on it was that the foreign chapters would be interesting to people other than friends and relatives."

"You've lived a lot of interesting places."

"I take that to mean no, the general public would not be interested."

"I don't know why you're asking me."

"You think it's too plodding, too . . . bland?"

I wanted to protest, but the word bland seemed so fitting that I could not bring myself to summon the energy to dispute it.

"Perhaps I've had a bland life, then."

"Oh come on," I said.

"I suppose I could have dragged up all my wounds but it just didn't occur to me that it was relevant."

"Of course not." Everything I was saying by then seemed reflexive, inadequate.

"It's not as if there are no ghosts."

"Everybody's got some." I half-sung this cliché, hoping he'd pick up on the parody and sense my reluctance to continue. But then he said something which both increased my dread and weakened my willingness to change the subject.

"My entire adolescence is one big graveyard. I could have written an entire book just about that."

"What do you mean?" Though my question was begged, I wished that I could take it back: was it really worth it to find out how he viewed his life?

"You know what I mean," he said, but I didn't. I thought those years were happy ones for him—his happiest in fact. And I said so.

"Where have you been?" His question infuriated me. I've been here, in Trent, at home; it might be easy to romanticize or embellish the facts of our youth in Cairo or Dublin but here the ghosts roll by on bicycles, press against you in the stacks of the public library, cough recognizably in the next voting booth.

"Sometimes I don't think I've ever gotten over it," he said. "In a way, everything I've done since has been affected by those years."

"Wilson, what are you talking about?"

"I thought you knew. I thought you all knew how horrible those years were for me. One day I'm here, bored in school maybe but here, home, with my family. Next day

I'm eight hundred miles north in what really is another country."

I managed to look enthralled because I was—I could not wait for his next word, I wanted his sentences to come faster. At that moment, Elaine backed out of the screen door carrying a tray. Since she'd left I'd been pleading silently for her return; now her arrival annoyed me. Her presence would change things. Wilson would go back to being his old stalwart self, and we'd start in on the Brie and realign our talk onto an innocent track of daily things.

"Wilson's talking about his prep school years," I told Elaine a little too enthusiastically. Toning it down a bit, I added: "About how hard it was for him."

Elaine nodded and handed me my drink. I tried to catch her eye but she looked to Wilson, who began to speak again.

"I remember when I got up there, nobody could understand a word I said. When they did make out a word, they made fun of my accent. For the first month I rarely spoke at all. Of course, even if I'd come from Connecticut, I'd have had little to say to that crowd. At table in commons everyone talked about European vacations.

"One day I came back from class to find a group of guys going through my closet. They were all in damn hysterics. You see, Mother had sewn my name twice in every article of clothing I owned, so that if one tag came off I would not lose a sock. My roommate discovered this when I lent him a T-shirt. He invited everyone on our hall in to examine the double-billing. From that point on I became known as Wilson Carleton, Wilson Carleton."

I laughed then—a sudden puncture of a laugh—and both Wilson and Elaine turned to me, shocked. Surely he meant this to be funny. Surely he was not still upset about such a trivial adolescent prank. How horrible—they made fun of his accent. All these clothes my mother sewed his names twice into were bought for him at a time when Peter and I shared a drawer full of frayed shirts. This is what I'd wanted to hear. This is what I'd wanted to read in those dull pages instead of stiff descriptions of Haiti's terraced hinterlands.

Wilson and Elaine were staring at me still, as if I'd just made fun of one of their children during a school play.

"I can't believe you have the gall to say these things," I said.

Elaine put down a cracker she'd spread with Brie and said, "Matthew, what is wrong with you?"

"Why don't you ask what's wrong with him?"

"He's only trying to tell us a story," said Elaine. "Are you feeling all right?"

I had lost her; I could not count on her any longer.

"I'm amazed. He expects us to feel sorry for him because our parents bought him a trunk full of clothes and sent him North to a school where he had to study Latin, where people he ate dinner with spoke a little French?"

"My God, Matthew. Wilson was fourteen years old when he went away to school. It's very difficult socially at that age. You must have forgotten how awkward it can be."

"Not at all," I said. "I haven't forgotten at all. I'm reminded of that awkward age every time I'm around him."

Elaine said, "What happened while I was gone?"

"Nothing. We sat around being polite and saying anything but what we were thinking, like we've been doing for the past fifty years."

I picked up my drink and slugged down a third of it. Through the side of the glass I could see Wilson watching me. Behind frosted glass and ice, he appeared blurry and magnified. "This isn't just booze talking," I said.

"Would that it were," said Elaine, which was what it took for me to turn on her.

"I can't understand why you're acting so *shocked,* Elaine. As many times as we've talked about this before. You always agreed with me in private."

Wilson swiveled in his chair, toward Elaine. The sun was behind him now, spotting his profile against the house next door.

"Matthew," she said, "what is this? How do you think we're going to have dinner now, after all this . . ." She noticed Wilson staring at her and said, "Oh, to hell with the damned dinner. I don't know what all this is about, Will. If Matt holds you responsible for his childhood it's none of my affair. Both of you have gotten on my nerves over the years, I'll admit that. I've complained about you both and always will, but I find it easier to blame myself for the big things."

During the course of this speech her voice grew stronger. "Right now I can't stand the sight of either of you. I don't know what this is about, but if you can't work it out before the others get back, you'd both better leave now."

She stood. "What you little boys call your psychic wounds strike me as mosquito bites. Who in the hell cares where you went to school? Oh, I know it's more than that to you, but it's not to me. I thank God I'm the baby. None of this is supposed to matter to me, and you know what? It doesn't."

After Elaine disappeared into the house we sat on the porch in silence. It was this moment, with its thick current of confusion and regret, desire to take back everything undermined by the stubborn idea that things had not gone far enough, that I recognized as a moment I was most familiar with. I had spent many a similar moment trapped in this muddle while my family life swirled and shifted around me.

"Say something," I said, thinking as I spoke: there are so many things I want to say to explain myself. Yet there in his shadow my strongest pull was toward apology.

"I had no idea you felt that way about yourself."

"That's a typical response from you," I said. "Turning it all back on me."

"I should never have asked you to read it. I see that now."

I thought back to the manuscript, trying to remember that sentence which stuck with me all day long, but I couldn't. For the life of me I could not.

"I'm afraid this is not about your book at all, Wilson."

"What this is about is jealousy," he said. "It doesn't surprise me that you'd be envious of my advantages—God knows you should have been. What surprises me is that you've cultivated this envy for so long."

I started to deny it but was silenced by the sound of familiar voices sweeping up the street. Seconds later my wife and in-laws climbed the porch steps in giddy camaraderie. They apologized for staying away so long yet were obviously delighted in having staged such a rebellion, which was fueled, apparently, by a prolonged cocktail hour down the street. The way they wielded their collective guilt, acting as if they'd done something which would banish them from the Carleton family forever and were proud of it, softened me a bit. Elaine stormed out on the porch and said, "I was about to call the cops."

"Dinner's burned. Carbon and fumes. Ancient history," said Wilson.

"We ate it anyway," I said.

AND THEN WE went inside. Conversation between my brother and me resumed in the kitchen, where we all settled down to help prepare dinner. It was strained—it came in trickles—but I don't think it was noticeable to anyone besides Elaine. There were moments when I wanted to pull Wilson into the dining room and take up where we left off, refute his charge that I had "cultivated envy," which I had not been able to answer. But this would no doubt lead to other charges which there would not be time for either of us to deny, and so I remained in the kitchen with everyone else. Bill and Alex chopped vegetables for a salad at one counter, Elaine and Jen worked at another. I sat down at the table and began to slice and butter a baguette, and from my seat in the middle of the room I had a view of everyone. Wilson stood at the sink running water into a pitcher, and as I looked up at him I noticed the water overflowing, bubbling over the sides as he stared out the window into the dim backyard. I looked out the window myself, into the shadowed stillness, black trees and grey sky, and I remembered last night, how we'd sat in Wilson's Florida room and waited for darkness to come to excuse ourselves, as if we all adhered to a sundown curfew. And it did not come and did not come: a fermata held above the final note of the symphony which had all the listeners rustling in their seats.

Now it was upon us again, this borderless time. At first it made me uncomfortable, for it was a lot like not knowing, a lot like the thick confusion I had been feeling all day— and all my life—about my brother. Darkness was past due, and if I had been at home, away from my family, in my own exalted sphere, I could obstruct the seamlessness of this time of day by turning on floodlights and piercing yellow cones from the gloaming. If I had been on one of my walks I could have looked straight up into the buggy streetlights, and the imprint of the light would have lingered, an aureole against which the world would darken. In my study I could pick up a book and become engrossed, only to look up from a page minutes later into pitch blackness. I have devised ways to get through it, and because of these ways I had never felt such impatience before.

There was a lapse in the chatter which had filled the kitchen since we'd come in from the porch, and it was during this lapse, during this moment—forever in coming— when darkness arrived. And though we lingered at Elaine's until late that evening, this is really the end of the story of how I tried to stop my brother from writing his autobiogra-

phy—of what Elaine once called the story of my life—
because this is how that day ended. This is how, in my
family at least, days end.

But there is one last thing I thought of that night while
sitting at the table, something that I looked forward to. In a
couple of days, I thought, I will give Wilson back his book,
and when he starts to type it up to distribute among friends
and relatives (as he has since done), more than likely he will
choose to thank me in his acknowledgments. As darkness
settled in the corners of the crowded kitchen, the thought
of my name in those pages was pleasing, because while
there was nothing I could really do or even say about content, Wilson has always been careless with his spelling. And
though I understand such a contribution to be cosmetic, I
am glad to have been of some help.

Commit to Memory

Occasionally, during those nights when the ring would cut through the late night quiet, one of my brothers or sisters would beat me downstairs to the table in the hall where the phone sat in the dark, but more often than not, I'd be the first to reach it. I'd pick up the receiver quickly to silence it, whisper my slow, hoarse hello. Sometimes they didn't even wait for me to speak before they started in with their pleas, and when I think about it, those years seem permeated with voices—with the whiskey-slurred words of the penitent, the frightened, the defiant and the adamantly innocent. There were times when I couldn't understand the first word, especially during produce season when the Mexican and Haitian migrants, midway through their grueling northward sweep, were locked up for knife fights, drunk and disorderly, misdemeanor B and E. But it really didn't matter what they said: they all wanted the same thing, wanted my father down there pronto to go their bail, and I understood everything from the tone, which was always the same: the tone of someone with only one phone call.

My father has been dead for ten years now, and the thing that I remember most clearly about him is how heavy a sleeper he was. For a long time this fact was less memory than fleeting image: his bulk beneath a quilt, curled and turned toward the bedroom wall, would appear briefly then fade before things became detailed and emotional. Not until one night a few weeks ago was I able to connect this image with our life together.

Because of my father's work as a bail bondsman, I grew up used to the phone ringing in the middle of the night. That sudden postmidnight ring that seems to so many a signal of certain tragedy was commonplace in our house. And because of my father's ability to sleep through sonic booms and thunderstorms I came to hear, almost nightly, the voices of those he called his people: people who would night-blind deer with foglights that bug-eyed from truck bumpers; people who would crouch beside cars with garden hose snaking from mouths into gas tanks. Utterers, forgers, passers of bad checks—his people, who acted as if every day was the end of daylight savings time and every odometer in every last-leg Buick on the lot was a clock begging to be turned back.

I suppose he was good at his work, if gaining the respect of hundreds of dubious characters is any measure. Financial success was a different matter. My father's people, if they paid at all, were not the most punctual of debt-settlers, a characteristic which drove the only other bondsman in our county to declare, before he closed up shop for good, that all the honest crooks had either died or moved away. My father hung in there, encouraged by the diminished competition. He nickled and dimed his creditors, nickled and dimed my mother with promises and charm.

From her he withstood a great deal of pressure. One winter we were so poor that we couldn't afford to retrieve our wool clothes from the laundry where they'd been put in storage during moth season. My mother would take my little sister and me down every other Friday to try and haggle another sweater out of hock. The laundry clerk was a girl my mother once taught in her refresher Civics class out at the high school—a Tindall from way out in Tindalltown who had it in for us because my mother had once reported her for necking on campus with her soldier boyfriend.

"I'd like to get the red pullover and the children's car coats today if I may," my mother said one afternoon at the laundry. She pushed a five across the counter, anchoring it with two fingertips so that the breeze from the huge floor fans would not blow it away. The Tindall girl, who adopted the blank, bored manner of a student in a postlunch study hall whenever she waited on my mother, looked down at the fluttering bill and erupted into a spiteful spray of laughter.

"You got to be kidding coming in here with just five dollars," she said. "I can rip one of y'all's vests in two for five. Maybe cut a foot or two off one of them scarves."

When my mother complained my father said only: "At least we have the woolens to store. Something to look forward to is how I see it. If we got them out all at once, think of the void it would create."

MY FATHER had not set out to become a bondsman. As he was fond of saying, it was not something one went to school for. What he'd always been passionate about was geography. He seemed to have been born with an unfathomable curiosity about the names of places, mostly places he knew he'd never lay eyes on. Maps, charts and globes were like icons to him. There wasn't a corner of this earth that you could point to without him ticking off a squall of place names.

Like most children of obsessed people, we sometimes suffered. Instead of more passive endurances, like being carted off to Civil War battlefields during summer vacation or spending the occasional weekend at an antique car show, we lived with one who insisted we share his passion. Each

of us had to learn by age eight the fifty states and their capi-
tals—*commit to memory* were the words he used. On the
Fourth of July following our tenth birthdays a ritual quiz
tested our knowledge of the hundred counties of North
Carolina as well as their county seats. The entire family
gathered in a circle of saggy lawn chairs in the backyard
while whoever was in the hot seat spouted off the names of
obscure coastal plain counties—Currituck, Pasquotank,
Perquimans—followed by a feast of field peas, corn, cold
ham. After each correct answer we were awarded small
prizes—a handful of Tidewater salted-in-the-shells, a sip of
icy Falstaff—and we were awarded larger prizes when we
completed the quiz. I got an old bitters bottle that one of
my father's people had unearthed in the woods behind the
dog pound while digging for worms; the bottle was the
color of cobalt, shaped like a fish. After their county quizzes
my sisters both got chokers. One of my brothers received a
biography of Woodrow Wilson, who had once lived just
down the road from us in Wilmington, and the other got a
leatherbound copy of *A History of the Johnstown Flood,*
which I spotted on his bookshelf just a few years back.

The field of geography, as my father often explained,
constitutes much more than the memorization of place
names. It is a complex and multileveled discipline, and if
what led him to it was his curiosity for names, what kept
him intrigued, after he'd memorized all the maps, were the
other emphases: demographics, population control, statisti-
cal studies. Geography, my father soon decided, was really
about helping people live on this earth.

He had little trouble distinguishing himself in the Geography department up at the state university. The only student in his class to finish with honors, he was accepted at
several of the top graduate programs in the country, but the
summer after graduation his father died, leaving him with
debts and a dependent, my grandmother, who was too old

to work. He came on home to the house he grew up in, the one I grew up in as well. Six months later he got engaged to my mother, who was just through her first year of teaching Latin and Civics. At home, married, he set about finding something to do.

I don't know how he first got the idea of being a bondsman. I have a feeling it was something as simple as walking through the bottom end of downtown and seeing Charles Hatch's neon BAILBONDS sign blinking through the haze of dusk. Whatever it was, it happened suddenly: one day he was in the management trainee program at Dusselbach's Furniture; the next day when my mother and I came in from school he was sitting at the kitchen table, filling out forms for the state bailbondsman license.

My mother was aghast.

"Aren't bailbondsmen usually sort of, well . . ."

"Sort of what?" he said without looking up from his paperwork.

"Riffraffy."

"I'm not so sure that's even a word," he said. "But if you mean are they usually married to teachers of Latin, the answer is no. But what the hell, why not? Let's us deviate from the norm."

"I thought bailbonding was something of a sideline," my mother told him, "something one runs out of the back room of a pawnshop."

"I don't happen to have a pawnshop to run a business out the back of," my father said. "Hatch is getting old and tired I hear. In a few years, when he retires, I can have his clientele."

"But think about what you're saying when you use the word clientele," said my mother. "Thieves and drunks and felons and who all knows what. You'll have to deal with them every day of your life."

"This is the closest thing I've found to what I want to do

with my life," he said. "This is the closet thing to geography available to me around here."

My mother said: "I don't mind telling you that I completely fail to see the connection."

"Of course you do. Most folks would fail. Most will. If I can't help people doing what I was trained to do, I'll help them some other way. You might not understand that, since you're getting to do what you want."

"Right," she said. "Teaching a dead language to comatose students. One out of every fifty might go on to use Latin, and then only in the Sunday crossword."

He capped his ballpoint and smiled. "You don't need to be pessimistic on my account. Not only are you doing what you want, you're good at it to boot."

"So by bringing the do-goodness of geography to selling bail bonds you're going to change lives?"

"I doubt it," he said. "But if I have to be here I might as well be doing something I think is worthwhile. I figure if I'd gotten to pursue the geography, I'd be off in some tiny African nation or traipsing through a South American rain forest. I'd be seeing things I wouldn't normally see, spending time with folks who are different from the run of the mill around here. Same with this career."

He hung out his shingle. For a few weeks he sat idle in his office, killing time by poring over his maps and atlases. Then he had his first client, and news of his willingness to extend credit, as well as his lenient repayment plan, brought in more. I don't think he changed lives—don't think he even tried—but he did develop a sense of worth I doubt he would have gained selling couches at Dusselbach's. He felt, somehow, as if he was making it easier for people—his people—to live on this earth, and he quickly became as dependent on his clientele as they were on him. Since so many were unemployed, or worked only when the sun went down, his office was always filled, and he kept up with everyone; he always knew who had a meeting with a probation officer or who was due down at the jailhouse to wash the deputies' cars as part of a parole. "Call me if you need me," he would say as the office emptied and invariably he'd be taken up on it, usually when the house had gone as quiet as the town outside, when he was too deeply asleep to hear the phone ring.

MY FATHER WAS thought of as odd, but his choice of employment didn't really ostracize him any further in the community. Most folks seemed pleased by the fact that my father, who'd been quiet and aloof all the way through school, had had his notions of becoming a globe-trotting geographer debunked and was now working out of a shabby storefront across the alley from the auto parts store.

I never paid much attention to what he did for a living when I was young. I got as used to criminals calling in the middle of the night as the children of the newspaperman must have been to old ladies interrupting supper with complaints about the wild pitch of the paper boy, or the doctor's kids to the harried calls of a first-time father-to-be. There were lean times but we got by, mostly on my mother's salary and the bizarre but often useful barters my father's people exchanged for bail: stovepipe, a new roof, a septic field, a series of root canals for my brother from our dentist, who had a bad habit of driving everywhere with a quart of beer between his knees.

My father kept my mother at bay during those lean months by cutting a deal with the Tindall girl, whose boyfriend had gone AWOL and gotten himself arrested for trespassing. She agreed not to pitch our woolens in exchange for free bond.

"You should have bargained to get everything out at once," my mother said when he told her of the deal, but it wasn't his way to push, and as a result two winters passed before he could save enough money to rescue that natty tweed overcoat he had affected while an honors student in Geography. He weathered the February winds with a flimsy parka, and it became apparent that unless something miraculous happened my father would have to abandon his bail-bond business.

EVENTUALLY SOMETHING OCCURRED that bolstered my father's business considerably: a family with too many kids to count moved to town and my father suddenly had enough new customers to draw every last woolen out of hock. The boom in bond writing was traced to the repeat offenses of four teenaged boys who were seen regularly going in and coming out of the new family's house, across the street from the post office. Our chief of police described them publicly as "accomplished criminals," yet despite their experience they seemed to get caught at everything they did. They continuously underestimated the local law enforcement from the day they moved to town, when a sheriff's deputy had caught the two youngest inching a paper stand down a back alley, armed with hacksaws they hadn't even bothered to conceal.

They weren't at all smooth, but they paid their bills. Every time one was arrested their father would show up within minutes, and he always paid in cash. He never seemed surprised at being summoned to my father's office: he bailed his boys out of jail with a curious mix of alacrity and concern, as if he were simply picking them up sick from school.

The presence of this family—they were called the Pasteluccias—was felt immediately. The way the younger kids played right out in the street made our paltry two-block business district seem suddenly very urban and deprived. People who saw them playing hide-and-go-seek in alleys previously used only for deliveries and trash removal would think, someday somebody's going to get hurt back there, or, isn't it awful those kids don't have a yard to play in. This town certainly has grown, people would think when they'd spot those kids kicking deflated balls across empty parking lots on a still life Sunday afternoon.

The strangest thing about these Pasteluccias was how you'd suddenly see one of them you'd never seen before. Anna showed up at school one day, walking down the hall with a lit cigarette in hand. Classes were changing, and I was drifting toward my locker when I saw her. The way she held her Marlboro so heedlessly—the ember nearing her knuckle, her jean jacket sleeve an eighth inch from ignition, stopped me.

Later that week, Anna showed up in the Rec Room. The only other female we'd seen there was Star, a dancer from Fayetteville who wandered over sometimes when the Fort Bragg maneuvers were underway. Star was pretty tough but she still played pool like a girl. Anna was the first female pool player any of us had ever seen who didn't use a bridge for the awkward shots. When the shot called for it, she'd hike herself across the table with an irresistible agility, one leg cocked perpendicular like the automatic arm at a railroad crossing. Her black hair would graze the fabric of the table top, making it look like a field that you want to stop and lie right down in.

THE PASTELUCCIAS had been in town awhile when word started around that attempted to explain their presence. I'm not sure who it was that spilled the story first—some say the Thornton boy the sheriff had specially deputized during a brushfire, who got drunk down at Williams Lake and couldn't keep it in any longer. But soon everyone in town knew that the Pasteluccias were wards of the Federal Witness Protection Program, that Mr. Pasteluccia had either seen something he shouldn't have or knew something he had no business knowing. The fact that the specifics of this case were so vague had little bearing on the many versions offered, all of which had Mr. Pasteluccia acting with a valor unknown among apathetic urban types. The unpronounceable name and the number of offspring made the leap of logic easy for most folks. Those who couldn't pronounce mafioso simply whispered "mob."

Mr. Pasteluccia immediately gained respect. Whatever he had done, it had been bold enough to warrant a new identity, which struck us as unreal, like something off "Sixty Minutes." How odd it must have been to wake up and be someone else, having a strange town, a strange climate and strange ways to contend with. The general consensus was that they came for him in the middle of the night, that his car was still parked by a curb somewhere, parking tickets thick under the windshield, battery and hubcaps long gone. People wondered why he wasn't given a local name like Tindall or Strickland, but someone pointed out that he didn't really look like a Tindall or a Strickland. The more his situation was discussed, the more the man was pitied. Plunged into unknown territory, not allowed to work, and he always, always had to look over his shoulder.

But Pasteluccia didn't seem to mind his new situation. He worked out a pretty good schedule for himself. Mornings he sat around on his front porch, waiting for the call from my father's office to come through. Soon he grew restless and took to strolling down the hill after lunch to hang out all afternoon, lounging in the corner on the bus-seat sofa. He and my father became close. One night I overheard my father tell my mother that Mr. Pasteluccia was sensitive to the fact that some of the more narrow-minded folks in town put him and his family in the same category as welfare recipients. Down at my father's office there was no such prejudice. Mr. Pasteluccia's reputation among my father's people—and the fact that his sons were basically keeping the business afloat—led my father to extend him full credit, the generous terms of which allowed for a quarterly, as opposed to the usual monthly, tab.

ONE DAY AT SCHOOL, Anna Pasteluccia appeared behind me in the hallway and laid a warm hand on my shoulder. She pressed down a little with her palm. Smoke rose from between her third and fourth fingers.

"Translate," she said, her fingers half-curled around my collarbone. "You look like the type."

"I barely know English," I said.

"This isn't English I want to know, it's local. What do those boys mean when they come up to me and say: 'Whattayasay?'"

"Oh that. It's a greeting. Like hello."

"But why do they say that when I haven't said anything?"

"It's a rhetorical question," I said. "One that does not require an answer. Like 'How are you?'"

"I've been telling them, 'I didn't say anything.' I even asked one was he deaf."

"What'd he say?"

"All my questions must be rhetorical. I haven't gotten a straight answer from anyone but you since I've been down here."

Anna Pasteluccia leaned in close. "In study hall," she said, "I look at you out the very corner of my eye."

I stared hard at the very corner of her eye.

A FEW WEEKS LATER Anna said to me, "Don't ever come by my house after supper. Don't you even call. We drink wine with our meals and after supper I get real sentimental. In a big way, you know? All of us go sappy, even the little ones; we don't even answer the phone for fear of being so soft on wine we'll say yes yes yes to anything."

I had tried to call her at night before but there was never any answer. No one saw her past seven o'clock, nor did any of the other Pasteluccias, even those four wild brothers, ever turn up after dark.

It bothered me that I couldn't see or talk to Anna at night. I hardly ever saw her at school and that left only late afternoon for us. She usually wanted to shoot pool, and it was hard to talk in the middle of that dark space, with the swampy jukebox ballads echoing off the divider blocking poolroom from plate glass and passersby, with Jay Jay Drawhorn drooling in the corner, propped up on a broom. I'd walk her home at dusk and this is when we'd talk.

Our conversations were careful, restrained. She never alluded to her previous identity, and I certainly never asked. The only part of her past that was admissible was the six weeks she'd been in town; the future seemed equally forbidden, filled with the threat of retribution from whatever dangerous parties her father had so gallantly exposed. When I'd try later to reconstruct our conversations they were filled with gaps, like censored wartime correspondence.

I slowed, then, to the moment, strolling with Anna through the settled, suppertime downtown until we reached her house. Her brothers and sisters would be swarming in the alleyway, engrossed in some enigmatic city game played with found equipment like sticks and trash can lids. They made that last hour of light look grey, gritty, industrial. The sight of Anna at the door calling them all inside for supper turned my town into someplace else. Everything seemed burgeoning then: my chances with Anna, my father's business, even the town I'd long since begun to tire of. I waited all day for those moments.

It occurred to me one night that Anna might have been using a little psychology in begging me not to call or come by after dark. Maybe this was just her way of encouraging me. I tried her number and when I got no answer I walked on over.

No answer at the front door either, although all the lights were on. I went around back: two vans were pulled up to the porch, both with out-of-state tags. I didn't mean to look in the window—I'm sure this is probably the hackneyed defense of all Peeping Toms, but it's true, people should put up curtains. Most of the kids were there, and in the bright kitchen light I noticed something odd, something I'd never noticed before: none of those kids really looked much like each other. They were all busy moving things around—stereos, televisions, boxes—and while I stood there in the shadows, the back door kept opening, kids kept coming in and out, some carrying boxes, others empty-handed. I saw Anna. She was walking around the kitchen opening boxes, writing things down on a yellow legal pad; as she passed by the window she looked right toward me, and I ducked.

The next evening in front of the Post Office we sat down on the wall and I said: "So what do y'all do with all those TVs and tape players?"

She looked at me and smiled. I think she was pleased. It meant she had a past now, and a future, although these were things I'd never hear about.

"Opening a Radio Shack franchise. Do you think it'll go over better downtown or should we move out to the mall?"

"Maybe try another town," I said. "We already got Parson's Electronics. He sells that same crap except it's new, not used."

"We thank your father for our lovely stay here." She stood then and kissed me on the forehead. "We never would have been able to manage without his generous assistance."

She crossed the street, calling to all those kids who looked nothing like her, and disappeared inside the big house that was vacant by morning.

FOR AS LONG as I could after Anna left I kept my mouth shut and avoided my father. The late night calls began to bother me so much that I secretly unplugged the phone when I went to bed and replugged it in the morning. The little bit of pleasure I got from this sabotage soured immediately when my father would sit down to his morning coffee and say with surprise: "My, what a quiet night."

The way he sat in his armchair after supper, bent over his dog-eared Rand McNally, brought out such resentment that I was forced to leave the house. The fact that he was a bondsman—a common bondsman—I suddenly found intolerable. The Pasteluccia incident raised questions I'd never let myself confront: what type of man does it take to equate the study of geography with writing bonds for street scum and hoodlums? And what kind of reason is it that purports to be "helping" people by bailing them out of jail?

My father never commented on the sudden departure until after Mitchell Thornton came forward with his story about how Mr. Pasteluccia had approached him at Williams Lake and offered him five hundred dollars to spread the rumor that he was a part of the Federal Witness Protection Program. By that time the local law enforcement, the same stalwart outfit we all thought the Pasteluccia boys had underestimated, linked the recent rash of burglaries to the culprits, a month or two late of course. Rumor held that none of the Pasteluccias were kin or even Italian.

Because he and Mr. Pasteluccia had been so tight toward the end, and because he had represented the financial interests of the family in their dealings with the state, my father was questioned by the sheriff, but nothing ever came of it. Privately my father expressed doubts about the sheriff's theory, which held that Pasteluccia had instructed his boys to blunder their petty daytime crimes so as to cover up for the more lucrative moonlight larcenies. According to the sheriff, Pasteluccia suspected that no one would believe his boys were into anything big if they were picked up constantly for so many amateurish offenses. My father called the sheriff's reasoning "malarkey." We argued about it every night at the table, until one night when I said something which allowed us never to speak of it again.

"Why do you think the sheriff would come out with a theory that casts his department in a bad light if he didn't absolutely have to?" I asked him that night. "He's admitted they were duped. We all were."

"Nonsense," my father replied. "I know my people."

"You don't have a clue, Dad," I said. "You know your geography, and that's about it."

He looked at me for a long time without speaking. My mother came out from the kitchen, watched the two of us stare at each other, then disappeared again. I didn't regret saying it. I didn't think then that it came close to saying all I wanted to say. I was ashamed of the way he'd allowed himself to be used and I could not forgive him for turning Anna into one of his people: someone with only one phone call, another disembodied voice of the night.

OF COURSE PASTELUCCIA, or whatever his name was, left without settling his tab, and my father had to make good on the bonds. Soon after the sheriff cleared him of any wrongdoing, my father declared bankruptcy. He hung around the house for a week and a half before taking a job selling insurance.

As totally happy as he was studying geography, as totally

satisfied as he'd been as a bondsman, he was that unfulfilled selling insurance.

"Selling insurance reminds me of those dances they do with poles down in the Caribbean," I heard him say once. "It's one big limbo, this business. I get lower and lower each year. By the time I retire I'll be a snake in the weeds."

Because I still held him responsible for what happened with Anna Pasteluccia, I didn't allow myself much sympathy for his whining; selling insurance seemed the sensible thing to do. For years when I was visited by those flashes of him I forced myself to think that his life in the end was decent, that he was lucky not to die destitute, in the middle of the afternoon attended only by someone accused of transporting a minor across state lines. For years when I thought of my father at all it was as a quilted mound snoring through another night of desperate calls, dreaming no doubt of a tilted, spinning globe.

And I continued to think of him this way until recently. Late one night the phone rang, and although I had been asleep for hours I found myself racing to answer it, just as I had done when I was a kid. Hurrying down the stairs I saw my father, sleeping soundly in a room as dark as the one I'd just left. It never occurred to me that the call might be bad news, nor did I think that it might be—and at that time of night the odds are higher that it will be—a wrong number, a mistake. As I moved toward the ringing in the dark and curled my hand finally around the cool receiver, I was too busy wondering if I was doing what I wanted, and if so, if I was doing it at all well.

Golden Hour

Nancy McFadden, Ph.D.

Late on the day that Mr. Register referred to me as a morose individual I noticed the bus.

It was parked on the shoulder of the highway directly in front of my office window, eclipsing my view of sunset. This is probably the only reason I noticed, as I always make it a point to be in my office during that time of evening, and I like to eat dinner at my desk while watching the sun descend into the pine grove across the highway. I am sure that it was this disruption of daily ritual which called my attention to the bus, and not the fact that another disabled vehicle had appeared by the wayside. People around here are inclined to operate vehicles prone to disrepair, a recurrent source of annoyance for me in my capacity as chief recruiter and dean of evening study at Sawyer County Vocational-Technical Institute. Often I must act as chauffeur to those with unreliable transportation. An inconvenience surely, but only one of many extras performed for the good of the institute and the community which are overshadowed by the more public means passing for philanthropy around here—the civic clubs and charity organizations to which Mr. Register's name is often linked in the local paper.

For a long time no one got off the bus. I stood by the

window, studying it. It was a badly painted blue, its windows tinted; I could make out no insignia, no name of church or private school on the side. Because the sun was setting I could see movement through the tinted windows, backlit silhouettes. After some debate I decided the bus might belong to a migrant crew, although it seemed unlikely that a crew leader would go to the expense of tinted windows. Crew leaders are almost all cheats and manipulators, and the fact that they have many things to hide led me to suspect that conditions within did not meet specifications required by law.

The plight of the migrant laborer has become a special interest over the years, as each summer more than five thousand migrants pass through this area. Like so many locusts, they sweep through the fields and this is what the majority of the people around here know about them—that they are hard workers, that they transform the landscape, that for the six weeks of harvest local stores stock tortillas and jalapeños. Natives know little of, or choose to ignore, the hardships: deplorable living conditions, low wages, the duplicity of some prominent landowners, who conspire with crew leaders to keep these migrants shackled to an inescapable system.

Though I have lived here for seventeen years, Mr. Register maintains that I know nothing *about* the place. Of all the things that he insinuates about my character, this is the most annoying, for I have given my life to this community and I did not *have* to. It was not as if I was marooned here by lack of options elsewhere. I could have easily found a job in my native Cincinnati or anywhere else in the country. For that matter the world. And I could have easily chosen to make the hour commute to the institute from the nearby Research Triangle, yet I would have found it hard to reconcile the commuting life philosophically. My life's work has, after all, been concerned with making Sawyer County a better place to live, and what kind of message would it have sent if after eight hours I got in my car and returned to the land of pita bread and art house cinema?

I have dedicated my life to the education of those whose circumstances require basic skills, skills which will equip them for survival in a perennially depressed economy and allow them to be (how I dislike this word, though it is in this context apt) *competitive.* These are not people whose survival depends on esoteric knowledge. It took only a few weeks here for me to concede that familiarity with Keats and King Lear will not necessarily, as I'd grown up thinking, change your life. I no longer have the luxury to ponder the question which once plagued me in graduate school: whether anyone who works hard enough can "get" Hegel. These people need to know how to read the newspaper. They need to know how to fill out tax forms and job applications.

Of course I could have chosen to spend my life among those whose circumstances and tastes more closely resemble my own. I've more than passing interests in both poetry and history and could easily have ended up teaching rhyme and meter, or made my living conversing with eager graduate students about Prescott and Parkman. My decision to pursue administration rather than these scholarly interests was based on the realization that educational systems in this country ignore the needs of the majority. One grey day in graduate school it dawned on me that I would have to go where I was needed most or live life with the needling awareness of having chosen cultural comfort over true need. And so, answering the call, I came to this region of eastern North Carolina, as desolate and impoverished a place as can be found in the Upper South even in these 1970s.

Within weeks I saw that the efforts of those like Mr. Register—powers that *try to be,* as I've come to think of them—would require as much of my patience and toil as the ignorance of the populace whom they'd been hired, ostensibly, to remedy. I had several advantages: the broader and more worldly vision an outsider can bring to such a place, and the fact that I was unfamiliar with certain slothful and wily tendencies inherent in the native character. For despite his claims to the contrary, Mr. Register's knowledge of "the way people think around here" doesn't prevent him from similar logic. After all, he is a native. Familiarity breeds complicity.

As I stared at the bus, a student cutting across the lawn happened to look inside my window, catching me in the act. Smiling self-consciously, I returned to my desk, ashamed of how much time I'd wasted. By nature I am curious, and this trait has stood me well during my time here—I have found out quite a bit about the area, its history, its odd customs—yet I have come to view curiosity as a force which must be strictly channeled, lest one waste time pursuing things of no value. The story behind this bus was of no value while my dinner grew cold and work awaited me. Mr. Register and I are the only ones around at night save the students and evening instructors, and being one of two in authority—and the only one who takes authority with the seriousness required—I had no time to waste. Mr. Register has a habit of eating dinner in Trent, at one of the franchise steakhouses or the fish camp, and he often exceeds his allotted hour. If his absence meant anything at all I would protest, but the truth is I'm glad to be rid of him.

Not that he is totally incompetent. As they say around here about people who fail to make their mark, he's got plenty of sense. Over the years I have laid blame for his failings in various places, but the one factor I keep returning to is his education. His doctorate in educational administration is from a large land grant institution an hour away. I have had occasion over the years to attend workshops and seminars at this "university," and while I won't waste time ticking off its obvious academic deficiencies, I will tell you that I find the very sight of this place oppressive. The boxy, monolithic buildings, the ubiquitous red brick, the miles of parking lots and courtyards of patchy grass; it's as if the place were designed to discourage any inkling of an aesthetic. There are no musty reading rooms or gabled dormitory garrets in which indulgent undergrads can read of madwomen in attics and stare down upon quads forlornly moonlit.

The drabness of the grounds encourages students to treat the educational experience as a transaction to be completed as quickly as possible. Shouldn't a college campus reflect an intellectual climate? Don't the dreaming spires of Oxford and even the Spanish-tiled roofs of Stanford feed the hungry mind? Not long ago I discovered a passage in Chekhov which commented on this very situation. I quote: "The student whose state of mind is in the majority of cases created by his surroundings, ought in the place where he is studying to see facing him at every turn nothing but what is lofty, strong, and elegant . . . God preserve him from gaunt trees, broken windows, grey walls and doors covered with torn American leather!"

Perhaps you find my opinions hypocritical. I've admitted, after all, to a no-frills educational philosophy, one which emphasizes basics. Yet I've adopted this philosophy for those who lack the skill or the inclination to aim higher. I don't advocate it for everyone—not even for Mr. Register, as, like it or not, it's his job as well to shape this philosophy. My vision has been enriched by having been on the other side. I know what these unfortunates are missing, and having known the rarefied beauty of early intellectual engagement, I feel at liberty to make decisions about what is and is not relevant.

Not so Mr. Register. Simply put, he has not the experiences upon which to base such decisions. It distresses me that he does not realize this. According to him, a degree is a degree. Mr. Register seems to view his education and education in general as a distracting but ultimately innocuous flood of paperwork.

I find him fascinating as a case study of how the educational system can fall short. Despite his doctorate, Mr. Register in many ways resembles an illegal alien in the nation of higher education. He is bilingual. Just yesterday I overheard him conversing in the hall with one of our new drafting students. "Ain't no big thang if you miss class, but don't go making a habit out of it," he said. An hour before he used the words "facilitate" and "implement" numerous times in a meeting with myself and the vice president. Ostentatious rhetoric is Mr. Register's safe haven during meetings. For many years he has favored such verbiage in his dealings with me in particular, and I have always interpreted this as a sign of his insecurity, an attempt to prove that he is my intellectual equal. I have become an expert at decoding it, and to be fair to Mr. Register, he is not the only one employed by this institution who prefers such jargon. At first I attributed this habit to the growing pains of autodidacts—verbal stretch marks, if you will—yet I've come over the years to lay the blame on those red brick villages of higher learning.

I was midway through my baked potato, glancing over some enrollment figures for next quarter, when I noticed the bus doors unfolding. A young man climbed down the steps, opened the hood, pulled himself up on the bumper and peered at the engine.

He was not dressed like a migrant farm worker. Instead of soiled work clothes, he wore bright red Sansabelt trousers with flared legs and a blue shirt with bell sleeves. His boots were not the type one would wear in the field. His dark hair was pulled back into a ponytail, his cheeks and chin were darkened by whiskers. He moved his hands from his hips to hug his chest and back, and his body language conveyed his confusion even before he was joined by the other young man, a gaunt fellow with stringy yellow hair grazing his waist, dressed identically in sharp trousers and flowing shirt. A peculiar uniform, I remember thinking. Both stared at the engine for some time, appearing at a loss even from such distance.

There was a knock at my door, and a student entered with a question regarding course offerings for the spring term. I pushed away my plate and spent a few minutes explaining curriculum requirements to her, and when she finally left—I hoped it wasn't obvious to her that I was rushing—I looked up to see that the men had been joined by a stunning black woman. She wore her hair in the afro fashion and was dressed in a short red skirt and a blue shirt with bell sleeves—a frillier version of the men's outfit, but definitely corresponding. I began to harbor all sorts of conclusions, but the only definite thought was that these were not migrant workers. The woman said something which caused both men to laugh, and after this outburst the three of them turned toward the institute.

Though there has definitely been progress in the racial climate since I arrived here, this area remains predominantly black yet predominantly controlled by whites, and there is still a great deal of friction between the races. Here at the institute we have had to deal with that friction, since our student body is almost evenly divided. There is less institutional segregation in terms of curriculum, since all students are here to learn the basics, and no classes are targeted to corral minorities as is often the case in the public high schools. We are all on equal footing here academically, yet it is rare that interracial friendships are formed. The snack bar remains segregated despite my eternal efforts to remedy this situation. "White people don't like to eat with black people and they don't like to eat with us," one of my Heat-

ing and Air Conditioning students told me when I stopped
him one night to inquire about this phenomenon. In a
tone carefully pitched to conceal my disgust I asked why.
"Don't like the same kinds of food, I reckon." This I knew
to be untrue, since all of our students and most of the faculty subsist on the snack bar's inedible short-order fare.
Still, men who dismantled carburetors together, women
giddy from giving their first permanents, would ignore
each other moments later at dinner, and though it reflected
badly upon the institute, I found there was not much I
could do to change it.

It is rare, then, to see the races commingle, rarer still for
young people of both races to be traveling together—and in
similar dress—through this part of the country. Though I
have always prided myself on my lack of racial prejudice, I
must admit that the scene outside my window bothered me.
It seemed potentially incendiary even before the attractive
black woman approached the ponytailed gentleman from
the rear, wrapped her arms around his chest, drew herself
obscenely close; before he spun her around and the two engaged in a long and (I realize how hackneyed this sounds,
yet no other term will suffice) *passionate* kiss.

This brand of passion, served on the shoulder of the road
in dwindling but discernable daylight, would be distracting
to our students regardless of the color of the perpetrators. I
tried to return to my paperwork but could not. Despite my
agitation I could not stop watching. The couple was no
longer entwined, but remained suggestively close. It seemed
they were in debate; I was doing the same, debating
whether or not—or rather when—to approach them when
a familiar figure appeared in the corner of my window, and
though it might seem that I would have been relieved not
to have to rouse myself from the sanctity of my office and
confront these people, my dread increased as I watched Mr.
Register lope toward our visitors.

Mitchell Register

I had just got back from Kiwanis which that night we met out at Golden Corral and I ate too damn much to want to go back to work. I'd daydreamed through most of the speaker, some Baptist missionary Arthur Strickland found, he comes up with the boringest programs, guy talking about spreading the gospel in British Guyana. Whenever I'm in charge of the program I get the bell choir from the Methodist Women to come clang us out a half-hour's worth of hymns and even though I catch hell for doing the same thing every year, nobody falls asleep and if anybody mouths off you can't hear them over the bells.

Once for a change I brung in my collection of Little Cedrick and the Royals memorabilia but those Kiwanis who knew me had been down in my basement and seen most of it already. I went back to the bell choir next time my entertainment came up because I had to do all the talk- ing with the Royals collection, too damn much work. Plus it involved opening up a private part of me, going through that stuff and holding it up for those sleepyheads to nod at. And some of the older members treated me funny for a while after that. It was like they knew something about me that I didn't know myself, like I'd revealed something that made them think different of me. Sometimes older men make me feel funny anyway. I'm talking about men my daddy's age. A bunch of us'll be standing around in the churchyard between Sunday school and the service, and I'll feel those older men looking at my tie and I'll start worry- ing if there's something wrong with me. I think it might have something to do with me having my doctorate and being a dean out at the institute and most of them barely finishing high school; I'd like to think they're proud to have me out there, local boy and all, but the truth is I think they believe it's not the kind of work a grown man should be doing. Not manly. Even Musselwhite, who's been my best friend since high school, calls my Ph.D. a posthole digger when he's tight. And he's a CPA, graduated from Wake. Still, Mussel gets right strange sometimes when I talk about work or Little Cedrick and the Royals.

Arthur Strickland was acting aggravated with everybody for nodding off, but hell, you bring a boring speaker, you got to expect people's attention to divide. This is what I'm always telling my night teachers out at the institute who come complaining their students are dropping off in class. Seems obvious that when you're dealing with people who've already put in a full day and not behind any desk either but in a garage or the blender factory or the sewing plants you can't just stand up and read out of a book and expect them to stay right with you. Plus some people are born without a knack for public speaking, like this missionary. Reminded me of somebody the whole time he was up there, though I was halfway back out to the institute when it came to me who: Fancy Nancy McFadden.

Once I made the connection I started thinking about how Fancy acted like a missionary herself. She even dresses like a missionary, plain garments chose to last. Lives like a missionary in that puny cottage over in the hysterical district. The time she had us over there, back ten, twelve years ago, Debbie liked to have had a fit over that place. Hardly any furniture, had all these African masks, tapestries, stuff from her world travels hanging on the walls. Missionary decor. Only thing it's got to offer is a fireplace covers one whole wall. Square footage of a step-van. Hot as hell in the summer: she's convinced air conditioning causes cancer, wouldn't take the window unit we tried to give her. Still, she is so damn proud of that house, though it isn't a thing but the summer kitchen of the Wilton T. Smart homeplace. I happen to know that Roy Tart took her on the deal too, which makes her seem even more like a missionary, since as

I understand it part of being a missionary's getting took by natives.

Some ladies from the neighborhood came to see her about six years ago, wanted her to paint her house. Not wanted, ordered—the ordinances they got in that neighborhood, you wouldn't catch me buying over there. What it was, they were trying to tell Fancy she had to paint it a certain color and she was trying to say that the color was not "period." She was trying to tell that particular crowd of DAR Confederamamas it was not "historically accurate" to paint a summer kitchen beige and that if push come to shove she'd produce the records to document it. She asked me, I told her, said either way you lose with that bunch. She didn't think much of that at first—too damn naive and uppity to understand who she was dealing with—but a couple of days later she come back and thanked me. Even said I was right. Said she'd decided to bite the bullet because she had settled here and what she really wanted to do was blend in.

I didn't tell her she could paint her hovel chartreuse and she'd fit in about like those Mormon boys who ride bikes through town wearing three-piece suits in August.

She talks like a missionary too. Preaches. People who don't know her think she don't waste words, but it has got to the point everything she says is wasted on me. Tired of hearing her proper diction I guess, tired of being talked down to. What I like to do is give it back to her, fight fire with fire. I can ascertain deficiencies till the cows come home but I'd just soon figure out what's broke.

Heading back out to school, I started thinking about how Fancy and I had got into it earlier that day and decided I should of kept my damn mouth shut, but hell, I'd been putting up with that woman for seventeen years, every once in a while I had to give it back to her.

What it was, back here last year they made this movie down in the south end of the county. A film, Fancy kept calling it. She was about as enthusiastic as she ever gets, not so much because of the local angle but because this film was made out of one of her favorite books. Literary classic she called it. I had to read the thing in college, and I thought it was about the boringest book I ever read. Didn't anything happen. About some woman living alone in a swamp. Figures Fancy would love it because the woman in the book was big on not having any conveniences, doing for herself. Making things just as damn difficult as possible, like Fancy, who tried to block us buying a microwave for the institute snack bar because she said it wasn't safe and did our students really need encouragement in the poor diet area?

Nobody around here had heard of the book, much less read it. Everybody was all excited. The movie people were staying at the Carolina Pines and the Sir Trent, and most everybody I knew laid out of work to go down there and watch. The starring actors nobody'd ever heard of but still, they were filming at Debbie's uncle's old homeplace and it was a kick to see these Hollywood types coming out of their RVs to traipse around the Little Coharie Swamp.

Fancy kept saying she couldn't believe they'd chosen to film her favorite piece of literature so close to her home. Which, this shocked me, her calling Trent home. I have always thought of her as just visiting, on loan from Ohio. Soon as she puts in her twenty-five years with the state I figure she'll be out of here, back to Cincinnati to spend her retirement volunteering and protesting and telling her neighbors not to boil water in aluminum pots.

I tried to get Nancy to go down there and watch, even told her she could ride with Debbie and me, but she said she'd wait for the movie to come out. I wouldn't want to gawk, she said. "I'm sure the day-to-day process is not all that fascinating," she told me. "From what I've heard, film-making is a laborious endeavor, not at all a spectator sport."

Well, she got that one right. Boringest day I've spent in years. A real hurry-up-and-wait situation: they didn't shoot but for about an hour that day. Waited until the sun was about down, then went hard at it until dark. *Golden hour* is what one boy we got to talking to called it. He said it's the best time to shoot because it made everything look better. Way he said this, sounded like he thought things around here didn't look so hot to start.

Which they don't. He was right. And I don't blame them for waiting until they could shoot the best side. If people all over the country are going to see Sawyer County, I want them to see it at its best. We made a pot full of money off the movie people and wouldn't mind making some more. See, you got to look at the promotion side, not only the art. My bachelor's is in marketing, and one thing I learned is that you can sell anything if you take a sharp enough picture of it.

Movie came out a few weeks ago, started showing out at the Coharie Mall last week. Like I said, I thought the book was just about boring, but they did a damn good job with the movie. Myself, I favor a faster-paced flick, more action and character development, but they added some stuff wasn't in the book to move the story along, and you would not believe what they did with that swamp. It looked like you were dreaming it: crisp and clear and colorful, not a bit like it really is down there.

Everybody I talked to raved. Had a bunch of articles about it in the paper, and some of the people who got work as extras threw parties, and the week it premiered reminded me of our sesquicentennial back in 1972. Same kind of pride in the air. You could feel it buzzing in the courthouse and the Post Office and all the stores up Main, like something happened to bring us together, like we all had something in common to feel proud of.

I got so caught up in the feeling I forgot about Fancy. I guess since I don't ever think of her as belonging to this place—I meant, I don't see her socially and don't know of anybody who does—I didn't think about her all week. Then one day Wanda, my secretary, told me she knew somebody had been sitting next to Fancy at the theater, said Fancy walked out forty-five minutes into it. Said she pushed past all the people on her aisle, whispering the word "disgusting," like this was some triple-X tits and ass kinda thing instead of family entertainment. Somebody out buying popcorn said she stormed up to the manager and demanded her money back, and when the manager asked her what was wrong, Fancy got to criticizing the movie. Manager told her said, "Well, there's no accounting for taste." Said Fancy looked him up, down and sideways, said, "The one thing we are held accountable for is our taste, actually, and neither that movie nor the superficial reaction of this town toward it displays anything other than wretched taste."

Soon as Wanda told me about it, I grabbed some papers off my desk and headed for Fancy's office. I wanted to hear exactly what was so wretched about my taste. One thing I'll say about Fancy's that she can surprise you. Ninety-five percent of the time I know exactly what she's going to say or how she'll react, but for somebody as tight-assed as her, five percent of unpredictable's a serious wide margin.

"Come in, Mr. Register," she said when I knocked. She always calls me Mister instead of Doctor, but I got over that years ago. I handed her some forms, asked some questions I knew the answers to, wasted a few minutes of her precious time. Thanked her, reached for the door, turned around and said, "By the way, how'd you like the movie?"

"Read tomorrow's paper," she said without looking up from her desk.

Fancy'll write a letter to the editor, now. This is something has always surprised me about her, since the editorial page of the *Trentonian* is not any great intellectual forum. Most letters are written by crackpots who'll quote Scripture on the subject of raised taxes or annexation plans or else somebody from out-of-state writing to thank an unidentified local for carrying them up the road to a pay phone when their car broke down on I-95. It's not like people read it to learn which way to vote. Plus, Fancy always claims she likes to stay out of the limelight. I do my work in the dark, she's always said. But over the years she's weighed in with four or five letters a year at least, all calling attention to some issue: nuclear power, defense spending, PCB spills on the interstate. Only time I mentioned seeing one of her letters she told me, said, "If I manage to raise one person's consciousness, I will have succeeded." I told her that was fine but she ought to try to raise consciousness on some other page of the *Trentonian,* since everybody skips editorial. She asked me did I mean the funny pages? I wanted to say hell yes, wouldn't hurt you to loosen up and have a laugh once in a while but instead I played it straight and said what she ought to do is figure out how to get her message across via the crossword.

"You mean politically aware clues?" she said. "Like: four-letter word for industry which each day slaughters millions of innocent cattle?"

"Yeah, or the horoscope," I said. "Something like: Confidential to Sagittarians. You will live to be ninety and enjoy excellent health if you withhold the portion of your tax dollars designated for defense spending, start recycling and get rid of that mink in your hall closet." I'll be damned if she didn't smile then, first and only time I can remember her laughing with me.

But she wasn't smiling when she told me to check out tomorrow's paper. Bet I was the only one in town flipped to the editorial page first that day. There it was under a skimpy editorial calling for new sidewalks on Buford Street, and damn if it didn't take up near about the rest of the page. Timmons, the editor, had put a note up top saying he'd waived the length limit to allow for a more complete response. Give her enough rope is what he means, I thought as I started reading. Debbie clipped the thing—she always has been scissor happy—though I'm damn glad she did, considering what it led to.

TO THE EDITOR:

A unanimously favorable reaction to the movie currently playing at the Coharie Mall Theater (the title of which I cannot bring myself to utter even in print, since it is borrowed—stolen?—from a book which happens to be one of my favorite pieces of American literature) compels me to write this letter not so much to decry the rape of a literary masterpiece, or to chastise moviegoers for their taste, but rather to elaborate on what I see as an unforgivable insult to our region.

The offenses of this film being too numerous to catalog in mere column inches, allow me to focus on those most detrimental in the attitudes they express toward our county.

(1) THE LIGHTING. Though I am certainly no expert on the technical aspects of film direction, I do feel that I have seen enough cinematic masterpieces to recognize when lighting obtrudes or manipulates the audience. It seems to me that those in charge of lighting this film had two clear choices: to do, or to overdo, and consequently undercut. That they chose the latter is in keeping with the overwhelming cynicism of their attitude toward this county and its landscape, not to mention the masterpiece butchered by this gaudily lit spectacle. In my capacity as dean of students and chief recruiter of the Sawyer County Vocational-Technical Institute, I have logged many hours on the back roads of this county, many in the vicinity of the Little Coharie Swamp. What I saw on the screen bore no resemblance to the swamp I have come to know and, after a long period during which, frankly, I was rather repulsed by its

appearance, to respect. The beauty of Little Coharie, as readers of this paper will recognize, is an acquired taste: its brooding lushness is off-putting initially. Yet once acquired, one's appreciation deepens with each contact: after numerous car tours, short hiking expeditions and a half-dozen canoe trips, I have come to love the very ambiguity of this place. The spell it casts is one of shifting moods; its beauty is eternally enigmatic. No time of day nor season of year is optimum for discovery of its "true" nature. Summer or winter, dawn or dusk, it hides its deepest recesses, and it is this refusal to reveal itself which I have come to identify with the fierce independence—and resilience—of those native to this area.

What a shock, then, to witness its bastardization on screen. Each frame was "bathed" in an overstated light indigenous only to movie studios. I have no doubt that many viewers might think my preoccupation with lighting inconsequential. Allow me to quote a few lines from Bluestone's seminal *Novels into Film: The Metamorphosis of Fiction into Cinema* (Berkeley: University of California Press, 1968). "The (camera) can distort light to fit a desired mood— deepen shadows, highlight faces, amplify contrast, turn night into day . . . the light pattern is the key to the composition." I do not find it in the least bit difficult to link such technical maneuvering with similar ignominious practices in our culture: silicone implants, buttock tucks, airbrushed photographs to name but a few. We have become all too accustomed to the tampering of images, resulting in a deplorable loss of individuality.

Although I promised not to dwell on how this "film" butchered the book I feel the need to point out how this timeless classic's central themes—man against nature, or, more specifically, a single woman's struggle to gain independence and survive in a society whose antagonism is mirrored in the harsh and formidable landscape into which she

escapes—were completely subverted by the meretricious
lighting. To quote again from Bluestone: "Like a precocious
child . . . the camera can become offensive through sheer
virtuosity. The technique of the camera has, after all, been
evolved by the demands of men making films for a specific
end. Consequently, *the apparatus should be subservient to the
idea*" (italics mine).

For the first few minutes of the film I allowed myself to
think that the brightness of the projector might well be
maladjusted, but a quick visit to the projectionist's booth
convinced otherwise. Within moments I realized that the
"apparatus" of this project, far from being subservient to
the idea of the book, was subservient instead to a Hollywood aesthetic committed not to our minds—and not even
to our emotions. Purse rather than heartstrings were the
object of their interest.

The simple truth is that our county does not look like
this. No place looks like this unless cheapened by the
cosmetics of klieg light. Why should we accept a visual
rendition which ignores all nuance and depicts this region
as a kind of coastal plain Oz? It demeans us, strips us of
our individuality, which is one of the few verifiably positive forces left in this county, and one we need to protect—as it is, and as it is represented to millions on the
overly silver screen.

(2) THE MUSIC: Nauseatingly saccharine. A barrage of
cloying strings and synthesizer which lends itself to story
and landscape and the intersection between the two in
much the same way as the lighting. The natural orchestra-
tion of the swamp—the symphonic sweep of cicada and
tree frog, the vast and varied wind section of bird song—
would certainly have provided a sound track more conducive to the work at hand.

(3) CAMERA ANGLES. Our Little Coharie is not a
landscape given to wide vistas. Why, then, did this viewer

feel that she was witnessing a landscape as expansive and panoramic as those best described by Dinesen or Cather rather than one in which a claustrophobic thickness plays a pivotal part? Bluestone again: "The apparatus should be subservient to the idea." If, as seems to be the case in the film in question, there are no ideas, then the apparatus is subservient only to the whims of its operators.

I will leave the more theatrical concerns to the discretion of the viewers. A great work has been defiled, but of more interest to readers of this publication, a fascinating region has been stripped of its subtlety and beauty and served to an unknowing, yet unforgiving public.

> Nancy McFadden, Ph.D.
> West Church Street
> Trent

Well good, I thought when I finished, at least she had the sense to be difficult in a way that's damn difficult to read. I don't know but five people in this town would get past the parentheses in that first sentence. Skimmers might pick up the word rape—that particular word blinks like neon in our paper—but when they read what it was got raped, they'd flip on over to the court docket.

I pushed the paper away and scrambled myself an egg, but as soon as I sat down to eat the phone rang. Debbie handed it over, said it was Musselwhite.

"Mussel, what?"

"Nope. It's Mussel*white.*"

"What are you doing calling over here this early?"

"You're up and you know it. Seen the movie review?"

I said I wondered why Timmons ran it.

"Hell, I don't. He'll run anything to keep from having to write his column. Even give his wife a cooking column: Martha Timmons's 'Let's Cook with Onion Soup.'"

"I'd a hell of a lot rather he run her recipes than Fancy's letters. That woman just don't get it, Mussel," I said. "She won't ever get it."

"Oh, I don't know. I kind of agreed with her about the lighting. You know how you usually come out of a movie blinking? Well, when that one was over I walked right out into the mall and my eyes didn't even need to adjust."

"Don't you dare tell her that. A movie lit like a mall. To hear her talk, a mall's as bad as TV and drug pushers."

"You going to say something to her about this?"

"No, hell. Why should I? It's a movie review. She's entitled to her fancy-ass opinion."

"Yeah but, Mitch, you got to admit she comes across a little strong. I meant, what she's doing? You know what she's doing: she's talking down to us."

"That woman has *been* on a soapbox. I thought you agreed with her. Besides, what do I care how they light up the Little Coharie Swamp? It's just a movie made out of one of the boringest books I've ever read. It'll be forgotten about in a week."

"Yeah, but she won't," said Musselwhite. "People around here won't forget her raining on the parade and making fun of them to boot."

"Seems like to me she was trying to say somebody else was making fun of us. Somebody named Holly Wood."

"Yeah, well," said Musselwhite, "I didn't make it through the whole letter."

"Neither will anybody else except me and Timmons."

"And Evan. He's already called me about it this morning."

"Evan Miller?"

"Mr. Mayor."

"What'd *he* want?"

"Wanted me to speak to you about speaking to her."

"Good he didn't call me because I'd of . . ."

"No you wouldn't of either," said Mussel. "Tell that lie."

"Look, Mussel. Tell Evan even if this was worth wasting my time on, I'd be the last person she'd listen to."

"You're the only one ever sees that woman. Evan said— and I believe he's right on this, Mitch—that this movie's been good for the town, inspired civic pride, brung us together, made us feel like we have something to offer. He don't think it's right for that woman to be spouting off, criticizing every little thing about it, putting doubts in people's minds."

"She's crazy as a bedbug, Mitch. There isn't ten subscribers who'd finish the letter, much less believe it."

"Well, she might be crazy but she's smart. She's crazy-smart, and that's the worst kind. Something risky about her, makes you want to consider what she's saying. Especially if you're young and don't know no better. You know how you are about authority when you're eighteen."

"It's too early in the morning for me to be thinking about when I was eighteen, Mussel. Too early for you to be calling me up, too."

"You going to talk to her, then?"

I said I sure as hell was not, and hung up.

Chewing cold eggs, I thought about Mussel's call. Seemed strange that Fancy could write letters about every bleeding-heart cause came down the pike and nobody around here would bat an eye, but here she comes out with this movie review and the mayor's calling people up before breakfast.

But Fancy had struck a nerve. Nobody likes to be told they're being made fun of, especially around here. We're proud of our pride, since we don't have much else—no restaurants, no ocean, no ski slopes, no jobs, no nightclubs, not even liquor by the drink. All a politician has to do to get the vote around here is claim the other guy's condescending or patronizing—and explain what the terms mean.

"What was Mussel wanting so early?" Debbie asked when she came back into the kitchen dressed for work.

I handed her the editorial page, which she read with a string of "My land's."

"Lord, that woman," she said when she was through.

"What did you think it was all about?"

"That letter?"

I nodded.

"About a waste of good trees."

"Think she's trying to make fun of us?"

"I sure do," said Debbie.

"Think I ought to say something to her about it?"

"I sure do."

"So does Mussel. And the mayor."

"What has got into her, Mitch? She is so depressing. Why does she want to always be so *down* about everything?"

I pushed my chair back and thought for a long time before I told Debbie that I believed Nancy McFadden had not had a happy childhood; that I didn't know that for a fact so don't go spreading it, but that certain clues in her behavior suggested to me some early trauma.

"Whatever happened, she's all dried up inside."

"Go easy now," I said. "She can't help it."

And all morning long, while I messed around in the yard, waiting for time to go to work, I thought about how Fancy couldn't help it. I figured there was something inside her that makes her pick and scratch until things bleed, just like there's something in me that says, let it go, Mitch, it ain't worth worrying over. It wasn't until I was headed to work that I realized she could help it. Happy childhood or no, you still have to learn to see the worth in things, and Fancy has never met a situation she couldn't find fault with. At first, reading the paper, listening to the reactions of Mussel and Debbie and them, I thought her letter was silly but not all that big a thing. Seemed like the letter of a woman who's both lonely and needing to prove she's smarter than everybody. But the closer I got to school, the more I realized that this letter was different from all the ones about Brunswick Nuclear plant, boycott grapes, public health needs of migrants. This one letter struck me as summing up her whole attitude toward this place, my home. Summed up also her so-called innovative educational philosophies. This letter wasn't about a movie or any old godforsaken swamp. What it was, she'd written down her true opinion of Sawyer and its people, put it in a code she figured nobody could crack.

Which she was right, mostly. Those that got it, got it wrong. They read at it instead of through it. I'm no Plato but I do have my doctorate and I've been working with the woman long enough to listen to what she's leaving out. And she underestimates me, for a whole lot of reasons: because she don't think a thing of my alma mater; because she knows I started out in education as a coach and she's all the time talking about the "coach mentality"; (she's one of those thinks football turns boys into moron wife-beaters, won't admit to the discipline, teamwork, logic and technique involved) because I have two ways of speaking, the way I talk to her and the way I talk to Mussel and the students and near about everybody else in the world. Fancy can't accept this. She dismisses anybody with a master's who occasionally lets an "ain't" fly.

Well, I don't trust anybody with just one way of speaking. Good grammar is fine, but you want to take some shortcuts when you're with people who understand you, and if you don't take shortcuts, how you going to let them know you understand them? Just because I have a terminal degree don't mean I need to terminate my friendships with all those who don't. Hell, if I went around talking like she does, my friends would be wanting to terminate me. She should understand that it's an appearance to this world and a reality, and if you speak the same way in both worlds you're lying in both of them.

At work that morning I went on about my business, put off seeing her as long as I could because I knew I had to say something to her about that letter. I wasn't sure what, but I knew I had to confront her. Seventeen or ever how long it's been years ago she comes in here and tells me and everybody else that what these people need to survive is the basics. Cut the fluff and the frills, she says. Don't waste your breath or our tax dollars trying to teach them something they don't need. Now she's saying that our county's been ruined by a bunch of lights pointed in a place so dark you couldn't see your foot in front of you at the height of gospel-hot July.

Well, it's all connected. The one way she talks and her ideas on how to prepare these bumpkins for a life of heartbreak and trailer house and now this movie which tried to pretty up a place she wants the whole world to know how ugly it is. As soon as I put all this together, I knew I'd have to call her on it, being the only one who'd even come close to seeing what she was saying.

After lunch I turned up some forms for her to sign. She wasn't any different from ever when I went in there—acted polite, but busy, didn't ask me to sit, just went to signing. I sat down. She looked up.

I upshifted into Meeting Speak.

"I read your letter in this morning's edition of the *Trentonian*."

Her eyes went back to her desk. "And?"

"I found it disturbing."

"Then you agree with my assessment of the film?"

"No. I could not disagree more."

She pushed my papers away, found some more to study so she wouldn't have to sit there doing nothing while we argued. "What was it about the letter which disturbed you?"

"I found your response uncalled for, to be honest."

"Uncalled for?"

"Much ado about a hill of beans. Mountain from a molehill."

She smiled again, but tried to hide it. "I felt it was rather much, obviously. I wouldn't have been moved to write a letter on the subject of a molehill."

"I am sure that you felt the issue was worthy of your attention," I said. "I'm not saying you can't write a letter to the editor about any subject you see fit. I've read your letters before and I've always enjoyed them."

"I'm glad you read them," she said, "but I'd rather they change your mind than amuse you."

I started to tell her I said enjoy, not amuse. But hell, she was right: they did amuse me, and I didn't enjoy them. "So you wanted to change people's perceptions about this movie? Was that your objective with this particular letter?"

"My objective was to touch upon some less obvious technical things about the film which I thought needed to be brought out. I could have taken up a page with the obvious banality of the script and the acting, but one thing my background in literature has taught me is if you want to convince people that a work is sentimental or banal, you must approach it on technical, rather than thematic, grounds. Had I come right out and commented on the sappiness of the movie, I doubtless would have been called a cynic. But yes, to answer your question, I did want to change people's perceptions. Though it's a bit more involved than that, really."

"I know. That's what disturbs me."

She leaned forward. "It seems you read the letter carefully, Mr. Register."

"I read it once, Dr. McFadden. It doesn't take a Ph.D. to figure out that you're not talking only about that movie. You're talking about us. Sawyerians. How we don't have a clue, according to you. How gullible and naive and thick we are, how we allow ourselves to get took"—here I lost it, lapsed into tongue number one, won't nothing I could do but pick up, dust off, go ahead on—"by sophisticated outsiders. You seem to enjoy thinking that every one is out to get you. Myself, I think you're laying false blame. If anyone is making fun of us, it's you."

Smiling, she held herself so straight it seemed she didn't need a chair—hell, seemed like she'd turned into a chair. "I think you need to read the letter again," she said. "My thesis was quite simple: why allow a place of such idiosyncratic charm to be trivialized? Did you see the movie?"

"You know everybody in town did. Most of them twice."

"And did you enjoy it?"

I always get nervous when she starts in with her questions. She holds her head a certain way that makes her eyes bore harder, and she gets on a niggling roll, like she's some kind of Vo-Tech Socrates.

"My cousin Walter was an extra," I said. "That last place they filmed at, that Victorian with the wraparound porch? That's Debbie's uncle's old homeplace."

She could of pounced, or laughed—she knew I was nervous—but she spared me. "You didn't find the lighting atrocious?"

"I thought the swamp looked real pretty," I said, regaining ground and hoisting myself straight up in that swivel chair. "And personally I don't see a thing wrong with pretty."

"Well I certainly don't . . ." she started, but I cut her off.

"If there's a patch of idiosyncratic charm to be found anywhere in the Little Coharie, I've yet to come up on it, and I've been hunting and fishing there since I was five."

She said that sometimes it takes an outsider to see the beauty in what you've looked too long and hard at.

"Don't I know it. Just like it took you to come in here and see the ugliness in how we educate our students. Come to find out we had got the lighting all wrong, were making those students' education look too pretty by offering them electives. What it was, we were making fun of them and didn't even know it."

"I'm not sure the analogy totally fits, but offhand I'd have to say that I follow you, Mr. Register. Yet I still think you misunderstand me. I never meant to sound sanctimonious, and I'm not convinced that I did. I merely wanted to point out what I saw in hopes that others might see it similarly."

"People don't want to see that swamp the way you see it."

"Precisely."

"They want a little sunshine in their lives, and don't care whether it's manmade or natural."

"They do. I agree. A little sunshine. But is that what they need?"

"Tough call, Doctor. But look at it this way: they haven't outlawed tanning booths, trashy romances or soap operas yet, and I don't think you're going to get them to."

"Oh, I don't want anything *outlawed*. I only want things *recognized*."

"And who says you're the one always gets to do the recognizing. I mean not trying to sound too pushy or anything."

"No offense taken. I'm glad we're having this talk, actually, and that is certainly a valid question. I don't have an answer for it, though, except to say that I've always been able to see things in black and white."

"Well, that's true," I said. "It's a talent of yours. But there's more to life than black and white, and people around here, well . . . I just wouldn't want them to get the wrong impression about you as a individual."

She sort of sighed and smiled at the same time. "I would doubt that the community has formed any impression of me at all, Mr. Register."

"Well, about those letters though, I've heard several make the comment that you seemed to be, I meant at least you come across on paper as right much of a morose individual."

"A morose individual?"

"Gloomy. You know: not wanting to take the time or energy to search for the silver lining."

"Is that what it takes to cure an individual of morose-ness? A tireless search for the silver lining?"

I shrugged, held up my hands like what the hell, search me, I don't know, I've said too much and you know it and I know it.

"What do *you* think, Mr. Register? Do you think of me as a morose individual?"

I told her I understood that she felt an obligation to call it like she saw it.

She said, "Good. I'm glad you understand that need."

"But," I said, "sometimes I'm not so sure you don't take things too far. Take this movie thing. I went down there to watch them film one Saturday. Got down there after breakfast and damn if I didn't stand around most of the day, watching the trailers for the doors to open, which they didn't until late afternoon. I got to talking to one of these Hollywood guys, best boy he called himself. Anyway he was carrying a walkie-talkie and seemed like he knew the lay of the land down there and we got to talking and I asked how come they'd just wasted a whole day and he explained to me the concept of the golden hour. Said it's that time just before nightfall when the sun's coming in kind of sidearmed right through the trees and things are lit so they look a thousand times clearer. Prettier too. It's like magic, this fellow said, but it's all natural. He looked like he was into natural, too. Now if they were willing to pay a crew to sit around and drink coffee all day to wait on a pretty shot, why shouldn't they do that instead of rushing it and coming out with something that pardon my French looks like hell. It's just like when I hired that fellow from Fayetteville to come out here and shoot some pictures of the campus for the catalog. He came back with some photos that made this place look like the projects. I rode into town, showed the pictures to Joe Bunch has that studio on Water Street? I said to Joe, showed him the pictures, said, Joe, if you saw these in an ad would you want to attend an institution looked like this? Joe said not unless a court ordered him to. I told him, said, let's see if we can't improve on this situation. Joe found some different speed film, used a different lens, shot from across the highway instead of right up on the cinderblock. Now you got to admit he made this place look attractive. And didn't do a thing but take his time and try to pick out the good side. Because there's one to everything and everybody and every place."

I leaned back to rest my case. Knew I had her, too. This year's enrollment was up by 7 percent and though I've never said as much to her, I know it was me hiring Bunch that did it instead of her driving around the county all summer, talking Basic Skills to people's mamas while they kept right on looking at their stories on TV.

"Of course it's possible with today's technology to improve the appearance of almost anything. But why should you? Don't you sacrifice a certain integrity when you ameliorate through artificial means?"

I told her I didn't see anything artificial about goddamn dusk.

She said she admired my capacity to take people at face value but that in this situation she thought maybe I had been duped. When I did not respond she said, "Took, as you put it." Then she tried to say that old boy from Holly-

wood had to of been lying. That there's no way they could
of gotten the swamp to look that way with what she called
available light, and that even if they had, it would make the
swamp look like a thousand other places, stripped it of its
idiosyncratic charm, rendered it bland.

Listening to all this, I had come back to thinking that this
was some dumb movie made from a boring book, and I was
ready to forget all my big ideas about her letter being about
something else besides this movie when she spoke again.

"If that movie was filmed entirely during the so-called
golden hour, then half of the so-called naturally blond hair in
this county did not derive, as I've long suspected, from a bottle. And I am wrong. But I doubt it. Sincerely, Mr. Register."

Later, she'd tell somebody—one of the secretaries I believe, or maybe it was Miss Wilcox teaches Cosmetology—
that she was not referring to any specific head of hair, but at
the time I think she knew what she was saying, knew exactly how I'd take it, too. Debbie's hair was legal pad yellow
when we started dating in high school and I've always liked
it that way and I don't see that it's anybody's business but
hers if she's chosen to preserve its natural tint. As for there
being lots of bottle-derived blondes in this county, I have
never seen figures on this and though I haven't traveled
what you'd call far and wide, I have been around enough to
know that people dye their hair in Ohio where Fancy de-
rives from.

What it was, she hated being called a morose individual.
It wasn't me saying her letter was uncalled for that got away
with her, it was this morose individual business which did
not fit at all with the way she saw herself. So she had to get
back at me on a real personal level. Still, talking about
somebody's wife's hair.

But I could tell by her expression that she enjoyed it.
And so I wouldn't have to look at her anymore, I scooped
my paperwork off her desk, stood up and left without even

a thank you. That was around four o'clock and I managed to keep away until I went to dinner.

When I pulled into the parking lot, I was scheming about how to avoid her for the rest of the evening. Her letter, our I guess you could call it a scene, pressed on top of all the food I ate, and all I wanted to do was close my office door, put my feet up and snooze until time to go.

I didn't see the bus until I was right up on it. Normally, an odd-looking vehicle like that parked in front of the institute, I'd of been on it from the get-go, but I didn't think much of it until I turned up the sidewalk, looked real quick over my shoulder to see was there anyone working on it or was it abandoned. If I'd of kept going without looking back or turned my head a second later, everything would of been different: everything. I know I wouldn't have messed with it considering what kind of day I'd had up till then. But I happened to turn around right when the white fellow and that black gal decided to engage in a little tongue-pull, right in front of the institute, right in the middle of the golden hour.

Franklin "Cisco" Reed

If I still believed in the convenience of cause and effect, if I wasn't so needled by the suspicion that history might well be controlled by forces beyond human control, I would blame the whole incident on what happened the night before.

We were playing Wilmington, a college for pothead surfers, and King did not want me to mention the Wilmington Ten.

"I know you are a militant, Franklincisco," said King, "but dredging up that shit just when it's died down good's not going to change anything but our accommodations for the night. Go spouting off and we out of here, spend the night beside the road."

"So give the people more groovethang opium, right?"

"I know you some kind of Commie philosopher, Franklincisco," said King. "But I hired your ass to play guitar, not preach. Keep right on, I'll have your mike cut off."

"As if it'd make a diff," said Candace. She was picking King's afro, and seemed impatient that he would actually spend time talking to me about such things when they could be lolling about on their waterbed. Candace tried to keep King sequestered in the back of the bus, his royal quarters. Besides the waterbed, King and Candace had a tiny bathroom, a sound system, a television; the rest of us had bus seats and overhead cubbyholes for our belongings. The walls of their compartment were covered with carpet—the royal padded cell, J.T. called it. As soon as we dropped below Baltimore and I saw for the first time the kind of crowd King drew down there, I told him he should get rid of that thin leopard print and put up shag.

Shaggers, not surfers—that was our audience in Wilmington. Not the surfer boys with the bleached hair and baggy shorts we'd seen around the campus that afternoon. The house filled with older guys, white, balding, pasty-faced, paunched. They wore a uniform: khakis and starched white button-downs, and their wives wore sundresses, espadrilles, wide hairbands. Before we went on we stood in the wings watching the warm-up, some local cover boys mangling Motown, and looking out in the audience, I saw a whole fucking gym full of these people, and *they all looked alike.*

Being from California, I was clueless about this "beach music" scene. Beach to me meant that surf-twangy Jan and Dean stuff—"Wipeout" and early Beach Boys—but down here what they call beach is really R and B. Some of them, according to J.T., even go so far as to claim that Otis Redding, Sam Cooke, Solomon Burke and Jerry Butler were beach music stars. As soon as it was explained to me it seemed simple—another case of whites ripping off black music, pretending we invented it, trying to make it our own—but it turned out to be a bit different, since the white "beach" bands weren't half as successful as the black ones. Apparently these shaggers were loyal fans. They bought albums and paid admission prices even now, fifteen years after the music peaked. King probably would have been capping tires if not for this beach music cult: college kids happened to catch the Royals at a club outside Myrtle Beach, brought them onto the frat circuit and within two years King had built his mom a ranch house in his hometown of Waycross, Georgia, had his own Corvette, was recording at Muscle Shoals.

He was Little Cedrick back then, of Little Cedrick and the Royals. They say he was bigger down South than Little Richard, though like I said I'd never heard of him or any of these bands until halfway through this tour. King likes to keep his other life a secret; I'm getting to why.

About his former fans, King seems to me terribly confused: on the one hand he despises them, remembers all those years when they'd stumble up to him after he played their mixers and, slobbery drunk, swear he was going to be famous. They'd slap him on the back and offer him beer bought with their daddy's money but the next day, if they'd have seen him walking through frat court, they'd have assumed he was the cook.

But King also understood they paid his mortgage, and kept his mom from cleaning houses. Back in the fifties, singles sold in the black-owned record shops, but not albums, and as beach music grew more popular with young whites, and word got around that the Royals and similar groups had become house bands for the spring break crowds, the black stations quit playing it. Blacks quit listening. King, bewildered by his suddenly palefaced audience, blamed black preachers for organizing against him. He said they should have either stuck to their Scripture or sympathized one. Man's got to make a living, King said. He didn't see where it made a bit of difference to *the music* that whites were buying it, since he didn't change his tune to please them, kept right on playing R and B the same as when they sat up in rib and juke joints across the South.

When I first heard King railing about how black preachers involved themselves in things that were none of their business, I hailed this stance as common ground, and prepared to pounce. I was sure I could use this distrust of organized religion as a way to broach our ideas to him, but soon I realized that King had nothing against *religion*. In his own loose way he's a borderline Bible thumper, and according to Janice he used to gather everyone in the dressing room for a preconcert prayer. Preachers who organized boycotts were what he was opposed to—a sign of economic autonomy and social activism that theoretically I approved of.

What was I supposed to do, King asked me once, quit playing as soon as white faces started showing up? If they wanted to call it beach music because they first heard it at the beach, that was fine with him. Matter of fact it was better for them to think of it as their own thing; that way he could keep a part of it hidden (the soul is what he'd hold back, he said, and this was way before that word became popular, before the cynics divorced the word from its implied spirit and turned it into four letters stenciled on a record store bin). His music didn't have nothing to do with any beach, he said. What's a black man from South Carolina going to sing about a beach for when he couldn't hardly set foot on one unless he was picking up white people's trash? King played clubs down there but the beach was just another town to him, he didn't even care for shrimp.

You're probably wondering how someone like me, an avowed Marxist, urban guerrilla, confirmed Californian, ended up gigging two-bit towns down South with a beach music band. In retrospect it seems almost as hard to understand as it does to explain, but back when I made the decision to go on the road, in light of the trouble I was having with the party, the details of which I'd rather not go into at this point (let's just say that I was trying to square certain disparate elements in my life, and had met with some opposition from those who felt my commitment was wavering), it seemed not only simple but *right*—as right as anything I'd done since joining the party.

I met King at a bar in the Haight. I was back in school again, working on a double major in philosophy and economics at San Francisco State, playing guitar with a funk/fusion band nights to make rent and tuition. I've been playing in bands since I was twelve, and though it does seem incompatible with the other area of my life, especially when playing with a band like King's, it's something I've refused to give up.

King had been in Oakland since 1971, trying to come back from those Little Cedrick days, playing house with Candace. He'd been working hard on a comeback, and he'd written some new songs, more in a funk vein than the ballads he'd been singing since his time with the Royals. He was visiting some clubs, trying to put together a band to take on the road, and one night he came into the place I was playing and sat almost right under me. If my playing impressed him, I couldn't tell it by looking at him: he sat there with his legs crossed, and this dead-eyed church-sermon stare. I'd gone through my Dimeola/Hancock/Bitches Brew thing and was into straight-up funk à la Parliament and Bootsy but with Hendrix fuzz tones. "He may sound like a funkier Ernie Isley," one of the alternative rags described me in a review, "but he's still a white boy." Though I haven't experienced a fifth of what my black brothers and sisters have in the area of discrimination, I am living proof of the reverse discrimination in the music business in America. A white boy playing funk, even around the East Bay, has about as much of a chance as a black man on the harpsichord. King was looking for the next new thing, and he had an ear for it; when it comes to music the man is prescient. Even if he doesn't really *like it,* he'll incorporate it if he thinks it'll splash.

A few days later he came around and offered me a job. He didn't even try to schedule an audition with the rest of the band—later I'd learn that except for Ronald, Janice and Candace, I *was* the band. King picked up a bass player later that night but the guy didn't even make it past Tahoe, where King heard J.T. playing in a casino and hired him on the spot. Janice and Candace had worked with King when he first came to Oakland, and as for Ronald, the drummer, he hardly spoke to me until Wilmington, so I didn't know what his story was.

King didn't say where we were going, either. He just said we'd work our way across the country and back, which sounded fine to me. I'd had it with school; classroom work once again seemed irrelevant to my real education. King also mentioned that we'd be playing some college campuses, and one of the things I'd been doing in my spare time was working campuses in the Bay Area, talking to students about the party; I saw this as a chance to reach new people, as San Francisco had grown stale, insular. I saw only my comrades, a small group of disillusioned Marxists, and we had the same conversations and I felt we weren't going anywhere. I became convinced that if socialism was going to work for me, I would have to remain in touch with the working class. Little did I know that the King's audience on those campuses would be made up mostly of forty-five-year-old bankers.

I told King I'd need to gig with the others first. King found the bass player, set something up at his place in

Oakland for the next day. The new stuff he was singing was easy enough to learn and not bad, and I drove back across the bay feeling okay about the music end of it—at least I wasn't compromising myself by signing on with a bubble gum group just to leave town. Whatever else I can say about the man, King can sing. He had Janice and Candace coming off three months of voice lessons, and they were sounding good. Looking good too. Between songs, Janice and I spent most of that first night talking in the corner, and though I'm not given to sappy ideas of romance, I will say that with me and Janice it was instantaneous. The proverbial whirlwind courtship thing, especially considering the cultural barriers of an interracial affair. Of course there were less problems with that in the Bay Area than when we went on the road.

We were in Chicago before I even got around to asking about the itinerary. Those first few weeks I just climbed off that bus and did the thing, went straight to the motel room with Janice and got back on the next morning. I didn't even notice how shabby and uncomfortable the bus was, didn't even listen to the others complaining about how we'd never make it to the next gig. I trusted we'd get there, wherever there was—it didn't matter to me. I liked the way King handled the finances—his manager collected the fees directly from the promoter and held on to them. We were to collect our lump when we got back home. One of the first things Marxism taught me was how to live on very little; it was a relief for me not to have to debase myself with divvying up money each night. I grew quickly accustomed to the nominal per diem and to supper among the proletariat at those truckstops King favored.

"Week each in New York, Philly, D.C., and then we headed South," King told me after the show in Chicago.

"How South?" I asked.

"Far as you can get without habling Español."

"You mean the Deep South?"

King went off with that chunky laugh of his. "All of it's deep," he said. "Can't wade into it. Get down past Maryland good, got what they call a sudden drop-off. Ain't nothing gradual about it. Sink or swim, baby."

"Can you swim?"

"I come out the womb stroking. That or drown."

Ronald said, "King's born in Georgia, just like J.B. and Little Richard."

"'Cept I can sing," said King. "And this is the hair I was born with."

"No way, King," I said. "You were born down there, you escaped and now you're volunteering to go back?"

King laughed and said some things had changed, they weren't lynching down there like they used to, that to him other parts of the country were worse on black people. He personally felt more nervous in Iowa where he'd never seen a black man except on television.

But as we worked our way through Ohio and Pittsburgh and across to New York, I started to wonder just what I'd gotten myself into. I'd never been down South, never been the least bit interested in going there, and here I was headed into the thick of it with my brand-new black girlfriend. One night, I think we were in Harrisburg, Pa., Janice and Candy had gone out shopping and I went by King's room and tried to feel him out on this part of the tour. I said I was a little nervous, wondered if playing down there was the right thing.

"King got a lot of fans down there," said Ronald, who was lying on one of the twin beds, watching "Star Trek." King shot him a look that shut him up and then, as if this look could only be trusted to silence him for seconds, tossed him a bill and sent him out for a bottle.

When Ronald was gone, King switched the channel and

said without looking at me, "What you worrying about now, Cisco?"

He called me that, though I hated it and told him so. No one but tourists used that cheesy nickname. When I complained he started calling me Franklincisco.

I told him I was worried for Janice, not myself.

King flopped back on the bed and said, "She's *from* the South, boy. What's the big thing?"

"Wrong, King. Janice is from Pomona, California."

King laughed. "She may of been born out there, but she ain't *from* there. Ain't no black people from out there. Janice from down there"—he pointed to the pocked green wall above the TV with such assuredness that I did not question it was South—"just like the rest of us."

"You're wrong, man," I said. "She's got the birth certificate to prove it."

King looked away from me like he was in terrible pain, like I'd come to see him in the hospital and had overstayed visiting hours. "You're not listening to me, Cis. People get out—up to Baltimore, Chicago, out to L.A., wherever—but they forget. Case of what they call selective amnesia. Clothes they wear might have come from up North, but everything else they got come from down South. Way they talk, food they eat, music they play. Hell, all the music in this country come from down there. Gospel, blues, R and B. Country, straight on jazz, even that freestyle haywire shit you play for people to smoke herb to? Even that."

I said that Janice would be surprised to learn that she had a Southern accent. She spoke generic L.A., in mass-produced model's "I'm from inside your TV" tones.

"It ain't the accent, boy, it's the rhythm. People born out there, they try to talk all white and shit—no offense now, Cis—but it still comes out sounding black. And black's South. Black people started out down there, that's where we from. I wish it won't so sometimes—lot of bad stuff went on down there, still do—but they ain't no use in denying it."

I took offense, though not as a white man. I took offense for Janice, the kind of offense any self-respecting black would take at this Uncle Tomish line.

"It sounds to me like you've been conditioned to feel loyal to a system—and a region—which has manipulated and oppressed you. White Southerners want you to think that way so that you'll continue to be shackled to a system of institutional racism which, despite the decline in lynchings and the so-called improvements in civil rights, still holds. You might as well deny that all major decisions in American society are dominated by the industrial-military complex or claim that the social-political institutions which rule this country respond with fairness to the needs of workers and minorities."

King was stretched across the bed with a big grin on his face. "Listen," I said, leaning over to him. "In bourgeois society, the past dominates the present. You're buying into an idea that will keep blacks down forever. Modern bourgeois society perpetuates its reign by establishing new forms of struggle to take the place of old ones. If you retreat into the past you will be treated as you were in the past. I've told you this before, I'll tell you again: all previous historical movements were movements of minorities. It's time for blacks to stake a claim in the now."

King was smiling. "I love to hear you spout that mousy-tongue shit," he said. "But look: if Janice and you so goddamn now, why y'all so nervous about going down South?"

Janice wasn't as nervous as I was, but I didn't tell King that. I told King that they didn't exactly have the greatest track record down there for welcoming black people with open arms. Especially black women with white boyfriends.

"Everybody gets a little nervous when they get ready to go home," said King.

"Now it's you who's not listening," I said.

"Oh, I heard you," said King. "About this salt and pepper thing? You got to hide that all over this country, don't matter if you in Ohio or the Okefenokee. Out in public y'all got to keep your hands to yourself."

"And live a lie, King?"

"Sometimes living's lying," said King, "and that's the way it's got to be if you want to keep right on living. You telling one lie, but you only doing it so you can tell the truth someplace else. It's like back when all the white boys started showing up to hear us play. I had to act like it was fine with me if there wasn't a black face in the house, and that was a serious lie. But it's like I said: didn't a thing about the music change, and I didn't do nothing different for a house full of white boys than I did when it was black people out there listening. I didn't smooth it out any, didn't go talking dirty to get those college girls giggling. I didn't get down on the stage and wallow like an alligator, which some of them around back then did all that. They was lying about the music, and that was a worse lie. My music didn't lie, see. So one lie let me keep on telling the truth."

I was about to call him on that when Ronald returned with the Smirnoff's, brown bag wrenched around its thin neck.

"Tell him, Ronald," said King, and Ronald said, "It's the gospel," as if whatever King said was the unqualified truth.

JUST BELOW RICHMOND, I noticed the change in the crowd. Shaggers started showing up at every gig, calling out the names of songs I'd never heard. Before the show I walked out to check the house, and took my first look at what I'd be staring into from then on: puffy-faced white people in their forties acting like teenagers. That first night I nabbed Ronald and told him we'd better go out and check the marquee, because it looked like they'd advertised the wrong band.

"Told you King's got a lot of fans down here."

"But white fans? Fat middle-aged white people? King?"

Ronald said, "Man, don't you know by now who King is?"

I shrugged. "You mean his real name? Cedrick something."

"Little Cedrick," said Ronald, leaning heavy on the "little."

"Named after his old man?"

"Of Little Cedrick and the Royals." Ronald managed to say it both slowly and impatiently.

"The Royals?"

"'Baby, Play House with Me'? 'That Summer Eve'?"

I stood there, staring, lost. Ronald got right up in my face.

"'The Night We Met'? 'Before We Were Three'?"

I must have *looked* deaf. He was shouting now.

"'Shaking and a Baking'? 'Only Wanted Love'?"

"Ronald, man," I said, unable to hold the laughter back, "what the hell are you talking about?"

Ronald shook his head. "How you get to be so ignorant? Wouldn't of been no Drifters, no Tams, no Platters, no Coasters, probably wouldn't of been no Motown if they hadn't of been the Royals."

"You saw them play?"

"Hell, man, I was one." He let me stare at him awhile, then said, "Well, I won't in the first original band, believe it was the third or fourth."

I remembered what King had said about the sudden drop-off. Sink or swim. It looked to me like sink: into the seat of an airplane whisking me back to California.

"I got it now," I said. "This is like one of those oldie-goldie reunion tours. Sentimental journey, right? Now that we're down here where everybody knows the music, we're going to play this old twist and shout shit, make these fat shaggers relive their carefree youths."

"Who?" said Ronald. "You ain't even heard the titles, how you going to play the goddamn song?"

"Can't be that difficult. Three chords, right? Doo-wop-wah."

Ronald snorted. "Harder than that tripped-out fusion shit you into."

"Right. I'm sure. Lots more improv. Ohbabyohbaby-ohbaby," I sang. "I want you, girl. With this ring I pledge my trough."

"You needn't worry. King ain't playing nothing but new stuff anyhow."

And he didn't. Each night the house would fill with these white faces, each night King would grin and bow and act like he was just about to break into some "Little Deuce Coupe" thing. But he didn't. We played the same set we'd practiced at his place in Oakland, and the crowd let it go, because here was this God from their past. No matter that he wouldn't sing the old songs, it was still *that voice,* the same one which had serenaded them in those cramped backseats of their '57 Chevys, same Little Cedrick who had provided the sound tracks for those sappy little red-letter dates these people love to love—prom, first kiss, graduation weekend, bachelor party.

I found the whole thing fascinating: that they'd let him be who he was, let him grow. I'd underestimated these people: I would have predicted that they'd start walking out after the third funk tune. Here it is 1977 and these people turned out to hear the 1963 model King. They definitely weren't into funk, probably hadn't even bought an album since the Beatles broke up. They wanted Little Cedrick, not another Kool and the Gang. But they went for it, shagging away as if Kennedy was still prez. And I began to think I might learn something down here, that King was right, things had changed.

Until Wilmington.

When we pulled onto the campus of the surfer college we were coming off six straight nights of double sets in these beach towns dot-connecting the coast highway. We were tired, and the bus was too—it wouldn't start, and Ronald, who did most of the driving, had to take it into the shop twice while the rest of us set up equipment for the night. King had bought the bus cheap from some church and he'd been burned: the odometer had been rewound, the "rebuilt" engine turned out to be a new set of plugs. King wanted to hold off on major repairs until Myrtle Beach, where we had three weeks at a Ramada Inn, but it smoked holy hell all the way down to Wilmington and we were all wasted and short-fused, looking forward to the next day, our first night off in more than a week.

All this might have influenced my perception of the crowd, but I don't think so. Wilmington may have been a night to be *got through,* as J.T. put it, but the crowd seemed whiter and richer than usual, and there was something about the way they seemed so oblivious to King's new music that pissed me off. It woke me to the truth, too: while I had thought all the way across the country that audiences were accepting the new Little Cedrick, in Wilmington it seemed they were patronizing him. *They weren't even listening to the man.* Before they knew the latest dances—the glide, the rock—but in Wilmington they went right on shagging as if the gym was a time capsule.

That night in Wilmington I remembered a girl I'd gone out with a few times in college who was from a wealthy family. They had a maid who rode the bus up from the Fillmore every morning, and long after she'd quit, the children she'd raised, grown now, would visit her and revert to their needy preschool selves, ask her to make them her special pancake recipe, beg her to tell humorous anecdotes from their childhood. I wondered why this woman put up with it, decided that these forty-year-old kids would never accept the fact that the maid was there to make a living, that she indulged them for the money. They pretended as if nothing significant had happened to her in the hours she was away from their million-dollar Victorian, during the twenty years she spent wiping their noses or the twenty since. King's fans were similarly time-warped. J.T. could thump his bass like Stanley Clarke, Ronald could go off on a Buddy Miles solo, I could pump my wah-wah and slash and burn like Hendrix, and they'd still hear some prom night slow dance. Still they'd shag.

Plus, this was Wilmington. Home of the Wilmington Ten. The Ten got a good bit of coverage out in the Bay Area, I guess because it happened down here and the situation seemed more hopeless than it would had it happened in Watts or Oakland, where there are more people around willing to ask questions. Amnesty International dubbed them "prisoners of conscience," and there was even a statement from the Soviets criticizing their prosecution as an egregious violation of human rights. It had been in the news again because the Ten—nine black men and one white woman sentenced for firebombing a white grocery store in what was one of the weakest set-ups in the history of conspiracy—were up for pardons. So it was on my mind from the moment we pulled into Wilmington, and looking out into the crowd during the first song, I saw, instead of a lot of white people patronizing us with their clumsy shagging, a gym full of bigots whom the Ten, by organizing a boycott to desegregate the local school system, had sacrificed so much to help. All of a sudden I felt as if I'd been hoodwinked into playing South Africa.

In between songs, King turned to Ronald to decide what to play next, and I saw my chance.

"Hello, Wilmington," I said into the mike. Generic rock star fare, but it worked. They all stomped and waved and, polite Southerners that they were, said hello right back. Out of the corner of my eye I saw King stop talking to Ronald and motion to someone off stage; I figured I had five seconds. "Been reading about Wilmington in the paper lately," I said. "Wilmington Ten, right?" Sudden quiet, the crowd grew benediction-still. "What I want to know is, when are you people gonna own up to what really . . ."

King's "Babeeeee"—a capella but summoned up diaphragm-deep—washed over my "happened down here." He filled the house like Pavarotti. "Babbeee, play house with me . . ." sang Little Cedrick, and Janice and Candy came winging in on this twenty-year-old Royals standard, their first big hit, and then J.T. plunked in with a basic bass line and Ronald picked up the beat right after him. I stood there holding my guitar like a terrified contestant at a talent show until the chorus, then fell in with some riffs cribbed straight from Muscle Shoals. To me we sounded terrible, but the audience didn't seem to share my opinion and any-way, it worked: my little diatribe was wiped from every memory in the house as Li'l Cedrick took them back down Sapster Lane. I looked at King after he sang the last note, saw him sweat and quake as the cheers rose and the crowd surged toward the security guards in front of the stage, a bulwark of thick-necked, crew-cutted cops linked at the shoulder like paper dolls. I saw one old cop glare up at King like he was responsible for pinning them against the stage. *Inciting a riot* his eyes suggested, and it was then that I real-ized what I had done.

After King left the stage, the rest of us waited in the wings for him to return. Ronald and even J.T. looked at me once in disgust then ignored me, and even Janice kept her distance. They knew we had a long ride on the jalopy ahead, knew King would find some way to punish them all for my sins. Finally Ronald said, "Fuck it, he ain't coming." We sent some surfer boys out to break down the stage, discovered that King had paid a security guard to take him back to the motel. He'd left us the bus, but we had to hide in the locker room for two hours while security cleared the fans from the exits.

That night everyone but King and Candace congregated in J.T.'s room, pulled a baleful drunk. Dark Bacardi and Campari sloshed bloody in our glasses, beauty pageant on the tube with the sound turned down, contestants performed dramatic readings to the new Earth, Wind and Fire pounding from Ronald's portable stereo. But there was no real pleasure in this trick. Nobody said anything, and we were so tired that each drink equaled twice its weight in misery. We'd only just bitten into the crust of the South. What lay ahead was eternal, rough going and all my fault.

Or was it, I wondered that night as Janice slept beside me. Every time I closed my eyes I saw the crowd shift as King sang "Baby, Play House with Me"; felt King's eyes sweep across me like prison yard searchlights. I didn't make him sing that song—didn't do a thing to harm him. I helped him really: at least they were listening when he crooned his hokey ballad. At least they were doing their shag to a tune you could shag to.

To keep my mind off things and to make what amends I could, I volunteered to drive the next afternoon when we left Wilmington. We were headed up to Raleigh, where we had a night off before three days in a beach club. I still hadn't laid eyes on King—he and Candace had boarded before the rest of us, and had barricaded themselves in the royal padded cell—but I felt as much trouble rumbling from the back of the bus as from under the hood, and of course since I happened to be driving when the engine coughed and choked, when we coasted alongside that decrepit campus, the unstated opinion was that the breakdown was my fault too.

For a long time—five minutes I'd guess—we sat there. Just sat, in stupid self-pitying silence. "*Can you believe this shit?*" someone said, and it echoed in the hollows of the bus, a tinny consensus. Trucks flashed by, shaking the bus; tractors passed, trailing strange implements of destruction, rows of what looked like saw blades bucking and spinning as the driver shifted gears. I looked over at the school: peeling white brick buildings linked with rusted-out breezeways, a fleet of ghost ships doldrumed in dead seas. SAWYER VOCATIONAL-TECHNICAL INSTITUTE. The sign was chipped, crudely lettered—the vocational offerings obviously did not include sign painting. It was a pitiful-looking place, yet the longer I studied it, the more I detected in its utilitarian squalor a perfect training ground for the proletariat, an ideal place to enact our plan of free education combined with industrial production. I imagined a single signboard announcing a simple name—Training Institute—and a slogan in plain script: FREE DEVELOPMENT FOR EACH IS THE CONDITION FOR FREE DEVELOPMENT FOR ALL.

In the rearview I saw Ronald walk down the aisle, knock on the door, slip inside. A minute later the door cracked and Ronald, when he reached me, said, "King said tell you get this thing back on the road."

"I don't know a thing about cars, much less buses."

"Find somebody who does," said Ronald.

"I'll call a wrecker," I said.

"No cash for that. You now how King works it. Manager's holding it for us till we get off the road."

"We'll pool our per diems," I said, but between us we came up with twenty-odd dollars, which even in the sticks would not pay a mechanic to put in a quart of oil.

"So where am I going to turn up a bus mechanic in the middle of outer space?" I asked, but Ronald went back to his seat and sacked out. I watched the rearview as if he would pop up and tell me he was just kidding, then looked to J.T. for help.

"Just check out the oil, man," he said. "Look up underneath and check to see if anything's leaking."

"I'm sure it's nothing major," I said. I opened the door and stood blinking in the frontal attack of five o'clock sun. There was nothing to catch it but flat field, parking lot, the buzzed-out lawn of the campus. I felt deprived of gravity out there in that nothingness, and I thought of a passage in which Marx refers to the idiocy of rural life. I stared at the windows of the institute; it looked closed, but I thought I saw a figure standing by one window. Checking us out, no doubt: strange bus, tinted windows, California tags, and each of us, out of coincidence or habit engrained by nine straight working nights, wearing those ridiculous disco outfits King insisted we perform in.

I popped open the hood and studied the engine until J.T. joined me. But he knew less than I did and kept asking where the oil them-ma-jig was.

Janice came out in a while to console me. First with a joke about our mechanical ineptitude; a minute later, when she realized how inept we were, with more persuasive gestures. As we kissed I remembered King telling me to keep my hands to myself in public, and I slid my tongue further into her mouth, darted it around desperately—a crazed and frantic kiss, like I was flat broke, famished and groping for lost change between couch cushions. While J.T. examined the greasy innards of the engine, I pulled away from Janice, saw the figure still standing at the same window.

We didn't notice the shagger until he spoke. "Evening," he said and the three of us wheeled around as if choreographed. Except for the blue blazer and madras tie, he was dressed exactly like one of the thousands in the house down at Wilmington: khaki chinos, starched white shirt, spit-

shined loafers. He had the characteristic shagger's bloat, a
ruddy overfed face, the beginnings of a capitalist corpu-
lence.

I said "evening" back, but rotely, flatly, as if to acknowledge that this was the only thing we had in common—both
citizens of the day, and a day soon to go dark.

Janice took my hand, sidled up close. The shagger
looked at J.T., then away.

"Trouble?"

At least he's not a talker, I thought. He crossed his arms
over the ridge of his gut, and there was something coachlike
about his stance, as if he were poised on the sidelines affect-
ing calm while waiting to humiliate some clumsy kid who
bungled a pop-up.

J.T. spoke up. He sensed the *real* trouble, checked my
eyes and the way the shagger would not look at me since
Janice had suctioned herself to my side.

"We need a mechanic. We're on our way up to Raleigh,
need to get there tonight."

"I'm with the institute here," he said. "Y'all are welcome
to use the phone, call a wrecker."

"Well, we're a little short on cash, see," said J.T. "You
wouldn't happen to know of anyone around who can work
on cars, would you?"

The shagger smiled. A beefy grin, neither friendly nor
sincere. Thanks but no, I thought. I would rather push this
bus to Raleigh than be indebted to this sniveling bourgeois.

"There's an Auto Mechanics class meets tonight," he
said. "Doubt they can do a thing with a bus, now."

"I don't think it's anything major," I said. "An engine is
an engine, right?"

He studied me carefully, as if I were under glass. I decided it was my accent, or lack of, which he found curious,
and not the fact that I had my arm around a black woman

and was accompanied by a man who could tuck his hair into his hip pocket.

"Where y'all coming from?" he asked, and J.T. told him Wilmington.

"Y'all working your way up North for the season?" It wasn't until later that I realized what he meant—he thought we were migrants. At the time I thought he was referring to the beach music season—what did I know? J.T. must have understood because he stepped in again.

"We're in a band. Think you could check it out for us, see if someone from your Auto Mechanics class . . ."

"What kind of music y'all play?"

"Funk," I said, angered by his interruption but intrigued by the way he looked us over. It was like he couldn't decide whether to call the police or an anthropologist, as if our status wavered from threat to curio. I spit the word out, biting and forming its dull vowel-into-k-click with the harshest emphasis I could muster. Saying it, I thought of the term "soul," marveled at how bland and palatable it sounded in comparison. A white P.R. man must have come up with it, I decided. Not so funk, which has an earthiness, a hint of the get-down bawdy designed to scare away white people.

He chose not to follow up on the subject of funk. I believe he lacked the vocabulary.

"Y'all welcome to use the phone, but those boys don't know a thing about buses," he said. "Besides, it being so close to the beginning of the quarter, I wouldn't let them wipe my windshield here for another month or so."

"Surely they have an instructor who knows what he's doing," said Janice.

The shagger brought himself, finally, to look at her. "Sure do. He might even be sober tonight, but sober for him's a relative concept."

"Could you ask him to take a look?" I said.

"He's in class right now. Wouldn't want to disturb him. Got a pay phone in the snack bar, or if you're short on change, just tell the receptionist Mr. Register said let you make a local call."

He turned to go. What motivated me to do what I did next I have not yet nailed down. I think it was something simple—the sight of the man walking away from us, his profile silhouetted by that magnificent last hour of light, which turned him into a head on a coin commemorating the generic Little Cedrick fan. He looked like every man I'd seen since Richmond—a specter haunting not only the South, but me. Away walked this archetype of capitalist greed, and it occurred to me as I watched him waddle in his tight loafers and bulging chinos that I must find a way to confront him and everything he stood for, or sink weakly into the bourgeois.

"Somebody better go tell Little Cedrick," I said. Loudly.

The shagger jerked, as if he'd reached the end of a leash. He snapped back open-mouthed, his face flushed brick red. "You said Little Cedrick?" He sounded stricken, his breath wavering from hyperventilation.

J.T. and Janice sent serious vibes my way. They realized the enormity of my betrayal while I was still marveling at the change in the man. He stuck his sweaty hand out to me and told me to call him by his first name, Mitch. I felt like I was on a public television documentary, introducing a socio-logical phenomenon into thousands of living rooms simply by uttering two simple words known to transform them from chubby adult to gawky teen.

"Yeah," I said, "Little Cedrick." In control now. I could spit on the guy and he'd rub it into his skin like suntan lo-tion. I pulled Janice close, snaked an arm around her midriff, settled my hand beneath her breast. Mitch only grinned. What King had warned me about had been made acceptable by the mention of his name. I hoped he was looking, and turned toward the back of the bus, but saw only the dark curve of window, brutal sun bouncing off the glass.

Mitch was talking. The fervency of his fanhood was evident not only in what he said, but in his breathless delivery. He had seen the Royals twenty-two times . . . every last one of their records, including bootlegs and the two Japanese imports . . . charter member of the Royal Loyal fan club . . . V.P. in 1963, Secretary in 1964 . . . had backstage beers with the original band down at Myrtle in the spring of 1965. He reeled off the names of various production companies, sidemen on forgotten sessions, obscure song titles, legendary concerts, a string of managers.

He was a type I'd run into a couple times before. I'd bet he never even listened to music now, didn't care much for the *concept* of music, but King's stuff had come to him through that narrow window open only for a few months of postadolescence, brief as an eclipse, but as powerful. He was a collector; his interest was materialistic rather than aesthetic. He'd held onto his interest like a cache of molding baseball cards, and the only way he knew how to enjoy himself, so warped was he by bourgeois society, was to transform what should have been aesthetic pleasure into private property. Facts, trivia were stored in his head, and these details were inextricable from his passion. He wasn't faking it—I could tell that King's music had sincerely moved him—it's just that he'd *collected* rather than listened to it.

"Think I could stick my head in, say hello?" he was saying to me. "Little C. might not remember me but what the hell, like I said I was a Loyal, he might."

"Cedrick's resting right now," I said. "We had a gig last night, and we're all wiped out. That's why we need to get this bus fixed so we can get on our way."

"I might be able to work it out," said Mitch. "I meant, now that I know who y'all are."

Who y'all are. I could paw my black girlfriend right before his eyes, and did so.

"Tell you what," I said. "Get your mechanic out here and get this bus fixed and I'll see if I can't get you a few minutes with King."

"King?"

"Little Cedrick. He goes by King these days but he's definitely Little Cedrick still."

Mitch stared at our uniforms. "Say y'all play funk music?"

"King's got a lot of new songs, but he'll dust off his old set on occasion. If he can find an audience old enough to remember."

Mitch lowered his voice. "Some of us had got to wondering if Little C. was still alive," he said. "Nobody's heard from him in years. You don't know what this means to me."

"It'll mean a lot to him, too," I said. "Little C. loves his fans."

"Well, it's not every day your favorite singer turns up on the side of the road in front of your office. Still, I'd hate to take my man out of class just so I can shake the hand of a hero." He leaned forward. "Lots of people around here kind of old-fashioned. I meant, racially and all. Music's the great common denominator, though, isn't it? Soothes the savage, I swear. Here at the institute we do what we can to promote racial equality."

"In February, right?" He looked bewildered, like he had no idea when Dr. King's birthday rolled around, when the token flag of black history is unfurled and flown for a few weeks.

"Be good for all our students if y'all could just put on a short show. Give them a chance to hear a living legend and . . ."

"Sorry, man," said J.T. "We're just off nine straight two-show nights. This is our one open date for a week and besides, even if, it would take hours to unload and set up."

"I could have your stuff set up in the snack bar in no

time. This being primarily a vocational institute, plenty able-bodies around. None of these folks here afraid of work. Plus while y'all playing I could get my auto mechanics man out here, get this bus ready to roll."

Mitch grinned at me, his eyes glinting in that last light. The sun struck his face, pinkening it. I led him through an unendurable silence, then nodded.

"Shouldn't you ought to stick your head in, check with Little Cedrick?" he asked before hurrying off to make good on his end.

"No sweat," I said. "Little Cedrick loves his Loyal Royals."

Nancy McFadden

It is not uncommon for me to hear Mr. Register well before I see him, as once he leaves his office he behaves like a grade school student who undergoes a transformation upon leaving the classroom and entering the corridor. Surely you remember that pathetic figure clowning about the open doors of your childhood afternoons, supposedly on the way to the rest room but dawdling to distract each class, performing obscene gestures which drew first the laughs of classmates and finally the attention of your teacher, who depending upon strength of character, either stepped out in the hall to deal with the perpetrator, or mumbled that most benign of elementary school platitudes: "Don't laugh, you'll encourage him."

I have never been tempted to laugh at Mr. Register, upon whom a hallway has a similarly disastrous effect. The slap of his shoes against the water-cooler pedal echoes like a pistol report through my office; his voice booms. Though I am sure he disrupts others as well, I've never heard anyone else complain, and have therefore refrained from comment. "Don't acknowledge or you'll encourage him" has become—I admit to this sadly—my tactic. I have assumed many compromising tasks during my tenure at the institute, but I stop short of hall monitor.

If ever I was tempted, it was that particular evening. The seven o'clock class was five minutes underway, the halls were quiet and I had just settled down to the evening's paperwork, having watched Mr. Register's conversation with the stranded motorists only briefly before realizing that between the bus and Mr. Register I had squandered hours. And so I put them out of my mind, convinced that the situation outside was not worth my falling behind over. Mr. Register would handle it—whatever it was—in his inimitable way.

I heard the front door swing close, followed by footsteps, unmistakably his. Whistling—whistling!—with classes underway—and then knocking. And then his booming voice. Words themselves I could not make out, yet his tone reached me clearly, and its manic waver conveyed emergency. The man sounded frantic.

By the time I reached the hallway, he had turned out three classes: Missy Lassiter's Court Reporter class, Harold Underwood's Accounting Principles, and a continuing education Flower Arrangement attended by half a dozen slow and lonely widows. The hallway was clogged, and continued to thicken as other teachers emerged from their rooms and assuming the worst, as I had—that the cafeteria was engulfed in grease fire flames, or that the withered infrastructure of Building B had finally succumbed to the ravages of neglect—turned their classes out as well.

At one end of the hallway stood Mr. Register, still talking. It took me several minutes to force my way through the crowd.

He was dispatching students to various places—the brawniest young men to the cafeteria, one of Missy Lassiter's prospective court reporters to the Auto Mechanics class. Though I stood close enough to touch him, and since working my way within earshot had been calling his name repeatedly, he did not acknowledge my presence. He looked odd—really rather happy—and much younger.

I knew within seconds that tragedy had not struck, but something fortuitous, and briefly Mr. Register's exuberance infected even me. I quit calling his name and listened to him give orders for a few seconds before I could grab his arm and calm him enough to look at me.

"What is it?" I said. "What has happened?"

He put both his hands on my shoulders—the only time I can remember him touching me—and drew me close.

"Little Cedrick and the hot damn Royals," he said. "I shit you not, Fance. Guarangoddamtee you."

We were, you'll remember, surrounded. By students whom I had recruited with the promise of improving somewhat the quality of their barren and—oh, I might as well admit it, as it had been clear to me for years before that fateful day—doomed and unpromising lives. Mr. Register spoke to me in the way in which they talked to each other, and right in front of them. Just when I felt drawn to an effervescent side of him I had rarely seen, he chose to humiliate me.

Immediately I tried to usher him out of the hallway and into one of the empty classrooms, but he would not budge. He went back to barking orders, demanding that tables be cleared from the cafeteria, telling Mike Harmon, our electronics instructor, to hook up the public address system. People were coming from other buildings, as news of Mr. Register's behavior had ostensibly spread to buildings B and C; everyone did what they were told without question. I was mystified.

"Begging your pardon, Mr. Register," I said—and I spoke slowly, patiently, determined to retain my composure lest he attempt to humiliate me again in front of the students.

"Ain't too proud to beg, oooh darling," sang Mr. Register. He placed his hands on my shoulders again and shook his hips in a manner which he no doubt thought lascivious but which struck me as buffoonish. "Please don't leave me, don't you go," he sang as the students, and even some members of the faculty, snickered, laughed outright, even slapped at each other's outstretched palms.

"Mr. Register getting on down," a voice behind called out, and from another corner came, "Do it to it, Big Mitch."

"I would very much like to speak to you in private," I said.

"Ain't got time for that right now," he said.

"Then will you kindly tell me what's going on? Using words which make sense?"

"You best settle for my words, if you want to know what's happening." And in a string of solecisms—all the more intolerable since we were surrounded by students for whom Mr. Register, as administrator, should at least be setting a verbal example if not a social one—in this grating localese he told me of a musical group that he had been inordinately fond of in his youth. He named albums and song titles, none of which I had heard of, and at one point launched into arcane trivia about record labels, radio stations and racism, the most socially aware thing I have ever heard him say. He then digressed to describe that sub-genre known as beach music, which this group had reputedly pioneered. Just when I had decided to interrupt him in order to ask what all this had to do with him disrupting my classes, he revealed the occupants of the disabled bus to be none other than these lost musical idols of his youth. In exchange for repairs performed gratis by our Auto Mechanics class, this Little Cedrick and the Royals had agreed to put on a performance in the cafeteria.

"You can't be serious," I said.

"The hell I can't."

"The only legitimate reasons for canceling classes are in-clement weather and/or an electrical outage. It's in the handbook. I suggest you consult it."

"Lighten up, Fancy," said a voice behind me. And when I turned to see who had spoken I gazed into a thicket of malicious grins. I felt myself waver—I almost, as they say, "lost it"—but one glance at Mr. Register's barely contained smirk and I found it once again.

"Any decision to cancel class must be reached by the two of us, since we are jointly in charge here. I was not consulted, which of course means that your decision is in-valid."

"What the fuck's she talking about?" This was not whis-pered but slung defiantly into my right ear.

"Get back in class," I said, over my shoulder.

"Right," said Mr. Register. His laugh was fatuous, false. "Tell them we're getting ready to have a concert but can't any of them come. Tell 'em go on back to Court Reporting. Look, even our flower ladies are wanting to hear Little C."

He gestured toward the widows, whom I had thought long gone. They stood along the wall in their felt hats and top-buttoned sweaters, clutching their shiny black purses, looking horrified but clearly not bored.

"Even if they were to go back to class, they wouldn't be able to get nothing done," Mr. Register was saying. "Cedrick and them like to play loud."

"I heard that," someone mumbled. Mr. Register was working the crowd like a sidewalk preacher, inviting inane responses with his call.

"That's neither here nor there, since there will be no concert."

"You going to tell those poor stranded people that? You going to let them sleep 'side the road tonight?"

"Since when did we take responsibility for each mechanical failure which turns up along our right of way?"

"Look at it this way: be good practice for the boys in Auto Mechanics."

"They have plenty of legitimate things to practice on without swooping down on road kill."

"Road kill?" Mr. Register seemed to enjoy this, and I must admit I was pleased to have come up with the analogy so quickly. For the first time I felt I'd gained an edge.

"That's a living legend out there, that is not your road kill."

Then came the audience reaction, delayed of course, like all human response in this place.

"What the hell's she talking about road kill?" and, "That's a hard-hearted bitch right there."

"Hey now," said Mr. Register. "Watch your mouth."

I had turned around again, and was on the verge of demanding the name of the speaker when I realized the futility of facing them. Mr. Register's feeble reprimand ruined me forever in the eyes of these students. I knew how they gossiped. Within minutes this scene would be replayed in every corner of the school, with the obligatory embellishments, none of which would favor my side.

Not only did it seem futile to face the crowd but it seemed suddenly futile to remain at the institute. Standing there in the crowded corridor, I realized that it was time for me to go, and I let myself be overcome by spreading melancholy which deepened and darkened into self-pity.

"She look like she about to cry," a young woman behind me said. And though I struggled against it, her words unleashed a torrent of doubt and defeat. Suddenly my stint at the Sawyer Vocational-Technical Institute appeared to me in that ephemeral term—a stint. Seventeen years! Yet it was not a stint but a life, one lived falsely it seemed, seen through the flickering light of ego, vanity, naïveté. Oh how could I have thrown my life away among these people, how could I have ever thought that my selfless devotion to improving the quality of life here was anything but a charade?

I will not die here, a tiny voice whispered. I listened as it repeated itself again and again until it became the very rhythm of one foot in front of the other, a way out, a path cleared through this blissfully ignorant, ultimately unsalvageable throng.

Mr. Register was watching me, his expression suggesting concern. I suppose my own had conveyed the despair I felt as I pushed past him on my way through the crowd. I smiled—sincerely—and said, "I was wrong."

"Say what now?" He moved closer.

"About the golden hour."

He looked baffled.

"The truth is—and I thank you for helping me see this—*my* entire tenure has been one long golden hour. Every hour of every day falsely tinted, seventeen years of hair dyed daily."

"Thought I was through talking to you about that damn movie," Mr. Register said curtly.

"You are. I'm going back to my office to type up my resignation. Enjoy your concert."

And there I left him. His bewilderment did not last; before I was out of earshot, he was back to giving orders. Yet it did not bother me so much then. On my way back to my office I composed my resignation *(I hereby resign; I will not die here),* and I planned to slip it beneath the president's door, load my car and leave this life forever. Freedom awaited. Wide, wide world! I was so busy contemplating the limitlessness of a New Life I did not even notice that my office light, which I had certainly left on, was off, nor that my door, which I was sure I left wide open, was closed. Not until I pulled the door quickly to and reached for the switch did I feel those hands on my shoulder, pulling me away from the light switch. As I opened my mouth to scream, a hand clamped over my mouth; I smelled oil and grease and felt the clammy palm skin tighten, and this sensory gust made the moment all the more terrifying as I thought again, *I will not die here,* this phrase having gained a new, an inordinate weight.

Franklin Reed

I wish I could say that the way I acted when she walked into the room was out of character, a frantic reaction to dire straits, a bounce back from the bottom I had hit. I wish it had been that easy. The truth is, the way I sneaked up behind, truly spectral, invisible and inaudible after having been severed from the capital-making machine, seemed a thing I was put on this earth to do. We all commit criminal acts in our lives, though of course what one defines as criminal another might see as a necessary act of social justice. The moment I felt her breath hot and quick on my hands, I knew that the time had come for me to pursue at whatever cost and by the most effective means available what Marcuse once described as "that freedom which has nothing to do with, and wants nothing to do with, the freedom practised in senile society."

Seconds before, during that moment when J.T. and Janice slammed the bus doors shut in my face, it occurred to me that I had become the walking definition of the proletariat: member of a class who live only so long as they find work, and can find work only so long as their labor increases capital. I knew that if I wanted to survive I had to sell myself piecemeal, that I was only a commodity, that I had become an appendage of the machine.

Since the only place around to sell myself was this institute, I plunged in with the idea of offering myself piecemeal for bus fare home. I planned to find Mitch, tell him King declined but I'd be glad to go on solo. But when I spotted him at the end of the hall, it appeared he'd already announced the concert; the corridor was clogged and buzzing. Because I could not figure out how to tell him in front of all those people, I ducked into an office. Turned out the light, closed the door, stood in the dregs of dusk waiting for the halls to clear.

When I grabbed her, her shoulders tightened, and then she went limp and fell against me, trembling. I reached over to flip on the light switch, thinking that would calm her. Her mumbled words hummed against my palm, damp and unintelligible vibrations. In the light I studied her: she was short and lean and the way she wore her hair, grey and so long, an older woman in a backwater place like that—I don't know, I guess I expected beehives or wigs on every female, and for an older woman to wear her hair that way takes a certain amount of courage. There's something both brazen and defiant about it, a refusal to give way to age, a sensual statement.

Of course I'm no fashion king, and had never even thought of such a thing until then, but I remember clearly thinking that I had not snagged a secretary. I looked quickly around the office for the first time. A Post-Impressionist still life hung on one wall, Georgia O'Keeffe cattle carcass and cactus flower on the other. Sorority girl art. Two bookcases crammed with textbooks mostly, higher education holding sway, but there were a couple of shelves of fiction and poetry, which I scanned: Greek tragedies, Penguin classic Austen and Eliot, a half-dozen Virginia Woolf diaries, collected Dickinson and Cummings, Rilke's *Letters*

to a Young Poet. On the next shelf some philosophy—Nietz-
sche, a withered anthology called *A Casebook on Existential-
ism,* and a half-dozen similar titles no doubt left over from
that four-year lobotomy called college which most come
to consider the high point of their intellectual lives. Books
kept for the sake of display, as if to claim, I READ CA-
MUS, books-unto-materials, the spirit of them unpos-
sessed. Books displayed like fading photographs of a dorm
room, a homecoming date. Pathetic, I thought as I dragged
my eyes appraisingly across the spines, enjoying the pre-
dictability of each title until a color caught my eye—the
bright red of a frayed paperback—and I recognized the
Penguin edition of Cockburn's *Student Power: Problems, Di-
agnosis, Action.* A book I've read tens of times. I carry a
copy along always, had one right outside in my suitcase on
the bus. And beside it, as if she'd shelved her library thematically, *Das Kapital* and a crisp copy of *Marx/Engels
Reader.*

When I pulled my hand away from her mouth, words
which had fluttered on my skin spilled out: "Not die here,"
she said, which shocked me. Did she think I was a murder-
er, a rapist? You've got it all wrong, I started to say, but
stopped myself when it occurred to me that she had no reason to think I was not there to harm her physically. So far I
was only a hand to her, a violating presence in the near dark
and a smell—not a very good one, either.

I let her go, asking her as she pulled away what in the
world she was doing with a copy of *Student Power.*

I suppose it was a strange first question from someone
who had just grabbed you from behind. The cords in her
neck trembled, and her face drained; I thought she was in
shock until she half-whispered in a voice low and careful,
"You're with the band."

"What band?" As I spoke I realized that I was wearing
my uniform still, that whatever I said to her was going to be

tempered by my outfit: sky blue polyester bell-bottoms, a bell-sleeved, French-cuffed gigolo shirt, zip-up pointy-toed super-pimp boots.

She pointed out the window to the bus, as if too shocked to speak.

"Oh. Yeah, I used to be with the band," I said. "But no longer."

"What do you want?" Her half-whisper again. She made it seem as if I'd permanently damaged her vocal cords. She shook still, and I could see that she was terrified, that I needed to outline my agenda immediately.

"Don't worry. This isn't sexual, it's political."

A glint of suspicion showed in her eyes which made me realize what I'd said, and how lame and ridiculous it sounded. Without words, with only a slight narrowing of the eyes, she reminded me that the sexual was the political, that what she no doubt thought I intended to do—rape her— was as political an act as if I planned to take over this miserable institution.

Take over this institution. The comparison occurred as naturally as if I'd said it aloud. Playing oldie-goldies for the pasty bourgeois had dulled my thinking, yet as an old lefty once told me, there's no such thing as an ex-Communist. They can kick you out of the party like they planned to do to me, but if you were committed to begin with, you continue to live your life inside the dialectic. If I was to survive this night, it would be because I fell back on agitprop tactics, not because I was crafty or canny or quick on my feet. What I needed to do was to break the situation down; what I had here was not a psychological relationship between two people in a bland office, but an economic schism between social forces. *Frivolous* was the charge they brought against me, but if I was so frivolous would I ever have thought of taking over the institute at such a crucial moment?

Politicize, radicalize, resist, revolt, disrupt: the old structure came flooding back, and though I never seriously planned on taking over that decrepit campus in the middle of nowhere (if I took it over I'd have had to stay, and I'd rather the capitalists use it to churn out sheep than be imprisoned there) I saw the worth of acting the part. So much of the movement was theater; this would not be the first time I'd put my militant left foot forward and my complacent, bourgeois-leaning right foot had followed.

Maybe there was something to be gained from an actual takeover of this place, I thought, but certainly this was not something I could pull off alone and overnight. What I could pull off was a way out of there, and this woman whose office I'd chosen to hide out in was going to be my travel agent and escort.

I don't believe in luck or coincidence. That I had landed in a room with copies of a *Marx-Engels Reader* and Cockburn's *Student Power* had nothing to do with either of these irrational concepts. Many would see this as a sign, a stroke of good fortune, but to me each bourgeois, regardless of his intellectual facilities, is alike: someone to be educated. It has been my experience that the more education he's had, the harder he is to convert. College campuses have proven to be fertile spawning grounds for the cause, yet the truly committed workers, the ones who come to see the struggle in every aspect of their lives, usually come from factory or foundry, bindery or brewery. I've had more success with workers, as I seem to have been born with the ability to translate complex ideas into a brand of low-prole rhetoric guaranteed to turn drone against boss. Truthfully? Given the time, I could turn anyone around—even the most God-fearing, law-abiding, red-baiting naif. I was almost there with Janice before Wilmington and the bus fiasco, and I had been working on King since Vegas.

King, though, was a harder sell. He claimed to have run into Huey Newton during his Oakland days and he found ludicrous how the New Left had deified Huey, who King described as just another "crazy cokehead who'll shoot anybody calls him 'Baby.'" I tried to explain what Huey P. and the Panthers represented to the more radical fringe of the movement—a domestic Vietcong, an embodiment of the old SDS notion that the black ghetto is the real battleground of the now, and in minority insurrection lay the seeds of the next revolution. King laughed at this and said to the people of Oakland the Panthers were just like any other street gang, pimping and pushing, extorting and robbing. He refused to believe in their political possibilities.

The lady frozen in the shadows across from me wouldn't exactly be a pushover either, but she was convertible.

"Sit down," I said. I leaned past her to pluck her copy of *Student Power* from its shelf. "What are you doing with this?"

"I bought it to read," she said. She looked baffled, but a smugness cropped up in her clipped tone.

"But didn't get around to it yet, right?"

"On the contrary." She barely moved her mouth when she spoke, as if conserving energy for an escape attempt. This and the way she sat, so stiffly that the orange plastic chair seemed to slouch beneath her, intimidated me.

She must have sensed my hesitation, because she relaxed slightly and said, "I don't want to sound presumptuous, but I'm confused. You say your intentions are political, yet your purpose seems to be to make sure I've read every book on my shelf. Exactly what kind of criminal are you?"

"I'm not a criminal and I'm not here to hurt you," I said, marveling at her prissy diction. Her speech was a parody of bourgeois academic arrogance, designed to make the student—or listener—feel removed and inferior. It was obviously a tactic, and a tired honky one. "I'm a member of the East Bay October Coalition, a splinter of the Marxist Workers Party, and I don't really care which books you've read."

"Thank goodness you're only a Marxist," she said. "For a moment I thought you were some kind of vigilante library scientist, going door to door. I was afraid you would have your work cut out for you down the hall."

"Why is that?" I asked. She did not seem quite at ease, but she didn't seem frightened either, and I wondered if I should have kept up the threat of physical harm, but violence has never really been my scene. Though I was hip to how valuable the Panthers were to the movement, I secretly agree with King that they were a hard group to back, considering they raped and murdered more people in a year than passed through our splinter.

Not that she seemed to think me capable of violence. The vibes I was putting out must have calmed her, as each minute I spent with her she grew more haughty and mocking.

"Once you leave this office, books become merely decorative. What is the quote from Schopenhauer?" she said. "'As a rule the purchase of books is mistaken for the appropriation of their contents.'"

"Not that anyone really reads Schopenhauer," I said, "which is just as well. The callow intellect worships him because he's curmudgeonly, but he's not really read these days, and not really worth reading."

"He produced some splendid aphorisms." She sat straight up to say this, and beamed. She seemed to have completely forgotten that five minutes before she'd thought I was some kind of sex offender, and had feared for her life. Suddenly I understood: this woman was lonely, stuck way out here with no one to talk the witty literary with, starved for what she thought of as "stimulating" conversation. Having done some time in factories where I had to endure endless conversations about things I had no interest in—conversational common denominators like meatloaf and pro hockey—I could relate.

This lady needed to talk, and once I realized this, my whole plan fell into place. All I had to do was let her wax pseudo-intellectual for a while, play along until she trusted me, and then, slowly, with the secret curves and straight lines of irrefutable party logic, I'd shape the conversation into something more useful, and get myself a ride out of here in the bargain.

"Exactly," I said, leaning forward, faking enthusiasm. "Exactly my point. He's an aphorist! A stand-up comic, not a thinker. Sententious wisecracker at an open-mike night."

"I suppose Marx is your idea of a thinker."

"My ideas are not needed to validate the purity of his thinking." This shut her up, but I wondered if I'd aimed too high. It had obviously been a while since she'd had a real conversation, and I wanted to be careful not to leave her behind. I knew from organizing that coming on too cerebral was a fateful mistake. "Back to you: you've read all these books?"

"Goodness, no." She actually laughed, but there was something authoritative in her laugh, a hint of that judgment with which parents approach the improbable questions of children. "Do you think I'd actually read an entire textbook entitled *Serving Their Needs: Implementing a Collegiate Community Among Lower Income Adult and Special Population Groups.*"

"So that one is a prop?"

"No one is completely without them. Back to you," she said, leaning forward. "Are you a member of the band?"

"I told you: I was."

"And do you have any trouble reconciling your political ideology with this brand of music you play?"

"Why should I?"

"Well, the Marxists I've known are not exactly . . ." She

hesitated, her eyes brightening beneath the yellow blaze of fluorescent light. "How to put this," she said, drawing it out for effect. "Not exactly fun-loving."

"Lots of Marxists around here, I guess."

Another flicker in her eyes, as if she welcomed such obvious irony.

"I'm not originally *from* here."

I told her that I didn't think she was. I did not tell her it was clear that she was here by default; that some huge failure had exiled her to this place, with its shaggers and shelves of unread books.

"Mr. Register is under the impression that your band is about to perform in exchange for some automotive repairs."

"That's up to them. I told you, I'm no longer with the band."

"Then you *could not* reconcile your ideology with the music?"

I thought of the night before in Wilmington, the sudden stillness of the audience when I mentioned the Ten, King coming in smooth on the hit from his Uncle Tom past.

"I don't want to sound impertinent, but I'm wondering just how you ever reconciled the two in the first place."

I was getting annoyed: at the rate and timbre of this exchange, at what seemed her sudden upper hand. I tried to ignore her, but this last question reached me because of what happened back in San Francisco, my situation with the party. It was hard enough to defend myself against their charges of frivolity while gigging with funk outfits; it was impossible now that I had become a lead guitarist in a beach music band. To the party, what I did for a living was inconsistent if not counterrevolutionary. Officially they brought me up on charges of racism, citing the fact that I had turned down a job with a black-owned manufacturing firm in West Oakland, and rather than suffer the humiliation of defending myself I accepted King's offer. What could I possibly have said in defense? I've seen people expelled for being physically attractive, charged with "superficiality" and sent packing. I did turn down the Oakland job, but it had nothing to do with race and everything to do with the fact that playing music I could make seventy-five bucks a night for a four-hour set, most of which of course went straight back into the party as dues and the rest of which paid my tuition and rent, which I never could have afforded on $2.65 an hour and I know it's counterrevolutionary to concern myself with money, but what was I supposed to do? Call up my capitalist dad and beg a loan? Like he'd even take a call from his Commie son. I had no intention of moving into another one-bedroom apartment collective with six other comrades and staying up all night for "struggle sessions" discussing the same things we'd stayed up the night before discussing, and getting into spats over whose turn it was to do the dishes and who was sleeping with whom and slimming down to tendon and bone on brown rice and steamed peapods. I'd seen twice as many comrades leave the party over whose turn it was to swab the john than over ideological rifts. Sartre said it best: "Revolution is seeing each other a lot."

Her question brought back all this baggage I'd not thought of since I'd met Janice and left Oakland. I studied her: she squared her mouth in a prim, slightly smarmy smile. At first I thought she resembled a psychiatrist, but the more I looked at her, the more she reminded me of what led me to join the party in the first place: loneliness. I wanted to respond to people on a serious level, to be with people who shared more than a taste in music or surfboards or beer. It was an emotional thing, and contrary to bourgeois misconceptions about humorless automaton Marxists, there is always a deeply emotional—and spiritual—core to radicalization. Never in my life have I felt more alive than when I joined the party. I wanted this lady, who was obviously as lonely as I had been, to know that, but I wasn't sure how to tell her without explaining all I had been through with the party lately, and I had neither the time nor the inclination to bare my soul.

She had me fixed with her shrink gaze, feigning patience while I drifted.

"People need money," I said, which was both a lie and the truth: people don't need money, at least not as much as they think they need, yet she'd asked me how I squared music and politics, and I'd always rationalized it by pointing out how much more dough the party gained from my gigs. She was smiling again, as if she saw through me, and I scrambled for the upper hand.

"Back to you," I said. "Surely you can relate, or you would be in a place where books are read, right?"

"An ideology brought me here. One similar in some ways to yours, in fact, though much less rigid. But heavens, what am I saying? I still haven't nailed 'yours' down yet, and how rigid could it be if it allows you to travel with a beach music outfit?"

"We don't play beach music," I said, spitting the word beach back at her.

She perked up at this. "Then Mr. Register is either mistaken or lying."

"Mr. Register is a fool."

She shifted in her chair, and the flash of bright orange plastic startled me. "Your politics might be murky, but you seem to be a sharp judge of character. Mr. Register most certainly is a fool."

I was so pissed at her reference to my "murky" politics I almost missed what she said—and how she said it. Alerted by her tone, I detected in her words something I could use.

"You work closely with Mr. Register?"

"Too closely," she said, "although I must say that the

term work must be used loosely when applied to Mr. Register."

"He's a beach music fanatic," I said, and she shrugged
and claimed to know nothing of his personal life. I asked
her what they both did at the institute and she told me
what I wanted to hear, that they were co-directors of the
evening study program, and essentially ran the place at
night. Eager to talk, she explained in too much detail her
theories of education, which were a muddle of innova-
tion and boilerplate liberal cant. As she put it, she had
"dedicated herself to equipping the have-nots with the
minimum skills necessary to their economic survival."
Though I was bored, I listened politely, keeping a tab on
what might be of use: her attitude toward the proletariat,
for instance. She seemed at once to hold them in con-
tempt and think them noble and pure. Right away I understood that, like most of my comrades, she'd rather talk
about than *to* them.

"What kind of jobs are waiting for these students when
they graduate?"

"This is a vocational and technical institute," she said, a
bit defensively. "A high percentage of our graduates find
work in their field of study: Auto Mechanics, Heating and
Air Conditioning, Cosmetology, Electrical Work. Those
who don't often are employed with local service industries
or drift into semi-skilled jobs with local manufacturing
concerns—there are several textile plants in the area and a
large pork processing plant."

"So you're teaching them to slaughter hogs?"

She tensed. "Employment opportunities are limited in
rural areas such as this one, Mr. . . ." She held this constipat-
ed look on her face until I told her my name, wondering as
soon as I spoke if I should have used a pseudonym. She in-
troduced herself as Nancy McFadden, asked that I call her
Nancy and picked up her tired lecture. "I can't be expected

to be both an educational administrator and an employment counselor. Of course it upsets me to learn that students aren't able to make use of their training, but you have to understand how provincial the residents of this area are, Mr. Reed. They would rather stay home and slaughter hogs, as you put it, than move to Raleigh and make four times as much in the field they've been trained for."

I was about to interrupt her to make my point—that her "ideology" was futile if students were corralled back into capitalistic enslavement—when she said something which showed me my shortcut out of town.

"Of course it doesn't matter now that I no longer work here."

"You no longer work here?"

"Surely I would not have time to sit around and explain my educational philosophies to a complete stranger—and one whose presence in my office is still rather a mystery I might add—if I were still 'on the clock,' as Mr. Register so mundanely puts it. I've had to adapt to the lax ways around here but I've never succumbed to them."

"If you're no longer on the clock, what are you doing here?" I asked, and what she told me next allowed everything to fall into place. She explained how she'd been working away when she'd seen me and Janice on the shoulder (she didn't mention the kiss, but I'm sure that's what drew her attention, sure it offended her lily-white sensibilities) and how a little later she'd heard a commotion in the hall and had come out to find Mr. Register turning out classes. She described how he had humiliated her in front of the students when she'd tried to stop him from putting on this concert, how it was in fact turning out to be a positive experience as it had led her to an understanding of her misguided idealism. But now it was over, and she was too exhausted to allow herself to indulge in regret or ill will. She was leaving here tonight, and would never return. I will not die here, she said, and the histrionic way she held herself when she said this, as if she were the lead in the community theater production and had arrived at the denouement, made me want to laugh.

But if there ever was a time not to seem frivolous it was then, as I had found our common goal: to stop Little Cedrick and the Royals from performing. And though at the time I was tempted to get up and walk out, I knew I could not leave until I had turned Little Cedrick back into King. Oh, I could have rationalized bolting if I'd tried hard enough; as a matter of fact a quote from Stalin comes easily to mind—something about the validity of selling out one's country for the larger good of the worldwide struggle. But I liked King, and I wanted King to like me. The notion that one person can have responsibility for another rather than the collective is dangerously bourgeois, but I was King's Judas, and we both knew it.

Looking out the window, I saw Ronald talking to Mr. Register on the shoulder of the road, and I realized I had to act quickly.

"Not only is Register a fool, but he epitomizes everything I am against in this world," I said. "From what little I've seen of you two, I'll bet you differ in the old ideology area as well."

"Mr. Register has no ideology to speak of. Oh, in meetings he's capable of spouting off an assemblage of educational clichés. If I had to summarize what passes for his ideology, however, I would quote the motto of this supposedly progressive state, which in the original reads, 'Esse Quam Videri.' Shall I translate?"

"You better. I've never bought that ethnocentric hype about Classical education. Seems to me that time spent learning the dead languages of imperialist, white supremacist civilizations would be better devoted to cataloging the atrocities performed by them against the Third World."

"In other words, you opted for Civics in high school rather than tackle Latin. 'To Be Rather Than to Seem.' This is the phrase which appears on the garish state seal, yet Mr. Register's ideology, as I understand it, is the antithesis. Appearance over Reality would, I believe, be its translation into pop terms."

"And I suppose you are an example of someone infinitely in touch with the objective reality."

"Oh no," she said, shaking her head and feigning a laugh. "You'll not drag me into that futile debate. I don't have the time or the energy to open that can of worms, especially with someone of your so-called convictions. In fact, I really don't know why I'm lingering here now that I know you're not going to hurt me. And I have to admit, Mr. Reed, that it was apparent to me almost immediately that you were troubled yet harmless. You seem incapable of violence. You couldn't hurt a flea, as they say around here, and especially not in that outfit."

Suddenly I was aware of my French cuffs and bell-bottoms. Polyester chafed my skin and my feet felt cramped and pinched in pointy-toed confinement. Polite conversation was not getting me anywhere. I knew that action was needed, but what I failed to realize in that irrational moment was that ideology without structure leads to anarchy, and anarchy to fascism.

Looking past her, I noticed that the blinds were open, that we were visible to anyone outside. Ronald and Register were gone. I walked over to the window, lowered the blind, crossed the room to her desk, jerked the thin directory from beneath the telephone, slammed the phone down on the desk. The ring echoed in the dead office air and she stiffened.

"Get me the number of the local newspaper," I said, flinging the phone book in her lap.

She looked as if she regretted calling me harmless, which was what I wanted her to feel, but her words were pitched in the same stiff, smart-assed tone. "There is something which covers this county, but I wouldn't go as far as to call it a newspaper. A circular perhaps. Grocery store ads and columns listing last week's sick or shut-in."

"Just give me the number," I said.

"This is all wonderfully romantic, but unless you've news of a wreck or a silver wedding anniversary, I doubt you'll garner much . . ."

"Give me the motherfucking number," I said, slamming the phone onto the desk again. The word worked its magic, as usual. She flinched, flipped through the pages, found the number, recited it without looking up.

A man answered. I asked to speak to the editor. The man said in a voice both slow and bothered, "Call back in the morning."

"This is important," I said.

"Miss your paper? Tell me where you live and I'll drop one by on my way home."

"The Sawyer Vocational-Technical Institute has been taken over by members of a radical Marxist organization. They're rumored to be armed and dangerous." I said this in a voice as unnaturally stiff as Nancy McFadden's, a counterpoint to the character of this character on the other end of the line. I was careful to choose clichés which would appeal to the most sensational instincts of the bourgeoisie, and to suggest a physical threat. Since I obviously wasn't too convincing in the flesh, I wanted to pull it off on the phone at least. The m.f. word had shut the lady up, but that smirk hovered in the corners of her mouth, suggesting she wasn't exactly terrified.

"Any hostages?"

"Let me speak to the editor," I said.

"Speaking. Jeffrey Timmons here. Not like we got a news staff. I write it, I typeset it, I sell the ads to pay for it, I roll it up and pop a rubber band round it and sometimes when one of my boys don't show I carry it right up on your porch for you."

"It's up against the wall motherfucker time out at the old Sawyer Vo-Tech," I said. Timmons didn't sound too alarmed either; he only asked my name.

"Never mind who I am. You should feel lucky that I've chosen you as my link to the outside world." The clichés kept coming, I was amazed how easily. Obviously the fallout from six weeks with the Little Cedrick Fat Capitalist Tour. "Listen closely and you'll definitely sell some papers tomorrow," I said, thinking that if I reduced it to money he would listen.

"Next Wednesday you mean. Hold on a minute, let me get a pen." The phone clanged dully on what sounded like a metal typing table. I cupped my hand over the mouthpiece and said, "Is this a morning or an afternoon paper."

"Wednesdays between the hours of 6 and 9 A.M.," she said. "Though he has been known to miss a Wednesday."

"Still there?" Mr. Timmons said. "Hold up a minute. First things first. What kind of weapons y'all got out there?"

"Weapons?"

"Didn't you say y'all were armed?"

"There's only one of us. And what does it matter what kind of weapon I have?"

"It'd help to know, see, because around here people know guns. That's the first thing they want to know in a situation like this. Plus, say you got an assault, I'd run that page one, double column."

"Today's Wednesday."

"Say what?"

She was trying not to look at me—a bad sign.

"Your paper just came out today?"

"Yes, sir. Matter of fact, you're lucky you reached me,

I'm usually out of here early on Wednesdays. I just came back by here to pick up my cigars."

"Look, Mr. Timmons, here's what I want you to do. As soon as I hang up, I want you to call the television stations in Raleigh, and the newspaper up there, and AP and UPI, and anyone else you can think of."

"I'd just soon not do that," he said. "You see, that'd be stupid, wouldn't it? I mean, in a business sense, for me to give away my scoop would not be smart. A newspaper is a business, you know. People around here think it's just a public service, they're all the time forgetting it takes money to print the damn thing. So it would be right stupid for me not to keep this piece for an exclusive."

"Until next Wednesday?"

"Be whole lot better for me to come out with it first, especially it happening in my own backyard."

"You mean you want me to stay here for a week?" I said, careful not to look at her.

"Well, I'd hate to ask you to stay put for that long. Why don't you just come back next Tuesday. Let me know when you're planning on taking over out there and I'll be ready to roll."

"This is fucking ridiculous," I said. I did glance at Miss McFadden then, and caught her trying to convert a smile into an unconvincing yawn. "You do what I say now or this woman's going to get hurt."

"Wait once," he said. "Calm down. You said a woman? Only woman administrator works out there at night's Miss McFadden."

I kept quiet. I hadn't meant to bring her into it, but on the other hand it felt thrilling to finally have broken through to the other side. I had just communicated a threat to the editor of a newspaper and knew that, whatever happened next, I could not back down.

"Oh hell. You must have read that letter of hers."

"What letter?"

"And I swear, the whole time I thought this was a joke. I never would have fed you that stuff about coming back next Tuesday if I'd of known you were serious. I hope that didn't tick you off too bad."

"There are ways for you to make up for it."

"This always happens," said Timmons. "Crackpots drawing crackpots. Give one their say and it opens the gates for a hundred more."

"I don't know what you're talking about."

"The mayor called up here asking me not to print her trash again. Said it would be bad for the town. Called her a subversive. I told him she had the right to say whatever the hell. And do you know what? He claimed that people don't quite understand such things, said somebody'd take it the wrong way and think Miss McFadden was making fun of us all, and that she was liable to get hurt."

"She is liable to get hurt if you don't listen," I said.

"I never would have figured him to get involved in something like this," said Timmons. "I never have liked the man, I didn't vote for him, but I didn't figure him for something this damn stupid. You must owe him money, right? Now he's got you working off a debt by calling me up, acting like some kind of crackpot terrorist. Trying to scare me from printing her letters, right?"

I cupped the receiver and said, "You didn't happen to write a letter to the editor, did you?"

"Y'all better leave that woman alone," said Timmons before she could answer. "She's been spouting off about things ever since she came down here, and so far as I know she's not changed a mind. I give her the space because it makes her feel good and God knows she needs to get some feel-good from somewhere, since she sure doesn't get it out there at the institute."

"What do you mean?"

"Well, according to Mitch Register, she's a joke to everybody out there. She's got all these progressive ideas about a no-frills basic education for the working class, always talking about the rights of workers, blue collar this and that. But nobody pays her any mind."

"I see."

"Ask me, she'd done a lot more for the institute than they want to acknowledge. Just in terms of her educational philosophy, seems like she's got her head on about providing people with the kind of schooling that will make them competitive. Thing is, she doesn't know how to talk to people. She's all *stiff,* you know what I mean? And those people out there, hell, they don't want to think of themselves as 'blue collar.' She gets up in front of 'em on Careers Day and starts in about workers' rights and there isn't a soul in the gymnatorium who don't see themselves as middle-class. Working class is all those that don't attend Sawyer Vo-Tech to get an associate degree in Heating Refrigeration. It's everybody *beneath* them. You still there?"

I was, very much, and told him so.

"Despite the fact that hardly anybody listens to her, I still believe she's done more good out there than harm. For one thing she's tough—ask any of the teachers out there, who hate her because when she was working on getting that place accredited she made them all go back to school and take a couple courses. Man, they hated that—had to *do* some homework instead of give it. No, she means business, and without her I don't believe the institute would have even gotten accredited. The administration out there— well, you know how it is around here, know how it gets when people start hiring their in-laws and double first cousins. You're from around here, right?"

"California."

"California? Well how'd you ever happen to get up with the mayor?"

I hesitated, thinking of the various identities I'd assumed over the last few hours—bass player in a beach music band, terrorist/abductor and now, flunky for some cracker mayor. But—and I know how trite this sounds—we have to play some kind of role to get what we want. To seem rather than to be: it had become as much my motto as Mr. Register's.

I should have hung up then, but I wanted to hear more about this letter.

"Never mind how I know him. You don't think she meant to make fun with her letter?"

"Meant to?" said Timmons. "Doubt it. She did come off sounding that way in places. I saw what she was trying to say, and with all the rest of the letters of hers I've run, the no to a nuclear incinerator ones and national health care and woman's right to choose and quit spraying soybeans with pesticide, all those—I heard something in it I thought people needed to hear. When it comes to letters I don't have to necessarily agree, now. You'll notice I run a little disclaimer stating the views of the letter writer don't reflect the views of paper. That doesn't mean I haven't had people call me up to tell me off after I've run one—especially the abortion ones. I lost right many subscribers over that letter."

"But you'd run it again?"

"Oh hell yes. Wasn't anything but the flip side of the coin. I give the Scripture quoters a couple of column inches a week—you'd be surprised the things people can quote the Bible over. Here I run one letter in a decade disagreeing and they up and cancel in droves, claim this paper's gone to the devil like the rest of the world. No, but it's good for people to hear what she's got to say. Like today—I didn't agree with her, but I saw what she was saying, and figured it wouldn't hurt to print the thing. There *was* some logic in it: to me what she was basically saying was that the world's guilty of prettying things up too much, that around here we don't want to see ourselves as we are. Spend too much time and money on cosmetics: parades and decorations and planters to put in front of the courthouse while half the people in Johnsontown are still using outhouses."

"You don't agree with that?"

"Of course. But to me she chose the wrong vehicle to make her point, because when she started talking about that movie, using it as a comparison, well it seemed to me like apples and oranges. I mean, it was just a *movie*—it's not *real*. People don't go to movies to get all depressed and think about the poor."

Mr. Timmons chuckled. "They read my paper to get that stuff."

"So movies are supposed to make you feel good?"

Long silence. "You sure you're a friend of the mayor's?"

"I'm just trying to figure out what she was trying to say in her letter," I said, a little too quickly.

"Why don't you ask her?" he said. "You holding her at gunpoint, right?"

"The lines of communication are not exactly open between us," I said, watching her shoulders for signs. They held, mannequin stiff, her half-smile similarly frozen across her face.

Timmons laughed. "She does kind of speak a different language, I'll grant you that. Writes in one too. I'd love to get in there and edit her stuff down some, but it's too intimidating. Be like clearing out a patch of kudzu. Where would you start? She can damn sure get behind a sentence, though. Good God almighty. Reminds me of the Henry James I read in college. You ever read any Henry James?"

"Of course," I said.

"Now I know damn well you aren't a friend of the mayor's. Which must mean you were telling the truth. I have to say I still didn't believe you were a real terrorist. I mean, I still thought you were some trusty from the county jail working off a drunk driving charge in turn for a little favor from our law-abiding mayor. Here I'm spouting off about movies and Henry James and you really are holding a gun on that woman?"

"I've never held a gun in my life," I said. "Back to the movie. You didn't agree with her opinion?"

A few beats of silence and he started up again. "Like I said, a movie, to me it's not real. It's a story, and what I want is to come out of there feeling good. But Miss McFadden, see, she obviously wants something else from her movies—or, she calls them films. And she got all bent out of shape about how they prettied up the swamp. Took it as some kind of symbol, said Hollywood was making fun of us by not showing the swamp like it is, filled with snakes and ticks and no-see-ums. It gets so dark in there you can't see the bow of your boat in daylight, and it just seems natural to me that they'd wait until the light was just right—golden hour they called it, way late in the day—to start shooting. But she didn't even think *that* was right. Doesn't fit with her idea of what's real."

"So let me get this straight: you agree in principle, but feel her using the movie to make her point detracted from her agreement?"

Five seconds of silence. "You read the letter. You saw the movie. What do you think?"

I stammered. Watched her watch me. Felt a fraudulence which extended well beyond being put on the spot with his question. And as he waited for an answer, I felt as if I was being challenged for a lot of other things I claimed to know without ever having experienced.

"She's got a point about the golden hour," I said.

"How do you mean?"

"It's hard to trust what it does to you. The light is—well, it's like the light sometimes in California. The way it back-lights things, turns them into symbols and icons when they're really only buildings and trees."

"Well if you agree with her, why are you holding her hostage?"

"I'm not," I said.

"So you're saying this is a crank call?"

"I guess so," I said, glad to have a name for it.

"Well it's the damn strangest one I've ever gotten. Most people know whether it's a crank call they're making or a real one. I mean most people don't call up the drugstore and ask if they got Prince Albert in a can, then say, 'Just kidding, I know y'all can't really let him out so I take it back.'"

I was watching her watch me, wondering if things had really deteriorated to the point where I could not even make a convincing crank call.

"Still there?"

"Yeah."

"Must be something in the wind today, second crank call I've gotten. Both from the institute, too. Somebody called up while ago, said for me to send a photographer out there because some band was getting ready to play a surprise concert. Said it was some big-time group from the sixties, but I never heard of them. Beach music. Hold up here, I got it written down somewhere. Oh yeah: Little Cedrick and the Royals. Ever heard of 'em?"

"No," I said. "Don't know a thing about beach music."

"That's right, I forgot you come from California," said Timmons. And he laughed in a weary way that made me see him as a good-hearted skeptic before he hung up the phone.

I held onto my end for a moment, listening to the dial tone, before I laid it softly down in its cradle and looked over at her.

"Quite an expansive conversation for a terrorist," she said.

"You're free to leave."

"Thank you, but since this is my office, I'd rather you leave."

"Of course," I said. I turned to look outside at the bus, trying to think of a way to get back on. I could promise the band the remainder of my wages, make some kind of sniveling deal. But I saw only the blind slats slightly yellowed by the fluorescence, and it occurred to me that the bus was probably long gone by now.

As this thought occurred to me, I regretted it, pushed it away: I was thinking like the guitarist in a beach music band instead of a revolutionary. I was through with the Royals, and I still owed King much less than I owed the party. The bus may have been gone but my ride was still there.

I turned to ask her for a lift into town, but as soon as I laid eyes on her I sensed the change. She had gone rigid again, and I knew before she even spoke that she had decided to hold me to the laws of senile society.

"I could press charges," she said. I thought of what they'd try to pin on me: trespassing, communicating threats, maybe even assault and battery. No jury, after learning of my politics and my black girlfriend (and I was sure Register would be happy to testify about our public display of affection) would let me off with less than ten to twenty, especially down there. I imagined being stuck in some Southern jail, recalled every horrific detail I'd stockpiled about the Dixie brand of justice: Bull Connor's firehose and attack dog tactics, midnight lynchings, voter-registration workers run off the night roads by carloads of beer-fueled rednecks. I would never walk away from this; there was no sense in trying.

"Maybe we could cut some kind of deal."

"I'm not inclined to negotiate with people who break into my office and act as if they plan to abduct me."

"The door was open and you said yourself you didn't think I could hurt a flea. Did I lay a hand on you?"

"A hand, yes."

"That was only to keep you from screaming. But I won't waste time apologizing. I did what I had to do to get what I wanted."

"Whatever that is."

"Actually, neither of us have accomplished much if you stop to think of it. In a few minutes, Little Cedrick and the Royals are going to take the stage. Not only will Register have succeeded in putting you out of the picture, but he'll have staged a coup in the name of white supremacy and the doomed-repeated past, and all your years of work will be wiped out overnight."

"As they say around here, Mr. Register will get his."

"Pretty lax attitude from someone who loves a good fight."

"It's been a long day, Mr. Reed. And a long, futile stint here. I'm tired of the fight."

"So you're giving up?"

She shrugged and said, "Call it what you want. Perhaps what I am about to do is similar to your deserting your party to travel across the country with a beach music band. And while we're on the subject, I'm still unclear about why *you* don't want this band to perform."

Because I saw no way to win her over without telling the truth, I told the truth: how I happened to leave the party, the frivolity and racism charges, my fears about traveling down South with Janice and King's retro Uncle Tomish answer to them. I told her about Wilmington, how interrupting the concert to mention the Ten had started all this, and how I was glad I had spoken up, because it showed me that with or without the party, whether living in a filthy collective and sitting through endless struggle sessions or crossing the country in a broken-down bus, my commitment was manifest. The more I told her the better—the less frivolous—I felt. I explained to her about King, how I sold him out, how he had succeeded in doing something which I aspired to do myself: reinvent himself. King's music, I realized as I spoke, was like my politics, and he was true to the song in the way that was dignified and constant. He had taught me a lot about judgment, about the dangers of reducing everything I came up against to a pat formula of economics and allegiance.

"What about the woman?" she asked.

"What woman?"

"Your girlfriend. You hardly mentioned her except to tell me how much you feared traveling with her down South."

"Strange things happen when you are on tour," I said, aware that I was resorting to the flabby clichés of rock stars who blame all their indulgences on "the road." "It's a desperate life, and people react unpredictably under the pressure of bad food, no sleep, and nightly gigs in shitty bars."

"So it was only a convenience? You were never serious about her?"

"We had our problems, like any other couple," I said. And it was only then that I realized this was true. The thing that I liked the most about Janice was that by hooking up with her I was subverting taboos, and I think she saw me as a distraction from the boredom of the tour. But sooner or later we would have split, and our breakup would have less to do with culture and race than with the fact that we really didn't have much to talk about. I went to the window and pulled back a blind slat. It was dark out, but the bus was still there.

"Well, it's over now," I said. "The sun's almost down and things will return to total darkness unless we get off our asses and do something about it."

"Something tells me I'm in store for more party rhetoric."

"This has as much to do with you as it does me. Both of

us. You know that if you let Mr. Register have his way you'll never be able to forgive yourself. And if I sell King out, I might as well move to Myrtle Beach and start my own beach music band."

"I suppose you want to call Timmons back and tell him you've changed your mind again. Forgive me for interfering, but I don't think he'll take you too seriously this time."

"No, I doubt he would," I said. "But I'm not going to act this time, I'm going to *do*. It's time to be rather than to seem."

"Spoken like a true Tar Heel," she said, "but what is it you're planning to do to stop them?"

"Nothing I can accomplish alone. I need help. A comrade."

"A few minutes ago I was talking of bringing charges against you. Now you're suggesting I collaborate with you on a plan which no doubt will involve charges against both of us."

"I couldn't hurt a flea," I said. "Violence is not my thing, and besides, considering your years of spotless service to the community, if there were any charges, they'd never stick. Remember Patty Hearst? Your lawyer would claim that I'd brainwashed you, you'd get up on the stand and claim to have forgotten everything from the point that I . . ."

"And risk perjury?"

"Okay, forget it. Walk out right now and leave Mr. Register in charge. In a week's time he'll be offering shagging courses. You can enroll and reinvent yourself as a professional shagger."

That feisty gleam returned to her eyes, and seventeen years of professional and emotional frustration melted away in a second. "I'd rather go out as Patty Hearst than come back as a shagger."

"Let's get started, then. We don't have much time to act."

"No acting," she said, standing up. "No seeming. Only

being." She delivered her hokey slogan so sincerely that I was moved to turn my frivolous first reaction—a stifled grin—into a genuine smile as my little grey panther and I went about planning our revolution.

Mitchell Register

There's a whole lot I'll never be able to figure out—how that Reed boy ever got up with her for one thing, and what in the world he said to make her give up all she'd worked her entire adult life for. It's one of the saddest incidents I have ever witnessed and one of the most aggravating, and in at least one way it's changed me forever: now I see you can't ever really know another, and that if somebody as tight-assed and predictable as Fancy can one day up and go off like that, we're all time bombs ticking. What happened out there that night made me nervous for my own I guess you would call it mental stability, though I swear, if I'm going to snap I hope I don't do it at work.

Lot of them around here don't think what she did had a thing to do with the institute, though. They believe it was all about sex. Underneath all the hair, that boy wasn't bad looking and when he appeared in court with a shave and a trim people stopped talking and started whispering. It would of killed her to know people were thinking she did it because she was love-starved. But I have to say, and your psychology will back me up on this, there is usually a sexual element to people's bizarre behavior.

Fancy had to have been right lonely, and when her lawyer started comparing her to Patty Hearst, people around here ate it up; Patty Hearst went off with that slime because she wanted a walk on the wild side but didn't want to take responsibility for it, they said. In other words, she was *pretending* to be brainwashed. Same with Fancy; some of them said she was tired of who she was and wanted a fling, but didn't want to pay for it. How anyone could brainwash that woman in an hour is beyond me; took me years to get her to change her mind about how to implement a fire drill.

I haven't told a soul this, but I couldn't help but feel like she did it to get back at me. I believe it was a cry for help, like the judge said, but there was also a little bit of tug-of-war to it, an attempt to stop me from bringing a little sunshine to our students. Course who it *really* hurt was the students more than me, and that is the saddest part of all.

But I'll have to admit that even while that whole mess was taking place I had the feeling that by letting Little Cedrick perform, I was in for more than a concert. When I went back to the bus to tell the band all they had to do was bring their instruments, rest was ready (Mike Harmon who teaches Electronics had rigged up a little light show, and damn if those biddies from Flower Arrangement hadn't pitched in and decorated the stage like a fresh grave) I was thinking about how Fancy kept too tight a lid on that place. You had to go through a triplicate set of carbon-copied forms before you could move the piano from one end of the snack bar to the other. I don't want to sound sacrilegious, but it was like Cedrick had turned up to right my wrongs of the past seventeen years, point me toward a new life.

The door split open after I knocked on it awhile, and this older black fellow pushed his face through the crack.

"You come to fix the bus?"

I was too shocked to talk at first, thinking "Here's Cedrick!" But of course he wouldn't answer the door of his own tour bus, and besides it didn't look like him—too skinny—though the guy looked familiar. About my age, salt sprinkling his stubby afro. Right then his name came to me: Ronald Little, bass player on Cedrick's last two tours.

"Ronald Little, I'll be damned. Didn't know you were back with L.C."

But Ronald didn't seem like he cared one way or the other about me recognizing him. "You come to fix the bus?"

"Me? Naw, I'm a way-back fan," I said. "Last time I saw you was in Raleigh in '72. Y'all played three nights at Johnny Goodnight's and I was there for every show." I went on to lay out everything I knew about him: who he'd played with before he joined up with Cedrick, how many Royal albums he'd played on. I knew more about his professional career than his mama, but he still didn't seem too impressed.

"No show tonight, King said tell you."

There were trucks passing by on the highway, and even though I heard him, I leaned over and acted like I hadn't. "Say what now?"

"That boy you made your deal with? Skinny dude with long hair? He might of cut some deal with you but he neglected to check it out with King. Now he's gone. Took off out of here on foot. We won't going to play before, and we damn sure ain't going to play now."

When I asked him how come, he said, "Told you we don't have nobody on guitar."

Long as King's singing I don't even hear the rest of the band, I felt like saying. I didn't want to insult the man, but see, Ronald Little always was a weak link. "How you planning on getting your bus fixed, then?"

"Same as before," said Ronald. "Only now we're depending on the support of way-back fans. King'll be glad to give you an autograph. You can even get your picture made with him if you want. Something you can take home and frame: you standing upside a living legend."

"Naw," I said. "That won't do. I meant, I'd love to have my picture taken with Cedrick if y'all got time after the concert, but the thing is this isn't just for me. What I'm trying to do, Ronald, I'm trying to help y'all out here. Increase your audience. This is an educational institution, and tonight I'm going to educate those students who don't know a thing about real music. I'm going give them a history lesson. Beach music started up down here, and it's something local about their heritage they need to know."

Ronald Little was shaking his head. "Beach? King hasn't played beach music in ten years. Cisco didn't tell you King play funk now?"

"You mean that hippie?"

"Damn Communist is what he is."

I stepped forward. "Say he's a Commie?"

"Oh yeah," said Ronald. "All the time talking that down-with-fat-capitalist-pig, power-to-the-people stuff. I bet he got a card he carries in his wallet like a driver license say he's one. Man, they got all kinds of 'em like that out in Oakland, though. It'll blow your mind how many kinds of Communists they is out there. Don't got too many around here, I bet."

"None that nobody knows about," I said.

"I guess there's one just about everywhere now," said Ronald. He lit a cigarette, opened the door some, took a seat on the top step.

"Yeah, and it don't take but one if you think about it."

"Damn sure don't," said Ronald. "Won't but one of Hitler."

"People like to forget the past, though, don't they?"

"Lot of it I want to forget."

"You must of had some damn good times back in those first Royals days."

"Oh yeah," said Ronald, his snort leaking smoke. "Get-

ting turned out of motels and restaurants. Sleeping in the
van side the road. Promoters was all the time stiffing our
asses, won't thing we could do about it. One time right
down the road here, believe it was Kinston, North Carolina, there was a robbery committed while we was playing.
Cops come hauled us off stage in the middle of a song, put
us in a lineup. See, people love you when you're singing
and playing, but as soon as you stop you better get your ass
back over to colored town fast."

I hate to hear a grown man whine. Especially someone like
Ronald Little, who nobody wouldn't have ever heard of if it
hadn't of been for King picking him up out of some fourth-
rate soul combo, making him famous and probably rich.

"Look here, Ronald," I said, mostly to shut him up,
though I made it sound like I was looking out for him.
"Tell you what I'm going do. I'll pay y'all whatever your fee
usually runs for a night's work plus get your bus back on the
road. What do y'all usually take home for a gig?"

"Couldn't say right off," said Ronald. "King's the one
decides on a fee."

"Let me talk to L.C., then."

Ronald held up the lit end of his cigarette, studied it
wearily.

"How else y'all going to get out of here tonight? Isn't a
mechanic on duty now anywhere around here."

There wasn't any way I was going back in there and tell
them, "Concert's off, get back in class." Not after the way I
stood down Fancy. Hell, I'd never hear the end of it from
her. I'd have to take early retirement, spend the next twenty
years selling cars.

Finally Ronald said, "Wait right here," tossed his smoke
over my head and was gone. I waited a few seconds before I
hoisted myself into the bus. It was dark, lit only by tiny map
lights above the seats where that black girl I seen the Communist hugging on and that other long-hair were stretched

out reading. Both looked up but neither of them said jack to me, just went back to their magazines like I wasn't worth studying.

I stood up front checking out the tour bus until Ronald came out of the back, motioned me down there. All of a sudden I got so nervous I could hardly walk. It was dark and cramped in the compartment, which made me even more nervous. I could make out this young thing slinked across the side of a waterbed like a skinny ridge of kicked-up sheets. When I came in she shifted and the bed squished and rolled and she gave me a look like I ought not to be coming in there.

The only light in the room was coming from one of those tee-tiny, battery-operated TV sets stuck up on a shelf. Little Cedrick was lying beside her. My eyes had to get used to him, but the way he stared back right wide-eyed made me think his eyes were used to me before I even stuck my head in there.

I said in a way-loud voice, "Mitch Register, Little Cedrick, I'm one of your biggest fans. Been following you for twenty years."

"You got to be tired, then," he said, and he and Ronald laughed.

"I'm serious," I said, and soon as I said it I felt like a fool. I got the hot-skin rash all over and I remembered how, so many times, I'd regretted being so serious about Little Cedrick, especially back in high school when all my friends worshiped either athletes, '55 Chevys, Sandra Dee or Elvis. None of them was as *obsessed* as I was, and my Little Cedrick thing got to be embarrassing. But still I kept up with it because hell, I believed the man had talent, and I loved his music.

He stared at me for a minute, then said, "Leave us alone, let me talk to my man here."

When the door shut tight behind them, I felt goofy

standing there talking to a man sprawled across a waterbed, so I crouched down like I was on the sidelines of a ball-game, getting ready to draw a game plan in the sand.

"I was a Royal Loyal," I said. "Vice president for three years. Remember Marlena Underwood? She was president when I was vice."

"That's been a long damn time," said Little Cedrick.

"Oh, I'm not saying it like you ought to remember me or anything."

"You look kind of familiar," said Little Cedrick, and for some reason he smiled.

"Put on a few pounds," I said, and out comes this kind of nervous laugh like haven't we all, but Cedrick didn't say a thing, and he quit smiling.

"You know that boy told you we'd play?"

"Ronald said he was a Communist."

"He don't really know what he is. Thing about it is, I like that boy," said Cedrick. "It'd be easier if I didn't."

He was rocking back and forth on the waterbed, his hands behind his back, staring up at the ceiling. "I figured he'd drop his politics once we left San Francisco. Figured it was just a act. But whenever he pulled that shit down in Wilmington, I saw what he was about. And even though he messed me up bad down there, I saw how come he had to do it."

"What'd he do?" I asked, even though I didn't really care.

"Turned the clock back on my ass is what. Looks like Cisco time's going to last awhile, too."

I didn't really want to hear about the troubles L.C. was having with his band. Like I said, he's the only one I cared about, hell, he could sing solo if it came down to it. "Sounds like y'all had a hard week. But classes'll be over here in about an hour and I want to make sure everybody gets to hear you play. Plus, as soon as you go onstage, soon-er I can get my man out here to fix the bus."

Cedrick shifted, rolling a waterbed wave my way. "Be a lot easier on all of us if you'd just take what cash you told Ronald you were going pay us with and call a mechanic."

I told Cedrick, said, damn, L.C., wish I could. I explained that this wasn't my own personal funds I was using. What it was, I was accountable to the institute. Said it wasn't just for me but for everybody out there.

And saying it made it true; it made me feel like I was representing the best interests of Sawyer Vo-Tech, made me proud of my job for the first time in years. To be honest, I got into education because it seemed like there won't a whole hell of a lot to it, but I always did care about the students, and I guess that's what has kept me going out here. They like me, see, and I don't see that it's a damn sin to be liked.

Here was something I could do for them that Fancy would consider a frill, an extra, the kind of thing would ruin them. But they needed it, and I told myself I'd make it happen for them no matter what it cost me.

"Like I said, been a long time since those Royal Loyal days," Cedrick said suddenly. I wasn't sure how to take it. Was he saying I wasn't loyal to him anymore, that if I was I would have forgotten about the concert and done anything he asked? I thought about it for a minute, then I figured he was right in a way, things had changed; I had responsibilities I didn't have back then. Back then all I had on my mind was Debbie and cold beer and getting my ass home without wrapping the car around a tree. Now I had an entire institute counting on me.

"That's true, things have changed," I said. "I'm still a Royal Loyal, but I told my people there'd be a concert, and I told them it'd be the best show they'd ever seen. Those people are counting on me. I've let them down before. Been letting them down for years, in fact."

For seconds after I finished talking, nothing in that room

moved. Then Cedrick said, "I was wrong. Ain't nothing changed."

"I don't get your meaning, L.C."

"Can't expect that to ever change. One set, my man. Thirty minutes. You can have this bus on the road in a hour?"

"You damn right I can," I told L.C. and I went off to see if I could.

The administration building was weekend empty; everybody was already out in the snack bar. As I hurried down the corridor humming an old Royals tune, all of a sudden I was back in my old room over on Park Avenue, the attic room with the A.C.C. pennants and the bookshelf/desk Daddy built from a kit and the twin beds with wagon wheel headboards I hated my friends to see but hated worse to part with and the Little Cedrick album covers stuck all across one wall. In there playing Royals forty-fives as loud as my little portable would go, singing into a white buck. Then, just as sudden, I was driving a car, Deb and me in her daddy's new Ford barreling down 701 on our way to Ocean Drive, an early Friday evening in June, three weeks after we graduated high school. On our way to see L.C. play and Deb had to close that night at the Dress Box and we were scared we were going to be late and all of a sudden the first three notes of "Baby, Play House with Me" came on the radio and the deejay announced he was going to play a whole half-hour of Royals in honor of their playing down at O.D. The sun was dropping behind the piney wood back of the fields, last blaze of it lighting the head-high corn and I smelled dirt and rain in the clouds to come, I smelled the heat stored up in the blacktop all day long and pesticide sprayed from crop dusters and in the sandy driveways of roadside shotguns little dizzy kids were playing crazy games with rules that changed every thirty seconds so you could goddamn win if you were *it* and I didn't have anywhere to be or anything to do until Monday when my job at the hardware store started for the summer and the weekend spread out before me like an afterlife. It was like I had died and gone to a heaven that looked exactly like the grand strand down at O.D.: free beer and good music and girl angels walking the beach in little clusters of skin and bikini string and guy angels goofy shy and talking all out of their heads up toward the dunes trying to act cool but sticking out like red neon devils. The next dirt road I saw I took, Deb and me and Little Cedrick and the lightning bugs together in that last quarter hour of backseat summer light. What Fancy and those best boys call the golden hour.

Then I was in college, standing in the basement of the house at the bitter end of one of our Hell Week parties for pledges and I could tell by everybody's sideburns that it was right around when everything starting getting goofy and serious and the sixties stopped being fun. Not that it mattered down there in the basement that night because we had all the leather couches stacked along the wall and were dancing in a row to the best of the Hot Damn Royals even though everybody else on campus was down at some coffeehouse drinking I guess coffee or sitting yoga-style in some dorm room smoking grass and nodding along to Purple Harum or the Electric Prunes, making posters for another march up to the Post Office and back. In this dream I could see everybody, but I just wanted to return to the party so I willed myself back down in the basement where things were just about to break—I believe this was the very night we run out of beer at five in the morning and raided the liquor cabinet across the court at the Deke house and a bunch of the pledges ended up chugging mouthwash in the court wearing only their boxers but I didn't get to finish that dream because when I came up on the door to Fancy's

office everything disappeared and there I was back in the
hallway again.

In front of her door, which was closed. Count on Fancy
to rain on my parade even when she's nowhere around. I
knew she wasn't there because her door was closed, and
Fancy is big on an open door. She never closed it, it was a
vital part of her educational philosophy. Of course leaving it
open was the same difference as if she deadbolted it in
terms of traffic in and out of there. Nobody visited Fancy
unless they had to; the woman has no talent for small talk,
she thinks it's a sin. Ask if it's hot enough for her and she
will look at you like you don't speak good English. I would
rather tell her to go to hell than to ask her how her weekend went and I swear I think she'd rather me insult her than
tell her have a nice day. For years she dropped hints about
me closing my door (she wanted to act like I'm in there
sniffing glue or getting it on with big Wanda, my secretary)
but you take a gregarious individual such as myself, if I
didn't close my door I would not accomplish half of what I
do in a day.

I was so put out with Fancy for interrupting my dream
that I stopped right in front of her door and just stood
there. It was like the ghost of Nancy had got away with me
and was keeping me from the snack bar, like when her old
leftover sourpuss spirit mind-read my idea of heaven and as-
certained that it included Beer and Bikini Clad Coeds and
smelled like Hawaiian Tropic Coconut Blend and rather
than the tired cloudbank and mist of most people's pictured
heaven there was sand packed by a parade of Vettes and
high-rise motels like a mountain range behind me and the
sound track featured not only half a dozen of the Royals
greatest hits but also cuts from The Dells and Jerry Butler,
Trammps, Embers, Platters, Drifters, Coasters, Chairmen of
the Board and Dee Dee Ford.

But hell, the woman killed my dream. I stood there getting madder and madder and I started to wonder what her idea of heaven was like and decided probably some city she talked about but hadn't really ever been too like Paris or Toronto. Art museums six to each block and a sound track by that guy she like to had a fit to get tickets to when he played Friends of the College last year—Yo Yo Ma? Or else Dave Brubeck, she's into jazz. The people in her heaven are dressed like missionaries, only skin showing is their ears. They are healthy skinny but look worse for wear than most sick fat people. They don't look at each other but from the neck up, as if all that counts in terms of body parts is ear eye nose and throat. There I was, still frozen in front of her door, when a boy from the Electronics class come tearing up the hall. "I've been looking for you all over," he said. "Where's the band at? You got a lot of people getting ill at you, Mitch. They're tired of waiting."

"Everything's all set up down there?" I asked him. "Lights and equipment and all?"

"*Been* set up."

"We're ready, then. Tell them to cut off those overheads, put on the houselights."

I led the band in through the kitchen, and was about to take them right up on the stage when Ronald stopped me, said they had to warm up some.

"Hope not for too long," I said. "Natives are restless."

"I guess we know how to tame 'em by now," Ronald Little said. Little Cedrick hadn't said a word since I'd gone to get him. On the bus I asked him would he mind honoring a special request for me and without looking at me he said he was fixing to. Took me a minute to understand—this concert *was* my special request. I didn't say a word about what all he was gaining in return, knowing how stars can be kind of touchy before a performance.

"Music soothes the savage beast," I said, and that stringy haired bass player said, "Funk ain't exactly what I'd call soothing," and the girls went to giggling and Cedrick gave them a look which shut them up quick. Then he turned to me and said, "You realize we ain't going to sound too swift with only one guitar."

I smiled, shrugged. Didn't want to hurt anybody's feelings by saying aloud how it would be fine with me if L.C. went on by himself.

"You got to roll with it has been my experience," I said as I left for the stage. "Got to learn to adapt."

It was so dark and crowded in the snack bar it took me a few minutes to push my way up to the front to where Debbie and Mussel and a crowd of them up from town were pressed against the stage. I'd had Wanda call home earlier to tell Deb to round up who she could from the old crew. Right off they started in on me—where in the hell had I been and what was taking so long and how in the world could I have gotten Little Cedrick and the Royals to play the institute snack bar on a Wednesday night and no cover too. Thank God the band chose that moment to come on stage and I did not have to explain all I'd been through that day.

It was all going to be worth it when Little Cedrick showed and when he did my crowd went wild, screaming. When L.C. opened his mouth, I was right back in the basement of the house, my brothers and I dancing in a drunk line to "Before We Were Three," and I was way down on it when I turned around and saw I was the only one dancing. Students were pointing and laughing and slapping each other's hands. I reached for Debbie's hand, got ready to show them some real moves—half of them didn't know a shag from a funky chicken—but Debbie hung back.

"I can't dance to that mess," she said.

"What?" I acted like I couldn't hear and kept right on moving, though Debbie and Mussel and them were standing there like they were listening to a political speech. Some of the students got into it, but the kind of shaking they were doing embarrassed even me.

Musselwhite came over, yelled into my ear, said, "Why don't he play his old material? I can't get behind that jive-ass stuff."

I told Mussel to relax, the man had to make a living, cut him some slack. No matter what he was singing it was still the same voice we'd worshiped twenty years ago, I said, and there we were hearing it again, live.

But all of a sudden we weren't hearing it. The lights switched off, the music stopped. Ronald Little banged on his drums for a few beats and those backup girls were stranded on a bridge of ooh and aah but after a few seconds even their echo faded and around me there was quiet and dark.

Somebody behind said, "That crew could not wire a doghouse," and I realized what must have happened: Harmon's boys screwed up with the juice and all those amps blew a fuse.

"Will Mike Harmon please approach the stage," I called out, and I felt my way through the crowd, anxious to reassure L.C. that it wouldn't take but a minute to plug things back in, when somebody way in back yelled out that the fire doors were locked, and this remark upset the crowd. People went to shoving and some girl up against the stage screamed holy hell and for a minute I let go and drifted blind helpless terrified, thinking I was just about to damn die in the snack bar of the Sawyer Vocational-Technical Institute, crushed to death at a Little Cedrick gig. The last part seemed okay—I'd dreamed of checking out to an L.C. tune—but I told myself I'd just be damned if I wanted to die at work, trampled to death by a bunch of wanna-be cosmetologists and some of the no-wiringest electricians ever to string a fuse box. Administration would remember me with a granite bench out in the crabgrassy courtyard be-

tween Buildings B and C, my name and the date of this day
from hell etched all blocky in the side and nobody would
ever sit on it except Larry Underwood, the groundskeeper,
who would be eating his lunch and smoking his generic
cigarettes on the shrine to the memory. That will not do, I
told myself, *I ain't about to die here,* and I just climbed right
over the people in front of me like they were sand dunes,
had scooted right up on the stage when that voice came
over the intercom.

Soon as he started talking the crowd settled down. Feedback gobbled up his first couple sentences but the voice
sounded familiar right off. As soon it came to me who it
was I knew I had to act, and I took off, waving my arms
around in the dark. I had not gone a foot before I tripped
over an amp and stretched out across the stage. Just laid
there listening to the Communist's voice flood the dark
room.

Wasn't any cause for alarm, he was saying; yes, the
doors were locked but only to ensure everybody heard
what it was he had to say. He identified himself as a member of the Marxist Worker's Party and claimed he'd taken
over the institute. He apologized for interrupting the concert but said his message was more relevant than any old
frivolous nostalgia trip down beach music lane. Then he
proceeded to get off on how beach music "represented the
most ignoble characteristics of a bourgeois white supremacist society," how its hits were "anthems of racist and classist oppression, modern day Camptown Races to the one."
Beach music, said this voice from above, "had forced its
performers into a perpetual pantomime of blackface min-
streldom."

"What about the Embers, they're white as I am," Musselwhite yelled out, but of course he couldn't hear and
wouldn't have known who the Embers were anyway.

On he went for a good five minutes about bourgeois society, white supremacy, classist patriarchal imperialist capitalist somethinganother before people got antsy, started pushing again. I figured I had to find L.C. quick, so I lifted myself up and started crawling across the stage, calling his name. The Communist kept right on but people had quit listening, and it felt like the room was building up to a boiling point. He was droning on like he had got hold of one of Fancy's letters to the editor and was reading it out loud, and as soon as I had this thought I collapsed on the floor. I realized the Communist must have had help getting into the vice president's office where the intercom is located, that somebody had to have shown him where it was and how to operate it. And how could he have known that the locksmith class had reversed the locks on all the doors in this building so that the only way to secure them was from the outside?

There wasn't but one Communist sympathizer that I knew of between here and Chapel Hill, and I felt so foolish for thinking I'd finally got rid of that woman that I let every bone in my body dissolve and I lay there waiting for the crowd to trample me or the bomb to go off, whichever, didn't matter to me, I had given up.

Minutes later when the lights blinked on and Mike Harmon growled over the intercom for us to stay calm, don't move, he had apprehended the suspect and was on his way to let us out, everybody in that room looked up to see me lying in a puddle up on the stage. I had my hands covering my head and my knees tucked up in almost a fetal position and if this was not one of the most embarrassing moments in my life when I opened my eyes and saw them all—students, colleagues, best friend in the world, wife of twenty-two years—staring at me. I tell you one thing, it will not be forgotten in my lifetime and who gives a damn if it's forgotten after I'm gone? That night I was theoretically the captain of the ship and instead of going down with the crew a lot of them in the audience perceived I jumped overboard with the women and children.

It wouldn't of looked so bad if I hadn't been the only one up on stage. Sometime during the blackout, one of the band members discovered he had a cigarette lighter on him and had managed to herd the band back into the pantry where they were holed up when Harmon made it to the fuse box. I jumped up the moment there was light, brushed the dirt off my blazer and ran to kiss Debbie, but I could tell I had shamed her by the way she drew quick and stiff out of my hug.

Mussel shook his head at me.

"What?" I said.

"Duck and cover, Big Mitch, duck and cover."

But I didn't have time for any of Mussel's mess because there was a commotion in the back of the room and since technically I was still in charge, I pushed through the crowd to see the doors open and a pack of Auto Mechanics students leading that Communist up toward the stage. They had his hands tied behind his back with what looked like an old timing belt and they were strutting cocky like they were bounty hunters out of a Clint Eastwood. Right behind them came Mike Harmon, and right alongside him—he had his hand on her collarbone, guiding her through the parting crowd—was Dr. Nancy McFadden.

As the crowd closed in, I motioned Mike over to the side of the stage where we could talk. Mike told me how he'd happened to catch them. He won't interested in any beach music concert, being a country western fan himself, so he'd gone out to see if he could help with the bus. Wasn't a thing wrong with that bus but it needed a new timing belt, looked like those boys had it under control, so he come on inside and was headed back to his classroom to piddle when the lights went off and this voice comes over the intercom. Harmon went right back outside to grab flashlights from the mechanics, rounded up a bunch of those boys to come with him and went to the fuse box, found the main for Building B had been switched off. Because he didn't know what kind of danger he was dealing with, he told those boys to wait in the hallway outside the vice prez's office and was just going to snoop around, check things out when Fancy came out in the hallway and stood there looking at him. Now in court, Harmon would testify that she didn't seem to recognize him right off, looked at him right glassy-eyed— but that's not how he told it to me. That night he said Fancy had just popped out and said, "He's not armed, Mr. Harmon. I'm sure he'll cooperate fully providing you don't overreact."

Harmon said he asked her did that Communist touch her and she laughed but didn't answer. He said at this point he got confused as to whether she'd finally lost it or something had been done to her and because he didn't know what else to do he asked her to come with him in the next office. Said Fancy didn't react one way or the other to him calling the law and when he asked her for the key to the snack bar she handed it over without any fuss.

All this would figure prominent in her trial. Was she so brainwashed she answered to anybody or did she figure Harmon had come to her aid? I can honestly say that I don't think anybody will ever know what really happened that night, and I doubt if Fancy herself understands what she went through. Whichever it was, her heart did not seem to be in playing the part of a Communist agitator, which I have to say this surprised me then and still does today. Seems like something she would of taken to.

"What about this Franklin? How'd you get him out of there?" I asked Harmon.

"He give himself up, Mitch. He must of heard us out in the hall there, come right out and surrendered. Told me he'd said about all he wanted to say over the air and then he turned to Miss McFadden and said, unless you think a filibuster is in order. One of the auto mechanics boys said he'd filibust his head open if he tried anything. Harmon said Fancy turned back to the Communist and told him she figured they had accomplished their initial objective and it appeared at that point he would not be permitted to continue his speech.

Harmon did relate this bit in court, and I have to say it didn't help Fancy much. Kind of made it sound like she was the one in charge, especially that bit about their initial objective.

"You don't think he drugged her?" I asked Harmon. I'd been sneaking looks at her: she seemed as calm as I'd ever seen her.

"Beats me, Mitch," he said. "But I tell you what. You better get them the hell out of this room. From the looks of it, we're going to have trouble."

The crowd had tightened around them and some of the students were trying to break bad, talking all kinds of trash to the suspects. Harmon called off his bounty hunters and we hustled the suspects up across the stage and down into the kitchen. The Royals looked surprised at the sight of that Communist. That gal I'd seen him hugging on earlier got right up in his face, said, "What, Franklin? Have you lost your mind?"

"It's a long story, Janice," he said.

"You a long story," said Ronald. "Too damn long. Take his ass to the jailhouse."

Then Little Cedrick spoke. I had about forgotten he was there. He was leaning against a sink in the corner, smoking a cigarette, that thin thing sucked up to his side like a blond barnacle.

"Didn't I tell you to watch yourself, Cisco?"

"The way I remember it, King, you told me that it wasn't any different down here."

"Way I remember is I told you to watch yourself everywhere." He turned to me and nodded at Fancy. "Who is this woman?"

Fancy watched me coldly while I explained who she was, said we had reason to believe she might of played a role in the takeover attempt.

"What'd you do to this woman, Cisco?" L.C. said.

"Used her, probably," the one called Janice said.

"Actually," said Nancy, "if the truth be known, we used each other. But using others is not a crime."

Everybody in that room stared at her like she wasn't real, except for me and Mike Harmon, who knew how real she was. "You know they getting ready to hang your ass, don't you, boy?" L.C. said to this boy called Franklin or Cisco. "What were you thinking?"

"That I've been your oppressor. And that you were right about Wilmington. I should have kept my mouth shut and let you continue to be King."

I wished to hell they'd all quit calling him King. I was scared he might just turn back into this King, forget all about his past.

"I did it for you, King. I felt responsible, like I'd painted you up in blackface and put you on stage to play the token Uncle Tom."

"I really don't see what you're apologizing for," said Fancy. "If anyone needs to hear a lecture about the Wilmington Ten, it's the very crowd you entertained last night."

She hasn't been drugged, I thought, or if she had it had wore off, because she was sounding like her old self again. She turned to Little Cedrick and asked him what exactly was wrong with this Franklin bringing up the Ten?

"Nothing for him," said L.C. "Only people didn't come to hear about all that. They paid their money for a concert, not a demonstration. Demonstrations are for free."

"But can't you effectively combine the two?"

"You might can. I damn sure can't. Not down here, anyway."

"I think you'll find that people around here are more amenable to social criticism than you might think. Not everyone thinks of the Wilmington Ten as agitators. There are a good number of us who sniffed the odor of injustice from the beginning."

"Well none of you injustice sniffers paid to hear me last night," said L.C. "And even if people did believe it was a frame, they wouldn't want to hear it out my mouth. Anybody in my band either. Every time Ronald here plays a bum note it's me gets blamed, see? So I got to be careful about what's said and done up on my stage."

"From what Mr. Register tells me, you have quite a loyal following. Surely you'll admit that such fame carries with it a certain responsibility."

I thought Cedrick was about to tell her off finally, but he spoke slow and gentle to her. "What kind of responsibility?"

"To say the right thing."

"Easy for you to say."

"No easier for me than you," Fancy said. "I have not your power."

"And I have not your skin," said Cedrick. If he was hot at her I couldn't tell it. He just seemed the kind of tired you can't ever catch up from, like he'd heard every word of this before. "I think you'll find that things have changed a bit since you left the South," Fancy was saying. "Of course there is still progress to be made, but your voice counts here more than it did."

"The hell," said Cedrick. "Didn't ever count more than when I was singing every night for drunk white boys down in Myrtle Beach."

"Wait once," I said. "Your voice still counts for this drunk white boy."

Even the Communist laughed when I said this; all of

them laughed except King and Fancy, who tossed me a sad little sideways glance and shook her head like I was hopeless.

"Law is on its way out here to pick these two up," I told Cedrick. "You got anything you want to tell this boy, better say it."

Cedrick asked to speak to the Communist alone. The two of them went back into the pantry and talked until Musselwhite busted in with the sheriff, a half-dozen deputies. I asked Mike Harmon to ride into town with the sheriff, fill him in on what had transpired while I stayed at the institute, took care of L.C. and them. When I turned back around I saw they had put Fancy in handcuffs.

"There's no need for that now, fellows," I said. "She didn't hurt anybody."

"It's regulations, Mitch," one of the deputies said.

"But we don't even really know if she *done* anything."

"Don't you?" she said, as if she were wanting me to think she had a hand in it. "I don't know why I should be presumed innocent now, since for the past seventeen years I've been presumed guilty of one thing or the other."

"Not that you spent a whole lot of time trying to clear your name," I said.

"Of what? Speaking my mind? Working for change?"

I did not want to be dragged into it with her, especially at that point and in front of an audience, but what it was, the woman made me crazy.

"There's ways to work for change and then there's ways to work for change."

"There you have it, the capitalist creed," said the Communist. "Lie down and be counted. Believe it and die." He turned to Little Cedrick. "You believe it, King?"

"I believe in playing music, Cisco. Wondering if down deep you don't believe in the very same thing."

They took them both away then, and I did not see Dr.

McFadden again until right at a year later, when I hired her part time to teach a couple of courses in our college transfer program. Oh, I saw her picture in the paper, but out of respect I never went to one minute of her trial. As if I could of gotten in anyway; that trial was one of the biggest things to ever happen in Trent, bigger than that movie they shot down in the swamp, which everybody completely forgot about when it never came out in video. The AP picked up the story and wired it all over hell and back, blowing it out all of proportion in the process. Out of respect for Dr. McFadden and for the good of the institute I declined to speak to the media. (I even refused calls from Jeff Timmons, because I believe him printing those letters egged her on and led to her let's call it a breakdown for lack of a better word. I see why he did it—he's got a lot of space to fill, and nothing much to fill it with—but still I fault the man for not seeing how her little letters would (a) impact upon the community and (b) give her a false sense of empowerment which psychologically speaking could of led to her crackup.) Course there were plenty around here willing to talk to the press, including my old buddy Musselwhite, whose role got bigger with each interview until he and Mike Harmon had to forcibly remove the Communist from the premises.

But all the exposure turned out to be good for L.C. Everywhere he went the whole sordid story was dragged out by the media, and as a result his new album went platinum and got all kinds of air play. He quit playing juke joints and podunk colleges and within six weeks was getting himself booked with the big dogs at outdoor festivals and coliseums. Right off he ditched that rent-a-wreck and bought Lou Rawls's old tour bus, which is got up like Las Vegas inside according to some pictures they had in a magazine. He fired his whole band except for that blond girlfriend of his who never really did much singing anyway and he married her. For a while there was a run of articles about him in the entertainment magazines and they always said the same damn things, how he'd been born again as a funk star after a moderately successful but long forgotten stint as a b-string beach music relic. Debbie clipped them all and would lay them out for me to read when I got home from work, but after two or three I lost interest. Every article cited Little Cedrick's (or King, as he kept right on calling himself) "date of rebirth" as that night he played the institute (or didn't play the institute) which that got away with me. L.C. never said much about what happened down here, though he did mention that since that incident he had not performed any of his old material nor had he accepted any bookings which attempted to link him to his beach music past. He wouldn't allow himself to be called Little Cedrick either. Wasn't that he had anything against his old stuff, he said, just that he'd grown out of it. (He made it sound like it was nursery rhymes he'd given up.) What happened down there that night didn't really have nothing to do with him, he told reporters—it was more a case of disgruntled employees taking out their frustrations—but it had got him to thinking about his past, seeing the present in a new way.

Dr. McFadden and Franklin Reed were brought up on a slew of charges but the most serious allegations were conspiracy and a safety violation they drew for locking the only fire exits on a couple hundred people. Reed was tried first, and at first it seemed like he was going to draw some serious time, since he was an avowed Communist and didn't care who knew it. But the fact that he was not armed, that he attempted to take over a technical institute without a weapon and wearing a sky blue Englebert Humperdinck uniform worked in his favor. It's hard for decent people to throw the book at a fool, and the way he would not shut up quoting a lot of dead revolutionaries actually helped him; none of the people in that jury box knew Karl Marx from

Groucho, and all that mouthing off just made him look more like a smart-ass rich kid who'd had a lot of down time to memorize stuff out of history books. The boy's daddy hired a lawyer out of Raleigh and it come out in the paper that his daddy was a wealthy orthodontist in San Diego and one thing about people around here, they are tolerant of the flings of the young. If you're young and rich, it's all that much easier to cop a plea or a prayer for judgment. Even if your jury is made up of factory workers or farmers, nine times out of ten they'll go easier on a youth with money or a country club address than they will one of their own. Would of been better of course if he'd broke and entered a beach house or got caught selling a little grass, but seems to me judge and jury saw his politics as a phase, a way of getting back at Daddy and postponing his entry into the real world of responsible, law-abiding, gainfully employed citizens. They didn't want to mess up the boy's future I guess, so they let him off with six years' suspended and a big fine and ordered him to stay out of Sawyer County forever, which that seemed like overkill to me.

Some friends of Fancy's up in the Triangle organized a legal defense fund (turned out she'd give most of what all she saved over the years to various causes and charities) and tried to hire a do-goody lawyer out of Durham to defend her, but she wouldn't have it. She went with the court-appointed, and the court appointed a boy just a year out of law school, who took the Patty-Hearst, she-was-brainwashed line. Like I said, I guess a lot of people figured Patty Hearst was just pretending to be brainwashed, and what the trial come down to was if Fancy was pretending to go along because he'd forced her to or did she willingly plot to overtake the institute? Of course the real issue was if the woman was *all there,* and since everybody on the jury had read at least the first paragraph of one of her letters to the editor, there wasn't a lot of debate on this.

They let her off with three years' probation and two hundred hours' community service, which she worked off in the Literacy Center the public library had set up. They say in six months Fancy taught more people to read than the entire Sawyer County school system did in the same amount of time, and she liked tutoring so much she stayed on as a volunteer after her court-ordered time was up. As soon as our own college transfer program was approved, I called her up and asked her to come back and teach English and History. Hell, she knew more about both areas than the ones I could find with degrees in those subjects, and since the students in the program were transferring to four-year institutions and were going to be corrupted anyway, I didn't worry too much about Fancy's effect upon our impressionable youth. I did keep her coming back to work for me kind of quiet, and I made it clear to Administration that she was only with us on a part-time trial basis. Plus, I made sure to schedule her classes at night, and those few who might have had something to say about it don't know nor care what goes on out here after they peel out of the parking lot.

Well, she said when I called, she'd been thinking of a second career in teaching. She had certainly enjoyed her literacy instruction, but she didn't really feel that Sawyer Vo-Tech was the place for her to begin her career.

I told her I had completely forgot about that mess and as long as she was working under me I promised not to mention it. I told her I needed teachers and I knew she'd make a good one. Plus, I said, if you're planning on getting into teaching you need some experience, and at your age going back to school, being a single woman, it's going to be a long, expensive haul.

I had not even finished my sentence when I realized who it was I was giving advice to. For a second there I could taste the old vinegar, and I wished I could see her face. But when she finally spoke, she didn't sound ill at me.

"It is hard to reinvent yourself," she said. "I'm sure your Mr. King would agree with that." I was about to remind her of our agreement to let bygones be when she surprised me by accepting my offer.

What it is, she needs the money, I thought at first, but I knew deep down that Fancy would go without before she'd compromise herself for money. When it became clear what kind of teacher she was, I saw it in a different light. Dr. Mc-Fadden has never been what I would call a people person, and for that reason it always seemed like Administration was a better place for her than the classroom, but the truth is teaching brought her out. As long as she wasn't trying to figure out how to change the world, or the educational philosophy of the institute—as long as she was telling about a poem or some old war—Dr. McFadden got on good with the students, who appreciated her strictness when they transferred out of here. I'm proud to have found a place for her, and I plan on letting her stay on here as long as she behaves.

There is one more thing to tell, and to tell it I have to take you back down to that night at the institute. Ronald had strapped the last speaker up top of the bus and L.C. was standing by the door at the exact spot where I'd seen Franklin Reed kissing his girlfriend six hours earlier. This put me in mind of what all had transpired since and I turned to Ronald and said, "Lord, what a day," but he climbed on the bus without a good-bye. "Check you later on, Ronald," I called as he pulled the doors to. It didn't bother me because I didn't expect too much from Ronald Little in the first place and L.C. was there, waiting to say good-bye.

"I still cannot believe you showing up after all these years. I had about give you up for dead, you know."

This seemed to get away with him. He laughed and said, "Don't feel lonely. A lot of them think I'm dead."

I reached out and cuffed him on the shoulder and he took a step back. "Hell, man, you're on your way to a comeback. I can feel it. Five Satins got back together last year, did a reunion tour." What I wanted to tell him was that if he kept on playing his old songs he wouldn't have to worry—he would never die.

"Thing about a comeback is one, it don't last, and two, you got to go under before you can come back. I never did go all the way under and don't plan on it."

I started to ask him what did he call the last ten years but I held my tongue. If he wanted to think he was a contender, hell, let him. Positive thinking never hurt a soul.

I stuck my hand out and Little Cedrick studied it, grabbed it loosely, shook at it once, pulled away quick. I stood there grinning at him until it seemed like I was about to start crying. "It's a honor to shake your hand again, L.C."

He looked away, like he was embarrassed for both of us, but he didn't leave. I coughed. We stood there. Why doesn't he go? I wondered. I was afraid if he didn't climb on the bus right then I'd say something sappy and his last impression of me would be of a goofy fan and I did not want Little Cedrick to remember me in that light.

"Just that one thing left to settle," he said finally.

"What's that?" I said.

"Compensation, Mitch. The money you owe us."

"I was thinking we're even here, L.C. I meant, we took care of the bus and y'all didn't actually ever put on a concert, right?"

L.C. fished a cigarette out of a shirt pocket, lit up. A truck passed, and he sent a thin stream of smoke off in the direction it disappeared. "We set up, right? We started playing. Can't play without power, and I don't see it's our fault the power went off."

"Whose fault would you call it?"

"On a contract I believe they refer to stuff like that as a Act of God."

"More like an act of Karl Marx, Jr."

"Yeah, but look like to me he had some help. From the inside, too."

Was he trying to say Fancy brainwashed his boy? Even though it was Little Cedrick saying it, seemed like something I ought not to let slide.

"Well technically, she had resigned an hour before, so she wasn't actually what you'd call 'inside.' "

"I can play that one too, Mitch. Cisco was no longer with the band at the time he told you we'd perform."

"Well, hell, L.C., I meant, it's not worth us fighting over. Neither of us ought to have to claim responsibility for two crazies. They're locked up now anyhow. We ought to just wash our hands of them, you ask me."

"Hate to wash my hands of anybody, because I don't really want nobody to wash their hands of me. But if you want to, that's your business. I got people waiting on me. They weren't supposed to work tonight and they're tired. It don't matter they didn't get through a song, see? They give up their night off to play and the way it works is, as long as we show we get paid."

I told Cedrick, I said, "Damn, man, if it was my money I'd write you a check right here and now but the thing about it, I am responsible to the institute, especially since I'm the only one in charge, and you know how a bureaucracy works. Everybody out here knows there wasn't any concert and I'd catch holy hell paying for one."

"Well, Mitch," he said finally, "I'm sure you're doing everything in your power to help me out."

"Damn straight, L.C. Once a Royal Loyal, always one."

"You got that right. Some things don't change, do they?"

"Much as people want them to, they keep right on."

"It's like what Cisco was all the time saying about history."

I ignored this, because I didn't want to hear that boy's

opinions on history. I'd had enough and was tired. L.C. must of been too, because he climbed in and pulled the doors to. That rubber strip sucked shut right in my face and the bus lurched off and in a minute the only thing left of Little Cedrick was red taillights blinking up the road. And I will tell you something: I was glad to see him go. Out of respect I didn't say this to his face but the truth is I did not agree with anything he said when we were standing there on the side of the road. Things can change. L.C. changed that night to hear the news media and he kept right on changing into something I did not recognize. But what does it matter in the long run? Whenever I put on one of Little Cedrick's records I don't stop to think who he is, what he's calling himself, or which songs he's performing these days. I hear him just like he was when I heard him the first time, and I have him just like I want him, trapped in hot wax and spinning around in circles for as long as the power holds.

About the Author

Michael Parker is the author of the novel *Hello Down There*. He is currently Assistant Professor of English at the University of North Carolina at Greensboro.